Annette Motley was an only child with her nose permanently in a book. She spent several enjoyable years teaching English in schools and a college of art before becoming a full-time writer. She has published short stories, magazine serials and a string of historical novels. *The Oldest Obsession* is her first contemporary novel and she is now at work on its sequel.

Annette Motley lives in a village in Surrey with her husband, the inevitable cats and a lot of wildlife.

༄༅༄༅༄༅༄

THE OLDEST OBSESSION

Annette Motley

WARNER BOOKS

A *Warner* Book

First published in Great Britain in 1997
by Warner Books

Copyright © Annette Motley 1997

A CIP catalogue record for this book
is available from the British Library.

ISBN 0 7515 2069 1

Typeset by Solidus (Bristol) Limited
Printed and bound in Great Britain by
Clays Ltd, St Ives plc

Warner Books
A Division of
Little, Brown & Company (UK)
Brettenham House
Lancaster Place
London WC2E 7EN

For my friends

Chapter One

⦿⦿⦿⦿⦿⦿⦿

LAST NIGHT'S DREAM WAS GETTING into the painting. Not the events, which Chloe could not quite remember, but the mood, the sensuous swoon of absolute sexual bliss.

She had no idea who her lover had been, but it was certainly not Alain. His touch, soft as clouds upon her body, had made her bloom in an instant like one of those Japanese flowers which will open their petals only under water. The entire encounter had possessed a submerged, aqueous quality – the watery sliding of skin against skin, the washes of blue light surrounding and in some way shielding the fronded green shade where they lay. From what or from whom?

The strangeness of it had remained with her all day, so had its extraordinary weight of sensuality. They had made love, she was sure of that, although she could recall no detail. It had been perfect, the bringing to perfection of herself and her lover in a moment of true union when everything about the other was known. It had not felt like a part of the recent history of the world; it belonged to the legends and lies of high romance.

And now she could not remember him, not his look or his voice or anything about him except the kindness of his hands. Her breasts ached in memory of him but she had no power to summon him before the eye of her imagination. Whoever he had been, she missed him.

The heat did not help. It was the last of the summer, an azure afternoon with the sun coming down like Zeus in his shower of gold. There was a light sweat on the watercolours that sat in her lap like a box of enamelled sweets. She sighed, restless with nostalgia for her dream. She wondered if she would tell Alain about it. Would he laugh and say how lucky she was, or would he be jealous of her phantom lover? Both, probably.

She began to paint with concentration now she had found the key to the picture. She would use blues and greens with deep purple overtones and a cloud of gold sprinkling the cupola of the old house deep-set among the trees. This was the first sketch but she already felt the tingle of premonition which told her she had found her direction.

She had coveted the landscape as soon as she had seen it. There had been a sudden breathtaking moment of expansion as she left the path through the woods and its beauty had burst upon her like Beethoven's 'Hymn to Joy'. Her dog, who was beside her, had been similarly affected and hurled himself downhill in an ecstasy of speed and scent. As for him, this glorious freedom under the sky was what Chloe most needed. It was for this she had come here, her personal gain from the collective gamble they had taken in leaving the city.

During the last ten years she had earned a growing reputation for her work. People liked her honest, analytical portraits and the quirky, eccentric interiors in which she seized upon those small corners of a house which most resembled its owners. These and her lovingly detailed book illustrations had eventually enabled her to give up her job in the National Gallery where she had given lectures and guided tours to varied groups of visitors. Throughout these years she had yearned after landscape with what she felt to be an atavistic English longing. Naturally Alain had challenged any such nationalistic claim, pointing to the august line of French landscape painters queuing round the Louvre.

Last year she had felt that her work was becoming too repetitive; the need for some new development was urgent. She had tried to make do with parks but parks were not landscape, not even the royal park of Greenwich near their home where she could stand at the highest point and see the distance-enchanted city lying on the river, in all the beauty and degradation of a fine, small galleon that is being relentlessly refitted as a grain-carrier. To Chloe every tree looked as if it had been put where it was and dared not even to dream of moving, like the exquisite props in a Peter Greenaway film. These were tame trees, however elderly and magnificent; they were domesticated and obedient. What she wanted was recalcitrant wilderness, the ancient forests beloved of Malory and Shakespeare, where hermits haunted the crossways to chide the ghosts of disputatious lovers. She wanted unaltered skylines and unpolluted waters, the green hills of hymn and song, the untrodden paths of the fabled demi-paradise. Only in such half-imagined territory would she recapture the wild rush of emotion that had been at the conception of every good picture she had done. Chloe had always been given to wild rushes of emotion, which was why, if one believes in the attraction of opposites, she had married Alain, an engineer and a disciple of Voltaire who was apt to trap her in nets of logic. She was uncertain whether it had been her emotion or his logic that had inspired the move to Sheringham, but it had been accomplished with the minimum of fuss and a maximum of goodwill from the whole family.

So now here she was, sitting amid the greenest of English grass beside a thin river filled with sparkling light, gazing downstream towards a scene that ravished her eyes and squeezed a possessive fist on her heart. The river flowed straight and shallow through pasture dotted with sheep and resting geese, the close-cropped turf sloping gently toward the tree-line on either side. About a quarter of a mile before her the stream curved smoothly away to the left around a group of rosy brick buildings, farm cottages and an old black-slatted barn whose uneven roof was spotted with a summer snowfall of doves. Behind them ramped a flowering jungle, flame and magenta against dark, fleshy foliage, a century-old web smothering a long stone wall and shoring up the crumbling arch that broke its line.

Higher up among the taller trees, lazing half-hidden, half-clad by all this luxuriant excess like a careless woman who knows she will not be disturbed, sprawled the warm russet-toned house. Despite its languor, it seemed to Chloe to offer an immediate intimacy. She could see very little of it clearly, so closely was it screened by the trees, but there was a square, dark red tower with a weather-vane and bare flag-pole, two galleried turrets imported from a Florentine palace, several large Jacobean windows and, free of the trees and insisting on its own perky turquoise against the azure sky, the delicately humorous cupola that made her want to embrace the whole elusive edifice. The place gave out a sense of vigorous life, yet even from this distance there was evidence of a lack of care; it seemed much too overgrown to be occupied. What was its history and to whom did it belong? What was the extent of it? Since it plainly demanded to be the focal point of her picture she would like to know it better. She had once painted the portrait of a Saudi woman who had wished to remain veiled to the chin. Chloe had insisted that she should be allowed to look, just once, at the naked body which would sit so patiently beneath the enveloping *hijab*.

Now, as the light had changed and she was satisfied with her progress, she decided to take the dog and walk along the riverbank towards the house.

'Baskerville?' The dog was not to be seen. She whistled piercingly through her fingers. There was an answering bark from the woods and the animal came crashing through some holly brush and down the hillside, giving rise to the appalling sounds that had earned him his name.

'Come on then, boy! Oh no, what have you got?' There was something in his mouth; she prayed it was not one of the baby rabbits she had seen browsing in the field further back.

'Bring it to me. Good heavens, where did you find *that*?'

He brought the prize and dropped it adoringly at her feet. It was a book, old and bound in fraying indigo leather. She picked it up and wiped it on her skirt. Baskerville panted amiably while she made out the faint gold leaf.

'Elizabeth Barrett Browning. *Sonnets from the Portuguese*.' Moved by affectionate memory she opened it and began to read:

> If thou must love me, let it be for nought
> Except for love's sake only. Do not say
> 'I love her for her smile – her look – her way
> Of speaking gently – for a trick of thought
> That falls in well with mine.'

'Hello. So that's where it's got to.'

A tall man, evidently amused, was coming energetically down the bank. His head was lowered to watch his step and black hair fell over his eyes so that all she saw of his face was his smile. I know you, Chloe thought. I have seen your hair fall like that before. But when he looked up he was, after all, a stranger.

'I'm sorry,' she called. 'He's a fool of a dog. He likes to give me things. It doesn't matter whose they are. I don't think he's damaged it.'

She watched him pick his way across the tussocky grass.

He wore linen trousers and an open-necked shirt and moved fluently, as if he enjoyed it. His face was dark and lively and he looked pleased with himself. His eyes, now that she saw them, were as alert and glossy as the dog's. He reminded her of the nicer kind of pirate. She handed him his book.

'Thank you.' He looked at her in turn. 'Which one were you reading?'

'The fourteenth, where it fell open.'

'It would. I've been looking at that one myself.'

She could imagine this, could hear him reading it aloud. His voice was easy to listen to, warm and deep and vestigially furred like that of a countryman who has been long away from home. She wondered why she was not surprised; it was not as if she often met men who made a study of love poetry. He tucked the book into a pocket and bent to pummel Baskerville.

'What a splendidly outrageous creature. What is he, some kind of mastiff?'

'He's half Burmese Mountain, we're not sure about the rest. We found him on Dartmoor when we were on holiday. The poor thing was wandering about, lost and desperate, howling with loneliness and fear. We tried to trace his owners but I don't think they wanted to be traced. We didn't try very hard, anyway. We got besotted.'

He smiled, his face lighting up in a manner she had previously observed only in actors or politicians. The dog slavered happily over his hand.

'What's his name?'

She told him and he gave a whoop of pleasure like a boy. 'Of course, what else? I wish I had my own two with me.' His smile increased. 'They really ought to meet this fellow. You won't believe it, but they are called Holmes and Watson.'

'I can't decide,' Chloe said gravely, 'whether or not one may describe that as a true coincidence.'

'I believe that strictly it's a correspondence. For a coincidence to occur, two events have to happen at the same time. I only know because I looked it up recently,' he added modestly.

'So did I. My children have to write a story based on a coincidence.'

'Oh?' He knew this was his cue to introduce himself but he was enjoying their harmless anonymity and wanted it to continue. 'Damn the dictionary, it'll have to stretch a point for once. Two people meet in a field miles from anywhere; they both own Conan Doyle dogs and have both just looked up the word that describes them both looking up the word. Whatever you call it, it's amazing, astonishing, astounding!' He flung wide his arms and informed the cloudless sky.

'I call it hyperbole.'

'How right you are,' he sighed. 'It's a failing of mine. But so satisfying. All right, let's forget coincidence. You were painting before I arrived. May I look at your work? Or do you dislike such requests?'

'I don't mind.' She handed him the sketch that was drying on top of her portfolio. 'It's only a beginning, but I think it's what I want.'

He examined what she had done, withdrawing all his concentration from herself and giving it to her work.

'I like it immensely. It reminds me of tales I read as a child: sad romances like "The Little Mermaid" and "The Seal Woman". It must be all those underwater colours.'

Her dream came flooding back, surprising her into embarrassment at his insight.

'There's a sadness here too,' he said. 'A sense of loss.'

'Yes.' She took the sketch from him and slid it into the portfolio with the drawing-board, groping for some pleasant remark to cover her abrupt behaviour.

'Did you read Elizabeth Barrett as a child?' she asked.

'Yes, but I prefer her husband. How about you?'

'I love them both. They were so painstakingly honest. They looked so hard to find the truth.'

'Poets are rarely hypocrites, I think.'

'Robert and Elizabeth lived in a hypocritical age.'

'So do we. All ages are. Wherever there is inequality there is hypocrisy.'

'It's a form of self-protection. Especially in government or in large companies. That's why we need the honesty of poets.'

'And of artists. Think of Goya.'

'Or photographers. Don McCullin.'

He looked at her thoughtfully. She felt shy suddenly and wished to break his gaze but could not because that would make her somehow hypocritical herself.

'Do you—'

'Perhaps—'

'I'm sorry. You first.'

Chloe said, 'I was going to ask if you were a painter yourself.'

'It's something I've wanted to do, really, very much, but I've not had the time. There's never enough time in life. Things pass and we can't grasp them.'

She felt an instant sympathy. 'I know. With me it's music. The piano. I started far too late and I hate the fact that I'll never get any better.'

'We must make choices. We have to be sure we choose the things we feel most *passionate* about.'

The word leaped out at her and lay ticking between them. She saw then that she had failed to realise, just as one can miss a vital phrase in a play or a film, that she found this man, this complete stranger with his pocketful of coincidence, compulsively attractive. Enlightened, and a coward, she took refuge in her children. Their names would act as talismans against all untoward enchantment.

'Music is my daughter Tilda's passion,' she told him,

carefully detonating the dangerous word. 'I hope she might make a career of it.'

'I think she certainly should try. She is unusually determined and her talent is undeniable.' He lifted one eyebrow and waited. Chloe stared. He returned the guileless smile of the Monopoly winner. 'Forgive me, Mrs Olivier – but I do know Tilda, her brother too. I teach them English. The story about coincidence?'

'I see.'

He held out his hand. 'Luke Cavendish. I really am sorry.'

'You needn't be.' She smiled. 'Chloe Olivier. Your name is constantly upon my children's lips. They seem to like you. Good but tough, is the consensus.'

'They're nice children. Clever too. They're settling very well at Sheringham. They are not much alike, are they, except in looks? For twins.'

'They tend to exaggerate their differences; it's the latest phase in their personal power struggle. But they're very close really, very loyal to each other.' She hoped this was still true; they seemed to have struck a bad patch recently. She said politely, 'You're the Senior Master, aren't you? What does that mean, in terms of duties?'

'Theoretically it means I look after the academic side of the school and the Headmaster looks after the administration. In fact we tend to share most of it. Philip Dacre retires next year. I shall take his place.'

'Congratulations. It's a beautiful school and you've built up an enviable academic record. And the music, according to my daughter, is on a par with Leipzig in full flower.' She found she disliked the withdrawal to the level of parent and teacher.

'It's as I said earlier,' he smiled. 'Sheringham is *my* passion. It is what I always wanted. I love the place.'

'It's good to hear that. People rarely admit to having all that they want.'

'Do you have that?' The question returned them to their first intimacy.

'I think so. Yes. Most of the time.'

They had reached another pause. Luke looked at his watch. 'Look, I shall have to get back now. Will you walk with me? I assume you left your car on Friday Street?'

About to agree, she was revisited by cowardice. 'No, I'll stay for a while.' She watched him watch the changes in her face. 'I'd like to try another quick sketch.' She would not; she just needed to be alone, or at any rate not with him.

'Fine. Well, I shall be seeing you very soon – at least I hope so.'

'Oh?'

'You are invited to Philip Dacre's house next Wednesday, to drink wine and tell us how you think we should treat your children.'

'Oh, yes. Rufus told me.' (*Hey Mum, there's a piss-up for new parents.*)

'He should have brought an invitation.'

'I expect he lost it.'

'Will you come?'

'Yes, we'll be there.'

'I'll look forward to seeing you.'

Luke sat at the crossroads waiting for the lights to change. He did not see the road or the traffic. He saw a beautiful woman standing in the grass, red hair falling round her shoulders, a smile on her lips and her arms outstretched as though she were leaning out of heaven like the Blessed Damozel. That particular smile had been for the dog, but later there had been one or two, of lesser brilliance admittedly, for him. He would give a great deal to earn the Baskerville variety. He had wanted her the moment he saw her. Her. She, Chloe. The lovely unexpectedness of her, waiting there in a place he visited every week, had been a shock of pleasure. She had risen from the grass like some

Chinese river-goddess, her face washed clear of all the disguises we wear to guard or to reveal ourselves in company. She had been so much herself, so complete in her solitude. And her eyes. Dear God, her eyes; such candidness was scarcely to be borne. How could a woman reach her age and still have that clear look, that soft, half-humorous gleam that told you how unequivocally she looked upon life? He wanted to kiss her eyes, to close them against all horrors. He wanted her never to be hurt. Chloe. Chloe. His heart ached as he repeated her name and felt young, guilty and an awful fool. He was jolted from his ecstasy by a blaring cacophony behind him.

'All right, all right!' He shot forward, leaving the angry BMW growling. What on earth had got into him? Chloe Olivier watched TV and used the loo like every other human. As for her eyes, he was not even sure what colour they were. Blue, grey? Oh hell. It was no use trying to delude himself. He wanted her so much that he grimaced in real pain, not of the heart but, more prosaically, in the balls. This had not happened to him for a very long time and never so suddenly nor so strongly.

It would come to nothing, of course. It was both socially unacceptable and humanly impossible. Besides, his desire was an aberration, a trick of the sun. We were not accustomed to sun like this in England, it was making him behave like an Italian.

Chloe drove home slowly through cathedrals of trees whose green vaults scattered light like bright coins. The original pennies from heaven? Luke Cavendish would probably know. She made herself think about dinner. It was already organised but she counted over everything she needed once more, to give herself something on which to concentrate. She felt peculiar, light-headed, not herself. Perhaps she was coming down with a bug of some kind or an early period.

She grew calmer as she reached the outskirts of Sheringham. It was a pretty, muddled village with houses of every age and state of preservation centred around the ancient church and the triangular green with its single dominant oak tree. The green was the size of two snooker-tables and the game on fairweather Sundays was to see how many tanned young people could cram themselves on to it with the drinks they had bought in the Dark Horse across the road. In winter they would crowd into the warren of oak-beamed rooms inside the pub and roast themselves in front of open fires. It was a friendly community and had made the Oliviers feel welcome. The move, Chloe reflected as she waved to the receptionist from the Health Centre, had been a success. Each member of the family had profited by it. Alain, although he insisted that relaxing was something he did only when asleep, seemed nevertheless to have found a looser mode of being. Tilda loved the countryside and was thrilled with the challenge set by her new music teachers. Rufus had dropped into his surroundings with his usual easygoing optimism and had made as many friends in the neighbourhood as he had left behind in Blackheath. There was even an unexpected bonus with regard to Miranda, who had officially left home last year to share the top floor of a warehouse on the south-east bank of the river with a group of other students and artists. Her life had been satisfactorily hectic and, although she and Chloe had spoken on the phone once or twice a week, she had visited rarely and been badly missed. Since they had moved to Sheringham she had come home nearly every weekend.

Chloe turned her little jeep, chosen for its scene-spotting potential, into the curving driveway and through the hotly blooming shrubbery of St Aubyn. She still experienced the lift of pleasure she had felt when she had first seen the house. It was a good-sized Regency villa, dignified and not too picturesque, its white walls supporting clematis, wisteria and a strong virginia creeper that she must remember to cut back in autumn. There were broad bay windows on two storeys and a row of pretty dormers above. The paintwork was French blue and recent, and a foam of lavender flanked the shallow steps to the front door. This stood encouragingly open, which meant that the twins had arrived home before her.

She drove round to the garage and parked outside it, collected her portfolio and let Baskerville out of the back of the car. They entered the house by the side door to the kitchen, a large, square room filled with light from windows facing south and east over the garden. Inside, the old oak cupboards and dressers were stacked with the crockery, plants, and postcards which ought to be there and a hundred other things that ought not. A similar anarchy prevailed on the big, round table in the centre of the room where Rufus had dumped his briefcase, sportsbag and tracksuit top. He turned from an exploratory forage in the fridge as he heard Chloe come in.

'Hello, Baskerville, you soppy article. Hi, Mum.'

'Hello, Rufus. Had a good day?'

'Not bad. Chemistry sucked but English was brill.'

Chloe put down some water and biscuits for Baskerville. She had the uncomfortable feeling that she might be blushing.

'Is Tilda with you?'

'She called in at the post office. What happened to those sausages I left? I was *saving* them.'

'I expect the poltergeist got them, as usual.'

'Arnie more likely, greedy little cooking fat.'

'Arnie can't open the fridge.'

'I wouldn't put it past him. I suppose I might've left them in the pantry.'

'He can open that. I thought you were going to mend the catch?'

'I am. Tonight, honest.' He groaned as he found the empty plate. 'Horrible animal.'

'He can't help it, any more than you can.' She gave him an affectionate smile.

'OK.' Rufus shrugged. 'I'll have beans instead. Want some?'

'No thanks.' She never ate at this time but it was nice of him to ask.

'Cup of tea, then? The noble Earl?'

'Please.' She watched him produce beans on toast, and tea brewed to her particular taste in her favourite mug with a panther on it, and decided not to mention the clutter on the table. He shoved it all further on one side and sat down beside her.

'You know that essay I've got, on coincidence?'

'Mm.' Alarming things were happening in her chest.

'I've got this fantastic idea. You know that thing we talked about with Dad – how if you could kill a man in China just by thinking about it, would you do it, and would you be a murderer?'

'Yes.'

'Well, there's two brothers, right? One of them lives in Hong Kong and the other's in London. And they have this amazing telepathic relationship. So the London one visits his brother and meets his "bizniss" partner, yeah? And when he gets home he thinks, hey, wouldn't it be good if old Hung Feng dropped dead and my bro' will get the whole biz. So he beams him these really strong signals to murder him. And he does. But he doesn't *know* he's done it because it was his brother's idea not his. What d'you think?'

'I think it's pure Gothic and I quite like it.'

'Great. Oh, here comes the infant prodigy. Hmm, the bad guy could be a female.'

Tilda came in, eating a chocolate muffin. She looked pale and rather tired. The two cats were dancing hopeful attendance.

'Are you all right, my love?' Chloe asked, concerned.

'Beastly period came early. I had to stop at the shop for some thingies.'

'Shut up!' Rufus was offended. 'We don't want to know about your revolting periods.'

'I just wish you had them,' Tilda hissed.

'Ugh!' said Rufus, trying to imagine the possible mechanics of such a misfortune. 'Glad I'm a nice clean man.'

'You're not. You're just a grotty little boy,' she said furiously.

'Leave it out. You don't have to be such a complete cow.'

'Rufus! And I was just thinking I had half-reasonable children,' Chloe remonstrated.

'Which half?' asked Rufus, enviously watching his twin feed the remains of her muffin to the hulking ginger monster, Arnie, and his svelte black companion, Grace.

'I've changed my mind,' Chloe said darkly. 'Don't give Grace any more, Tilda. She's getting too fat.'

'Perhaps she's going to have kittens,' Tilda said hopefully.

'I *think* she's still too young.'

'If she was, though, would Arnie be the father?' Rufus asked.

'I think he's too young as well, but I'm a bit vague about it. I'll have to check. Oh Lord, just listen to that!' A mechanical symphony outside announced the arrival of the Oliviers' elder daughter and her ancient 2CV.

'It sounds like something by that cartoonist,' Rufus said.

'Heath Robinson,' Tilda provided.

'Yeah – or one of those horror films where people get pushed into machinery. Hey, that's what could happen to my Chinaman.'

'Not very original,' sniffed Tilda. 'Well, I'm off to practise.'

'I was going to do my homework in there.'

'My playing never used to stop you.'

'I need to concentrate more today.'

'Do it upstairs, then.' She flounced away, via the bathroom, to the room where the piano was, and most of the books, a TV, a computer and the pool-table with the cover that turned it into an ordinary table. It was known simply as 'the other room'.

The mechanical symphony had come to a shuddering conclusion outside and now Miranda wafted into the kitchen on a cloud of essential oils, one-part Rose Geranium to two-parts petrol. She uttered a strangled sound relating to the dry-cleaner's bag clenched between her teeth.

'And it's good evening to her,' said Rufus brightly. He got up and relieved her of the bag.

'Phew, thanks. Thank God for Fridays. How are you all?' She dropped several other bags on the floor and laid a large portfolio against the wall near Chloe's, then settled her black leather jacket on the back of a chair.

'I thought you were supposed to aim at the canvas.' Rufus looked thoughtfully at the pink streaks in Miranda's long hair, which was already coloured a rich garnet. 'You look like Morticia Addams, done up for a really good funeral.'

Chloe tried not to look as though she agreed. 'It's a good strong shade. And it matches your car,' she offered, returning her daughter's kiss.

Miranda seemed pleased. 'My art-history lecturer said it made him understand the expression "drop-dead gorgeous". I like it; it's fun. I just hope it'll hold up like this tomorrow night.'

'What happens then?' Chloe enquired.

'Nothing much.' Miranda inspected the hole in the knee of one black stocking and made it bigger. 'Just an arty party.'

'Nice assonance,' said Rufus cheekily, 'but you missed a word.' He was ignored.

'Nothing heavy,' Miranda continued. 'But there might be some good contacts. And I'm going with this really terrific guy.'

'Someone new?' asked Chloe.

'Yes. He looks like Alain Delon. No, honestly, I'm not kidding. He is absolutely stunning. But the best thing is – he paints like no one there's ever been. I don't know, like maybe Francis Bacon crossed with Bosch. He does sculpture too, stuff that really grabs your eyeballs and twists them.'

'Certainly sounds interesting,' Chloe acknowledged, 'if a little disturbing.'

'He's that all right, his work I mean, Well, his work too.' She flushed.

'Oh wow, now your face matches your hair!' hooted the ungallant Rufus.

'So will your assonance if I get to it,' replied Miranda cheerfully. 'How about glum drummed bum?'

'What's for dinner, Mum?' Rufus retired gracefully.

'Um – oh yes, it's the full taverna menu; kebabs, shashliki, hummus, taramasalata, tsatsiki, pitta, salad—'

'You mean you went to M&S?'

'Yes, you unpleasant changeling, but I did buy some decent meat from the butcher. You can cut it up if you like.'

'Well, there *is* my homework . . .'

'I'll do it,' offered Miranda. 'I haven't done any real cooking for ages.'

'That's not good news,' said Chloe severely. 'What do you eat during the week, if I'm allowed to ask?'

'Oh you know – salads, takeaways. Love.' She smiled shyly.

Chloe rolled her eyes.

When Alain Olivier entered the kitchen he was greeted by the attractive sight of his wife and daughter preparing a meal, the delicious aromas of lamb and oregano, and the celestial strains of Dowland's *Lachrymae* caressing his ears from the other room. Of a tidy mind, he put his arm around Chloe and kissed the nape of her neck beneath the heavy hair, then dipped a long and sensitive finger into a bowl of hummus and sucked it pleasurably.

'Every sense satisfied in one overwhelming second,' he announced gratefully.

'Sensational.' Miranda got up to kiss his cheek. She liked the tanned smoothness of his skin, smelling of sun and citrus and the Gauloises which he had just given up trying to give up.

'And so are you, *chérie*.' He raised a quizzical brow at her hair.

'Don't you start. I've had enough flack from Rufus.'

'Indeed I shall not; I should not know when to stop.' Alain touched the stiff mass of gules and madder as if it might bite. 'One must sleep upright if one wishes to preserve this?'

'If necessary.'

'My poor child.'

'*Il faut souffrir pour être belle,*' she reminded him.

'The concept of beauty, *ma fille*, is one of mankind's more elastic notions.'

'Stop tormenting your daughter and find us something to drink with this,' Chloe commanded. 'I think there's some of that retsina left.'

'Please not.' Miranda only insulted her body from the outside.

'My sentiments precisely,' Alain agreed. He went to look for a nice full-bodied burgundy.

The twins were recalled and the meal progressed in the orderly but enthusiastic manner characteristic of the family. The lamb was praised and Messrs Marks and Spencer toasted in various preferred liquids. When nothing remained except the coffee jug and a few tenacious crumbs of baklava, Alain looked across the table at Chloe, relaxed and glowing beneath the lamp, and experienced a moment of pleasure and deep love mingled with the fear of death – his own or hers or that of the universe itself, he could not have said.

'Did you find what you were looking for today?' he asked her tenderly.

'Yes, I think I did. I made some sketches.'

'Great,' Miranda said. 'Let's see them.'

Chloe washed her hands and fetched her portfolio. 'I'm quite pleased with this.' She produced the last watercolour she had done.

Miranda pored over it. 'I can see why. It's stunning. What's that house?'

'I don't know. I found it while I was walking.'

'Looks posh. Wonder who lives there.'

'I've no idea. Perhaps nobody. It seems to be empty.'

'Where is it exactly?'

'I'm not quite sure. I may not be able to find it again.' The lie felt uncomfortable, like pebbles in her mouth. She did not know why she wanted to keep the place to herself. She was not a secretive person. Miranda continued to appraise the sketch, admiring the sure flow of the brush, as exact and economical as that of a Chinese calligrapher. 'It's going to be really good. Don't hurry it, will you?'

'No. I'm glad you like it. What do you think, Alain?'

'It's beautiful. And very strong. But where does this melancholy come from?' He was half teasing, half concerned.

'I don't know. Perhaps it's in that house.'

'Yeah. It's really spooky,' Rufus said. 'Looks like Dracula's castle.'

'You are a cretin,' Tilda sighed.

'Oh yes? Well, if I'm one, you must be one too.'

'Not at all. We're not identical.'

'Thank God for that.'

'I couldn't agree more.' Tilda threw back her hair with her hand and glared.

'That is enough,' Alain said quietly. 'If you want to be unpleasant to each other, go and do it somewhere else.'

'Sorry, Dad,' said Tilda, biting her lip. She worshipped her father and hated to displease him. She wished Rufus did not get on her nerves so much, as he had lately. It was his own fault. He behaved like a little kid all the time.

Alain nodded dismissively and smiled at Miranda. 'Shall we go and look at your car? I have to work this evening but I'd like to satisfy myself that it's fit to drive.'

'I hope!' she grinned. They both rose and Alain put his arm around her as they left. 'Mind my hair,' she warned.

'Not really,' he teased. He loved language play, however foolish. Tilda watched them go out together, arm in arm, laughing.

'Are you all right, lovely?' Chloe asked her. 'Only you look a bit miz.'

'I'm OK.' She left the table. 'Shall I wash up?'

'Most of it's in the machine, thanks. Finished the homework?'

'All except that story for English. I can't think of a coincidence.'

'Well, let's see,' said Chloe brightly. 'How about something to do with music? Or a love story?' She might have suggested a vignette about two people who looked up the word 'coincidence' at the same time. Why not? Luke Cavendish would enjoy that. It would make him smile his pirate's smile.

'Oh, Mum. A love story? No way. I might have to read it out in class.' She quite often did; she was usually near the top in English.

'All right, how's this – two composers write simultaneous works. What shall they be? You say.'

'Requiems.'

'And they dedicate them to the same aristocratic patron who is furious with both of them because—'

'—because he has no intention of dying. But then he lets the requiems get to him so much that he drinks all day and all night until he has a stroke. He just has time, before he dies, to indicate whch one he wants for his funeral.' She made a staggering gesture with her hand outstretched. 'Great! That's it. Thanks, Mum.'

'You did the important bits yourself.'

'She couldn't have started without you,' Rufus declared, conscious of the purity of his own muse.

'Miserable toad,' said Tilda, swirling her long skirt crossly past his chair. 'I'm going to work upstairs, where I don't have to look at your smug face.'

When she had gone, Chloe said briskly, 'Rufus, I wish you would try not to upset Tilda so much. You know she has a bad time with her periods. There's no need to blush, you donkey. Just try to remember, will you?' She stroked his copper-coloured head to show there was no real problem.

'Mmm, I guess so.' He shrugged, expressing male helplessness in the face of the less enjoyable facts of life. 'I've finished my schoolwork for now. Is it OK if I go and play football?'

'Yes, off you go. Back by ten, please.'

Alone, Chloe gave the cats some milk, then sat with Grace on her lap, thinking about the place that Luke Cavendish had called Friday Street. She found that he too had somehow become a part of her projected landscape. She might put in two small figures, just to give scale, like an eighteenth-century painter.

When Alain came to bed that night, muttering distractedly about a cylinder-head gasket, he was treated to a soft ambush of warm, predatory flesh.

'*Mais qu'est ce que c'est?*' he murmured in the throaty accents that had made her go weak at the thighs when they first met.

'Whatever it is that it is,' she promised, 'you are going to enjoy it very much indeed.'

Towards morning she awoke. The underwater dream had come back. This time she had recognised the face of the lover who had brought her to such a pitch of carnal perfection. But now, as she opened her eyes to the shaft of early sunlight diving between the curtains, it was just as it had been before. Although she still retained some sense of his hands upon her body, she could no longer see his face.

Perhaps, after all, it had been Alain. Last night she had wanted very much to give him the greatest pleasure. She had felt herself to be overflowing with every sort of goodness. It must be the country air.

She rolled over and began to welcome him to Saturday.

Chapter Two

IN 1608 SHERINGHAM HALL HAD been endowed as a school for intelligent orphans by its owner and architect Sir Sidney Sheringham, an eminently successful merchant adventurer who had inherited much of the surrounding countryside. History had reduced the estate to the thousand acres of farmland and woodland which helped to support the manor house and its celebrated gardens (open to the public on selected Sundays). Distributed about the grounds were several smaller houses and settlements occupied by the boarding pupils and the academic and domestic staff. The foremost of these was the pretty, serenely proportioned Dower House in which, according to felicitous tradition, the incumbent Headmaster lived. It was here that Philip Dacre had brought his wife Catherine, twelve years ago.

Now, Philip looked about his humming drawing-room and decided his party was going rather well. Most of the new parents were interesting and energetic people, and many of them would prove useful to the school. He enjoyed the opportunity to display the elegant house with its damasked walls and fine fireplaces and the enviable collection of sixteenth- and seventeenth-century pictures. It did the place good to be opened up on occasions such as this. He did not entertain as often as he ought to do. He was alone now and felt it deeply. Poor Catherine had died of cancer three years ago and nowadays he occupied only two or three of the rooms. He had not thought of his wife this evening, which was perhaps a small advance on his painful journey towards an acceptance of her death.

He had thought, however, as he was beginning to do too frequently, of Dinah Cavendish, his Senior Master's wife, with whom he fancied he might be falling in love, or perhaps in lust – he was not sure which. He did not expect, or even hope, if he were to be honest, that anything much would come of it, but it was a comfort to him to know that his frozen affections had not, as he had feared, become a part of the permafrost. Dinah's glass was empty. He filled another from his private stock of exquisite Condrieu, which he knew she liked, and carried it to her.

'Philip. Well, thank you.' She sipped. 'Wonderful. All warm and round like apricots on a wall in summer.'

She peered at him kindly out of the corona of gold-and-brown-streaked curls that fitted round her face, he thought, like Garbo's hood in *Anna Karenina*. She looked especially lovely tonight, in a festive variation on her usual gypsy mode of dressing – soft layers of violet lace in bondage to a lot of oriental jewellery. Somehow she managed to suggest the stylish present rather than the unreconstructed horrors of hippidom. Philip was interested in fashion. His personal copy of *Vogue* was delivered with the one in the school library.

'Have you been flying since I saw you?' Dinah asked.

In a minor way a merchant adventurer himself, if only on the Stock Exchange, Philip kept a small, quite elderly Cessna at a local airstrip. Last month he had taken Dinah up with him and the intensity of her pleasure in the experience had brought him back, amazed and grateful, to the full sense of himself that had been missing since Catherine died. She had been like an excited child, asking a hundred questions, crying out in fear and delight when he banked sharply, speculating wistfully on their possible nearness to an improbable Heaven.

He smiled. 'Just once. I took Baines of the Fifth with me. It was his prize for improving his French.'

'Lucky Baines. Much nicer than a leatherbound Racine or a new Larousse.'

'Indeed. Your husband suggested a video of *Emmanuelle*. He claimed it would improve his French even further.'

Dinah laughed. 'Is that what *he* gives them?'

'Ask him.' He touched her arm upon the few inches of tanned skin between the lace sleeve of her dress and her long grey gloves. He found it astonishingly sexy.

'Come up with me again,' he begged. What he really wanted to say was, Come upstairs with me, come now.

'Oh yes. I'd love to. I suppose we couldn't take Belle? She being a pupil, I mean, and not having won any prizes. It wouldn't be fair?'

'No,' he said firmly, 'it would not. I'm asking you, not your daughter.'

'Never mind.' Her smile, warm and affectionate and very slightly askew, forgave him easily. 'Look, come and introduce me to that couple over there. I really like the look of the woman. She's beautiful, isn't she? And he seems interesting, sort of sharp and keen, like a jazzman or a great detective.'

'The Oliviers. Yes, I suppose she is. And no, he's an engineer. Come on.'

Dinah felt the tremor of his hand beneath her elbow and was touched by pity. She was well aware of his feelings towards her.

Before they could reach Alain and Chloe they were waylaid by Luke, who looked mischievous.

'Philip, you absolutely must come and talk to Mrs Cubitt. You remember? My scholarship boy?'

'That's right. I didn't meet the parents. You took him on yourself.'

'Why are you grinning like a gargoyle?' Dinah asked her husband.

'Don't be unkind. This is my society smile.'

'Good thing they haven't brought their horses. Oh Lawks! Is *that* Mrs Cubitt?'

A small, portly woman, who appeared to have a leg at each corner, stood stolidly before the buffet, having circumvented the butler, and poured herself a triple Glenfiddich. She wore a lot of orange make-up to match her curls and the flowers on her dress which, though very loud, were a whispering *pianissimo* to the triumphant double *forte* of her hat, a wide-brimmed crimson silk bawling with vermilion roses. Dinah, an eclectic shopper, had considered buying this hat in the Oxfam shop last week. She had thought of wearing it on its own to amuse Luke. She had to admit that on Mrs Cubitt it was nothing short of formidable.

'How nice to see you again, Mrs Cubitt,' Luke said. 'And what a marvellous hat that is.'

She beamed at him as he presented Dinah and the Headmaster. 'Nice to meet you, Sir, I'm sure. Hello dear, you do look nice. It's quite right, what you wrote in Dwayne's exercise book, Mr Cavendish. 'Ee *is* a lazy little sod and I got 'is dad to knock an 'ole in 'im just to teach 'im. They aren't going to give you no scholarship if you don't do the work, I said.'

'Good for you, Mrs Cubitt. You keep him at it. He's a bright boy but he does need a slave-driver. Shouldn't knock too many holes, though. It's supposed to be terribly bad for the brain cells. Shakes them loose.'

Dinah felt Philip stiffen beside her.

'Is your husband here, Mrs Cubitt? I should very much like to meet him,' he said.

'Not 'im,' she replied with fine-tuned contempt. 'Tonight's the night 'ee plays 'is guitar with 'is mates, down at the Dark 'Orse. Wouldn't miss that, wouldn't Morris, not for anythink short of 'is own funeral.'

'I'm sorry.' Philip produced his own society smile.

'Never mind, eh? Eee don't know nothink about education; 'ee never 'ad any.'

'What line of work is he in, Mrs Cubitt?' asked Dinah.

Mrs Cubitt chortled. 'Only line 'ee's in is the payout
down the Social. I don't mind. 'Ee's better off at 'ome
where I can keep an eye on 'im. I find plenty for 'im to do,
I can tell you.'

'I'm sure you do.' Dinah felt she might laugh, or
possibly cry.

The brave orange face fell into reflection. 'It's too late
for Morris, what with the recession and everythink, but
both my older lads is learnin' a trade. Clint's a 'lectrician
an' Elvis is a mechanic – good 'ee is too, if any of you ever
wants your cars fixin'. But Dwayne's a clever little devil as
you know, Mr Cavendish, and I want 'im to 'ave the chance
of somethink better. You wouldn't believe it, but I was a
clever kid myself, only I 'ad Elvis when I was sixteen and
Bob's yer uncle.' She sighed. 'Anyway, I've got the Institute
and the Church and me bits of work around the village –
that reminds me, old Mrs Carey's gone now, so I've got a
window in me week. If you know anyone what wants a
cleaning lady, I'm yer man.'

'I'll ask around,' Dinah promised. 'I wish you could
come to us, but we get the school cleaners free. Look, your
glass is empty, mine too. Why don't we do something
about it?'

'Are you sure you knew what you were doing, taking on
young Wayne?' Philip asked when they were out of earshot.

'It's Dwayne with a D,' Luke instructed.

'Good Lord.'

'Ours is a living language, Philip.'

'That doesn't mean anyone can do anything they like
with it.'

'Yes it does. Think of the United States.'

Philip shuddered. 'I'd rather not.'

'Have you taught him yet?' Luke asked seriously.

Philip made it his business to take each form in the school once a fortnight for a lively seminar on a current inflammatory issue.

'Indeed. His contribution was to inform me that drugs are here to stay and that Her Majesty's Government would be well advised to wise up and face it like they do in Amsterdam.'

'Good. He tells me that publishers will have to wise up in a similar fashion if they want 'the yoof' to keep on reading.'

'All very well, but is it worth a scholarship?'

'His written papers were surprisingly good. I followed my instinct. Time will tell. He's a likeable lad. A bit too fly, but we might alter that.'

'Not with Elvis and Clint at his back,' said Philip gloomily.

'Why don't you –' Luke took on his mischievous look '– give your next seminar on the use and abuse of the Social Services? Dwayne might give you a few fly points on that. But if you want to know what I think, he'll be a good influence around here. He's probably the nearest we've got to an intelligent orphan, intellectually at any rate. And we were never intended to be a school for the sons of company directors.'

'Don't accuse me of snobbery, Luke. You know it isn't that.'

'I know it isn't meant to be; but it's what it comes down to, in the end. It has to be. The boy's intelligent. He deserves his chance.'

'The chance to grow up speaking a different language from his parents?'

'An awful lot of us have done that. Myself, for one. But not you. You were born in the purple, Philip; that's why you need someone like me to translate the mouthings of the masses occasionally.'

'You are a horrible man,' Philip said warmly. 'D'you fancy a glass of Condrieu?'

'No thanks, I'll stick to mean red. To match my character.'

'Well if you don't need no one, no 'fence taken.' Mrs Cubitt was systematically peddling her talents among the scented ranks of well-dressed mothers, for several of whom she already provided a quick and very efficient service.

'No luck, Mrs C?' asked Luke, who was talking theatre to a familiar-faced TV actor whose daughter had joined the Upper Third.

'Never say die, dearie. There's a few left yet.' Her voice was less distinct than it had been.

Alain Olivier, whom fate had cast back to back with Luke as though they were about to commence a duel, overheard and turned around with a pleasant smile. 'Forgive me if I interrupt you.' He nodded at them both. 'But I think I may be able to help you. My wife tells me our house is descending to the level of a pigsty for the lack of a *femme de ménage*.'

'A what?' Mrs Cubitt's features made a rush for the middle of her face. 'You're foreign, ain't you?' she accused. 'French, innit?'

'I am.' Shamelessly, Alain could not resist capturing her plump hand and kissing it with exaggerated Gallic excess as he introduced himself. 'My wife is English,' he reassured her. 'If you would like me to fetch her, she is over there. In the black dress, with the chiffon thing in her hair.'

'Olivier, eh? You've got a decent English name, anyway. There's never been a truer Englishman than Sir Laurence, God rest 'im. S'all right. I'll go an' talk to 'er in a bit. Don't you disturb yourself.' She moved off magisterially in the direction of the buffet.

Alain and Luke did not duel. It soon transpired that they were both wearing white hats, or at least that they found themselves in agreement about the major points of education, politics and the finer things of life. Their discussion was so satisfactory that each recovered his wife from her separate conversation in order to present her to the other. Confronted with Luke, Chloe was suddenly struck with shyness. She accepted his hand and looked up at him gravely. Luke hesitated. Her clear eyes – they were in fact grey – told him nothing.

'Mrs Olivier, Chloe, how nice to see you again. Have you finished your painting yet?'

'Not yet.' She had thought that he would not mention their meeting. She saw now that this was absurd.

'I was out walking,' Luke explained. 'I was carrying a book, thinking about the best way to trap the free-thinking Fourth into considering the possibilities of nineteenth-century Romantic verse – and suddenly I was attacked by the Colossus of Rhodes on four legs.'

He continued in that vein and although he made her laugh Chloe wished he would not make it quite so amusing. Alain did not say so but surely he must be surprised that she had not spoken of such a hilarious encounter. But Alain was looking at his watch. 'I'm sorry, Chloe. I have to finish some notes for tomorrow. I'll walk back now, if you don't mind, and leave you the car.'

'I don't mind. It's probably too early for us both to leave politely.'

He laid his hand on her shoulder. 'Enjoy yourself.'

Dinah watched appreciatively as he wove through the crowd. 'Somehow I never imagine engineers looking like that. Or speaking English like delicious Dépardieu.'

'Sometimes he exaggerates,' Chloe said. 'He likes to be a frog out of water.'

'Only sometimes?' said Dinah. 'Aren't you lucky? Luke exaggerates all the time. I only hope his pupils realise that, otherwise they'll grow up believing the most extraordinary things.'

''Course they realise; they're all such clever little devils,' Luke murmured. His mimicry was excellent.

'Mrs Cubitt,' marvelled Chloe. 'What a wonderfully determined woman. She has just engaged me as her employer. She was extremely drunk but perfectly clear about what she wanted.'

'I hope you'll endeavour to give her every satisfaction,' Luke grinned.

Chloe found she did not want to meet his eyes. She was feeling uncertain of herself, especially in front of Dinah. She smiled up in the general direction of his chin, which was safe enough territory, and found herself contemplating his mouth, which was not.

'How are Holmes and Watson?' she enquired idiotically of Dinah.

'They've got fleas,' Dinah said. 'I thought we'd got rid of them but this Indian summer has brought them back. But never mind them; are you a serious artist or is it a hobby?'

'Serious.' Chloe was amused by her bluntness.

'Terrific. Is it an inherited talent?'

'Well, my grandmother sketched a bit. My mother had a terrific sense of form and colour; she was an interior designer. And my father is an architect.'

'I asked because I'm interested in reincarnation. I wondered if we get to carry all our abilities into our future lives or if we have to start the whole learning process every time. And where inheritance comes in.'

'Do you really believe in the transmigration of souls?'

'I'm just interested. But it seems to me more sensible and acceptable than a lot of things that churches have asked us to believe.'

'It is an attractive idea,' Chloe agreed. 'What do you

think, Luke?' She felt more confident now that she had managed to use his name.

'Oh, my mind is open all hours, but so far that notion has not walked in. Oh, Lord,' he added in Philip Dacre's patrician drawl, 'here's the idiot Frodsham's fire-breathing mother. Hand me the magical mirror and I'll go and do battle with her. That boy is *not* Oxford material and no number of snakes on her head will hiss me into submission on that. Chloe –' his smile was gentle '– I hope that we shall meet again soon. Thank you for coming tonight.'

She felt weak with relief as he descended gracefully upon a large woman in a tweed suit who carried her plump little husband on her arm like a handbag.

'Poor Luke,' said Dinah affectionately. 'Philip leaves him to charm all the snakes in the woodpile.'

Chloe looked at her and they both collapsed into laughter.

'Yes, well, I *am* inclined to mix metaphors. It's a sort of personal stand against Super-literate Man.'

'I know what you mean. With Alain it's logic, and the pre-eminence of technology. There are bits of engine all over the kitchen right now.'

'We don't get that. Just books. The entire house resembles the Sack of Constantinople. Literature, literature everywhere and never a bloody good read.'

'I'm halfway through a Ruth Rendell. Does that qualify?'

'You bet. Specially if it's a Barbara Vine. Meat and drink to the amateur psychologist in all of us. Anyway, why don't you come over and see for yourself? Our house, that is. How about this week? Teatime?'

'I'd like that.'

'Thursday OK?'

'Fine.'

They smiled with the artless self-congratulatory pleasure of new lovers. The beginning of a friendship is very similar to that of a love-affair, often possessing the same instant physical attraction, to be followed by the same happy discovery of a thousand things held in common.

That is all right, then, thought Chloe as she drove home. Luke had led her to Dinah and that, obviously, is what it must all have been about.

'You didn't say you'd met Luke Cavendish before,' Alain remarked as he abandoned the 2CV manual he was reading and welcomed her into their bed.

'Didn't I? I suppose I was too excited about my picture.' *Oh Chloe*, she reprimanded herself, *how very foolish you are*. Lies and guilt, and all for nothing.

Chapter Three

ᖆᖆᖆᖆᖆᖆᖆᖆ

THE CAVENDISHES LIVED IN A many-gabled Victorian house on the opposite edge of the village from the Oliviers. Dinah's kitchen was so similar in mood and degree of clutter to her own that Chloe felt at home as soon as she sat down at the big oblong table with its patterned oilcloth. The chief difference was that here nothing quite matched or toned. Dinah relished aesthetic clamour, even conflict, and anyway it was easier if you did not have to bother about mix-and-match every time you bought an eggcup.

'The locusts will descend soon, but we've got half an hour to ourselves,' she told her visitor, removing scones from a scarlet oven. 'Luke won't be home till later. He has a Governor's meeting.'

'What a pity,' Chloe said. But she found that the very certainty of his absence relieved her of a tension of which she had not even been aware.

Dinah buttered the scones and put the plate in front of Chloe. 'I've seen you a couple of times in the village and thought "she looks nice", but somehow we never managed to meet. Anyway, here we are.'

'Yes.' They shared a smile in celebration of this small achievement.

'Do you think you're going to like it here?'

'I already do. It was time to leave London, for us at any rate. It was getting too—' she searched for the word '—conscious of its own decay, decadence even. I got tired of listening to people complain. Everyone worries – about crime, diseases, money, their kids. All those shops and businesses closing down. All the new brave ventures, and then *they* close down. Sometimes there's a miasma of hopelessness hanging over everything like a Dickens fog. But the main problem was the drugs scene. I know fifty per cent of the kids are on something but I don't want ours to be part of it. We found that Rufus had been buying hash regularly from a lisping little entrepreneur in the junior playground.'

'We're managing to contain the problem at Sheringham, so far. But we're constantly on the look-out for it. Guildford's only a few miles away and there's plenty of it there. It's a pig, isn't it? Luke and I used to enjoy an occasional smoke but we've had to give it up completely to provide a good example. I'm not sure where that places us, morally.'

'Banging a tambourine among the saved. It's either that or "do as I say, not as I do". We made the same decision when we had Miranda. I used to wish I'd tried a few more interesting substances before I recanted. Alain didn't mind. He genuinely prefers his Gauloises.'

'It must be nice to be married to a Frenchman. Opens up twice as many possibilities, especially for your children.'

'It is nice, mainly because *he* is. And we're all more or less bilingual. And there's Paris. Alain's parents are there. They're both doctors but his mother only works part-time now, so the kids can go over there on their own. At least, Miranda does. Rufus and Tilda do everything together. Or they used to. That seems to be changing.'

Dinah responded to her hint of anxiety. 'That's only to

be expected. Different sexes. Not identical. It's normal, all the child psychology books say so. I know; that's what I was going to be,' she said with regret.

'What happened?'

'I'm just like Mrs Cubitt,' Dinah grinned, 'I'd only just started to practise when I met Luke. Then I had Oliver and Belle and I soon became so involved in the family that I forgot about my brilliant career.'

'Do you still think about it?'

'Sometimes. Not really. I've got it back in a way. I have a part-time post as the school counsellor, a cross between a nanny and a mother-confessor. It's an elastic occupation. I even refereed a football match the other day.'

'Fancy being able to.'

'I'm not. It was sheer anarchy. But we won.'

Their conversation continued on these pleasantly familial lines while friendship grew above and around it in the psychic space that has little to do with such subjects. They had just returned to the interesting notion of reincarnation when there was a soundtrack screeching of tyres on the gravel outside.

'It's Adam. Good. I wasn't sure he'd be back before evening. He's Luke's, by the way, by his first marriage.'

Chloe revised her mental notes.

Adam was very evidently Luke's son, tall and dark-haired with the wide-shouldered, slim-hipped grace that can make Solomon's glory of jeans and jumpers. He entered with the slightly wary confidence of those who are reasonably sure of themselves but not of others, nodded in response to Dinah's brightly welcoming smile and came to take Chloe's hand.

'So you are Dad's book-thief?'

'I only have amateur status,' she said modestly. 'The dog isn't properly trained yet.'

'You should open a school. We'll enrol Holmes and Watson.'

'Surely it would be against their principles?'

'They'd be undercover.'

'Now you've given them away.'

He was studying her. Chloe did not mind his direct, considering gaze. It managed to include her wholly in whatever was going on in his head. There must be a gene for this happy gift. His father had it too.

'Damn. I'll never make a writer at this rate.' He grinned engagingly.

Dinah rolled her eyes at him. 'Not working tonight?'

'No. Ruth's doing the interview. The ed said the situation needed feminine sympathy. I told him I had as much of that as Ruth and he said I could probably put that down to tight jeans. I've just started working for the *Surrey Clarion*,' he explained to Chloe. 'They haven't decided where I fit in. My next assignment is a fashion spread – "with the accent on youth"! It's a bit of a bummer. What do I do? Tweeds and Barbours for the horsey-set or lycra and leather for the druggy clubbers?'

'I'll help if you like,' Dinah offered eagerly.

'That's nice of you.' Adam struggled for words which would conceal his doubts about her opinions on style. 'But I don't think it's quite your sort of thing. I mean, I guess I ought to talk to some sixth-formers.'

Chloe took pity on him. 'You could talk to my daughter, Miranda. She loves anything to do with fashion. It's part of her course at art school. She designs and makes a lot of her own clothes. She'd probably know exactly where you should pitch your article.'

'Really? That's terrific. Just what I need.'

'Then why don't you come over and see her? Saturday morning would be the best time. She lives in town during the week.'

'Does she? So do I, on and off, but Helen – that's my mother – has gone on one of her provincial tours, so that the viewers can see her in the too too solid flesh.' His voice was warm with affection. 'The house is a bit empty without her so I'm taking refuge here.'

'Helen Cavendish is your mother?' Chloe had seen her dozens of times in TV dramas. 'I think she's splendid. She seems to be able to do anything. She was so sad and selfish and maddening as Hedda Gabler, and the next week she was making me laugh in that office soap. Have you any interest in the stage yourself, Adam?'

'Well, I want to write for a living, so I expect I'll try my hand at a play one day. 'I'm really aiming at novels, but it all comes a lot harder than it looks, so I'm going to take it slowly. And I have to eat so I'm doing a journalism course at Kingston. The *Clarion* job is to pay the fees. I did offer myself to Fleet Street – to the organs of the people and the guardians of the truth – but the *Clarion* was the only paper in the entire South-East that would actually let me write.'

'Don't be too modest,' Dinah said. 'He had a short story on Radio 4 last month.'

'Yes, but they rejected the next one.'

'Perhaps you picked a rather difficult subject. You've never been to Los Angeles; you haven't met a Mexican family.'

Adam stiffened. 'I didn't say you could read it.'

'I haven't,' Dinah said quietly. 'Luke was talking about it.'

'I see.' Chloe felt that were it not for her presence he would have spoken more bitterly. Dinah, too, seemed more hesitant with him than with others. 'So it's "write what you know", is it?' he challenged.

'I'm no expert,' Dinah defended herself, 'but I should think it might be a good rule when one is first starting.'

She offered him a piece of lemon sponge, a favourite of his. Adam refused and asked, 'Do you think that's true, Mrs Olivier?'

Chloe answered slowly, giving herself time to think. 'It seems to me that for a writer, just as for a painter, it isn't the subject that matters most; it's primarily a question of finding out how one sees or thinks of things and learning to get it down exactly as one does see it. As you say, it's not easy.'

'Finding one's own style,' Adam nodded. 'So that anyone can say "that's George Eliot" or "this is a Modigliani".'

'Yes, but that comes later, when you develop more confidence in yourself. At first you must learn to look out for your own wrong notes, to avoid imitation and pastiche and work as close to the truth as you can. One of the things that makes it about ninety-nine per cent impossible is that, in a way, the whole of civilisation and your own education is ranged against you as much as with you.'

'Because there's too much of it, you mean?' Adam said.

'Because you develop tastes and you can't help but follow them. You become a ... a realist or a romantic or a nihilist without intending to become anything except a person who tells the truth as they see it.'

'Yes. It's difficult to keep things innocent,' said Dinah thoughtfully. 'Even a cake recipe can be perverted over the years.' She chewed critically.

'I don't believe you! Let's try a bit.' Adam reached for the lemon sponge and demolished a slice in three bites. 'Nonsense. It tastes just as it did when you first made it for me. It says Dinah Cavendish as clear as Pablo Picasso.'

Dinah smiled. 'What Chloe is saying – I think – is, how can *I* know that?'

'I'm not sure,' Chloe said. 'I really only know what I mean where painting is concerned. But I think what I'm saying is that it's important to know how to use the influences in our personal environment. We must acknowledge that it is these which make us, whether by our affirmation or rebellion; but each of us does have an original, inimitable self – or mindset or soul or whatever you want to call it.'

'DNA?' suggested Dinah.

'Certainly if Modigliani had been able to sign his work with a DNA print we wouldn't have all those fakes. Anyway, call it what you like, it is oneself and it is unique and it is where the work has to come from.'

'You mean I should stop trying to write like Henry James?' Adam grinned.

'Yes, I'm afraid so.' She remembered, 'Miranda likes him.'

'I was thinking of giving him up anyway. The average modern reader has the attention span of a stuffed tomato. More tea anyone?' He got up to make it, wondering what beautiful Chloe's daughter would be like.

'Hello, here's Olly,' he said. 'Just in time.'

'Er – hello everyone,' said a quiet voice from the doorway. Oliver Cavendish, at seventeen, was as clearly Dinah's child as Adam was Luke's. He had her leaping aureole of streaky-bacon hair and an expression of calm unusual at his age. He was very thin.

Adam put down the teapot and threw his arm around the boy's shoulders. 'My brother Oliver,' he told Chloe. 'Younger, wiser and an altogether more hopeful specimen than this poor scribbler. Olly, meet your namesake, Madame Chloe Olivier.'

'Don't be an ass, Adam.' Oliver smiled shyly at Chloe.

'OK. Is that badger all right?'

His brother's face lit up. 'He's going to be fine. Alastair let me do the sutures. We should be able to let him go in a couple of weeks.'

'What was wrong with him?' asked Chloe.

'He was hit by a car. Luckily the driver brought him in. His ribs were badly bruised and there were some nasty wounds, but we managed to patch him up.'

'That must be one of the best things about your work, being able to send an animal back to the wild.'

'It is. But you musn't think I'm a proper vet. I won't be

for ages yet. I'm still in the sixth form. I only work for Alastair at weekends and holidays.'

'And every other chance you get,' said Dinah darkly. 'Just make sure you finish that biology tonight, that's all.'

'I will,' he promised. 'I've applied to both medical school and veterinary college,' he explained to Chloe. 'But I know now that I'd rather be a vet. Ma worries that I do too much on the practical side and not enough on the stuff that will get me my exam grades.'

'There's one practical thing you could do for me,' said Chloe, wanting to encourage him. 'We think our cat is pregnant, but we could do with a more professional opinion. Perhaps you could come and look at her?'

'I'd be glad to,' Oliver said. 'It's very easy really.' He looked shy again.

'Why did you choose animals,' she asked gently, 'rather than people?'

He had thought about this. 'Because they don't make such a fuss about everything. And because you don't have to talk to them. Not in words anyway. Oh, I'm sorry. I didn't mean—'

'I understand. Really. It *is* less of a strain. We communicate with animals by telepathy more than otherwise.'

As if in direct contradiction to her words a bestial explosion of howling and barking was heard outside, in which the assembled initiates could easily detect extreme pleasure.

'Dad,' said Adam.

Chloe began to examine the tablecloth. The blue and gold pattern was quite complicated when you concentrated on it, full of arabesques like a Koran cover. She felt a little sick.

The room was suddenly full of him. He loomed in the doorway, two dogs, a poised and disdainful red setter and a portly and amiable black Labrador, pushing insistently at his legs.

'Not staying. Forgot the accounts book. Hello, everyone. How are you, Chloe? What a pleasant surprise.' He beamed at her. 'Meet Holmes and Watson.' Both dogs trotted at her side and she bent gratefully to attend to them. They pressed their noses into her hands and she gave them pieces of scone. 'Don't let them mug you,' Luke said. 'Especially Watson, he's on a diet.'

She felt the weight of his gaze like snow upon her eyelids. She blinked and looked up. The teasing fell from his face as her look answered his. It was a very brief exchange, the smallest and yet the most significant of moments because it contained, between his easy strictures and his appreciative seizure of a slice of cake, the simple acknowledgement of everything they might become to each other.

Luke filled his mouth with the soft, lemony stuff, thinking that he would never taste it again without seeing her sitting there at the table next to his wife, with her grey eyes filling with wonder and fear. It was not the first time he had seen her since Philip's party. There had been many fantasies.

Chloe turned away quickly and began to say something, she scarcely knew what, to Oliver. Luke, with equal haste, began to search the appropriate drawer for his ledger. Just as both were fearing that the expansion of time in which they had momentarily existed had been accessible to others who might have caught the plighting of their eyes, a loud young voice was heard proclaiming at the door. 'Hello, it's me. I'm home! All be quiet; I've got Horace. AND I've got the part!'

'Sorry Belle, can't wait. Terrific about the play.' Luke found and grabbed his book and waved the rest of his cake at them as he side-stepped his daughter at the door. 'Hear all about it later!' Chloe subsided into her chair, feeling like an overstretched balloon from which someone has at last been kind enough to release the air.

Belinda Cavendish was fifteen and already far more striking to the eye than was good for her character. She was aware of it and made well-considered use of it from time to time. She was presently outraged, as evidenced by the flash of her large dark eyes and the toss of her golden-brown pony tail. She dropped her tapestry kitbag and secured a tighter grip on her pet. Horace was a rather nervous ginger kitten whom Oliver had rescued from a family of infant torturers. Belinda acknowledged Chloe's presence quickly and proceeded to scold her family.

'I found him *outside*. At the *front*. He could've been *run over*! You ought not to let him out. He isn't old enough.'

'I keep telling you he's a she,' said Oliver affectionately. 'She's at least four months old. She should start to wander a bit. She needs to discover her boundaries.'

'I did put her out at the back, darling,' said Dinah, 'but we can't stop her exploring.'

Belle ignored this unpalatable fact. 'Everyone knows there aren't any ginger girls,' she announced.

'Who knows? Where did you get your information?' asked Oliver mildly.

'*Everyone* at school knows.'

'Have it your own way. Horace won't mind.'

'It isn't *my* way. It's how it is. But listen, folks, I'm going to be Gwendolen in the play. But Kate Forest got Cecily and she'll be the pits. We're all well pissed-off about that. I'm going to see if I can put the frighteners on her. But it's brill I got Gwendolen. Isn't it, Mum?'

'Yes, Belle. I'm very pleased for you. Oscar Wilde is obviously just what you need. When do you expect to rehearse and which member of staff is directing?'

'Sometimes straight after school, sometimes later. Mr Day, Middle English.'

'Let me have a timetable when you get one.' Belle's sense of time was an expedient one and Dinah had great difficulty in keeping track of her whereabouts.

'I can't wait to tell Aunt Helen about it. I'll send her a postcard, one of those Renoir ones you gave me. She'd like that. Can I go out now? I don't want any tea.'

'Where?'

'Just to the swings. Lucy's there.' So were Thomas and Paul, but Belle saw no need to mention them.

'All right. We're eating at seven. Be there.'

'Aw wight. See you.'

Dinah groaned. 'The way she talks. I've decided that if I ignore it, she might get tired of it. But I've a hideous feeling I'm quite wrong and the idiomatic nasties will multiply like – like what?'

'Rabbits?' said Oliver.

'The baddies in a computer game,' said Adam.

'Royal rumours,' suggested Chloe.

Dinah laughed. 'At least she has stopped using "unreal" as her sole adjective. They don't watch "Neighbours" so much in summer.'

'I once tried to ban TV until after dinner,' Chloe said, 'but the twins threatened to go on hunger strike and claimed that they couldn't relate to their peer group properly unless they watched the same progranmes.'

'They won, of course?' said Dinah gloomily.

'Yes. I suppose they're right, in a way. To tell the truth, I sometimes watch with them. I think soaps are quite good for people, on the whole – sort of comforting, like a coal fire or a beloved children's book.'

Adam said, 'They're fine until they enter their baroque phase – when people start acting out of character and they try to hype up the storylines with unlikely love affairs and grisly abortions and unprecedented waves of crime.'

'Life does include these things,' Dinah said.

'I know, but you have to be careful in a soap. As Chloe says, they do represent security. We all want them to follow a pleasant, stimulating but not too exciting existence and go on doing it for ever.'

'Like us, you mean?' asked Oliver sweetly.

'Exactly.'

The phone rang. Oliver, who was nearest, picked it up. He covered the earpiece. 'It's for you,' he told Adam. 'Michelle.'

'Oh shit. Tell her I've just gone out.' He made for the door. 'And I won't be back!'

Oliver sighed. 'I'm sorry, Michelle,' he said kindly. 'He doesn't seem to be here.'

'I liked Michelle,' Dinah said. 'But she was much too nice to him. Adam needs a girl who'll give as good as she gets.'

Dinah walked part of the way down the road with Chloe. 'Let's do something together next week,' she said warmly. 'I don't often work in the afternoons. We could wander round a stately home, or go in to Guildford, or just walk. It's a great place for walking.'

'I'd like that. Any of them.'

'I'll ring you, then. Or you ring me if you have another inspiration.' Dinah touched her arm before turning back towards her gate. 'I'm glad you came to Sheringham,' she said.

'So am I.' Chloe watched her walk away. Her long red skirt roused the memory of a single hibiscus flower she had once seen, burning early in a garden in Rhodes. She liked Dinah, liked her more than any woman she had met since her college days when she and Jane and Lennie and Thea had been a gang of four. They had stuck together ever since, through affairs, marriages, children, divorces and, in Jane's case, through a cruel cancer until her early death. Friendship was a gift of irreplaceable value, ever more so as one grew older. She must remember that. She would remember that it was Dinah who was going to be important to her. She was not about to spoil such a rich possibility by allowing herself to have an undignified crush on Dinah's husband.

Chapter Four

〰〰〰〰〰〰〰

THE NEXT WEEK IT WAS autumn. It came with the single shake of a kaleidoscope, as sudden and theatrical as a magician's trick. Full blossom lay at one's feet and young leaves became old in a crackling consummation of gold and green. This year there was a new, fierce auburn that blazed in the lingering sun, filling the low reflective bowl of the sky with clouds of apricot smoke.

On one of these burnished afternoons, shortly after her visit to Dinah, Chloe returned to Friday Street. She parked the jeep outside the Thomas à Becket and went inside for a glass of wine and a sandwich. She chose tuna because it was good for her brain, and chatted briefly to the bartender, a young Australian girl who was working her way round the world. Chloe felt a pang of envy as she envisaged the complete freedom of such an enterprise. She had considered doing the same thing when she was younger, but there seemed to have been no space for it in her crowded life. At first there was school and her parents and friends, then college and the revelation of what painting would mean to her, followed by the job at the National that she had been so lucky to get. Then had come the immediate certainty when she met Alain: love, the children, painting. She saw that she was simply a person who had got what she wanted. The passing shadow of envy gave place to full-bodied awe as she contemplated this remarkable fact.

The walk to her personal paradise would take from fifteen to twenty minutes. A lane led up from the inn, past half a dozen cottages nestling deep in leaves, to a small fishing lake bordering the narrow road which was the only thoroughfare. Friday Street could not call itself a village because it lacked the amenities to support such a claim. There was no church, no post office, no shop and no natural centre apart from the lake – only the Thomas à Becket hidden down its lane and two or three more houses near the water.

There was, however, a new, self-conscious National Trust sign telling her, in case she should not have noticed, that she was in a place of outstanding natural beauty.

She crossed the narrow road and went down a steep lane past a white smallholding with geese and rabbits in the garden. This was a public footpath which meant that she might sometimes have to share her newfound land with hikers and tourists. Selfishly, she regretted it. As she began her descent the path was bounded on the right by dense thickets of hebe and rhododendron, snaked by an occasional rutted driveway. Behind, in the woods, she caught sparse glimpses of roofs and chimneys. It was mixed woodland, a lot of ash and birch backed by climbing pine forest, while on the left, hedged by tall holly and burning beech, the land began its gentle slope into the valley where the river lay.

Over her head the branches met and mingled and let fall their leaves, laying out a new palette in welcome before her feet so that she felt herself to be a privileged guest. It was the most peaceful place on earth and one of the most beautiful. She received its peace and beauty as a gift and knew that, should it ever be necessary, she would also receive them as a solace.

She heard no strains of Beethoven as she came out of the trees above the river, but there was a sense of homecoming and as far as her work was concerned, one of boundless opportunity. The change in the scene was one of urgency as well as of colour and texture. The grass she walked in was longer, a darker green, the ground softer. The river ran deeper, had become busy, flowed swiftly, swirling leaves along with a new, demonic energy. Chloe let it take her eye, hurrying her downstream past the giant trees in their singular glory, the oaks, the ashes and the flame-thrown beeches, to the red farmhouse and the black-slatted barn where the doves still roosted on the gap-toothed tiles. The evergreen jungle behind them had lost its parrot colours but kept its sheen as it streamed across the long wall to frame the empty arch in which it seemed a figure must surely appear. Had there been such a figure, it must have thrown up its arms and cried 'Fire!' For the house above it was engaged in a fierce dance of colour and light, red stone revelling in an orange crucible of leaves, the windows leaping as the sun beat them into bronze, towers and chimneys stretching gilded limbs into the apricot smoke. It appeared as a living thing, sublime, a creature touched by the Firebird.

She looked at everything for a long time. Then she set to work. In two hours she thought she was beginning to get somewhere. She used pastels, block on block of crude colour, to build the changeable effect. She might translate it into oil or acrylic later, but this was the real, the raw opportunity to get down the way she was seeing it in this extraordinary light. She worked rhythmically, conscious of having got over some kind of obstacle, of being where she wanted to be. Her brush-strokes leaped like small flames, for she was painting a conflagration, the sacrifice that Autumn makes to the future Spring. The beauty that she had felt so deeply on the path had been transformed; it no longer had anything to do with peace. She put down the amber crayon, reached for white. The sky was the hardest part, swimming with tiny motes of light like a bowl of barley wine sprinkled with spice. She must not lose that lovely liquid feel.

As she stretched her hand to the box of pastels a cold nose pressed into it. 'Hello, boy. Not long now,' she murmured. But the nose, when stroked, was unfamiliar. It belonged to Watson; she had not brought Baskerville today. Holmes bounded up, wagging his tail. The afternoon stopped.

'Chloe.'

She could not tell herself that she had not half hoped for this; it was just that, working, she had forgotten.

'Shall I leave you in peace? Say so, if you'd prefer it.' There was a curl of amusement in Luke's voice. She thought it probably meant that he knew very well that he had destroyed for her all possibility of peace.

'No. I was about to stop. Soon, anyway.' She put the pastels carefully into their box. Her hand shook.

He was looking at the easel. 'My God!'

'Well, that's how it feels.'

'It's how it *is*.' He sounded like Belle, emphatic, delighted. 'Do you dare go nearer?' he asked.

'What?'

'Further into the flames. I was going to walk that way. Come with me?'

'Yes.' She began to pack everything into her portfolio.

'We could leave it under the hedge up there, it'll be quite safe,' he said. They climbed the slope back to the path and tucked the package under the brushwood. They walked steadily, side by side without turning to each other, speaking infrequently. Chloe remembered the first time she had gone for a walk with a boy. She had been thirteen. They had walked like this, talking abruptly, keeping apart, apologising when they touched, yet longing to touch, to hold, to kiss. In the end he had taken her hand, nothing more, and it had been the first truly sexual experience of her life.

Would she feel like that if Luke were to take her hand? The thought filled her with nervous irritation and she moved to the other side of the path as they came to a waterlogged section. She told herself she was a silly bitch who ought to take her own juvenile imagination in hand. Why on earth should she suppose Luke Cavendish regarded her as anything other than the twins' mother and his wife's prospective friend? As for the look they had seemed to exchange across the clichéd crowded room – the *kitchen* for God's sake – it had almost certainly been no exchange at all, just a random collision that had become, briefly and unintentionally, an entanglement. She must stop this, she was embarrassing herself.

Preoccupied with her self-scolding, she forgot to watch the path and slipped, almost losing her footing. Luke stepped quickly across the mud to steady her, taking her hand and holding it firmly as he walked her like a child along the narrow bank of grass above the ruts. There was nothing sensual in the contact. She felt only numb and slightly apprehensive. He let her go as soon as the path was dry again. There, you see, she told herself, everything is as it should be.

They continued in silence until the path left the woods and they found themselves up on a ridge overlooking the red house. From that height, about that of a low-flying air balloon, it was possible to discern the shape of it, a shallow E with the central tine thrust out at the back. The details were still masked by trees but it was obviously a much larger house than Chloe had realised, and one of great beauty.

'Its name is Arden Court,' Luke told her. She nodded, a lump in her throat. The path, soliciting curiosity, had run behind a rocky outcrop. They saw it reappear below, coasting in a wide spiral towards the house.

'It's like one of those roads in a Leonardo interior,' Chloe said. 'You see them through a window, making off over a hilltop.'

'In that case, shall we walk into the picture?' The actor's light had returned to his face. His look warmed her and her awkwardness fell away, an unnecessary burden toppling over the ridge.

'Of course. We can't go back now.'

He raised a mischievous brow. 'We are steeped in mud so far . . .?'

She laughed. '"To go back were more tedious than to explore." Horrible! May the good Bard forgive us. And in Arden Court, too.'

'He will. Even misquotation helps to keep him alive.'

They began to walk briskly downwards, the dogs racing past them. Their pace accelerated as the ground became steeper until on a sudden turn they were tipped, wide-eyed and breathless, on to a stretch of cool green turf at the front of the house.

Chloe could only stand and shake her head in pleasure. It was a small, faithful replica of a Jacobean manor house in the style known as the *'ferme ornée'*, an ornamental country house built by a Victorian gentleman farmer on the happy principle that usefulness does not preclude beauty. He had set it down in perfect accord with its surroundings, as certain of its place in the world as his flocks, his herds, and his parcel of pretty children.

There was a walled garden in front of it, once formal, now romantically overgrown. A broad path hedged with lavender in its second flowering led from tall wrought-iron gates to a paved area before the canopied portico. A weathered escutcheon above the door featured running deer and some dumpy shapes which Luke identified as woolsacks.

'It's so lovely,' said Chloe. 'It's the kind of house that looks like a person, not just an arrangement of bricks and mortar. Do you know anything about its history?'

'The original estate belonged to a Squire Arden, which explains the name, but it changed hands after the Great War and became a convent nursing home. Later it was a school, and recently there was an abandoned scheme to turn it into a country club. I suppose it still belongs to the company.'

'Do you think anyone lives there?'

They stood close to the gates and peered through their iron foliage, trying to decide.

'It doesn't *look* inhabited,' Luke said thoughtfully. 'But not quite uninhabited either.'

'Perhaps there's a caretaker. He might let us look at it.'

'Bound to be, though not necessarily living in. Why don't we find out? These gates are locked but there might be a more hopeful entrance at the back.'

'It's odd. I didn't realise that what I'd been painting was the back view. I'd love to take a closer look, if you don't mind the brambles.'

It was Holmes and Watson who rootled out the old stone path along the left flank of the house, snuffing their way through a high-coloured wilderness that had once been a well-kept shrubbery. When this yielded to comparative order, it was clear that the back of the house was almost as pleasing as the front. The tall trees which had seemed from a distance to crowd too closely had in fact been carefully placed to allow plenty of light, a guardianship of honour rather than of custody. Led by the dogs, Luke and Chloe walked among them to get a full view of the house.

There were two paved courtyards on either side of an ornate central block whose ruddily reflective falls of Gothic glass suggested it might be a conservatory or perhaps a small ballroom. Upon every surface the flames were holding their own; gold and crimson pyromaniac creepers licked at the walls, shinned up the drainpipes and half choked the undefended windows. It was wildfire without constraint.

There were several doors in each courtyard. They knocked on them all but there was no sign of life. Tacked to the last one was an old printed notice which invited them to 'Please to ring and wait'.

'There's nothing to ring,' Chloe said.

'And I'm not sure how long I can wait,' Luke replied. There was a faint suggestion in his voice that brought back Chloe's earlier insecurity in a disconcerting rush.

'We can hardly break in,' she said, steadying herself.

'Oh, I don't know.' He felt inside his jacket and produced a pocket knife. He was looking at her in a way that made her fear he was about to say something that should not be spoken. But all he said was, 'Perhaps we can. These old windows are probably not difficult to open.'

'Luke, you mustn't.' She moved away from him and paced about the courtyard. 'I don't care about the inside,' she said. 'I just want to come back and paint this before the colours change.'

Luke abandoned his examination of the window. 'When?' he demanded.

'I don't know. Soon.'

He swung round impatiently. 'Why are we doing this, Chloe?'

'What do you mean?' She knew she sounded wary, childish.

'Come here.'

She did not move. He crossed the stones and took her by the arm. She flinched.

'For God's sake, woman, I'm not going to rape you.'

The words shocked her by provoking a uterine tug that left her no denial. 'I can't *stay* here.' She was near to anger or tears. 'I have to go home.'

He was still holding her arm. She wanted to press her mouth to the hand that held her. She wanted to sit down on the stones and hide her face. Luke pulled her closer, forcing her to look at him.

'When can you be here?'

'I can't.'

'When?' he insisted. 'Next week?'

'No.'

'Oh yes, I think you can.' He held her more tightly.

Their kiss was every bit as dangerous as Chloe had known it would be. It bound her to him instantly, she was reeled in as though by a rod or a lasso – caught, bonded, weak and giving up. She wanted to lie down with him now and be magically relieved of all that she felt. Until that happened, and the kiss had made it inevitable, she would no longer be in control of herself or her life.

He held her face between his hands and she felt, or recognised, their kindness. 'I know,' he said. 'But it can't be today.' He put his fingers over her lips. 'A week today. You will come?'

'No, Luke. It can't happen.'

'I'll be here at three.' He released her and at once she was lonely.

'I don't know.'

'Don't you? I do. Chloe, I am sorry, but we ought to leave now. I have a tutorial in half an hour. I haven't managed the time very well.'

'I'll stay. You'll be quicker alone. I want to. I'll be all right.'

'Then just tell me if you'll be here. Or not.'

'Yes,' she said quickly, appalled at the idea that she might not see him again.

'Good.' He smiled happily, disgracefully. He whistled to the dogs and they came running, eager to be off. 'You're sure?' She nodded. He left her and walked out of the courtyard. She followed and watched him go down through the uncut grass towards the vine-covered wall. He could take a shorter route from there. When he reached the archway he turned to wave. Although there might well have been, there was no cry of 'Fire'. Chloe stared at the empty arch. She felt bereft, then angry, first with Luke and then with herself. She had never believed that there were women who said yes when they meant no. But that was what she had done. Wasn't it? Or had her body meant yes while her head said no? What had she meant? What, now, did she intend? She must know. Her mind spun and gave no answer.

Soon she caught sight of Luke again as he climbed up to the path. Again she felt that visceral tug. Dear God, what did it matter? She did not care about intentions, or about consequences, only for one thing: they would be together again in a week.

Alain would be in Singapore. That made a difference, though it was not one she cared to analyse. She could not think about all that just yet. (She must remember to take his linen suit to the cleaners . . .) A week. A week was a long time, longer in love than in politics. Love. Was that what it was? How could she tell? She felt as if she had been hit by a car. Was that love?

She wanted Luke so much, not only to make love with him, although every atom of her was alive to that probability, but just to be with him, to revel in his company. The thought of being apart from him for any great length of time, now that they had come so much closer, struck her as akin to the idea that Catholics have about being deprived of the presence of God – it is the only way they can describe what they imagine it is like to be in Hell. She managed to laugh at her self-dramatising, but only just.

As often happened, Alain had to leave for the Far East on Friday evening. Although it was not her habit, Chloe found herself clinging a little. 'You're away so often, we are hardly ever seen together,' she remarked, hovering while he packed. 'People are beginning to think I'm married to Baskerville.'

'You make a lovely couple, but 'ow do you explain the children? 'Ave you seen my Asterix cufflinks?'

She smiled; whenever he dropped his aitches in that appealing way it still made her want to smile. She searched the dressing-table.

'Here. In my earring box.'

'*Bon*. I need them for good luck.' Chloe had had them made for him last Christmas. He was faithful to Asterix. Rufus, always the fashion victim, had transferred his allegiance to the Simpsons.

'Will this be a difficult job?' She understood very little about Alain's work, which was perfectly reasonable considering it was based upon the relationships between higher mathematics, vast temperatures and very large pieces of metal, damage to which could cost a terrorists' ransom and black out the power grid of half a nation.

'It's a responsibility. I think the turbine blades may be corroded. I 'ave to oversee the blading group who will take them out and clean them so we can find out. Part of them will be destroyed. It is a very delicate operation and a very expensive one.'

'How expensive?'

'If we were to allow the Japanese firm who made the turbine to do it, they would take out every blade and charge a million. I hope to do it for considerably less. But I don't yet know how much. So you see, I'm a little nervous. And I 'ave great need of the cufflinks.'

'It must take a lot of nerve to juggle with such enormous sums.'

He shrugged. '*C'est mon métier*. I chose to do it. I have to go now, *chérie*. I'll call you tomorrow from the hotel.'

Men, she thought; they were always leaving. She received his kiss, as familiar as the contours of his body fitting into hers, not exciting because it was not offered in order to excite but in extenuation of his absence. Towards the end of the embrace it promised, as it always did, passion on his return.

'Take care of yourself, *ma mie*.'

'You too.' She rubbed her nose against his cheek as he liked her to do. He looked at his watch. Thus summoned, the car that was to take him to the airport was heard to arrive. Chloe smiled; Alain was ever precise, even to the timing of a kiss.

After he had gone she experienced the usual sense of freedom and relaxation caused by the knowledge that, apart from the children, she had only herself to think about for a while. The relaxation was a normal reaction to the small tensions of any such departure. She had sometimes worried about the sense of freedom. This time it terrified her.

Their marriage, three months after their first meeting, was generally agreed to have been made in Heaven. Though not entirely without theological overtones, the fatal encounter took place more practically in the afternoon splendour of the Renaissance rooms of the National Gallery.

Chloe, scribbling notes for a lecture on portraits of women, took an absent step backwards from the sumptuous presence of the Duchess of Urbino and landed with an unmistakable sensation on a softly clad foot.

'*Mon dieu, mon dieu, mon dieu*,' her victim repeated fervently.

'O my God, I'm so sorry!' She teetered like a mad top on the other heel. Firm hands caught her shoulders, steadied her and turned her round. She saw a thin, interesting face, flickering with humour.

'*Alors, Mademoiselle*. Now we 'ave established our religious credentials, per'aps we might move on to another subject?'

Chloe shook with delighted laughter. 'You choose,' she said. 'I really am sorry. I hope it doesn't hurt too badly?'

'Not really,' he smiled, 'but for a complete recovery I shall require many cups of coffee and I shall need an arm to lean on.'

She realised that she did not want to relinquish his company. She offered her arm. 'It's the least I can do,' she agreed.

Relaxed and companionable, they walked together through the elegant chambers. He did not apparently need to limp. On the contrary, they kept perfectly in step all the way to the café. By the time they reached it they had exchanged the few obvious facts that would allow them to place each other. Chloe had told him about her job and her ambitions as a painter and had learned that he was a professional engineer who lived in Paris and was in London to visit a firm of consultants who had invited him to join them.

'Will you accept?' she asked, already conscious of an interest.

'I have not decided.' He pronounced the 'H' determinedly. She had noticed that he did so occasionally. His accent enlivened her. She liked the way it ran lightly up and down the scale; no Englishman employed as many notes. She might begin to find it addictive.

They found a table and he pulled out a chair for her. 'I will make the decision before I shall bring back the coffee,' he said surprisingly. 'You would like something to eat?'

'No, thank you.'

She watched him get what was necessary at the counter with alert economical movements that suggested he was aware of his body, like a dancer or a gymnast. With a flash of incipient jealousy she saw him pause for brief courtesies with the girl at the till. She grinned at her own foolishness. He sat down and poured the coffee exactly as she asked for it, without any nonsense about who should be mother.

'*Eh bien, j'ai décidé. Je le prends.*'

'Just like that? You're coming to London?'

'Yes.'

'But don't you need longer to think about it?'

He shrugged, delighting her further. She loved to see a Frenchman shrug. '*Mais pourquoi*? I already have all the facts. It is an excellent offer. The experience will be good.' He frowned. 'There will also be much travel.'

'Don't you like to travel?'

He had thought he did. He shrugged again, memorising the colour of her eyes. 'Sometimes,' he said.

She had an unwelcome thought. 'You're married. Your wife dislikes it.'

'No wife,' he said. He looked at her hand. There was an ornate ring on her third finger, as there was on the second.

'Me neither,' she said cheerfully. 'I mean, I just put rings where they fit.'

'So, you are free to 'ave dinner tonight? I should like you to celebrate with me.'

'Thank you. I should like that, too.'

It was a great relief to have that out of the way. She did not want to sit worrying about whether or not she would see him again.

They stayed in the café for two hours, after which he offered to drop her at her flat on the South Bank before going back to his West End hotel. In his car they suddenly realised that, in all this time, although they had heaped each other with information and anecdotes – they knew what were their favourite films, what perfume their respective mothers wore and who had been their own best friends at school – they had failed with superlative stupidity to effect the simple exchange of their names.

He braked with the cinematic suddenness of Belmondo at his best and ran the car on to the kerb near the London Dungeon. One famished look and they were cramming the names into each other's mouths, bruising them greedily between their lips like ripe, delicious fruit.

'Chloe. *Mon dieu, mon dieu, mon dieu.*'

'O my God. Alain.'

It had been very easy after that. A momentum took them over in which they rearranged their lives, organised the meeting and predictable friendship between their two pairs of superbly professional parents, paraded their old friends, planned their future and helped to orchestrate their marriage. Their only complaint was that these things were such wholesale consumers of their precious hours together.

Whereas it takes no time at all to fall in love, only an inscrutable blink of the heart that no scientist has yet been able to measure and no artist to comprehend.

That is why it is so dangerous.

Chapter Five

oooooooo

'**M**UM.' MIRANDA, CARRYING A MOTOR-CYCLE helmet, entered the kitchen with an air of smug ecstasy. 'Joel's here,' she announced breathlessly. 'He's just seeing to the bike.'

'Darth Vader.' Rufus eyed the helmet. 'Can I try it? Thanks. How do I look?'

'It does have the advantage of sparing us your hideous visage,' Tilda said loftily, suborning Grace who was making for her brother's knee.

'Piss off, pruneface.'

Miranda sighed. 'Are you two still at it? Wish you'd grow up a bit. Dinner smells good, Mum.'

'Coq au vin. Your father made it before he left.'

'Oh, yum!' Miranda went out again. 'There you are! Come in and meet everyone. Mum, this is Joel.' She stood back with the modesty of one who presents a well-chosen gift.

Oh dear, thought Chloe, this one really means something. And yes, he does look like Alain Delon. Joel took her hand and shook it once, very firmly. The smile that accompanied this courtesy reminded her for unfathomable reasons of a song she had sung as a child – 'Never smile at a crocodile'. This was ridiculous, of course, because it was

— 61 —

probably the most handsome and most dentally correct smile she would ever see. It startled forth, with the snowy purity reserved for the coifs of nuns, against unrelieved black; long, beautifully cut black hair; heavy-lidded, unreadable black eyes and as much black leather per square centimetre of his excellent body as there was of his skin.

'Joel, it's nice to have you with us,' she said hospitably. She was not at all sure it would be. Her instinctive reservations had nothing to do with his appearance. She could appreciate that as the epitome of a certain style, the purification of it, in a sense – no studs, no badges, no skull and crossbones scarf – but there was somehow altogether too much of him for a first impression.

'Thank you, Mrs Olivier. I'm glad to be here,' he returned unobjectionably. The words 'animal magnetism' slid into her mind.

He sat down at the table and began to talk to the twins. Tilda, overfaced by the white-linen smile, answered him nervously, her fingers working in Grace's fur. She was relieved when Rufus hijacked his attention for a thorough catechism on the merits of the various models of Harley-Davidson, one of which stood outside.

'The Superglide? Wow! Will you show me?' He was half out of his seat.

'Later. We'll go for a burn, if you like.'

'Yeah!' Rufus was enslaved.

Chloe awarded Joel minus points for encouraging every parent's nightmare, then almost rescinded it when she saw him field and return Miranda's shining look as she served him his food. When Chloe herself sat down he began to question her intelligently but not intrusively about her work. He obviously knew what he was talking about and she found herself responding with some respect.

'Show him your new landscapes,' Miranda begged. 'They're stupendous, Joel. The colours just *eat* you.'

'Burn-up first?' asked Rufus hopefully.

'Homework first.'

'Oh, Mum.'

'Just around the houses?' Joel bargained. 'Fifteen minutes. He'll settle down better afterwards.'

This was true. 'Oh, all right, then. Fifteen minutes, no more.' And if he falls off I'll kill you with my bare hands.

Tilda made her escape to the piano, leaving Chloe and Miranda to wash up and make coffee.

'So what do you think?' Miranda asked shyly.

'I'm not sure. I'd need to know him better. It's what you think that matters.'

'Me?' Her mouth stretched in a broad and beautiful grin. 'I fancy him rotten.'

'"Tell me where is fancy bred,"' quoted Chloe soberly, having her own reason for asking. '"Or in the heart or in the head?"'

'"It is engender'd in the eyes,"' Miranda continued gravely, '"With gazing fed; and fancy dies/In the cradle where it lies." It won't be like that with Joel.'

'Sorry. It was only that the word set me thinking. "Fancy". It sounds so light and inconsequential. Not a very robust emotion.'

'Shakespeare's is a noun. Ours is a verb. Verbs are stronger. Anyway, this is the strongest feeling I've ever had for a boy. A man. I just want to be with him all the time.'

'I know what you mean.' Chloe was pierced by her own treachery.

'So what do you think?'

What does one say to a beloved daughter who has whole constellations of stars in her eyes for the first time? He is probably a rat and will most likely break your heart?

'I'd like to get to know him. I hope he makes you happy. But don't get too serious, will you, sweetheart? Not yet.'

'Not if I can help myself.'

You can't, Chloe agonised for her. Any more than I can.

She wanted to ask if they had made love yet but she did not feel she had the right to intrude so far upon Miranda's privacy. She knew that she was unusually blessed in receiving so much of her confidence and would not test its boundaries. The state had decreed that it was no longer her business. She had done her duty as a modern parent. As soon as she had begun to menstruate Miranda had been told that she must go on the pill if a sexual relationship seemed likely to develop. The family GP would ask her no embarrassing questions and she need not even tell Chloe about it unless she wished. She should never risk unprotected sex. She had said that it all sounded like more trouble than it could possibly be worth.

'I enjoyed your playing. Won't you go on?'

Tilda jumped. She had left the piano and was standing in front of the mirror holding up a bunch of her hair behind her head.

'People don't usually come in here while I'm practising.'

'Don't they?' Joel was unrebuked. 'Your hair would look good something like that. You should put a bit of curl in it, perhaps.'

'It won't curl.' Tilda wanted him to go away.

'It will if you use a diffuser and the right kind of spray.'

She went back to the piano and waited for him to leave. She had a dancer's walk, smooth and straight-backed. Joel followed her and stood behind her.

'It has a marvellous deep shine. Like dark amber. It's lovely just as it is, but if you have a heavy date tomorrow I'd go for some curl. Boys like curls. They're sexy.'

He picked up a length of her hair and wrapped it round his hand. Tilda tugged it sharply and painfully away.

'I don't care what boys like,' she cried. She got up and ran for the door. Outside, safe, she was sure she heard him laughing.

Rufus had been in heaven.

'You picked the right boyfriend, Miranda. Now all he has to do is to tell *me* how to make six thousand pounds for a Harley.'

'That much? Really?' Miranda was surprised.

'I thought he was a student,' Chloe said.

'He is. But he does sell his work sometimes.'

'To that extent? Maybe his family are well off. Not to say wildly indulgent.'

'I don't know. He never mentions them.'

'That's only the second-hand price,' said Rufus knowledgeably. 'But Harleys are known for holding their price.'

'Well, just don't hold your breath,' Miranda advised him.

'I won't,' he sighed. 'But Joel's going to teach me to ride. Only off the road,' he added quickly. 'That's OK, isn't it?'

'No,' said Chloe shortly. 'You're not old enough.'

'But then I'll be ready to pass my test when I am.'

'There's plenty of time.'

'Yes, but—'

'Leave it, Rufus.'

'OK. But I can go pillion, can't I?'

'I suppose you may.' Chloe was reluctant but she did not expect it would happen often. Joel would have better things to do. And everyone knew that saying no was the worst thing to do when dealing with a cherished obsession.

Luke, she thought then. Just that, nothing more.

The name provoked a tingle of heat inside her as if she had swallowed a tiny glass of slivovitz. Hers was not an obsession. She did not know quite what it was. A fancy, probably, in Shakespeare's sense.

Let it be, oh let it be.

At nine Chloe went to check on Tilda and take her some hot chocolate. She had been very quiet this evening, even for her. Finding the other room deserted, she carried the mug upstairs.

Tilda was lying on her bed in her dressing-gown, watching the news and crying. Part of her hair had been inexpertly curled with Miranda's diffuser.

'What is it, darling? That poor little boy who was killed?'

'No.' Tilda sat up, looking wretched. 'Mum, do you think – Am I sexy? Or going to be?'

'Here, drink this.' Chloe regarded her thoughtfully. 'The word "sexy" seems to me to describe something very obvious – overt and superficial. I think what you are beginning to be is something more subtle.'

'You either are or you aren't. Which?'

'Wait. It really is not as simple as that. Except in the minds of ignorant little boys and rather stupid and insensitive men.'

'The kind who snigger over page three and shout "I wouldn't half like to get inside that" at bus-stops?'

'What a broad education you are getting. Yes. But a lot of them do grow up, eventually. Tilda, what I'm saying is that you shouldn't worry. You are going to be a very sensual woman. How could you help it when you are so close to music? And your dancing? It is all part of the same thing. Sensuality, sexuality – they are the interaction of the mind with *all* the senses; not just the eyes. As for sexual attraction, I admit it's hard to pin down, even harder to recognise in oneself.'

'With animals it's all to do with signals,' said Tilda hopefully. 'We are animals too.'

'Yes, and we do give out signals, sometimes consciously, sometimes we are unaware of it. Look at Miranda now; she's doing both.'

Tilda's face closed. 'Have they gone out?'

'Yes, why?'

'I don't like him. Joel.'

'Why not? What don't you like about him?'

'I just can't stand how he is with people.'

'He seems to treat them rather well, I thought.'

'I know not "seems",' said Tilda darkly.

'Very wise. But shouldn't you give him more of a chance. He may have "that within which passeth show".'

'I don't think so. I think he's a "smiling, damned villain!"'

'Touché. Or possibly cliché. I didn't know you were doing *Hamlet*.'

'We're doing an examination of the idea of romantic love. Cool Hand Luke says Hamlet's chances of a normal love relationship were ruined by having to watch his mother with his uncle.'

'Poor Ophelia,' Chloe said shakily.

'Well, she was a bit flaky already, or I suppose she might have made him get himself together. That's my theory, anyway. I like Luke. He really is cool. He treats us as if he likes us and he has the most amazing brain, really original. He's good-looking too, don't you think?'

'Yes, he is. Shall I take that cup?'

'Here. No, wait. Do you think I should curl my hair?'

'No, I think *I* should. Come on, let's have the hairdrier. We can watch the film at the same time.'

'Great. Thanks. Just one more thing . . .'

'Yes?'

'Do you think Joel is sexy?'

'It can't be denied.'

'OK. And how about Luke, Mr Cavendish?'

'Him too. In a different way.'

'Which is the most? If you don't count their ages.'

'For heaven's sake, Tilda, you just cannot quantify everything, that especially.'

Breakfast was over and Chloe's pictures were spread out on the table. Joel prowled around it, head down.

'You use the paint like a big box of fireworks. No, it's a compliment, honestly. You're pushing at the boundaries of landscape here. Isn't that part of every real artist's work – to keep pushing and ultimately to keep changing the definition of art?'

'Like a computer artist does?' Rufus suggested. He had been making recent experiments with some new software, using fractals and various random elements to make interesting three-dimensional shapes.

'I'd accept that example. Chloe?'

'I agree about the boundaries, but it isn't every artist's mission. Live and let live. If someone wants to do flowers or animals or academic portraits, that's fine with me. The true space missionaries so often take people into territory where they feel insecure or frightened and then all you get as a reaction is denial.'

'I don't believe that. If I can imagine it, they can follow it, some of them. The others will just have to try harder.'

Tilda said tightly, 'Isn't that just arrogance?'

'No. They have the choice. They don't have to look at my stuff. They can gape at perfect representations of sheep instead, in the mirror.'

'Oh come on; there's no right or wrong here,' Miranda declared. 'There's room for anything an artist wants to do. I don't feel I have to push at the boundaries of painting, only of myself.'

'It's the same thing,' said Joel.

'I don't think so,' she insisted. 'There's a big difference between self-discovery and determined iconoclasm.'

'What's that?' asked Rufus. 'Sounds like falling downstairs.'

'Not far out,' Tilda giggled. 'It's throwing down idols; icons, traditions.'

'Trust you to know.' But he was not sneering.

Chloe began to gather up her paintings. 'I'm sorry to

break this up but I have to go out. Not that you need my contribution particularly.'

Joel smiled. 'Is this your way of saying you've heard it all before?'

'Well, perhaps a few times.'

He stretched his long legs and nodded, still smiling. Chloe had never before seen such extremity of ease in anyone of his age. Perhaps it was because he was sitting in Alain's chair, which was more than reasonable as it had been the only one unoccupied, but he seemed to her to be making himself at home with the single-minded despatch of Richard III upon a vacant throne.

Joel and Miranda had been lying on their jackets in a sunlit circle of grass and leaves in the privacy of the North Downs forest. They had kissed and held each other and had gone as far as her unspoken limitation would permit. Now Joel was sitting on a tree stump smoking a cigarette while Miranda disentangled her hair.

'Want some?'

'What is it?'

'Just dope.'

'I wish you didn't do any of that.'

'You're missing out. It's good. Makes you mellow.'

'I am mellow.'

'Are you? Come here then.'

She came to him and there was more kissing.

'That's nice,' she said.

'It can get much nicer. It's time it did.'

'Yes.'

'Then let's not have any more of this schoolgirl stuff. I need to know that you really do want me.'

'I do. I really do.'

She did. It was beginning to hurt her how much she did. If only she could feel more sure of him. She never had, even when he was with her. She would not be surprised if he just strolled away and left her, anywhere, at any time. Now, for instance; she could imagine him tossing down his cigarette, picking up his jacket and wandering off into the trees without another word.

'I want you,' she said.

'I'm glad.' He set her gently on her feet. 'Go over there. No, not too far. That's fine.'

'Why?'

'I want to watch you.'

'You're not going to sketch me?'

'Not quite. Take your knickers off.'

'What!'

'You heard me. Take them off. Slowly.'

'Joel!'

'It's a very exciting experience, watching a girl take her knickers off for you.'

'I'm sure it is, but you'll just have to manage without it. What am I, some kind of sex-slave?'

He sighed. 'Don't go all virginal on me, Miranda.'

'Why not? I have a perfect right.'

'*Ah*, do you? I wasn't absolutely sure.'

'You could have asked.'

'Fine, fine. Well, if you are not going to take your pants off, come back here and let me do it for you.'

She came, displaying reluctance. 'You are not making it very romantic.'

'No, I am not. I don't intend to. Romance has nothing to do with sex. Or even with marriage – which, by the way, is another thing I don't intend to do. Romance is old books, old films, the lies and delusions of old people. It's history. Sex is far better. It's the best thing we've got: you don't have to call it something else to make it good.'

'What about love? You can't pretend people don't love each other.'

'You want me to say I love you?'

'No. Not if you don't.'

'I don't know if what I feel for you is what you would think of as love. I like you. I enjoy being with you. I think you're beautiful. And intelligent. And I want to fuck you. And I think I'll go on feeling these things for some considerable time. How's that?'

'That's – yes, that's pretty similar to what I feel, except—'

'What?'

'As well as all that,' she shrugged depreciatingly, 'I love you.'

'OK, OK, crazy girl. Whatever you like. Love, dove, moon, June, just read me the words.'

They fell on each other, laughing.

'So, show me how to fuck.'

'My pleasure.'

It was. And because Joel loved sex and had therefore made it his business to become exceptionally well-versed in pleasing his partners, it was Miranda's too. She had always expected to be either daunted or amused by the logistics, or was it the gymnastics of it, but they fitted together so easily and inevitably that she could not quite believe it when he was actually inside her. She had thought it would hurt but this was quite the opposite feeling. It had more to do with beauty than with pain. There was also an inkling, towards the end, that these two, beauty and pain, might be closer to each other than she had previously had cause to consider. The end itself was a pure astonishment of bliss.

'You're very good at it,' she said dreamily.

'How can you know?' Smoke circled their heads.

'It can't get any better than that.'

'I promise you, moon of my delight, it can and it will.'

'I can't wait.'

'Give me two more minutes and you won't have to.'

'Joel?'

'Mmm.'

'I'm incredibly happy.'

'I'm quite pleased myself.'

'Any chance of another trip on the bike?'

'Not right now, Rufus. Miranda and I are going out. Tomorrow for sure.'

'Great. Thanks.'

'That's OK. Do you smoke?'

'Not really. Oh, that. Well, yes, as a matter of fact—'

'It's nice stuff. Algerian. Your parents won't mind?'

'You're joking. Dad'd murder me.'

'Well then, it had better stay between you and me.'

'Yes. Thanks. It *is* good stuff.'

'When did you start?'

'At my first school, when I was seven. But it got found out and there was a mega panic. Tabloids and everything. You know – "Teachers Tricked by Turned-on Toddlers". It all dried up for a while. Then it went underground. I had to be careful. I don't smoke much now.'

'Really? Well, any time you want any, just let me know.'

'Yeah? That'd be ace, Joel.'

'No sweat. In fact why don't you – oh, well maybe not.'

'No, go on.'

'Well, if your parents don't like it—'

'They'd never know. They think they really put the frighteners on me.'

'OK. What I thought was, if there's nothing doing round here, at school for instance, you could – with my help you could make a nice little earner for yourself. Fill the hole in the market.'

'Be a dealer you mean?'

'That worries you?'

'No. Well, I've just never thought about it.'

'Nothing heavy. I'm only talking dope. Nothing hard.'

'I see.'

'Think about it. You could start saving for that bike.'

'How would I explain the money? To my parents.'

'You certainly like to think ahead. You could say you won it on a horse. But I wouldn't worry about that yet.'

'I'd like to think it over if that's OK.'

'Fine. I've got a bit more of this stuff with me. Why don't you use it to test the market? Give it to a few friends?'

'I suppose I could.'

'That's my man. And listen to me, you don't tell a soul, right? Not even your sisters.'

'I've never told anyone. Not even Tilda. She really hates drugs.'

Joel had an appointment in London on Sunday afternoon which meant that he and Miranda had to leave after lunch.

'I'm sorry you're going so early.' Chloe watched her daughter tossing a rainbow of garments into a black holdall with a screaming eagle insignia. 'This time all I seem to have seen of you is your smile, like the Cheshire cat.'

'That's the effect Joel has on me,' said Miranda creamily. 'I'm sorry too, but this man he's seeing could be important for him. He's someone who might get him an exhibition, or part of one. Joel needs that now. He's right on the edge. Mr Yamamoto has already done great things for quite a few young artists we know. He's a millionaire; he actually owns Picassos and Chagalls and anyone important after that. We want him to want to own Joel Rangers too.'

'Then I wish him luck. So do you think you'll be back next weekend? Your father should be grounded, and he wants to fix that car.'

'Joel too? If he can?'

'Of course.' (If that's what it takes.) 'Whenever you wish.'

'I don't really see much of him; he's a fanatic about work. Here, I can have him all to myself. When we're not together it seems such ages until we are. I know that's anti-feminist and reactionary, but I can't help it.'

'I believe the feeling is universal,' Chloe said gravely.

Miranda looked sympathetic. 'I suppose you'd know. It must be rotten for you sometimes, with Dad going away so much.'

'I'm used to it.' Again she felt shamed. What would her daughter say if she had any idea of the turmoil going on in her mind?

'All set?'

'Just a second.' Miranda placed a monumental boot on the bed and laced it more tightly. 'Fine.'

She thundered downstairs ahead of Chloe, calling, 'Come on everyone, time to wave your hankies.'

Rufus was already outside with Joel, saying a poignant farewell to the Harley.

'And you'll definitely bring it up to school?'

'The first chance I get.'

Miranda and Chloe came out carrying the luggage. Tilda idled behind. Joel swung his bag on to his back and helped Miranda with hers.

'It's a pity there's nowhere to stow them,' Chloe said. She felt this would be safer.

'Hard luggage on a bike is very heavy,' Joel explained. 'I chose this model because it has none. It looks a hell of a lot better that way.' He held out his hand. 'Thank you, Chloe. It's been a good time.'

'You're welcome.' When, she wondered, had he begun to use her first name? 'We'll see you again soon.'

'Thanks. Bye Rufus. Have fun. Goodbye Tilda. Hey, don't look at me like that. I'm not all bad when you get to know me.'

Tilda did not respond. Nor did she wave when they zoomed off into the autumn backdrop looking like a poster for the kind of movie she held in the deepest contempt. Then she said, 'Oh yes you are. If we opened you up we'd find badness running right through you like Blackpool through rock.'

'And what runs through you, Miss Piggy?' Rufus grimaced at her. 'J-E-A-L-O-U-S.'

'Don't be absurd, you grovelling little sycophant.'

'Yes, don't be,' Chloe ordered unconvincingly. Poor Tilda. How horrible it was to be old enough to envy your sister's romance but too young or just too far short of confidence to imagine ever having your own.

'What the badness is,' the unconfident young moralist proclaimed, 'is that Joel doesn't really like people; he just wants them to like him.'

'How do you know that?' Chloe asked.

'I just know.'

Out of the mouths. For Miranda's sake I hope her instinct is not correct. 'Don't judge him quite yet,' she advised. 'First impressions are often wildly mistaken.'

'You hope.'

Chapter Six

⟨⟨⟨⟨⟨⟨⟨⟨⟩⟩

CHLOE HAD BEEN SAVING SOME time when she could be alone to think seriously about Luke. He had come uninvited into her mind very often during the last few days but each time she had evicted him on the grounds that it was already too crowded. Alone in the bedroom she let him in at last. There he was, standing at the foot of her bed with his easy stance and his untidy hair and that optimistic grin that was the cock-eyed opposite of Joel's parade of pearls before swine. There he was, an instant hologram of masculine glory. Oh God, if *only*! No! This was not what she had meant to do. She was not to think *about* him, she was to think what to *do* about him.

She had agreed, she supposed she had agreed, to meet him on Wednesday. The thing was, ought she to go, or not? If she did go, he would think she was willing to have an affair with him, whereas – no, don't stop there, go on – whereas if she did not go, he might think she had simply been delayed or prevented and he would be left wondering. That would be a graceless way to treat him. Anyway, failing to turn up was a coward's way out. She could see, in the cold light of day, or reason, or some other inimical glare, that there had to be a way out. Because she was *not* going to have an affair with Luke. How could she? How could he? There was Alain, there was Dinah, there were six young persons and several innocent animals, not to mention the Sheringham Board of Governors, all lined up against them like a police force confronting a neo-Nazi demo. There was no question of an affair. She was not about to kick Doc-Martined over her principles. She was not the kind of woman who had affairs. She had never needed them. She loved Alain. He was the right man for her; she was the right woman for him. No one who knew them had ever doubted it. Nor had Chloe. She did not doubt it now.

She decided; I shall meet him and tell him, very quickly, that I can't stay, that there can't be anything between us. Then I'll – just go. There, that's it. But suppose he wants to kiss me goodbye? No, there is an absolute prohibition on that. That way madness lies. I will not think about how it was when we kissed. That is strictly for juveniles. Leave all that to Miranda; it is her turn, not mine.

I'll just go, and say what I have to say, and leave.

On Monday she could not work. She was quite unable to concentrate. The brush behaved as though she were the Sorcerer's Apprentice, while form and colour denied ever having had relations. Subdued, she took up a sponge and loo-brush and a bright blue bathroom cleaner only to be rebuked by the arrival of Mrs Cubitt.

'You punishin' yerself for somethink?'

'Oh, I just felt energetic. Have a cup of coffee and tell me how Dwayne is getting on at Sheringham.'

'Bothered if I know, Mrs O. Ee's such a bare-arsed little liar that we shan't know until we gets 'is report. *If* we can get 'old of it before 'ee doctors it. Don't mind if I do. Nice coffee, you 'ave 'ere.'

She slept poorly that night, and Tuesday was such a limp, struggling thing that she was glad when it was time to put it out of its misery. Sleep was absent again until two in the morning, when it crept up on her and threw her down a black shaft into a pit of hissing serpents without the ghost of a hope of an Indiana Jones to rescue her.

On Wednesday morning she spent twenty minutes in the bath soaking off the sweats and terrors of the night. The bath essence, a present from Miranda, contained something called ylang-ylang which sounded inappropriately threatening, like the clang of prison doors. It smelled gorgeous. It made her feel like a whore. The feeling was far more pleasant than otherwise. With the instinct which Mrs Cubitt had shrewdly recognised, she dressed in a long soft suit of pale grey wool which she considered to be severe. She added intricate silver earrings and took them off again.

In order to occupy part of the century before three o'clock she made a barely necessary trip to the supermarket. When she got back it was still only 10.45. She put the shopping away without paying it any attention, searching her mind for some small event that might help her to find her centre again. She needed it badly.

She thought of something almost immediately. She supposed it was extraordinary but it seemed the right thing to do. She picked up the phone and dialled. 'Hello, Dinah? It's Chloe Olivier. Thanks. You too. Listen, I wondered if you would like to come over for coffee. Well, now, if you can. Psychic counsellor? What's that? I see. That's admirably adventurous of you. I think I'd be a little bit scared myself. Well, yes, it *would* be wonderful to know who one had been. Sam Palmer? I doubt that, but he'd certainly be my first choice. Come with you? No, I'm afraid I can't. Yes. All right, then, Dinah, see you next week. I hope you turn out to have been Freud or Jung or some other founding father. Better still, founding mother.'

It was probably for the best. She would not have known what to say to Dinah had she come over. *Anything* she said would have sounded insincere. Or she might have tried, 'Hello, good morning and welcome. I'm just off to tell your husband I won't sleep with him.'

That was not the right attitude to see her through the next three and a half hours. She must not let herself get hysterical.

Luke.

At least – at last – she would see him again.

When Chloe entered the courtyard, ice-cold with apprehension, Luke was sitting on the step in an open doorway. The sight of him set delicate mechanisms turning over inside her.

'I thought you might not come.' His voice turned them faster. 'I'm glad you did.'

I'm not staying, she had planned to say, but if she said that she would have to turn right around and leave him, and now that she saw him this was not possible. Not quite, not yet. She just needed a little time, to look at him, to be near him.

'Hello Luke.' Her mouth betrayed her in a smile that was too joyful. She could not speak the words she had to say.

'Chloe.' There it was, the pirate gleam.

He got up and they clutched each other with the desperate grasp of refugees who had never hoped to meet again.

'I have missed you,' she said. 'How can I miss someone I hardly know?'

'You know me. Don't cry. I've missed you too. I can't stop thinking about you.' They kissed, very gently as if they were invalids.

'Luke, we have to talk about this.'

'Yes, of course, but inside. I opened the door for you.'

'Are you sure?'

'There's no one here; I've looked. You wanted to see the house.' He held out his hand.

She recognised the moment, the perfect opportunity to tell him her decision and walk away with a conscience as clear and as dull as still mineral water. She saw it and let it pass by. She felt a calm acceptance as if she had allowed a train she might easily have caught to leave the platform without her. She placed her hand in his and he led her over the threshold. Before her memory could add shame to its automatic nuptial comparisons Luke was kissing her again.

He was thorough, intense and very determined upon his objective, which was to transmute her entirely into liquid fire. Unable to wish it otherwise she began to employ a similar alchemy herself. When she could no longer think or breathe or move her limbs except in a caress, he said 'Come on. Come with me.'

He hurried her through the hallway, up stairs, through rooms and along passages she had no time to record, until on an upper floor he stopped and pushed at a half-open door.

The room rested quietly in diffused sunlight, sailing high among the trees, gazing through long medieval casements into the mirror image of her painted landscape. They stood together and looked out, she leaning against his shoulder. There was an exceptional stillness.

When the silence became heavy they turned and looked at the bed. It was a thing of carved and brocaded splendour, a frayed and faded relic of the halcyon days of the house. Chloe stared at it and began to shake.

'No, don't touch me, not yet,' she begged. She began to pull off her clothes.

Their haste as they undressed was unsteady, frustrating and slightly hilarious, so that they began with shared laughter, then quietened as nakedness made them serious with its vulnerability and demand for trust. They looked at each other's bodies with a complete and wondering familiarity. It was as if a voice in the room had spoken with infinite kindness: So there you are. I have been waiting for you all this time.

They sighed with the exquisite relief of it as they lay down together. The respite was brief. They touched, embraced, torched and were consumed in an intensity of need so extreme and so demanding that there seemed no adequate physical way to deal with it. Time, which until now had cheated them and would cheat again, and space, which had kept them apart and even now would not allow them to come close enough, were enemies. Chloe wept because she could never become Luke, could not live in his body or inhabit his mind, while Luke cried out in despair because he could never truly possess her, make of her his own flesh, never put back the missing rib that symbolised all that he lacked. Even in this strange, brave, pitiful conjunction when bone flowed into bone and thought went wheeling beyond the universe, no matter how great the strivings to be one, each must remain a prisoner of self, lonely at the last, on a pinnacle among stars.

'I love you,' Luke said.

'Yes.'

'What is it about sex? How can I know so surely, from what we have just done, that what I feel for you is love?'

'Is that how you know?'

'Is it not for you?'

'No. I think I knew some other way, when I saw you coming down the hillside after Baskerville.'

'And this has made no difference?'

'A great difference. It has made it real. Before, it was like a poem or a story I knew. I love you too.'

'There's no need to sound so tragic.'

'Perhaps it was a tragic poem.'

'Nonsense. It was a great romance.'

'Name one that doesn't end in tragedy.'

'Chloe, let's not talk. One thing that language is absolutely no good for is talking about love in real life.

Poets can manage it, but they recollect in tranquillity; they don't try to net the Bird of Paradise on the wing.'

'I only said I love you.'

'Hush.' He moved over her and emptied her mouth of words. No longer in desperation, but gentle and seeking, they began to explore each other and to test for what would bring delight.

Luke leaned on his arm and spread Chloe before him like a secret hoard, counting each discovered jewel with a kiss.

He kissed her hair, which clung to his mouth and fell away softly, strand by strand, each one meshed in amber light.

He kissed her eyes, and the snowfall weight of it recalled the time when his eyes had rested on hers and made her look up to see that all this was clearly foretold in them.

He did not kiss her lips, although they fluttered and tried to reach him, small wings clamouring at his finger-tips, but only looked at them, and touched them, and smiled at her.

She wanted him so much when she saw him smile that she made a small unkempt sound and carried his hand to her vulva, pressing the straight bones hard against it to quell its rebellion. He stroked her into a deceitful truce and continued his inventory, tracing her with his fingers and hovering with his lips until she brimmed and could bear it no longer. It was too much, too sweet, too soon.

She stayed his hand and eeled from under him, leaning over him now, their positions reversed. She began, in turn, to learn his body, the hardness of it, so different from her yielding surfaces, its deeper colours, brown and bisque, with the dark glow of the blood beneath the skin making it layered and luminous, like a lantern in a temple. She gave back his kisses, finding new places for them. She was amazed at the softness of the black hair, furred and curled like the cadences of his voice, that overlaid the shape of him, a permanent, portable shadow to his sun. He lay like a sultan in his pleasure while she licked that shape into her.

It was not the silken versatility of her tongue that made it impossible he should hold back any longer, but the steady brightness of her face as she looked up to see how well he liked it. He rose and put her on her back and let her feel the vibrating echo of her attentions, feathering her flesh and setting it among clouds, among fronds, among drifting weed. Chloe closed her eyes into perfect bliss and straight-away was returned to her dream, the dream that had heralded her need for him. The Japanese flower opened inside her like a soft fist unfolding. She flowed about him, the water and the wave. Time did not pass. The magic was made and they reached a place where they were everything that they could become. It seemed very familiar to them. When they left it they clung to each other as though they might be dying, as though they must be torn apart. Luke gave a lost, wild cry and Chloe wept like an abandoned child. She opened her eyes; tiny points of light exploded behind them as if the room were thick with stars.

'It's like loving a sailor,' she said. 'Except that you take me with you when you go voyaging.'

He murmured something indistinguishable into her hair.

'I have been to some legendary places. I was underwater for a while.' She told him about the dream. 'It means I was waiting for you,' she said. 'It was a kind of premonition.'

'That's how a religion is born,' Luke said, amused. 'You argue from the thing you have to the thing you want. If three pigs fly across the moon, Hamilton Academicals will beat Partick Thistle.' He spoke the names as if they tasted good.

'But I didn't know I was going to want you,' she said reasonably. 'It isn't the same. I'm not superstitious.'

'Oh, you can run the logic backwards or forwards; God

made us or we made God, it doesn't matter. It's what we do.' He stretched with feline luxury and furled himself round her again.

'It will matter, if it turns out that he did. Did you know that you have the body of a Greek dancer? On a vase. Preferably from Crete.'

'I wouldn't mind if the music were not a bit limited. Twenty-five centuries round and round the terracotta to the pipes of pan tends to make one two-dimensional. Now, what about you? A temple prostitute? Both lovely and generous. It suits you.'

'They did it for the money. I am not fat.'

'The priests got the money. No, you are not; you are the pattern of what a woman should be. Now I have made you blush. How beautiful that is. I didn't know it went down so far.'

She said, 'We should have music here. I should like a Magnificat. There is a beatifically triumphant one by someone called Marenzio.'

'You shall have it. Next time.'

'Thank you.'

'Next week.'

'Yes.'

Oh yes. Yes. My soul doth magnify the Lord and today I would even speculate that He does exist. In love, the body cries out for completion, and sometimes the spirit, for the term of a firefly's flame, achieves it.

Later she sat dreaming in her rocking-chair beside the drawing-room window, gazing across open fields to the downs and watching a copper sun descend behind the ruined church that crowned the near hill. She felt an immense sense of well-being, of liquescence at her centre as though the soft-edged orb had come down into her belly and melted there.

She closed her eyes and called up images of Luke, the things they had done, how he had made her feel. The liquefaction increased and she quickened with the memory, small wings fluttering inside.

A sound jarred and outrageous hands covered her eyes. She gasped, wrenched and deprived. 'Rufus!' She must not sound angry.

'Are my 'ands so small? Or his already so large?'

'Alain! You gave me such a shock. What are you doing here? I mean—'

'You mean "welcome home", *chérie*. At least I hope so.'

'Yes, of course.' Heart still knocking, she turned for his kiss. Did she feel like a Judas? Not exactly. What then? Nothing. Just the surprise. Followed by the fear that he might read something unprecedented in her face. But he did not.

'We finished the job far sooner than I expected.'

'So it went well?'

'We hope so. The tests seemed conclusive. The blading engineer was a marvel – so quick, so completely sure. We worked well together.' He rubbed his hand against her cheek; he did this to all of them when he was pleased; even Rufus liked it. 'So now I feel like celebrating. Let's go out for dinner. Chez Claudine, or anywhere you like.'

Chloe was still winded, as if she had been punched in the stomach. 'Yes, let's,' she agreed. 'It will be nice to see John and Claudie.'

As they prepared to change in the bedroom he said, 'I have something for you.' He handed her a long slim package that she knew must be a picture. He rarely gave her paintings, had said that choosing for her was too difficult, too great a responsibility. This time he had been certain.

'Oh, Alain, how beautiful.' It was a watercolour – a group of horses, chestnut, bay, palomino, painted with that particular oriental delicacy which combines rigorous economy of line with a perfect understanding of anatomy. 'There's so much movement in it. You can see their tails flicking. Where did you find it?'

'In a tiny gallery near the food market, a canvas-booth really. The artist is a woman. I'm glad you like it.'

'I love it. Let's hang it in here. Over there? We can boot Braque.'

'Fine. I'll fix it now.'

'Great. I'm going to take a shower before I change. What shall I wear?' Her clothes interested him; he had the Frenchman's unashamed appreciation of style, considering it a necessity rather than an indulgence.

'Mmm? The black velvet jacket with the peacock embroidery. And that chiffon skirt, or trousers if you are cold.'

'OK. Hair up or down?'

'Down. It's pretty today. I like that just-out-of-bed look.'

They were greeted warmly at the restaurant where they were fast becoming friends as well as customers. Claudine and her husband John Latham provided excellent French cooking in a well-judged and comfortable atmosphere. Careful to consider the thin pockets of the hungry young as well as the bulging belts of the stockbrokers, they had divided their space between a brasserie with checked tablecloths and candles, which the Oliviers preferred, and a panelled dining-room with silver, lace and chandeliers which owed more to the boulevards of St Germain than to Montmartre. 'I am a Jesuit at heart,' John had explained. 'Catch them early and you'll keep them. Besides, young people are so decorative.'

This was especially true in the case of his waitresses, who came over in relays from Claudie's native Paris to perfect their English, their popularity and the knack of keeping several men in the air without dropping any of them. The one who was making the most progress was Chantal, an extremely pretty girl who liked to demonstrate her skills to Alain. Normally, Chloe was amused by her flirtatious pout and flounce, and as willing as any man to admire her minuscule waist and the cascade of chameleon curls that changed colour from week to week. This evening she found her irritating – so much so that she interrupted the headlong French narrative which she and Alain were clearly enjoying.

'Do you think you might fetch that bread now, Chantal? We do need it to mop up the juice.' She was perfectly justified. They were both eating moules marinières and mopping up was half the fun.

'Yes of course, Madame.' Chantal tossed the curls, treacle-toned tonight. 'I will get it for you at once.' She gave Chloe a measuring look and clattered away with the air of conferring a favour.

Alain had registered the impatience. 'I do tend to get a little carried away by Chantal. She is like an express train.' He smiled, testing.

'I thought she was here to speak English.' This, she knew, was not justified.

'Well, yes – but, you know, I like very much to hear some French occasionally. She is aware of this, I think.'

Chloe was instantly contrite. 'Alain, I'm sorry. I didn't think. I'm so accustomed to your English, I just forget. You must feel quite homesick when you come here.'

He smiled. 'I wouldn't put it as strongly as that. And anyway, you are my home now, you and the children.'

She returned his smile but his statement, far from flooding her with warmth, made her unaccountably angry. I am not your home, she thought; it makes me sound like one of those horrible motor caravans. I am myself, that is all. Her anger acted as a warning, she saw how unstable her mood had become. She covered Alain's hand with hers, pushing down the guilt aroused by the action. Very soon, they would go home and go to bed and make love. She pushed that thought down as well.

'Do you think we could have another bottle? I don't know why, but I feel like getting a little bit drunk tonight.'

'Why not?' He made a sign to Chantal.

The wine helped. Chloe recovered her composure and began to glow. She made a point of being nice to Chantal, to make up for her tartness, and was appreciative and amusing when first Claudine and then John left the kitchen to join them at their table.

They were invited to stay for more coffee and some of John's beloved Armagnac, but Alain refused, saying he needed his bed. He looked at Chloe as he said it, so that she nodded and touched his sleeve. On the way home in the taxi she leaned against him and closed her eyes. Although she tried hard to hold on to it, all her wine-coloured confidence drained away during the brief journey. She was an unfaithful wife; she loved another man. She loved Alain too, of course. That could not have changed. She loved him, and now she was even looking forward to the certainty of going to bed with him. She no longer felt strange about making love to him. She wanted it. She would take it now if she could, here in the back of the taxi with Mrs Cubitt's Elvis surveying them imperturbably in the mirror. The idea excited her in a new and uncharacteristic fashion. Was she changed already by her deeds? She had become an adulteress. She had taken Luke inside her, into territory which Alain must regard as exclusively his own. That was the meaning of marriage when you looked at it truthfully. It was a witnessed exchange of genital rent. She laughed.

'What is funny?' Alain wanted to know.

'Oh, nothing.' She must have drunk more than she thought.

'We're home,' he said. 'Wait. I'll help you out.'

She stood solemnly on the pavement and looked up. There was a huge moon, as big as a sun. Chloe smiled at it.

'The Guinessy Man,' she said. 'Or is it the Porridgy Man? I can't tell.' It was funny how childhood caught up with you when you were drunk.

Alain undressed her and laid her on the bed. Another of those thoughts that she did not want was circling somewhere near the ceiling. Did she still smell of Luke? When she had showered, earlier, she had not wanted to wash him out of her, had needed to keep that little bit of him. She supposed this to be tasteless and juvenile, but there you were. Her lips, she couldn't seem to control them, widened in a rubbery smile. What a reprehensible state she was in. She ought to feel disgusted with herself. But she didn't, not at all. What she did feel, by some paradoxical trick of self-deception and psychological mirrors, was a lubricious desire for her husband. If it was partly the fault of the wine she was grateful to it. She moaned and drew the attention of Alain's fingers to her condition.

'I need you to fill me right up,' she said carefully, trying not to lose the little syllables that tried to get away. 'So that there is no room for – anything else.'

If Alain was intrigued by her phrasing he was soon too occupied to consider it further. She was behaving, he found to his surprise and huge pleasure, very much in the manner of a young prostitute he had known in Hong Kong – a quick, golden girl like a dancing cat. Chloe showed him the same voracious greed, the same restless athleticism, the small, cruel encouragements of her heat. She had never been so demanding or, in a sense, so crude in her demands. 'Make me come,' she cried. 'Make me all yours.'

He set himself to bring her frenzy under his control. 'You *are* mine. And you will come when I tell you.' He gave her instructions, made her hold back until he was ready to let her go. In purely physical terms, it was the most tremendous orgasm she had ever had.

But at the end of it, all she saw behind her closed lids was

Luke. Luke watching over her happiness with intense concentration as he recognised first love and then responsibility. 'Why us?' he had asked, suffering an acceptance that was as painful as denial. She began to weep, harsh, rending sobs that tore at her throat.

'Chloe, my darling, what is it? Did I hurt you?' Alain raised himself in concern and stroked her wet cheeks.

'No. I'm all right.'

'Then why are you crying like this?'

'I'm sorry. I don't know. I'm sorry.'

Tears splashed on to her breasts. He wiped them gently away. '*Chérie*, you have not been yourself tonight. You had such tension in you. Why?' She continued to weep. She felt dirty and guilty and very lonely.

'I am away from you too much,' he said penitently. 'That is the cause of all this. It's bad for you to be always waiting for me to come home.'

'It isn't like that.' A leftover spark of anger flew. 'I don't just sit and wait. I have a life of my own. I always did.'

'I know. Nevertheless, I feel accountable.'

'Horrible businessman's word. For what? There's nothing wrong. I drank too much and got tearful, that's all.'

Alain was unconvinced. 'I'll try to be at home more in future.'

The phone rang next morning as she tried unsuccessfully to work.

'Chloe.'

'Oh Lord, it's you. I hadn't thought of your *phoning*.'

'It's eleven o'clock. Break.'

'I remember. Frozen milk and jammy dodgers.'

'Fresh espresso and Danish. And now you.' The voice was velvet. 'How are you?'

'Well, I haven't caught anything lethal overnight. Sorry. That was nerves. I haven't got used to you in my kitchen yet. And I'm well, thank you.'

'And happy?'

'Yes, now.'

'Me too. I love you.'

'Are you sure? No, I mean is it all right? Over the phone. Isn't there a switchboard or something?'

'Yes, but this is my private outside line. No one will break in. How about you? Shall you mind if I call you sometimes? I think I'm going to need to.'

'No. I need it too. It's magical to hear your voice; it's one of the things I love most about you. Like Irish coffee on a cold night. I can feel it in the pit of my stomach.'

'And yours is the perfect instrument to play havoc with my erotic responses, especially when you laugh like that. God, next week is a long time ahead. I don't think I can survive like this. It's a particularly fiendish form of sensory deprivation, this telephone. I need to see you, hold you, taste you, roll about in the scent of you.'

'*Don't*. I know. Luke, Alain came back last night. He was two days early.'

'You slept with him.'

'Yes.'

'Damn. I'm sorry. How do you feel about that?'

'Confused. I was a bit drunk. I cried. He thought it was because he's away so much and felt like a heel. I felt like a worse one.'

'And?'

'What?'

'Does it make you want to stop? Us.'

'No. No, I couldn't.'

'Thank God. It's the same for me, you know. Dinah and I have always lived very close to each other. I can't change that now.'

'No, of course not.'

'I'm glad you – oh hell! Someone on the other line. I'll have to take it. I'll try to talk to you again later.'

'No. Please, it's better not. Too nerve-racking. I'll see

you next week. I love you. Goodbye.'

'Yes, oh yes. Goodbye.'

She replaced the phone. He had left her limp, tearful and sexually aroused, a state that showed every evidence of becoming permanent. She thought that she might have to do something about it, there and then, but it seemed a tawdry act, a betrayal of yesterday's shared splendour. She would not face her other, enormous betrayal, not today, perhaps not for a very long time. She was not afraid to do so but she knew that, even if she did, it could make no difference.

One day, no doubt, the reckoning would be delivered. Today what she wished to do was to follow her instinct somehow to get down what she felt about Luke on paper. It was a need that was as fundamental as sleep. How do you paint love? How to choose its colours, make still its shape? What was it he had said? That language was no use for describing love in real life. Line and colour were her language, just as words and constructs were his. Would she find herself unable to express what she most wanted to say? The fear was a divided one, half the sensible, established knowledge that she was not, and never would be, Rembrandt hymning his Saskia, half a new hesitation born of the newness of her emotions themselves. She knew, certainly she did, how to embody vitality and mass with the merciful collusion of charcoal. Very well then, why didn't she get on with it?

She made a beginning. Slowly, over what remained of the morning, she brought Luke's naked body back to her. At first she used lighter strokes than she normally did, erasing and repeating until she became confident, her hand remembering what her eye did not. The rough paper took silk from the smooth surfaces of skin with their suggested complexities of musculature, of the weight and hardness of bone. She did not stop before she drew his face, it came to hand as a thing known by heart. When she had done, and

Luke lay looking at her from the page, she sat perfectly still and breathed him in, drawing him into herself, her mind open to visions that she could not yet paint.

Later, when she put away the drawing in an old college folder, she hated the concealment, foreseeing it would be the first of many. She had little choice. Anything she had done recently was subject to Miranda's licensed scrutiny.

She forgot then, she had forgotten almost at once, her conversation with Miranda who had called her to say that she would not be coming home at the weekend. There was a party, a private view at some West-End gallery. Mr Yamamoto had invited them. All sorts of famous people would be there. Wasn't it exciting?

She did not remember until Friday evening, just before dinner, when Alain remarked with a trace of worry that it was not like their older daughter to risk missing a home-cooked meal. Had she mentioned to anyone that she might be late?

So shaken was Chloe by her forgetfulness that she was subdued throughout the meal and could only feel that she was served with perfect justice when Alain spent the greater part of Sunday repairing Miranda's car.

Chapter Seven

Wᴴᴇɴ ᴅɪɴᴀʜ ᴄᴀᴠᴇɴᴅɪsʜ's ɪᴍᴘʀᴏʙᴀʙʟʏ ᴘʀᴇ-
ꜱᴇʀᴠᴇᴅ half-timbered Morris coasted into the
driveway on Monday morning, Chloe's first
thought was that it was all over. 'He has told her. She has
made him promise never to see me again. She has come
here to tell me what she thinks of me.' Baskerville, to
whom she had spoken, waved his tail and looked troubled.
She opened the door and waited.

'Hi, Chloe. I love your garden. It's like a terrific head of
hair that's been professionally dishevelled. Ours is more an
Old English sheepdog run wild. Now, you're not to say no,
this time. The psychic counsellor didn't quite work out.
She's passed me on to a past life regressionist and I have an
appointment right now. I'm a little nervous and I need you
to come along and hold my hand.' She smiled brilliantly
and produced a paper bag. 'Here, have some of this fudge,
I can't stop eating it. Mrs Kelly at the post office has just
made a new batch. Ginger, or apricot? Here's some for
you, Baskerville. Good boy.'

'Ginger, please.' Chloe felt as if she had been blitzed.

'You will come, won't you?'

She hesitated, letting her mind click back into com-
monsense mode. 'Yes, why not? Just let me get my jacket.'

The reason she had not refused, she realised as she ran upstairs, had nothing to do with guilt or remorse, or even her ridiculous relief; it was the simple wish to spend the morning in Dinah's company.

Sunk in the old leather bucket seat of the Morris, she asked, 'What happened with the psychic counsellor?'

'It was interesting. I went to her because she's been a tremendous help to a friend of mine. I know she believes in reincarnation so I wanted to hear what she thought about revisiting past lives. She said what she mainly did was to put one in touch with one's higher self. She would act as a channel for my spirit guide, to whom I would bring my questions and problems and generally sort myself out over a long period. Raking about in past lives is apparently not considered helpful, oddly. For true spiritual growth we need to examine our present selves, both conscious and unconscious. The way she put it was, "Why do you want to dig for boxes when you already have the treasure?"'

'I like that.'

'Yes. She's an impressive person; there was this absolute certainty that you could trust her. I think I will go back and sign on with the spirit guide, but she said I should get my interest in the past over first or it might block my spiritual path. So that's why we're going to see Kenneth Clery. We take a left here, then all the way up the hill.'

In architectural terms, the regressionist had retreated as far as a modest seventeenth-century mansion which represented an immodest amount of twentieth-century money. A gardener saluted them with his secateurs. The door was opened by a pleasant young woman who took them through to an inviting, bookish room where white flowers gleamed among comfortable lumps of furniture.

A small, delicate man rose from an armchair, alert bird's eyes assessing them behind thin spectacles. 'Mrs Cavendish. How nice to see you. And your friend too.'

Chloe was introduced. 'I hope you don't mind. I can wait elsewhere,' she offered.

'Not at all, if Mrs Cavendish feels easier for your company.' His voice, light and dulcet, remembered County Cork. They found its music reassuring as he explained to them what would take place. First, Christian names were exchanged, as being less formal, and Dinah was placed in a high-backed wing chair closely opposite Kenneth, with Chloe on a sofa a little apart.

'I am not about to hypnotise you,' he told Dinah, 'though you may feel that you are falling asleep, and afterwards, that you have indeed slept.' To Chloe he said, 'You may think that I ask her a great many questions. Well, the precept that has been most strongly established in the history of these exercises is that the subject is quite unable to describe anything she may experience unless specifically asked to do so. I shall, of course, record everything that is said on tape.' He asked Dinah to close her eyes and relax her body by degrees from the toes upward, flexing and loosening the muscles, taking as long as she needed.

'How is that, now?' he asked after a while.

'Lovely. I feel as if I'm floating.'

'Yes, you may feel a little drowsy. Don't mind that. Go with it. You can relax your mind as deeply as your body. Let it clear itself of everything except my voice. Let all the thoughts flow away. It will become quite empty. It is a great relief, this emptiness. To be conscious of nothing at all. Sleep. Let go your consciousness. Let go altogether.'

Dinah grunted. Her eyelids fluttered.

Chloe jerked and opened her eyes very wide.

'You are asleep now, are you not?'

There was no reply.

'You are sleeping and perhaps you are dreaming. You can experience the past as a dream. You can travel backwards in your dream, backwards through a tunnel. Back, back you go. How far? A hundred years or so?

Something important happened to you thereabouts. Where are you now?'

'In the tunnel.'

'What are the walls of the tunnel like? Put out your hands and feel them.'

'Red bricks, small and old and crumbly, covered in moss.'

'And the ground?'

'Earth. Grass ruts. A bit muddy.'

'Keep walking. When the tunnel ends, what do you see?'

'It's misty. I can't see.'

'Look at your feet. What are you wearing?'

'My clogs.'

'What about your clothes?'

'Just my working dress.'

'Describe it. How does it feel?'

'It's dark blue; rough wool, with a high collar that itches.'

'What else are you wearing?'

'My striped shawl and a pocket-apron.'

'Is there anything in the pocket? Feel inside.'

'Herbs. Plants.'

'Now you have left the tunnel and the mist has cleared. Where are you? Indoors or out?'

'I'm outside, in the garden.'

'Where is the garden?'

'At the back of the house, beside the river.'

'What sort of weather is it? What colour is the sky?'

'Blue and bright, but it's chilly.'

'What are you doing in the garden?'

'I'm picking the leaves off this valerian plant.'

'Why?'

'It helps you sleep.'

'Do you have trouble sleeping?'

A giggle. 'Of course not. It's for sick people, and old folk. For the shop.'

'Which shop is that?'

'My father's. The herbalist's.'

'What is your father's name?'

'Matthew Mottram.'

'And yours?'

'Margaret.'

'Is anyone else collecting herbs with you, Margaret?'

'Yes.'

'Who is it?'

'My sister, Miriam.'

'What are you doing now, the two of you? You have the herbs you need.'

'Walking along, eating apples.'

'Where are you walking? Where are you going?'

'Down the lane, back to the shop.'

'Where is the shop? In what street, in what town?'

'It's in our village. Thorpe Barton. In Middle Street, just round the corner.'

'What is happening now?'

'Miriam is pulling at my sleeve. She wants to look in the haberdasher's window.'

'What do you see?'

'There's a cap she fancies, with blue ribbons. Oh my! No. Be careful!'

'What is happening?'

No answer. The cry had been urgent and fearful.

'Where are you now, Margaret?'

'Up here.'

'Where?'

'Above the street.'

'Tell me what has happened.'

'It was the brewer's dray. It came round the corner at such a lick, far too close to the wall. I gave Miriam a great shove out of the way of the horses but something struck my shoulder as I turned. I went down under the back wheels.'

'What did you feel?'

'Fear, very quick.'

'Pain?'

'No.'

Chloe bit on her hand, not daring to breathe, uncertain of her reactions beyond an hysterical need to laugh. It was so bizarre. To see one's own death like that, so sudden and casual in the daylight, the apple flying from her hand. Dinah sounding so unconcerned. She found she was weeping.

'Do not think about it any more,' Kenneth said. 'Don't think about anything at all. All is well. You have been asleep and dreaming and you will wake feeling refreshed and cheerful. You are almost awake. You can open your eyes now, Dinah.'

Dinah did so, dazed and blinking. 'I must have dozed off.'

'Indeed. You are an ideal subject.'

'You mean something actually happened?'

He smiled. 'You shall hear for yourself. I should warn you that you chose to visit the occasion of one of your deaths.'

'I don't believe it!'

'It is quite usual. Especially if the passing was sudden or violent.'

'Violent!'

'Don't worry. You'll be surprised how well you protect yourself.' He started the tape. Chloe watched as Dinah listened, her face re-recording each tiny change, her hand twisting one of her curls into a spring. When the end came she let go and it spiralled free.

'Oh my God, was that real? It was, wasn't it?'

'I think it was,' Kenneth said quietly. 'There is something I want to ask you.' He led her away from that last stab of terror. 'Your sister Miriam; is there anyone in your present life with whom you are able to equate her? Purely by instinct.'

'Oh yes,' said Dinah without hesitation. 'I am quite sure of that.' She smiled shyly at Chloe. 'It was you who were with me.'

— 99 —

Alarmed, Chloe rushed under the skirts of reason. 'I suppose it must have been because I *am* with you. I'm in your mind.'

'It depends how you look at it.' Kenneth looked mildly amused. 'I sensed the energy between the two of you as soon as you came in. I think you will find, if you care to travel further, that you have known each other in many different guises: sister, mother, lover, brother, friend. Your families and intimates, even your animals, will have been intertwined time after time, life after life.'

'Oh Lord,' wailed Chloe, whom reason now abandoned, 'Dinah – it was my fault. If I hadn't made you stop at that stupid haberdasher's—'

'Now *that*,' said Kenneth severely, 'is something I do *not* allow.'

'Are you OK?' asked Chloe, in the car. 'How do you feel?'

'I don't know. It's so weird. I just don't know if I can believe it. Perhaps I made it all up – and put you in because you're here, as you said. But how could I do that in my sleep? I *was* asleep.'

'No doubt about that, you were almost snoring.'

'So it was a sort of dream, then?'

'More like a guided tour where the client provides the local colour instead of the guide.'

'Oh, well, I don't know what to think. I'll leave it to soak in for a while, then take it out and look at it again later. Thanks a million for coming with me, Chloe. I'm so glad you did; it has made me feel much closer to you. It seemed so natural, somehow, that we should have been sisters.'

In the fizzing Molotov cocktail of Chloe's emotions, the base ingredient proved to be instinctive agreement. She wanted to throw her arms around Dinah, and also to tell her she should be less generous with her trust. She contented herself with a warm smile. 'I call that handsome,' she said, 'in view of the brewer's dray.'

'Pure bathos.' Dinah pulled a face. 'But it wasn't your fault. You couldn't have known what would happen.'

Chloe was reading the notices in the Sheringham church porch. She did not expect to make use of them, but they gave her a sense of the continuity of an order of things that were good, or at least well-intentioned, in themselves. The unchanging calendar of services, the choir, the bell-ringing, the societies for spiritual and social refreshment, the rotas for cleaning the church and arranging the flowers: surely these were the activities of people who cared about each other as a community, many of whom, perhaps most of them, believed in the existence and potency of a Supreme Being who cared even more. If Chloe, no longer able to believe, could not be one of them, it did not prevent her from conferring a modest blessing on the work.

Looking idly down the list of lady cleaners, she was amused to find that two of them shared Mrs Cubitt's services with her. Another signature leaped out, destroying any hope of the equilibrium she had come to seek – 'Friday a.m., 9–10, Dinah Cavendish'. She reacted physically, as though the name were Luke's, heart pumping. To think of Luke and Dinah on the same accelerated breath; how did that compare, on the scale of falls from grace, with sleeping with Luke and with Alain on the same day? And why did it hit home now, at the sight of a name on a piece of paper, rather than yesterday when she and Dinah had moved closer to what seemed, however absurdly, to be a natural and inevitable friendship.

'Oh God,' she said aloud.

She grimaced apologetically at the venerable west door. Having survived the attentions of Henry VIII and Oliver Cromwell, it was quite impervious to such small blasphemies. But as she reached for the latch the blackened oak shuddered and jumped; it stuck fast, then shrieked in outrage as it was dragged backward from inside. There emerged a large, energetic-looking man in a grey cord suit. Beneath this the neck of a white polo jumper stood a visible inch above a black one. This was the preferred clerical collar of Nicholas Bannister, the rector of St Mark's.

'The devil take it,' he said cheerfully. 'I rehung the thing only last week. How are you, Chloe? Look a bit pale. Are you coming in?'

'I'm fine, really. I was considering a visit to Catherine Chandler – but if your door is averse to agnostic ex-Catholics . . .?'

'Heavens no, it gobbles them up. Nothing it likes better. If you don't mind my saying so, you sound so perfectly certain in your doubt. I wish I were as perfect in my faith.' He smiled to remove the sting.

Chloe had met Nick Bannister at Philip Dacre's and had liked his friendliness and forthright attitude to his work. If his breezy accents and boyish air of challenge seemed to belong to the UN officer he used to be rather than the bishop he might become, his kindness to the living and gentleness with the dying were legendary among his parishioners. They also enjoyed his often hilarious and sometimes merciless sermons.

'But I'm not perfectly certain,' she said. 'That is what agnostic means.'

'Of course. It was your tone of voice that fooled me.'

'I just don't want to come here on false pretences.'

'Why do you come?'

'Because it's peaceful and beautiful. Because although I have left my own Church, I still feel happy in churches.'

'Then be happy here. So you've made friends with Catherine Chandler? She has many, I believe. *She* left us, you know,' he added mischievously, 'but she came back.'

'Yes. She intrigues me. I wish I could understand.'

'It is difficult, isn't it? Let me know if you succeed. I must be on my way. Parish meeting. Lovely to see you, Chloe.' He shook her hand and marched off between the ranks of green-shouldered gravestones standing drunkenly to attention.

Chloe entered the church and found it empty. She stood for a while at the foot of the nave, allowing the tranquillity of stained glass and old stone to lap about her like warm water. As she moved down the aisle the pointed arches of the crusaders soared and closed above her head like praying hands. As she glanced along the pews the crooked rows of kneelers, embroidered with small woodland animals, met her with a bright-eyed attentiveness that disowned the stone rows outside.

In the chancel, beyond the winged chariot of a lectern, carved and painted in the form of the lion of St Mark, there were no more pews, only a calm space before the altar. Here a knight lay buried beneath his brass self; and by grace of the saints in the luminous east window, he wore a memorial wreath of coloured light.

Nearby, in the north wall, two openings were driven into the Bargate stone, one a worn and misshapen quatrefoil, the other a bias-cut shaft known as a squint. These, and a glass case containing three documents, were all that remained witness to the life and sacrifice of Catherine Chandler. The documents, letters between churchmen, told her story with the frugal economy of a medieval ballad.

In the summer of 1329, Catherine, the daughter of Wilfred the Chandler of Sheringham in the diocese of Winchester, had informed the Bishop of her wish to become an anchoress. She would take vows of continence and perpetual chastity and suffer herself to be enclosed in 'a narrow place' adjoining the wall of her parish church, to spend her life in the service of God. It was not written how old she was, or whether she was fair or ill-favoured, who were her friends or what was the pattern of her life, or if she had ever exchanged the urgent, secular vows of a lover. Her petition was granted and she went into the narrow place that was built for her in the cold north wall.

The second letter, three years later, recorded that she had broken her vows and returned to the world, putting herself in danger of excommunication, even of death, and her soul in the power of the wolf. Here, the reader feels relief – thinking the price worth paying – but Catherine was not a modern woman; to exchange her sacred vows for freedom was to rob herself of the hope of Heaven. Once again she counted the world well lost for the love of God, and, throwing herself on the mercy of the Holy See, begged most humbly to be re-enclosed. Rome agreed. She would be given absolution if, within a further four months, she caused herself to be sealed back into her cell. There was no further information.

Did she obey? After four more months in the light of the sun, could she bring herself to keep forever to that narrow place, in the cold, in the dark, to take her food and offer her sane counsel, if she had any to give, through an iron grille, her only rewards in this life to look aslant and unseen upon the altar, and to receive, between the leaves of the quatrefoil, the daily mercy of the sacrament?

Chloe shivered with anger each time she thought of her.

And yet, Catherine had chosen her fate, not once but twice. Anger was uncalled-for, an ignorant anachronism. Chloe had no idea why she should feel so deeply about a woman who, had she been able, would undoubtedly have replied to any observations of hers in terms she would not like to hear. They could have nothing in common other than their shared womanhood. Why was it that she wanted there to be more? All she knew was that Catherine mattered to her in some way. It made no sense. Why should it?

'It's a neat opposition, isn't it?' she asked the blank shape of the quatrefoil. 'You locked yourself away to avoid all occasions of sin – medieval morality was so cruelly practical – while my lover and I lock ourselves away to sin in peace. I need not ask what you think about adultery. Perhaps you are right. Perhaps freedom is too risky a business. We give in to temptation and turn it into licence, become weak and permissive and all the things I want my children to guard against. But here I am, calling after a married man like a cat in heat, quite unable, despite these worthy sophistries, to think of anything else. Children, I implore you, do as I say, not as I do! There. I was bound to come to it in the end. You are not impressed, I know, Catherine. I feel a bit feverish. I meant to talk to you about Dinah. I *want* to think of Dinah.'

Any imaginable reply was postponed by a new alarum of protest from the west door, followed by an influx of sibilant noise and murmur as if a flock of birds had come to roost among the branching pillars. A horde of boys and girls poured in, their blazers writhing with the triple SSS of Sidney Sheringham School. One of them was Rufus. Behind them, their Ghengis Khan in a blue greatcoat, was Luke.

Chloe had fainted only twice in her life. Now she was going to do it again. She leaned against the wall and felt for the edges of the quatrefoil, knowing that in a moment she must fall. The children streamed over the church with surprising care, moving in groups in predetermined directions. One of the boys reached her just as she began to sink.

'Sir! There's a lady here not well.' A thin shoulder supported her.

'Over here, sir.'

'Oh cripes, it's my mother!'

'All right, Jonathan, I'll take her now. Fetch us a couple of those chairs, would you, Rufus?'

Chloe felt his arms go round her and breathed in the scent and cold of his coat while the world behaved like a failing light-bulb.

'You'll feel better now, Mrs Olivier.' He touched her forehead with the back of his hand.

'Yes. I'm sorry.' She transferred her grip from his sleeve to the chair. With an effort she opened her eyes. She did not feel much better but at least she was not going to faint.

'Mr Cavendish,' she said politely. 'Thank you so much.' She smiled hazily at the interested semi-circle standing round them.

'You all know what to do,' Luke told the children, his voice filling the quiet space with reassurance. 'If everyone will get started, I'll make sure that Mrs Olivier has recovered and then I'll come to each of you in turn.'

The class – there were about two dozen of them – milled and separated again, moving into purposeful groups in different parts of the church. The nearest, two girls and a boy, settled on the chancel floor and began to take a rubbing of the brass knight. Others carried notebooks into the south aisle or one of the chapels. Someone began to play the organ.

'Are you OK, Mum?' Rufus hovered awkwardly in front of her with Dwayne Cubitt. They were together a good deal lately. Tilda would not be here, of course; although in the same class, the twins were separated for all group activities.

'I am now. You mustn't worry. I probably just didn't have enough breakfast. Hello, Dwayne. How are you?'

'Awrite, Mrs O. Good job we woz 'ere, though, innit?'

'Yes indeed.'

'You might of fell an 'it your 'ed on the stones an' bled to death.'

'That is a possibility,' Luke admitted gravely. 'But not one it is considered tactful to mention. Your assignment, I believe, is to make an illustrated report on the construction of the tower.' The boys grinned, shaking off the embarrassment caused when someone's mother does anything out of the ordinary, and obediently trotted off. Chloe began to relax. She and Luke sat side by side and did not look at each other. Behind them the organist began a subdued Kyrie.

'It's so unlikely,' she said dreamily, 'that you should be here.'

'Very. I'm standing in for their Social Science tutor. It's his project, finding out all there is to know about the church. You can imagine how I felt when I saw you. I thought you were a mirage until I realised how you were.'

'I'm sorry,' she murmured. The sense of his weight beside her made her uncontrollably happy, the feeling rising in her like yeast. 'I think it was a mixture of shock and lust. You were in my mind – you are hardly ever out of it – and then there you were in the doorway. And Rufus. I'd already had one small sort of shock. I saw – it sounds so foolish. I saw Dinah's name on a list outside, and I was suddenly overwhelmed by what we are doing—' She broke off. 'I know this isn't the time. Or the place.'

'No.' He turned and laid his hand on her brow again. 'For comfort.'

She kindled. 'Don't. Don't touch me or I *will* faint. Wait for tomorrow.'

'Chloe, I'm sorry.' He turned away again, not wanting to see her disappointment. 'I've been trying to call you. I have to go to Cambridge tomorrow. A language conference. I'd forgotten completely.'

'Oh, Luke.'

'I can't bear it either.'

'Another week.'

'Unless we can think of something different?'

'Yes, perhaps. Or – no, that's not good. There would have to be excuses. Lies. Smaller sins, but they make one *feel* smaller than the big ones.'

'It may happen eventually. Next week then – if you want to go on sinning.'

'Yes.' She moved a little away from him. 'Why does Dinah clean the church?'

'To show that, although she doesn't go to church, she is a part of the community and supports what is done here.'

'That seems like her; she's such a generous person.'

'You should know.' He sounded amused. 'She tells me you are sisters.'

'I like her,' Chloe muttered. 'More and more. It doesn't help.'

'Nothing is ever going to help,' he said firmly.

'No, I suppose not. What's that?'

A soft commotion had broken out among the children in the south aisle. Someone had opened the door to the tower stairs and a concord of sweet sounds drifted down from above. Two voices, one tenor, one still treble, chased each other round and round like rabbits in a field in a rollicking fugue of 'Glorias'.

'Rufus,' Chloe smiled.

'And Dwayne. His voice has been quite a surprise. He has even joined the choir. Rufus must be a good influence.'

'I wouldn't bet on it.'

In the tower, the two boys sang louder, for cover, while they extinguished their fat cigarette and tamped the stub hard down between the floorboards.

'Worrabout the stink?'

'Oh, it'll mingle with the odour of sanctity.'

'Eh? Oh, yeah. Come on, then. Grab 'old.'

They began now, without the least suspicion of the necessary skills, to see what it took to ring the bells of St Mark's. It took a lot more than they expected and the noise was horrible. Below, Luke sighed. 'I think, if you're quite well, you should go now, Chloe.'

She rose, smiling. 'Are you going to beat them or join them?'

'I haven't decided.' He offered her his hand.

She took it. 'You know what I want to say.'

'I know.'

Things seemed more simple than they had done before she came.

Chapter Eight

〰〰〰〰〰

S UCH A COMFORTABLE ILLUSION OF simplicity was
difficult to sustain. Chloe was forced to abandon it to
an alternating cycle of guilt, glory and periodic
forgetfulness that anything had changed.

On Saturday morning she answered the doorbell and
the guilt swung giddily to the top of the wheel. The visitor
was Adam Cavendish, who unnerved her with his inherited
smile before asking nicely for Miranda.

In the kitchen she said, 'Alain, this is Adam. You
remember, I told you – Luke Cavendish's son.' A swig of
bliss as she spoke his name.

'Of course. 'Ow are you, Adam? Sit down and 'ave some
coffee. Miranda is at home but she does not like to get up
early.'

'I'll tell her you're here.' Chloe escaped. She went
upstairs very slowly so that she could regulate her breath
and her thoughts.

'Why didn't you shout?' Miranda was sitting on her bed
in her dressing-gown, painting her toenails green. 'So
what's he like, this Adam? A chip off the old dish?'

'Why don't you come and see for yourself?'

'Like this?' Miranda's dressing-gown was satin, very
short, with dragons.

Chloe had not noticed it. 'Why not?' she said vaguely.

'What do you want, to *sell* me to this person?'

'I might do worse.' She had recovered enough to make private comparisons between Adam and Joel.

'My mother, my procuress. I'll be down in a minute.'

Half an hour later, passing the kitchen door and seeing the two intent heads meeting over Miranda's sketchbook, Chloe wondered what there was in the subject of fashion to provoke such explosions of laughter. They were already glancing sparks off each other, her daughter and Luke's son. She envied them.

'Any idea where your father has disappeared to?' she asked Miranda.

'He's working. Said he had a paper to do.'

Chloe groaned. It was not unusual for Alain to work throughout the weekend. She made fresh coffee and took it into the small, dark green room which he kept with obsessive neatness as his study.

'Thank you Chloe. I'm sorry about this. I 'ave only a week to write an 'undred pages for the Belgians.' He never told her beforehand when he planned to work. He said it made her angry twice when once would do.

'Blast the Belgians!' she said, with enforced cheerfulness.

'This blast – it would not, of course, affect their inestimable chocolates?'

'No, it would blow them all towards Sheringham. They would land in that field over there. Yum! And to think I nearly buggered them instead. Listen, are you going to have *any* free time this weekend? Only it's Mike and Maggie's party tomorrow. I'd like to go.'

'I'll try to make it, *chérie*, but I won't promise.'

'Try hard, or I'll heave your horrible firm before the European Court of Human Rights for cruel and unusual practices. *Nobody* is supposed to work all the time. Don't

— 110 —

they know it isn't even productive, in the end?'

'Times have changed. We used to work for the satisfaction, and perhaps for money. Now firms like ours work chiefly to survive.'

'I know. I'm sorry. I won't complain any more.' She pressed her head against his as he sat at the desk. A stray visual impression came to her of Dinah doing precisely the same thing in the house across the village, laying her head against Luke's in the jungle-lair of books and plants and haphazard heaps of paper which was his equivalent of Alain's ordered tranquillity. She found the image to be in bad taste and cast it out. It was promptly replaced by even less appropriate pictures of Luke and herself. What had he done to her? It was bad enough to have stumbled into unwanted love without having to put up with members of the love object's family moving into one's head and one's house.

When she returned to the kitchen she was not in the least astonished to find Belinda Cavendish sitting next to her brother at the table. Tilda, looking pleased, hovered with biscuits and the coffee-pot.

'Oh, another of you,' said Chloe. Her lack of surprise sounded less than hospitable, so she smiled and added, 'That's nice.'

'Good morning, Mrs Olivier.' Belle greeted her with the bountiful aplomb of one who will shortly be signing autographs. 'I've come to persuade Tilda to come out with a crowd of us tonight. If she's allowed, that is?' The request was spoken prettily, with widened eyes. It was not over-done. The child was evidently a *good* actress.

'What sort of outing is it?'

'Just a rave. You know – dancing.'

Chloe did know. 'Indoors or out? Drugs? Alcohol?'

'It's in the Ellisons' tithe barn. The floor's really ace. Some people do take booze and stuff along, but there's nothing on sale. I don't know about any drugs. But it's OK, really. Dad lets me go.'

'Adam, do you know this place?'

'It's a bit young for me. I'd say it would be all right. Jim Ellison's a councillor, he wouldn't stand for any trouble.'

Why was she hesitating? It was high time that Tilda began to behave more like other girls of her age.

'I expect you're right. If Tilda wants to go – do you, love?'

'Come on, it'll be great,' Belle pressed.

'I'm not sure. What would I wear?'

'Whatever. Anything goes.'

'Are you wearing that?'

Belle was dressed in an entertaining collection of brilliant rags. She gave a contemptuous hitch to her purpose-dropped shoulder strap. 'No, I like to get glammed-up at night.'

'I don't really have much stuff,' Tilda worried. She had claimed, until now, to despise the cult of clothing.

'You can have something of mine,' said Belle. 'I've got heaps.'

Adam said, 'Tilda may not want to look like an accident in a paint factory.'

'Why is it,' asked Tilda, taking pleasure in her newly found loyalty, 'that brothers always have to be so rude?'

'He isn't my brother,' Belle said quickly. 'Only half.' She looked at Adam over her shoulder, her eyes slanted in the style of Vivien Leigh as Scarlett O'Hara. 'It's a far more interesting relationship, psychologically.'

'Is it?' Adam shrugged. 'As far as I'm concerned you're as much of a liability either way.'

'Now you *know* you don't mean that.' Belle waved her lashes. 'You're just trying to disguise the fact that you love me madly.'

'Come on, Belle, give me a break,' he said mildly.

She means it, Chloe saw suddenly, only it's the other way round. She's in love with him, poor little beast.

'Ignore her,' Adam advised. 'She's practising to be a comedienne.'

'No I'm not. Well, I suppose I might do a bit of comedy, like I am now in *Earnest*. But I want to become a great tragic actress. If there *are* any when I'm ready.'

'Don't you think there will be?' Chloe was interested.

'I'm not sure. It might be like all those old romances we have to read. Sort of historical. Not about now any more.'

'What, no more great tragic lovers? No Tristan, no Lancelot?'

'I'm not really sure, but I don't think so. I mean you can't be tragic about adultery if no one really thinks it's such a terrible thing any more.'

'I think that depends,' said Chloe carefully, 'on how much trouble it causes.'

'What do you think, Miranda?' Adam asked mischievously. 'Are you for tragic love? Adultery and grand opera?'

'Not if I can help it.' She smiled at him. 'How about you?'

'I belong to the old school. I'd be happy to die for love, if love were ever to be worth dying for.'

'But it hasn't been?'

'Not so far.'

'Actually, he's foul to his girlfriends,' Belle informed Miranda with evident satisfaction. 'They're always ringing up and crying over the phone and I have to tell them lies.'

Adam looked embarrassed.

'Perhaps tragedy is more often one-sided than not,' Miranda suggested.

'*They* aren't tragic, they're just pathetic. No pride,' Belle said firmly. 'Anyway, Adam can't get involved with all that if he's going to be a writer. He has to observe, not take part. For a while, anyhow. I'm sure you understand, being an artist yourself.' She nodded at Miranda in a businesslike way as if the two of them had come to an agreement, then turned briskly to Tilda. 'Come on, let's go up to your room and see what you could wear tonight. Is that OK?' she demanded of Chloe.

'Of course it is. If you don't find anything it's more than time Tilda had something new,' she added hopefully.

'No thanks,' said Tilda. 'I'm not into panic-buying.'

'"Not into", eh?' noted Miranda as the two girls clumped upstairs. 'That little slip into the vernacular is the first sign I've heard of linguistic peer pressure on our peer-proof Tilda.'

Adam shuddered. 'Let's hope it ends there.'

'Don't worry. They'll be good for each other. They're very different, but I think, in the end, they're equally strong. I'm glad Tilda's found a friend. She needs one just now.'

'So do I,' said Adam plaintively. 'Are we doing this article, or what?'

Chloe left them arguing the merits of a becalmed Armani and the Milanese mafia as against a British New Wave set on its roll by a shock of young designers with shaven heads and surfboards.

'Mum,' Tilda said later.

'Yes, my love?'

'Do you think I ought to go to this thing tonight?'

She wanted to be persuaded, but which way? 'Not unless you want to.'

'Belle wants me to, lots.'

'That's nice. But you don't have to go just to please her.'

'I know.' The voice was frail.

'Belle is a lovely girl, but you might have a little trouble adjusting to her *speed*, for a while.'

'Perhaps.' Tilda digested this. 'Dad told her she looked elegant. Do you think the way she looks is elegant?'

'It's not the word I would choose. I expect he was just being nice to her.'

'What is? The word?'

'Oh – exotic, I think. Like a parakeet. When did she meet your father?'

'As she was leaving. He was in the garden, having a Gauloise and a think. I introduced her and she said she was *enchantée*, in a woman-of-the-world sort of voice, and gave him her hand to kiss.'

Chloe laughed. 'And did he?'

'Yes. And then he told her how elegant she looked. What did you mean about her speed?'

'Well, that Belle's is *molto capriccioso*, while you tend to be *adagio*.'

'I suppose you're right. But I might like a change. Do you think I should wear clothes like hers?'

'I think you should experiment and see what suits you.'

'Mmm. Perhaps I will. But not tonight.'

'Why not?'

'I don't know. It feels a bit too sudden. And I don't really know any of Belle's friends.'

Chloe saw her shoulders hunch with shyness and hugged her, filled with love and pity. 'But you soon would. When you wake up tomorrow you could have two or three new people in your life.'

'They probably won't like me. They'll be the sort who like pop music.'

'But you like *some* pop music yourself.'

'Yes, but it doesn't *matter* to me.'

'It doesn't have to. Couldn't you just enjoy the evening for whatever it brings, try not to be self-conscious, just live in the moment?'

'Maybe. I don't suppose anyone would bother about me too much, not with Belle around.'

'Why do you say that?' Chloe spoke gently.

'Well, you've got to admit she's special.'

'And *you* have got to admit *you* are. Come on, I've just thought of something I used to love wearing that will look terrific on you. Don't worry, it's a ten. And bang up to date.'

'But I don't . . .' Tilda sighed. She was talking to the air.

Chloe came back with a black bias-cut sheath made in the thirties as an infallible man and gin trap.

'There, you see?' she affirmed triumphantly as Tilda stood twisting in front of her mirror. 'Wait till your father sees *that*. You look exactly like Audrey Hepburn. He used to have a tremendous thing about her.'

'No, did he? Do I? I suppose I do, a bit. Was she sexy?'

'Yes. And warm and sophisticated and innocent and an extremely nice person.' She thought, I'll show him elegant, the perfidious frog, clod-hopping all over his daughter's sensibilities. She would turn Tilda into a confident young woman if it meant the entire Cavendish family moving into the spare room, Holmes and Watson too.

'Belle says,' said Tilda, still twisting, 'that if she didn't look like herself, she'd quite like to look like Andie McDowell.'

'Yes, well they don't make them like Audrey any more. We used to play that game at school – if you weren't you, who would you like to be?'

'So who would you pick?'

'Oh – no one else. Just me with all my opportunities to take again.'

'Mum! And not have us? You can't.'

'No, of course not. Not ever. That's not what I meant. Sorry. I don't know what made me say that. Look, keep the dress, decide later.' She patted Tilda's polished shoulder and left her. She needed to cry. She did so quickly and efficiently, using only one tissue, feeling that tears were a luxury she did not deserve. There may have been a vestige of compensating virtue in the fact that she was weeping not only for herself and for some lost, never-never life with Luke, but also, in her present over-sensitised condition, in

— 116 —

empathy both with Tilda's paralysing self-doubt and Belle's boldly chosen road to rejection.

The Harley drew alongside Rufus as he made for Dwayne's house after lunch.

'Hi, Rufe. I was hoping I'd catch you. Got something for you. And you for me, I hope. Get up behind and we'll find somewhere quiet to talk.'

In the woods there was a chill and a dank graveyard smell, like mushrooms.

'You did well. There's more than sixty pounds here.'

'Yeah. I did it for three quid for enough to get mellow, or fifteen for an eighth.'

'Fine. So this time, keep fifteen quid. I feel generous.'

'Great. Thanks.'

'You're welcome. Now here's some more stuff. Moroccan, pretty good. And how'd you like to try out a little acid and maybe a touch of speed?'

'I thought it was only going to be hash?'

'It's up to you, good buddy. But if you don't corner the market at that school, someone else soon will.'

'Yeah, I suppose. The seniors deal among themselves. They get their stuff in town. But they won't let us have it. Too much damage if they're caught. We're not even supposed to know.'

'Is that so? Maybe I could save them a journey or two.'

'No. Not yet anyway. I have this feeling we ought to go slow.'

'OK. As I say, it's entirely up to you.'

'Right. Well, I don't want anything really hard, no crack or anything. But I'll take the LSD, to go at, what, three-fifty a tab?'

'Yep. But the speed is strictly for partying. Fifteen quid a gram, OK?'

'OK.'

'You're doing great, friend. You'll remember what I

— 117 —

said? No dealing on school premises. Or anywhere you might be seen too closely.'

'I'm not an idiot.'

'Just checking. Lower the risk is the name of the game.'

'Sure, Joel, I understand.'

I can give it up, any time, he thought. I don't have to do it.

Miranda met Joel at the gate.

'Give me ten seconds to be sociable with Chloe and we're out of here,' he commanded. 'Think of somewhere comfortable, not too far from home. It's getting cold out there in the woods.'

'Don't worry, I know just the place.'

Inside, he gave Chloe his bag and thanked her for allowing him to visit again. 'It makes me feel like one of the family.' There were the teeth, two rows of little sepulchres, whitened twice daily.

'In that case, you can tell me what meals you'll be here for and whether you and Miranda will be in or out tonight.'

'Of course. Breakfast tomorrow. And out.'

'Thanks.'

'Not at all. You look beautiful today, Chloe. Your eyes have a clear, kind of washed look.'

'You don't have to flannel me, Joel. There's no point.'

'No, there isn't. I'm perfectly sincere. And we're going out for an hour or so, now, in case you need to know.'

'I don't.'

Up in the hayloft adjoining the local riding stables, Miranda spread her legs very wide and tried to get as much of Joel inside her as possible. This, that he called simply sex, was the only way she had found to get anywhere near close to him, and it seemed to her, although beautiful and increasingly painful to her in its beauty, to be a closeness of instinct rather than of spirit or even of body. They were two animals, warming and protecting each other, two animals fucking in a nest. They were not nice animals out of a children's picture book. Joel liked dirty sex. He had taught her to suck him and finger-fuck him and how to dilate her anus to accommodate him without too much discomfort. There was nothing they did that she did not like too. There was nothing he could do that she would not welcome. His mind was her temple. His body was her god. She had never been so happy.

Tired, a little sore, and with some interesting bruises developing, they lay back in the new hay and Joel smoked while Miranda asked questions.

'What do you think of my father, then?'

He had been briefly introduced to Alain's impeccable courtesy before they left the house. 'He seems nice, reasonable – like your mother. You have a good family. You're lucky.'

'Why, what are yours like?'

'I don't see them.'

'Why not?'

Smoke billowed across her face.

'Why not, Joel?'

He sighed. 'All right, let's cancel this curiosity. My father left when I was two. I don't remember him. My stepfather didn't want a kid hanging around and made a good fist at discouraging me. He also used his belt and odd bits of stick. My mother couldn't do anything to stop it. Soon she stopped trying.'

'Oh, Joel. Didn't she love you?'

'She "loved" him. It wasn't an emotion you would have recognised.'

'Poor little boy. I can't bear it.'

'I kept to myself and drew a lot. Drawing made me feel real, worth something, I don't know.'

'Did he leave you alone then?'

'No. I was in so-called care for a couple of years. It was worse than home. They certainly taught me to take care of myself.'

'Was there no one to help you, someone else in the family?'

'I'm an only child. I never met any of my mother's family. They threw her out when she married my father.'

'What happened?'

'I went back home the second time and beat the shit out of that bastard. Then I left. I've never been back.'

'Where did you go?'

'I knew how to make friends. I'd made sure of that. I got lucky. Lived with a girl for a while, then an older woman, Elizabeth. She's an art-freak. She got fired up about my drawings and stuff and made me see that I could go to college. She used to work there in the admin department. She really loves all of it. In the Renaissance she would have been a great patron.'

'Do you still see her?'

'Sometimes. She's a good friend. The best.'

Miranda felt anger heat her flesh as if she had been stung all over by virulent insects. 'Do you fuck her?'

'What's that to you?'

'I can't help hating the idea.'

'It's none of your business.'

'Joel?'

'Mmm.'

'Are you angry with me?'

'Not if you leave it there.'

'It's left.'

She would ask no more questions because they drove him away from her. She had taken the risk just now because she wanted to know the child he had been in order to understand the man he was becoming. She leaned to stroke his hair, soft and fine and thick. He must have been a most beautiful child. How could anyone have so hurt and betrayed him? It went a long way to explain the self-sufficiency that she found so unnerving. She would not be so easily rebuffed by it in future. Indeed, might she be wise to develop a self-sufficiency of her own? She found that a bleak prospect. She did not want to be sufficient unto herself. She needed Joel. And he needed her. There had to be a way to show him that. She would learn as they went on.

She said lazily, as if she did not care, 'It's a pity you have to leave.'

'Why? This way we get to fuck now – this is an excellent place, by the way – then we go on the town and come back to your place and fuck all night. *And* I get to work on Sunday. Seems to me like the acme of maximisation.'

'Love, dove, moon, June,' Miranda chanted. 'The last of the great romantics, that's you.'

'Don't concern yourself, Lady Caroline. Our ways have changed since you made it with Lord Byron.'

'Even he had his bad days. Poor Caroline was a case in point.'

'I tell you, romance does not exist.'

'You mean, like the figures in your work don't exist? The paint is real, like the fucking – but the fucking *concept* doesn't exist?'

'Now that's the most interesting thing you've said today.'

'What I mean is, the things that don't exist are often the most important.'

'I'll buy that. But I just don't buy romance. It's spare luggage. I don't need it.'

Mike Carter and his wife, born the Hon. Margaret Barnes, lived two miles from Sheringham in Westwater Hall, which was Maggie's inheritance. Unlike St Mark's, it had never quite recovered from Cromwell's depredations and Maggie had met Mike when she applied to his department for a grant to help shore it up. When she had asked for a portrait of the accomplished improvements to mark their engagement, he had produced a further miracle in Chloe, then his next-door neighbour. This had initiated a series of visits which had led to a comfortable friendship between the two couples and also to the growing affection for the area which had eventually brought the Oliviers to Sheringham.

Tonight two hundred guests were celebrating the Carters' eighteenth anniversary. Older children were invited and Miranda, at a loose end, had pinned her most expensive set of holes together and accompanied her parents. It was she who presented Maggie with their gift, a modestly-sized view of Westwater lake, done when the irises were out.

'Darling Chloe, that is sublime.' Maggie, who described herself as Junoesque, swept forward to engulf her friend in a spume of green chiffon and half a bottle of No. 5.

'Look, everyone – see what Chloe has given us. Mike, come and look. Bring Luke and Dinah with you – glad you could make it, you two, even if you are last, as usual. Isn't this sheer bliss?'

Chloe did not hear Mike's reply but she smiled and nodded, clinging to him as he kissed her in thanks. It had simply not occurred to her that Luke might be here. What a fool she was. Of course he would be.

'I suppose the four of you know each other by now?' Maggie gathered them in to her in mother-duck fashion. 'I wanted to arrange a little dinner, just the six of us, but I simply could not get you all at the same time.'

'Never mind, keep trying,' said Dinah greedily. 'I've never forgotten your game pie.' She came over to Chloe and laid a hand on her arm. 'Hello, you look lovely.'

'So do you.'

'If you are going to pay each other compliments, you leave us nothing to say to you.' Luke beamed upon them both so that Chloe felt like a member of his harem. She fantasised briefly about how pleasant such a life might be. 'Which is fine, because I want to talk to Alain. That is, if you have a moment?'

'But of course.' Alain began to follow Luke out of the circle.

'What about my present?' asked Maggie severely.

'Be patient. Give us ten minutes.'

'Ah, a surprise.' Juno was satisfied.

Luke led Alain outside to Dinah's car from which they extracted a long, oak garden seat, carved with flowers and leaves.

'Pretty, isn't it? I found it in a junkshop and Olly did it up. He's good at that sort of thing. Now, where shall we put it for the best effect?'

'I know a place where Maggie likes to sit beside the lake.'

'Ideal.'

They managed the transfer smoothly, Alain holding his end of the bench slightly upward to counter Luke's greater height. They placed it with precision, in exactly the right spot, and exchanged satisfied nods as they admired their handiwork.

'Actually, I have another favour to ask.' Luke spoke with a hint of apology. 'A rather larger one. I need someone to get the sixth-form interested in engineering – some good solid information on the various careers open to them, what qualifications they need and where the jobs are to be found. Plus an enormous helping of inspiration – what a uniquely useful and rewarding profession it is, what you personally enjoy most about it, money, travel, international networking, anything you can think of. Interested?'

'Oh yes, I am interested. I think it is important. For me it is a question of time. If I can find it, I will do it. Perhaps in two weeks?'

'That is very good of you.'

Alain smiled. 'Wait until you 'ave 'eard me. You may regret it. I am like Savonarola when I speak of my profession. You will 'ave the entire class, the girls also, renouncing all other *métiers* and begging to be admitted to Imperial College.'

'Why not? God knows, it's your turn to be fashionable. Why should the arts and the media get all the publicity?'

Alain shrugged. 'Because it is their business to do so. We have something to learn from them, I think. But you, Luke, you 'ave produced a future media-star yourself. Your little actress, at home.'

'Belle? I hope so, or we'll never hear the end of it. You seem to have made a hit with her, by the way.'

'She likes men, and she knows they like her. It is a good way to be, if you are a woman.' It was how Chloe was, and his lovely Miranda. Not Tilda, or not yet anyway. Chloe seemed to think there was something he could do about that, but he was not sure what that was. Tilda was already so determined in her opinions.

As they continued to talk Luke found Alain's personal mix of gravity and enthusiasm more and more sympathetic. The irony of this was not lost on him. What had Chloe said, about her affection for Dinah? That it didn't help. And he had replied that nothing was ever going to help. Well, now he was beginning to feel the truth of that. Feeling, he discovered, was more painful than merely knowing. But it made no difference. Even if he and Alain Olivier were to become the closest of friends – he would not seek this, but it might happen – he would still be the lover of Alain's wife. He could not stop. It was not even worth thinking about it; he *could not*. The lecture had been Philip's idea. Luke had not wanted to ask a favour of Alain. But he had and now he must suffer the consequences of finding him to be someone he might both like and respect.

Apart from the scintillating fact that most of the wine was

champagne, the party followed the traditional pattern of talk and drink, followed by food and drink, followed by drink and drunken dancing. It was not until it had reached the latter stage that Luke and Chloe came together, thrown upon each other by a sudden eddy of the swaying, sweating throng.

'Where's Dinah?' she asked, breathless, dizzied by his existence.

'Convincing Philip Dacre that he was once the Red Baron. What about Alain?'

'Not sure. He and Mike went off somewhere.'

'Where can we go? I've got to have you. Now.'

'Outside?' she gasped.

'Too popular. Too cold. A spare bedroom?'

A bed. Oh, please. 'No. People get curious when you lock a door.'

His eyes lit. 'Not if it's a bathroom!'

'Luke, I couldn't. I'd be terrified.'

'First floor, next to the master bedroom. There are two doors. Go in through the bedroom and lock them both. Let me in by the outer one when I knock.' He was gone, holding his glass above the crowd as if intent on refilling it.

In the Carters' blue and gold bathroom Chloe waited, crawling with nerves, and tried to pretend the lavatory was not there. How could they possibly make love in its uncompromising porcelain presence? She inspected it more closely, nurturing hopes of familiarity and contempt. It was a Thunderer, much prized by the *cognoscenti*, the deep bowl swagged with azure garlands of fruit and flowers. The fruit made sense, but did the Victorians really eat flowers? Perhaps she was being too literal? She drew back, worrying vaguely about 'Use' and 'Beauty'. She was jittering. The thing was grinning at her. Its expression was lewd.

She heard two taps on the outer door. 'Anyone in there?' Luke's voice was silky with tact. She wrenched at the door and they fell upon each other.

'Bloody clothes.' He pulled her top down and her skirt up and thrust her against the closed door. He moved his hands over her and inside her feverishly while she got him, the part that mattered, out of his trousers. When he lifted her on to him the pain of wanting ceased, only to be replaced by another, far more exquisite.

'Oh my God,' they shuddered, in a very short time. They collapsed beside the bath and slumped against it, propping each other up like puppets after the show.

'Well, that was sensational, for an hors-d'oeuvre. Chloe, it's been aeons.'

'Light years. What's the first course?'

'Electric eel, served in its own juice.'

'That's disgusting. We are disgusting.'

'Sorry. It must be the influence of Mr Crapper, there.' He sat up and stared at her, serious as a clown. 'Really, I *am* sorry. If you can't bear this, let's just go, and we'll meet next week, at Friday Street.' Friday Street. It seemed histories away.

'No, it's all right. I'm just drunk enough. More than enough. But I *don't* like being watched.' The Thunderer's grin had metamorphosed into a lascivious Cyclopean eye. Chloe struggled to her feet and threw a towel over it. 'Why can't it have a lid, like a decent creature?'

'I expect Maggie reminded Mike to close it once too often. More interestingly, have you any idea where your knickers are?'

She looked down, surprised. 'I don't know. I'm sure I had some on.'

'Don't worry. They're in my pocket. Remind me later.'

'I'd better have them now.'

'You haven't got a pocket.'

'I do have something similar that might interest you.'

The first course was so delicious and so outrageously satisfying that they decided to forgo the next one in favour of a little light dessert. They were enjoying this at a

— 126 —

civilised speed, spread upon a pleasantly thick bath mat, when there was an urgent rapping on the outer door.

'Can you hurry it up in there?' a tense male voice requested. 'Only, I'm absolutely bursting.'

Chloe looked at Luke who signalled silence. Everyone there knew his voice, and many of them would probably recognise hers by now. Holding hands tightly, they froze.

'Come on, I know you're in there.' The rapping was repeated.

'Are you *sure* there's anyone inside?' A second male voice.

'Yeah. I heard them moving around and sort of – *breathing*.'

'Come on then, Letsbe Avenue!' said the newcomer, a trenchant wit.

'Is there some problem here?' A female complaint now, hooting and plummy with authority. There was a short season of muttering.

'Now listen to me, whoever you are,' the female presence apostrophised, 'I don't know what you're doing in there – ' Luke and Chloe spluttered and stuffed their hands into each other's mouths. This provided its own peculiar pleasure. ' – but there are people out here in genuine discomfort.'

Their inebriated bodies shook with malarial intensity and Chloe's mascara ran hooligan races down her cheeks.

'I love you,' he mouthed, returning her hand. She nodded vigorously and let out a spurt of laughter.

'Just what *is* happening in there?' The tone was pure Betty Boothroyd.

Luke composed his features into a mask of fragility. 'I'm terribly sorry,' he uttered in throttled stops. 'I'm afraid I've been sick. Something I ate,' he added inanely, causing Chloe to shake the sides of the bath. 'I won't be long,' he called. 'Just need to clean up some of the mess.'

'Tut. Never mind, we'll find another bathroom,' Madam

Speaker decided unilaterally. They listened, weak with gratitude, while she marched her desperate party away.

'Do you think she'll send anyone up here?' asked Chloe.

'Neither Mike nor Maggie will *give* a damn, at least till tomorrow.'

'In that case . . .' She held out her arms.

When eventually the lust and the laughter left them like a departure of Maenads, to feel a little flat and a little foolish without their frenzy, they descended separately to resume their places in society. They danced with everyone with whom it was courteous to dance, and then with the people they most enjoyed dancing with. They danced, just once, with each other and became newly enthralled with the perfect fit of their interlocking limbs.

'This is lovely, but it makes me feel sad,' Chloe said.

'Probably a reaction to the foregoing comedy. There is always some sadness in a good comedy, towards the end.'

'Must you see *everything* in literary terms?'

'No. I'm just trying to understand your sadness.'

'I'm sad because I feel so right like this, and I know it isn't right. We're going to have to consider—'

'Excuse me, Dad.'

'What? Oh, hello Olly, what do you want?'

'Excuse me.' Oliver Cavendish smiled shyly at Chloe. 'This *is* an excuse-me,' he explained.

'Oh. Of course. I'd be delighted.' Shaken by the need for yet further emotional adjustment, Chloe transformed herself from Luke's arms to those of his second son and tried not to feel bereft as he wandered away. She saw him tap Claudie Latham's partner on the shoulder and fizzed with jealousy. Claudie's dress revealed everything to the imagination.

Oliver was talking to her, his words coming out in a tumbling rush. '—and I think you look beautiful tonight, Mrs – Chloe.'

'Thank you Oliver. You look pretty good yourself in that shirt.'

'Do you really think so?'

He seemed absurdly happy. She found it touching. She felt a surge of affection for Luke's child.

'Green suits you,' she affirmed. 'Let's see, do you have green eyes?' She looked. 'Yes, you do. Nice and slanty. Sort of Slavic. What is it Nureyev was?'

'A Tartar?'

'Yes. You have Tartar eyes. Is that good?'

'Very good. Thanks.' He glowed and held her tighter. He was a nice boy. His nerves were all on the outside of his skin. This was especially noticeable tonight.

'By the way,' he said, 'Belle was supposed to give you a message. I came over after school last Thursday when you were out. To look at the cat. Rufus got her. She is pregnant.'

'Oh, that's nice. I think. Thank you. Can you tell when she'll have the kittens? She's awfully fat.'

'A month, at least, I'd say. And if you want to give one away, Belle says Horace needs a companion.'

'We ought to give them all away, but the twins will have other ideas.'

'Chloe?'

'Yes?' He was looking at her oddly, as though something had suddenly gone wrong.

'Do you – have you ever – Oh hell, I don't know how to say this.'

'I should just say it.' Luke had left Claudie now. Good.

'Have you ever, well, been in love with anyone? Apart from your husband?' The swirling room seemed to stop and hold its breath. How and what had he seen?

'What do you mean?' she asked coldly.

'I don't mean it like that, not really.' He was now, she saw, in acute distress. 'It's just that I – I ought not to say this, I ought not to *feel* it – but I've been thinking about you ever since I met you.' He had said it. It was over. He had placed himself in her hands. They had stopped dancing. Appalled, Chloe began to move again.

'Come on. I need time to take this in,' she told him with gentle neutrality.

'I'm sorry. I probably shouldn't have told you. I just had to. I've never felt like this about someone before. I haven't slept for a month. There was nothing I *could* do but tell you. Please understand.'

'I don't know what to say.'

'Say what you feel.'

'I feel as if I had been hit on the head. It's such a surprise. A shock.' She paused, rallying. 'Of course, I'm tremendously flattered. Any woman would be. A woman of my age especially,' she added with dowager serenity.

'Really?' His seriousness fled, trounced by a swift radiance. He pulled her towards him, holding her against his thin body. She could feel his heart beat. He was so thin. His thinness seemed a measure of his vulnerability. She wanted to feed him, cosset him, make him happy. But this was not what was necessary. She stretched her arms, making a distance between them.

He was gazing at her as though she were the statue of a saint. Mary Magdalene was the one who came to mind. All right, Mary, if you will get me out of this – well, I'd be a fool to make promises. Just help me to do it without hurting him. Don't worry that I've lost my faith. It comes and goes . . .

'Dear Oliver, you are an extremely attractive boy,' she began truthfully. 'If I were foolish I might easily let that attraction lead me into something I would regret. And so would you.'

'I wouldn't. Never.'

'You haven't really thought it through, have you?'

'No. It's only been a dream up to now. I don't suppose I'd have the courage to tell you without the champagne. I don't drink, you see.'

'I know,' she said feelingly. 'Champagne can make one do things one would never have believed of oneself.' The Thunderer loomed, accusing.

'Chloe, what shall I do? How can I bear it? I know you're just being kind.'

'No, I'm not. You *are* very attractive. But the fact that I think so does not make it appropriate for me to seduce you.'

'No? I'd like that.' Now his expression was Luke's, lazy and speculative. She ought to smack him.

'How old are you, Olly?'

'Nearly eighteen.' A child's answer.

'And I am over forty.'

He shook his head, impatient. 'So what? It happens. I know it does. You see it in the papers all the time.'

'That's because it's sensational, not usual. And it isn't going to happen here.'

'I suppose not,' he muttered, despondent again. 'But you can't stop me dreaming.'

'No, I can't, but I think you ought to try to stop by yourself. Oh Olly, why me?' There are literally hundreds of lovely young girls around you every day and you pick on me. It makes no sense.'

'It does to me,' he said darkly. 'It just *is* you, that's all. And please don't tell me I'll get over it. I couldn't stand that.'

'I won't say any more. But you mustn't think I don't care about you. I do. Just not in the way you want at the moment. And now I really think it's time I went home. Will you be kind and help me to find Alain?'

'I suppose so, if you must.' He let her lead him through the dwindling number of dancers. 'But I won't stop,' he said angrily, on the edge of the crowd. 'It just isn't that easy.'

'I know it isn't. Believe me, I really do know.' Guilt settled on her stomach like undigested bread. 'I just want you to stop hurting.'

'Well, I won't.'

At the other end of the room Miranda had placed her holes and laces in the sensitive custody of Adam Cavendish, with whom she had spent most of the evening.

'What are *you* doing here?' had been her cheerful greeting.

'Following you.'

'I'm not allowed to have followers.'

'Then I'll turn round and you can follow me.'

They had got mildly drunk together, laughed a lot, eaten an enormous supper and discovered, like their respective parents, that they could dance together with an intuitive ease. Miranda particularly appreciated this as she was very fond of dancing. Joel disliked it, he did not care for close bodily contact outside of the sex act.

'Tell me about him – Joel,' Adam encouraged.

'I can't. You'd have to meet him. But his work is terrific, that I can say.'

'What kind of thing?'

'All kinds. Lately he's been doing big blood-boltered canvases that look like natural disasters. But then there are the frogs.'

'Frogs?'

'He likes them. He made a whole lot of them, a hundred maybe, out of wire as fine as hair. So delicate and miniature. They make me want to cry. They're sitting round this pool, with waterlilies. Pure magic. I loved it. He sold it to a Japanese collector. I wanted him to do another but he won't. He's always moving on.'

'Then let me know when he moves on from you.'

She frowned. 'Why do you say that?'

'Or you from him, naturally.' Had he hurt her?

'I hope neither will happen,' she said stiffly. He had. Damn.

'I see. I suppose there's no chance he doesn't understand you?'

'No.'

'Or that he beats you regularly?'

''Fraid not.' She smiled. He was forgiven.

He sighed. 'There you are – the tragic love we were talking about. Blighted before it could be born.'

'Idiot.'

'I mean it. You're getting to me, Miranda.'

'Then I'll go away.'

'No, don't. Come for a walk round the lake.'

'I don't think so. Anyway, I should go home. My parents left hours ago.'

'Then I'll give you a lift.'

'OK.'

In the car he asked her to go with him to a re-run of *Les Enfants du Paradis*.

'But that's my favourite film ever.'

'Mine too.'

'I don't know.' She hesitated. She knew Joel was too busy to take time out for a film. 'Yes, I do,' she said. 'Why not?'

'Good. I'll call you.'

'But you must promise, well, you know, not to—'

'Miranda. Have I touched you tonight except to dance?'

'Well no, but—'

'Have I said anything you didn't like?'

'No.'

'So what's the problem?'

'There isn't one,' she admitted.

'Then goodnight,' he said, and kissed her before she could see it coming. It was a light kiss, feathery and sensual and promising. Miranda was mortified to find that she would have liked to know just what it had promised, but she disapproved of infidelities, even small ones. By way of compromise she stroked Adam's hair. It too was soft and fine and thick, though not as black as Joel's.

'See you soon,' he said.

'Yes.'

As he drove away she thought how much of a relief it was to be able simply to like someone, without any tension or hot, crossed wires.

When Luke emptied his pockets that night he found a note in one of them – 'Love is a wound within the body that has no outward sign'. There was no signature. He recognised the elegant metaphor of Marie de France which he had used himself in his lectures on Romance and Literature. The handwriting appeared familiar, though he did not recall having seen Chloe's script. He was puzzled. The reference to the physical sublimation imposed by the doctrine of Courtly Love was outrageously inapposite to the Rabelaisian pleasures of their recent encounter. Perhaps she had felt a need to redress the balance? It might even be some sort of joke.

Chapter Nine

❦❦❦❦❦❦

On Tuesday evening Dinah rang Chloe. 'Henry Jeykll is doing a workshop on regression and re-incarnation. It should be the ultimate persuader! You must have heard of his cases?'

'I think so. The young girl who was burnt at the stake? The boy who thinks he was Robert the Bruce? When is it?'

'Tomorrow. Sorry about the short notice. I only just found out.'

Why, oh why did it have to be tomorrow? When she was meeting Luke. 'I can't,' she improvised, 'I have to see my agent; you know, the gallery.' She hated lying. Was life to be networked with lies from now on?

'That's a shame, but there'll be other chances. Hey, that was a good time we had on Sunday night?'

'Yes. Yes, it was.' I risked my marriage to do things to your husband that are on the way to being depraved. Oh yes, and your son wants to make me a cradle-snatcher.

'OK, I'll catch you later. Friday, maybe? I'll tell you all about it.'

'Great. Look forward to that. See you then, Dinah.'

Chloe took a deep breath. I don't know if I can manage this, she told herself. I thought I could but I'm less and less sure. And God knows self-disgust is no aphrodisiac. If Luke were here right now I believe I could tell him it was all over.

It was Alain who administered the short sharp shock that disabused her of this notion. 'It seems I 'ave a free day tomorrow,' he announced, ten minutes after Dinah's call. 'Why don't we go into town? We can have lunch and go to that exhibition you wanted to see. Then perhaps a film – there's a re-run of *Les Enfants du Paradis*. And afterwards we could take Miranda out to dinner.' He looked pleased with himself, as well he might.

'Wow. That *is* a surprise. I can't remember the last time you had a day off.'

'Cairo rang. They don't need me till Thursday now. So let's enjoy ourselves.'

But she must meet Luke, she must! She had to – to what? She did not quite know, but she needed to talk to him, there in that quiet house where there was time and space and peace to think straight. Something had to be worked out between them. She could not go on lurching from the swings to the roundabouts.

'Yes, let's have a day out. It will be lovely,' she said.

It was not lovely. It was an unmitigated nightmare.

First, there was the business of trying to phone Luke that evening. She waited until Alain went out for a prowl round the garden, then dialled Luke's home number. She got Dinah again and dropped the phone as if it had bitten her. Wiser, she called the school answerphone, leaving a message cryptic enough to fox the wiliest codebreaker.

Then, as she spoke to his ghostly presence on the machine, came the unlooked-for epiphany, a certainty that swept her with the joyful momentum of a Mexican wave – that however strong her feelings of guilt might be, her need for him would always overwhelm them. When she put down the phone she was faint with love.

*

On Wednesday she dressed festively, saluted herself in the mirror and promised to do her best to do her duty to Sod's Law and her husband and have a jolly good time. Unfortunately the Girl Guide approach no longer served her as easily as it had in adolescence.

It was a pig of a day. It rained, so they took the car into the city. Other drivers mocked them with alternate impressions of (a) a funeral cortège and (b) the British Grand Prix. When at last they had parked outside Alain's headquarters, a colleague rushed out and carried him off for twenty minutes. Chloe fumed. Alain apologised. The colleague grinned oafishly.

The taxi-driver who took them to the South Bank refused to stop just over Waterloo Bridge so that they could take the short cut down the steps. The croissants served with the coffee in a *soi-disant* French café were, Alain informed them in the language of Escoffier, fabricated of Bakelite. The exhibition at the Hayward was a disaster; both of them decided they loathed the Post Modernists and wished they had gone to the Tate.

Normally, none of these pygmy piques would have affected their pleasure in the gift of a day at play. Today was abnormal. Chloe knew it to be her fault, all her fault, her most grievous fault, and could do nothing to stop it. If anything, she made it worse. She picked at her expensive little lunch as if it were a school dinner and decided at the end of it that she did not want to see *Les Enfants du Paradis* just now because it made her cry.

'But *chérie*, you always cry.'

'Well, I don't want to today.'

They went to *Orlando* instead and were subtly and inexplicably disappointed.

'It was ravishing to look at,' Chloe said apologetically.

'*Quand même*.'

'Do you still want to have dinner?'

'But of course. We are meeting Miranda.'

'Oh yes, I forgot.' She longed to cut their losses and simply go home.

'Is 'ee coming with us, that Joel?'

'No. He's working, she said.'

'Don't you like him?'

'I barely know him.'

They took another taxi back to the car. This time the driver was talkative and pleasant. Alain seemed to find him enlivening but he got on Chloe's nerves. When they reached the unpromising warehouse which contained the studio flat that had once been Chloe's and was now Miranda's New York-style loft, there was no reply from her entryphone. When they tried her neighbour they were told she had been out all day.

Alain gave his characteristic shrug. 'What to do?'

'Go to the restaurant, I suppose.' Chloe's lips were tight.

It was a small trattoria, close by, that Miranda loved. They were halfway through their second Campari and soda by the time she arrived.

'Hi, everyone. It's great to see you!' she enthused, as warmly as though they were a crowd who had just cried 'Surprise party!'

'So – where were you?' responded Chloe. Her smile would not form, as if there were paste in the corners of her mouth. She had forgotten how little she really liked Campari. 'I thought you'd found something better to do.'

'Oh – you know. Just couldn't catch my tail today.'

Alain held out his arms and they embraced as if they had been separated for months. If only he would hug Tilda this way sometimes, Chloe thought resentfully. It was so unfair to make a favourite of Miranda as he did. On the other hand, it was a pity he could not be here with her alone tonight. As for herself, she would rather be in bed with the telly. And the telephone. Luke might answer if she tried later in the evening. He could always claim she was a nuisance caller.

'You're quiet tonight, Mum.'

Chloe waved her arms. 'Make noise, make noise, if that's what you want. I'll just listen, if you don't mind.' She looked away, aware of their surprise.

The meal proceeded gloomily. They did not linger over their coffee, nor did they accept Miranda's invitation to have some more at the flat. They dropped her at her door and drove home in a heavy silence which lasted until they left the M25.

'What's wrong, Chloe?' Alain then asked.

'Nothing.'

'Don't be foolish, of course there is. You are never like this.'

'Like what, for Christ's sake?'

'Irritable, depressed, bored – I don't know. And unnec-essarily rude.'

'All right, if that's what you think. Just leave me alone.'

'Very well, if you will not speak.'

He did leave her alone. There was no one who could do this more thoroughly than Alain. He had a unique ability to withdraw into himself completely, to swim out of her ken without rippling the water. Now he was with her; now she was on her own. Prestidigitation of the spirit. She might as well be driven home by an inflatable dummy. With a goblin malignancy that was all that was left of her day, she wished heartily that he were just that. She would let the air out of him the minute they got home.

In bed she lay awake in grey solitude while his granite absence softened imperceptibly into sleep. Her scapegoat had abandoned her, leaving her in a moral desert, his deep breathing giving the signal to her conscience to come out of hiding. Embarrassing herself with the weedy predict-ability of it, she began to regret her behaviour with a thorough-going contrition. She had hurt Alain, and for what? Not because he had stood in the way of what she wanted, but because she felt shorn of her glory before him when what she wanted was another man. She had spoiled his day and trodden his gift to her in the gutter. She was ashamed.

And Miranda? What had she made of her mother's pettish display? These were the people she loved. They deserved her respect. She had no right to treat them with such contumely. She had sat in their company with her heart and mind elsewhere and they had suffered for her lack of balance. She had not expected this of herself. She had thought she could keep things separate, that she would do so instinctively. But it was not like that. Perhaps it was something one had to work at, like a new language? She did not try to sleep at all, that night. When she closed her eyes Luke was with her. He lay on her other side, more palpable than the quiet form of her husband. She had only to turn to be in his arms. Her palmy Mexican wave collapsed, underwhelmed by a Hokusai of guilt. She began to be afraid of the possible extent of her selfishness.

In the morning she surfaced late, with a heavy sense of things being all wrong. Alain had left a note on his pillow. 'Gone to Cairo, Don't make a pyramid out of a sow's ear.' There were two kisses.

She had never disliked herself so much.

At eleven she decided to call Miranda, who would probably be out. She needed to apologise for her ill humour. They could meet later in the week. She would treat her to lunch to make up.

The phone rang as she reached for it. It was Luke.

'My secretary was intrigued by the cancelled performance of the Arden Consort. And also desolated. She is very fond of early music.'

'Oh Lord!' Chloe laughed, getting her breath. 'What did you say?'

'That in fact I was deeply relieved, and that she really

would not like to hear the noises they make. Can you manage today instead? I can.'

The sea pounded in her ears. 'Yes, but I was—'

'What?'

'Nothing. I'll be there.'

The vegetable inferno was dying down around the house and grounds, allowing the evergreens to come into their own again, a reliable Dickensian antidote to a nasty dose of Dante. Chloe let Baskerville run ahead through the crumbling leaves while she took the lane slowly and tried to think what she wanted to say to Luke. The dog galumphed away absurdly, lumpen paws crunching like a giant eating cornflakes. She arranged a few sentences, logical and damning, which she planned to voice immediately. She had made a similar plan once before.

In the courtyard she found Baskerville and Watson lying together in a leggy heap, slavering companionably over each other. Holmes sat aloof with his back to them, mentally playing his violin. She spoke to them softly and went into the house.

The halls and corridors were cool but struck no chill. She touched a radiator and found faint remnant heat. The caretaker was not, then, imaginary. She ran upstairs as if he might be at her heels.

She entered the room breathless, aware first of Luke and then of the music – Marenzio's *Magnificat*, containing all the light left out of the chamber on a dull October day.

He lay on the bed, watching for her pleasure. 'It's what you wanted?'

'I don't know what to say. It's part of my soul. Thank you.' How could she tell him, now, that she would not love him? She could not. An ache of emptiness had begun inside her as soon as she had looked at him. 'Do you like it?' she asked.

'It's like angels singing on their pinhead – the harmony

is as scrupulous as that. I love it. Won't you bring your beautiful soul over here?' He had piled the pillows against the headboard and reclined like a Roman, a small CD player on a table next to him. His hair flopped over his brow as it had when they first met. She came to him quickly, her nicely arranged sentences dropping in disarray at her feet. She stepped out of them and lay down beside him, slipping sweetly into his niches.

Because of the music they did not speak until they had made love to one another with famished joy and then great gentleness. They were honest enough not to reach their ecstatic conclusion at the same time as Marenzio, but allowed him to finish first so that they could concentrate entirely on each other. It was a glorious performance.

'Angels on a pin,' Luke said again, settling back against the pillows and carrying her with him.

'I feel as though I were made of flowers,' she said blissfully. 'All light and clear and clean.' Suddenly she frowned and turned on her stomach, facing him. 'But I'm not, am I? I'm an adulteress and my beautiful soul is covered in black blotches like the pictures of hell in the convent classroom.'

His eyes were closed. He was grinning. 'Chloe, what are you talking about?'

'No, listen, Luke, it's important.' She got to her knees beside him and shook him to open his eyes. 'You see, I've never *wanted* anyone like this. Such a strong feeling – to do with blood and bone and spirit and longing. And it's such a terrible longing. Elemental. It's always there. It takes precedence of everything else in my life, of all the people and things I should give my attention to, my whole and loving attention. It seems wrong. As if I were being corrupted. Or worse, knowingly corrupting myself.'

She had winded him, she could see. He sat up bemusedly, staring at her. 'You'll have to give me time.' His smile was for the first time uncertain. He said slowly, 'I had no idea you felt like this. Oh – not the wanting. I know how that feels as well as you. But I would never have expected such a stern sense of sin. I suppose they taught you to think of sex as a necessary evil, those excellent and ignorant nuns? So what happened when you met Alain? Didn't you feel the fire then?'

'It wasn't the same. How could it be? It was a permitted thing between us. Innocent. We simply enjoyed it, a marvellous prize for just being ourselves.'

'And now, like a modern Eve, you have done what you have been told is not permitted, and you are suffering. I am sorry for that.' He stroked her hand. 'I thought you had given up being a Catholic.'

'I have, but I haven't stopped knowing the difference between right and wrong.'

'And you think this is wrong?' He was incredulous. 'That you and I are wrong?'

'Yes.'

Her heart had stopped. Or possibly the world. They gazed at each other, stone on stone.

'Then, very probably it was you who sent me this.' He reached for his jacket among the pile of clothing on the floor and tossed her the note he had found. 'As an indication of how it ought to be between us?' His voice was thin and taut.

She read aloud, '"Love is a wound within the body that has no outward sign."' Her hands shook. 'No, I didn't send it. It's beautiful. It sounds like poetry.'

'It was written by Marie de France, a most accomplished lady who embellished the court of Henry II and Eleanor of Aquitaine.'

'I know. She wrote *The Nightingale*.'

His eyes glinted. 'Another part of your soul?'

'Why do you ask?'

With short-leashed savagery he said, 'Because in that exquisite moral fable the lovers bury their passion alive

— 143 —

rather than dishonour the sacrament of marriage. Is that what you think we should do?'

She waited for a moment, composing herself, like a Russian who sits down before making a journey. 'I believe we ought to stop and I don't know if I can. Will you help me?'

'To stop?' He laughed. 'Do you know what you're saying?'

'Yes. Before we hurt someone.'

'Chloe, has something happened to make you like this?'

'No. It's just me. I'm not very good at this. I suppose I am afraid that there *will* be an outward sign.'

'Don't be such a coward. You can't give yourself and take me into you like that and then say you want to stop.'

'It isn't just that, is it? Because if it is—'

'Don't hope for that excuse. My God, woman, what were we just talking about? It's the same now as it was in the Middle Ages. Love is love. It requires consummation or it must die. And yes, that is a magnificent thing. It's the engine at the centre of it all, a source of energy and inspiration for living. You know that.'

'Is that what you tell your students of romantic literature?'

'I tell them to read and think, and to write down what they think. I give them Donne and the *Sonnets* and the Brownings and Byron and Lawrence and anyone else who is honest about love. What's the matter, Chloe? I love you. I love being inside you. I love watching your face. I love your questioning, your sense of who you are. I love to hear you laugh and to see that solemn, preachy look you get sometimes. God damn it, what do you want? I want to be with you every minute I can. It's all one to me, the loving and the having. And I won't let you call it corrupt. We don't live in the Middle Ages now. We are modern lovers who may do as we please. You will just have to decide whether or not you think it's worth a little left-over childhood guilt.'

'Have you finished now?'

'Possibly. Is that all you can say?'

'You seem to have used up all the words.' She tried an unsteady smile. It worked; she got one back. Unexpectedly she began to weep.

'Don't. Please, love.'

'I'm sorry. Oh, Luke, I don't want to lose you.' She kissed him with a despairing premonition of how that would be.

'I won't let you go, you know that,' he said.

'I don't really want you to. You are right, I am a coward. I want the decision to be yours, not mine.' The terror of capitulation was like vertigo.

'It's made. Now, for God's sake hold your tongue and let us make up for the time we have wasted.'

'Not wasted. Now you know I'm a coward, and I know you're an emotional thug.'

When they came out into the courtyard they found Baskerville and Watson playing a dim-witted jumping game with a heap of leaves. Holmes, driven by their idiocy, lay glassy-eyed in a corner, lost in dreams of Cockayne.

'Luke,' Chloe said, observing them idly, 'who did send the note? If not me.'

'Why? Are you jealous?'

'Yes.'

'Then, if not you, my guess is one of the sixth-form girls.'

'Any particular one?'

'Yes. I ought to have recognised the writing, only you were too much in my mind. I'd already noticed the signs. If it goes on, I'll talk to her, and try to lead her out of it with her pride intact.'

'If she is daring enough to send you this, she probably doesn't care about pride.'

'Then I'll just have to hope she recovers quickly.'

'*Well I won't!*' Oliver's challenge rang in Chloe's head rendering dust of such a hope. She wished that they could speak about that, but it would not be fair to the boy.

'Poor child,' she said. 'It hurts so much at that age.' As at this.

'Yes. And she's a sensitive, dreamy sort of girl – a little like Tilda, but without her saving spark of irony. That's the bugger of teaching literature; so much of it is about love. It catches like the plague.'

'Then you and I have Elizabeth Barrett to blame?'

'Personally I blame Baskerville.'

Hearing his name, the outsize hound stopped playing and grinned in their direction. Then, floppy ears still comically pricked, he swivelled and cocked his head. At a distance, a faint hum modulated and ceased. Chloe stiffened. 'Wasn't that a car?'

'It could have been.'

'So close? It can't have been on the road.'

'No. It would have to have been somewhere at the front of the house.' They listened. There was nothing further. Baskerville had lost interest and the other dogs had barely lifted their heads.

Luke reached for Chloe's hand. 'Don't look so haunted. We'll go back by the higher path. If there is anything, we might see it from there.'

They stood on the rocky outcrop, staring down at the house. Leaves dropped from the trees with profligate haste. After five minutes they had heard and seen nothing more.

'Do you think it was the caretaker?' Chloe asked warily.

'Perhaps. If there *was* anyone. The noise was very faint and we have no idea exactly how sound carries around the building. Do you want to go back and look?'

'And risk meeting him?' She shivered.

Luke laughed. 'It isn't Pinter. There's no conspiracy against us. Anyway, it could equally well have been some farm machinery in the fields over there. It's that time of year.'

'I suppose so.' But Chloe did not believe that. And whether or not the sound had been attributable to a putative caretaker, she found the event disturbing beyond all proportion to its magnitude.

'The music,' she said. 'We had better not have that any more.'

'Possibly not. Or only very quietly, beneath the sheets. At least you are not refusing ever to come here again.'

She looked wan. 'Where else can we go?'

'Maggie's bathroom?'

She would not smile. 'That was sheer insanity. How did we *do* that, Luke?'

'With an element of risk, a dash of hysteria and a good deal of champagne. Don't *worry* so much.'

'I can't help it. I am just not accustomed to living life with a cutlass between my teeth.'

Their parting, despite their efforts, was subdued.

As she passed through Sheringham on her way home, Chloe elected to do some shopping. She did not need anything; it was purely a means of getting her bearings in her transposition from one life to another. Even thus, she mused, might Persephone have paused at the village stores after her connubial visit to Hades. She picked up a frozen pizza and a tin of baby clams and entered noncommittally into a conversation about the sexual accommodations of certain members of the government.

'Well, I mean, they're supposed to be above us, like, i'n' they?' demanded whiskery Tom Tremlett, the Second Oldest Inhabitant who hourly expected promotion now that centenarian Eva Allot had taken to her bed. 'If they're goin' to do their peccydildos, why should we be'ave ourselves? Eh? Eh?' He eyed Chloe's afterglowing body with remembered lust.

'A shitten shepherd and cleane sheep.' Pretty April Hollings surprised them from behind the counter. 'If gold ruste, what shal iren do?'

'If you're so clever, Miss, why a'n't you at school?' complained the ancient, having no truck with pert sermons.

'Cos it's exams, that's why,' triumphed April incomprehensibly.

Chloe slunk out, her pizza held across her bosom like a shield.

It was when she was passing Holly Cottage that she saw Miranda. It wasn't Miranda, of course; Miranda was in London. It was a doll. Or rather the amputated and abandoned head of a doll, its hair streaming like seaweed, lying in the grass in the small front garden, pale girl-face startling, macabre and piteously out of place.

It was one of those Victorian heads that often outlive their bodies, made of porcelain and ravishingly painted: eyes as black as midnight, skin as white as snow, lips as red as blood.

It was Chloe's child. It was Miranda.

She stood stiff and chilled before it, her veins filling with foreboding as though with embalming fluid.

It was an omen. It must be. Something dreadful was going to happen to Miranda. She began to shake. The pizza fell out of her hands and dropped over the wall. At that moment a small curly-haired girl ran out of the house. She trotted purposefully across the grass and picked up the head.

'Naughty!' she scolded, holding it by the hair. 'Mummy is very cross.' Shifting it maternally to the crook of her arm she retrieved the pizza and gravely presented it to Chloe.

'Thank you.'

'Sawlrite. She's always doing it. She does it on purpose.' Blue eyes disparaged the black glass ones which avoided further recrimination by snapping shut.

'She's very pretty,' said Chloe gratefully. 'What do you call her?'

'Annalise. Off the telly. She's blonde, but it doesn't matter. My name's Rosie.'

'That's nice. Mine is Chloe. Will you be able to mend Annalise?'

'My dad will.'

'Good. Well, it's nice to have met you, Rosie. I expect I'll see you again.'

'Spec so. Bye bye then, Chloe.' Rosie smiled, pleased with the interview. Chloe returned the smile and waved back at her as she left. She felt this to be a far from adequate recompense for the timely salvation of her sanity.

She drove home slowly, reflecting on her growing inability to handle her life as it was now. Her well-ordered world was turned upside down and she was madly dancing on her head, hoping against hope that no one would notice. Nevertheless, her reaction to the bodiless Annalise had come from the far side of unreason.

No outward sign? All very well for Marie de France. At the French Court they had probably given degrees in Necessary Doubleness.

Dinah screeched into the Oliviers' drive and flung her car askew in front of the lavender. Her hair appeared to have been up all night on its own and she wore an eccentric mixture of Romany rejects and psychotherapist suiting.

'You look a bit wild-eyed. What's wrong?' Chloe led her into the studio, whither she had just taken a pot of coffee and a comforting wodge of chocolate cake.

'It's Belle. She's had one of her bright ideas.' Dinah peered at the latest Arden Court landscape which was sitting on the easel. She began to relax in its languid warmth. 'I never knew landscape could be sexy. Is it finished?'

'I'm not sure.'

'I want it. But I'm going to want them all.'

'Don't have this,' Chloe said quickly. 'I'll do one especially for you, paint somewhere you really love.'

'OK, I'll think about that.'

'So what has Belle been up to? Tilda has said nothing.'

'She wants to surprise her. You see, the school's Lady Bracknell has been told she has glandular fever. Belle, without any consultation, has persuaded Helen to take over her part.'

'Helen Cavendish? In a school play?'

'Believe it or not. She's coming for the weekend – *this* weekend – so that she can rehearse with the family before she meets the cast. She always wanted to play Lady B, and, amazingly, she has the time.'

'Wow. That will certainly bring the audience in. Especially so soon after that Victorian serial she was in. So it's all fixed, is it?'

'Yes. Philip Dacre can't wait to count the extra money for the scholarship fund. He said it was a commendable notion.'

'It is. Good for Belle.'

'Well, yes. It is.'

'But?'

'Nothing really. Only my selfish emotions. Even after all these years, I can't quite feel comfortable with Helen. All that polish and performance, on *and* off the stage. Every time I see her I ask myself how in hell Luke ended up with *me*.'

Chloe said warmly, 'Well, I don't know her, but I don't need to make any comparisons. I'm sure Luke doesn't either.'

'You're probably right, and I'm the only one who does. And Adam, of course. He adores her, always has. I did try to mother him a bit, when he was little, but he just wouldn't let me. He kept me out. He still does. Oh, he's friendly enough, charming even, but I'm sure he classes me as hopelessly second-rate.'

'Dinah, I'm sure not. It doesn't seem like that when you're together. He may not always agree with you but that doesn't mean anything deeper. Adam likes to argue, that's all. You should hear him with Miranda.'

'Really?' Dinah brightened. 'Is there something going on there? I thought she had this James Dean character.'

'Alain Delon. She does. She and Adam just get on well. They went to a film together last week.'

'Hey, that really tickles me. I'd love it if they did get together.'

'Well, don't plan the wedding just yet.'

Dinah chuckled and sucked her chocolate-tipped fingers. 'I don't think Adam has a very good opinion of marriage. But what I *am* planning is an extended Sunday lunch party. Will you come, and bring the family?'

Chloe swallowed hard. 'What, all of them?'

'Sure. Tilda will be with us anyway, instead of poor Kate whom Belle can't tolerate. You can hardly have seen her since she's been understudying both Cecily, and Gwendolen. She's really very good, by the way – I've heard her. So anyhow, I thought why not dilute Helen's heady presence and get to see some friends at the same time. What d'you say?'

Chloe had been practising doubleness and lack of outward show for all she was worth, but so far only in her head. She was not sure she was ready yet to step out and spend several hours play-acting Happy Families in Luke's company.

'Thanks,' she said. 'I'll have to check with everyone. I know Rufus is up to something with Dwayne, and I'm not sure about Miranda—'

'Hey, I'm counting on you. You owe me for the brewer's dray, remember?'

What could she say? 'Don't worry. I'll bring as many troops as I can.'

'I hope so. Luke said to tell you how much he's looking forward to it.'

Sadist. 'Yeah, thanks. Terrific.'

Chapter Ten

❦❦❦❦❦❦❦

'I'D NEVER *DARE* PLAY LADY Bracknell in the ordinary run of things. Once you start doing older roles you never look back. And in my profession, I can tell you, we look back as far and as long as we can!' The familiar gilt-edged voice staged, screened and radioed its way toward the Italian plasterwork on the Cavendishes' drawing-room ceiling. Helen Cavendish in the flesh did not disappoint her audience. 'I don't mean I expect to play Juliet again – there are no Margot Fonteyns in drama – but I still get Portia and the Scottish Play; even Beatrice last year, which was delicious. But the great thing about a school perform-ance, my darlings, is that *everyone* is too young for their part!'

She had no need to worry, Chloe thought, as of course she knew. She was a one-hundred-per-cent professional who had judged every move in her career with a precise appreciation of her best advantage. The theatre had made her admired and respected; television had made her a beloved icon. Her talent was exceptional. She could in fact play any woman, from Juliet to the Wicked Witch of the East. Her beauty, by some extra grace, was of the shape-shifting kind that defies type-casting. She could make herself look like anything she pleased. Today she was understated, in rehearsal mode, the Rapunzel-spun mane tied and tendrilled, make-up minimised to a fine grey line around the eyes and a slick of bronze lipgloss. Her skin, like Adam's, was the freckled bisque of a nice brown egg.

'How old *is* she?' Miranda muttered to Chloe, large-eyed.

'Ten years older than she looks.'

'She's fabulous, isn't she? Love those beigy-gold pants.'

'She is indeed. To look at, anyway. To live with? I don't know.'

'It's funny,' Miranda had turned her attention to Luke, who was filling Helen's glass and smiling at her in what Dinah might well think was an unnecessarily affectionate fashion, 'she looks a lot like him. They both have that *bold* look – as if they were going to mug you and you wouldn't mind. And their bone structure's quite similar. See – the chin and the cheekbones? I guess that's why they didn't get on – they're obviously two of a kind. *Can* you see it, Mum?'

'I believe I can,' Chloe said neutrally. 'And they seem to be getting on perfectly well right now. Come on, we'd better stop staring. Dinah wants us to move into the dining-room.'

There were ten of them around the table, six Cavendishes and four Oliviers, Rufus having opted to spend the weekend in a tent on the common land behind the Cubitts' garden. Chloe, who felt she needed partisans every bit as much as Dinah, missed him. Rufus was good at parties, especially if one felt a bit alienated and sore-thumbish as she did now.

She experienced a moment of blind panic when Dinah directed her to the chair on Luke's right, opposite Helen. His nearness was the thing she dreaded. If she could just keep far enough away from him, she had told herself, she might be able to carry off the occasion with the semblance of *élan*. Her first exchange after sitting down was with Luke's knee under the table. It was not his fault, his legs were too long, but Chloe withdrew her own as sharply as if it had been a criminal assault. She saw his most mischievous smile appear and was relieved when he turned it on Helen.

'You ought to ask Chloe to paint your portrait,' he began conversationally, 'quite soon, I should think, before they start offering you Mother Courage.'

'Darling Luke, you are always so gracious,' she replied sweetly. 'I do have three portraits already, but I must confess I don't much like any of them.'

'Not even the one I gave you? When you were young and – well, young.'

'Especially not that one. I keep it in the attic. It's my Dorian Grey picture. It made me look like a startled virgin.'

'Really? I can't imagine how that could have been. I hope you check it regularly for the signs of excess.'

'Now why ever should I need to do that?'

'That, dear old thing, is no longer my business. But you really ought to have one done now you have reached your visual peak. You could call it *The Smile on the Face of the Tiger*. That is the animal the journalists like to compare you with, isn't it? What do you think, Chloe? Does she make you want to portray her with stripes and a tail?'

'Only if she is willing to lurk behind a tree,' Chloe said firmly. 'I think purely in terms of landscape at the moment.' It annoyed her that he would use her to fuel their skirmish. It might be amusing for him but she felt diminished by their obvious enjoyment of each other.

'Adam.' Helen applied to her son for ammunition. 'Will you tell your father that he would be wise to treat your mother with more respect or the tiger will remain in her lair for the run of his beastly play.'

'Adam,' Luke responded gaily, 'will you tell your mother

that I accord her the deepest respect for having given birth to you; it is quite the best thing she has ever done.'

'Oh, I agree absolutely. I can't think where I got him from,' Helen purred.

Adam clapped a dramatic hand to his brow and groaned, 'My God, parents! Who'd have them? Thank Heaven for divorce.'

'I do, every day,' said Helen smugly.

'Chloe, you mustn't mind them,' consoled Oliver's quiet voice on her other side. 'They always go on like this.' Tired of providing an audience, Chloe turned to him with relief. 'We're all used to it,' he continued, 'but it must seem a bit odd to a stranger. Not that you are a stranger. Not any more.'

'Thank you Olly. I suppose it's quite an achievement that they are still such good friends.'

'I guess so. But I wish they didn't have to act all the time.'

'It's only a comedy act.'

'But why act at all?'

'I imagine because they think it makes things easier for everyone else if they ham it up a bit. But I'm no expert. I've never been divorced.'

'No. And I suppose you never will?'

Oliver sighed.

'Well, try not to sound so regretful. It isn't exactly something to aim for.'

'No. I'm sorry. Oh, Chloe—'

'Hey, we're eating lunch, remember? No heavy stuff here.'

'OK. But it's difficult. Being so close to you. It just breaks me up. I mean, I could even *touch* you if I dared.'

Oh dear God of Irony, what did I ever do to you? 'I'm sorry too, Oliver. I don't mean to hurt you. Pretend I'm just another boring adult. Eventually you'll find it's true.'

'You're crazy.' Oliver laughed loudly and cheerfully.

People looked at him for a second. He seized a dish and thrust it at Chloe. 'Would you like some more pilaff, Mrs O?'

'No thanks. Ask Miranda. She loves it.'

'Yes please,' begged Miranda, turning to him and taking the dish. She had been watching Adam who had now become the focus of his parents' mischief, eavesdropping as Helen teased him about his legendary litter of cast-off mistresses and Luke deplored the lack of artistic satisfaction in his life as a Surrey hack.

'I can only cast off one at a time. Like knitting,' said Adam reasonably. 'As for the job, I like it. I intend to stay as long as they'll have me.'

'Look at her,' Oliver murmured, marvelling at Helen. 'She's really proud of his trail of bleeding hearts. She'd loathe it if he ever got serious with anyone. She wants him to be just like her.'

'How do you mean?' Chloe asked.

'Put it this way – if she could get the Great British Public to send her on a sponsored fuckabout, she'd soon be a millionaire.'

'Oliver! That's—'

'Really funny?' spluttered Miranda. 'The thing is, they love her so much they probably would. The *Sun* would come out twice a day to keep up. You would think,' she continued thoughtfully, her attention back on Adam, 'that they would have spoiled him completely, between the two of them – but they haven't, have they?'

'Not completely,' Oliver allowed. 'He's cool. He's OK. Maybe he could be just a little bit nicer to Michelle.'

Belinda Cavendish was in the process of inventing herself and so avidly collected material from which to work. Her role models had always been figures of formidable strength and allure: Cleopatra, Boadicea, Elizabeth I and that estimable scion of a base clan, Lucrezia Borgia, whom

History had so crassly misunderstood. Since Belle had known she was destined to become a great actress she had added to her pantheon; Sara Bernhardt, Isadora Duncan and her Aunt Helen were women who knew instinctively how to make themselves quite clear to History; Cleopatra (certainly) and Lucrezia (perhaps) had enjoyed the added advantage of sleeping with their brothers.

Today Belle felt that she had taken her first steps on the road to immortality. Like the Divine Sarah she was about to act a leading role. Like Isadora she had proved she could also be an impresario. No one else would have thought of getting Helen Cavendish for the play. Her cup ran lavishly over. The only fly in it was Miranda Olivier, unfairly named and far too fair of face. She had noticed a proprietorial attitude in Adam when he had presented that unnecessary person to Helen. And now the wretched girl was looking at him as though she had some kind of right to make judgements about him.

'Adam.' She tugged at his arm.

'What is it, Belle?'

'I thought Miranda Olivier was bringing her boyfriend.'

'He's in London.'

'Are they engaged?'

He frowned. 'No.'

'Oh. Someone said they were. I suppose it's pretty serious, anyway?'

'I've no idea.'

'Do you like her?'

'I like her.'

'A lot?'

'What *is* this, Belle?'

'I just wondered.'

'Well, don't. Miranda's a friend, that's all.'

'That's what you always say,' she said gloomily.

'Mum looks great, doesn't she?' Miranda had noticed that

Alain's eyes were frequently drawn to the head of the table. 'She and *La Belle Hélène* make a stunning contrast on either side of Luke Cavendish. Mum is sort of "and God created Woman", fresh from the Garden of Eden, and Helen is the epitome of the city sophisticate.'

Alain laughed. 'I like that. It has the pitter-patter of excruciatingly high heels.' He pronounced the aitches with care.

There was more laughter, a low, intimate sound that Tilda caught across the table. She sighed. They looked so pleased with each other. Miranda could always make him laugh. Rufus too. She missed Rufus. True, he was a bit pissy lately, since he had got so thick with the loathsome Dwayne, but he was her twin and today she needed his confidence to support her attempt to take Kate's place as Gwendolen. Even his scorn would have served. It was stupid, but she couldn't help it.

'Wake up!' Belle dug her in the ribs. 'Better hurry up with that pudding. We've got to get the room ready for the play-reading.'

'OK,' she said gratefully. She felt better at once. Of course she didn't need Rufus, not when she had Belle.

Helen pushed away her syllabub and stood up. 'My darlings, I have simply *got* to have a cigarette. Will anyone share my exile in the garden?'

'Go on, Dad,' urged Miranda. 'You know you're dying for it.'

'Am I? Bah, *alors*! Per'aps I am,' Alain agreed. He seemed still to be amused. He signalled to Helen who regally inclined her head.

Outside, they avoided damp drifts of leaves, taking the path into the grounds of the Hall. They conversed together with surprising ease, slipping into French now and again because Helen enjoyed showing off an unusually high proficiency. They discussed the Paris theatre and she told him about the Shakespeare season she was about to begin there. She would play Lady Macbeth and also Mariana in *Measure for Measure*.

'A strange play,' he remarked, 'where marriage is a judicial punishment.'

Helen shuddered delicately. 'I'm surprised there are not more. Perhaps the courts should follow Shakespeare's example. I'm sure it would act as a powerful deterrent.'

He smiled. 'Then I take it you have never remarried?'

'No, and I never shall. I'm too selfish. I enjoy being selfish.'

'I enjoy being married. But I am also selfish occasionally. I shall be in Paris for the last week of this month. I shall come and see you as Mariana. And then, perhaps you will let me take you to dinner?'

'That will be lovely,' Helen murmured. 'I shall even be able to repay you. I have taken a small flat in the *troisième*. I'm a passable cook.' She opened her soft leather bag and handed him a card.

'Call me when you arrive, Alain.'

'Immediately.'

She smiled. He lifted her hand and brushed it with his lips. Their eyes colluded briefly, then they continued to walk and smoke in silence.

Chloe followed Dinah into the kitchen, her hands full of plates.

'How is it going, do you think?' Dinah asked anxiously.

'Very well. The food was scrumptious and everyone is enjoying themselves like mad. You can tell by the noise.'

'Too right. Especially Luke and Helen. Does he *have* to play up to her like that?'

'I expect it's just a left-over habit. It's better than studious politeness.'

'Something in-between would do. Honestly, Chloe, I

have trouble not hating that woman.' She seized an unfinished glass of wine and emptied it down her throat.

'She does come on a bit strong, but I'm sure there's nothing to worry about. I wonder how she and Alain are getting on.'

'She's probably eaten him by now.'

'I doubt it. I don't think she's his type.'

'No? What is?'

'I don't know.' Chloe was vague. 'Me, I suppose.'

'You never can tell,' Dinah said thoughtfully. 'For example, would you ever expect Philip Dacre to be capable of nurturing a secret passion for *me*?'

'Wow! Does he?'

'At the Carters' party he asked me, very sweetly, and only a bit drunkenly, if I would consider becoming his mistress.'

'That's incredible. He's so – well, so full of rectitude.'

'Even rectors have sex,' said Dinah owlishly. 'Have a drink.'

'Thanks.' Chloe sipped sparingly, conscious of the need for control. 'How do you feel about him?' she asked mischievously.

'I'm fond of him. He's easy to be with and he makes me feel special. He's sexy too, once you start looking at it that way. But obviously . . .' She waved a negative hand. 'It's nice to be asked, though. Especially when one has Helen in one's life. How about you, Chloe? You must get lots of offers.' She despatched another glass.

Chloe could do nothing to prevent the flush that began in her pelvic region and roared upward to imprint itself on her brow, she was sure, in the form of a flaming 'A'. If only she could tell Dinah. Then it would all be over.

'Funny you should say that,' she began, fighting the nausea that accompanied her insane urge towards confession, 'because I did have one.' Don't be such a bloody fool. You're not even drunk. 'Not like yours,' she said more coolly. 'Just a kid with a crush. But I found it harder to handle than I would have expected.'

Dinah did not appear to have noticed the scarlet letter. 'You get on well with kids. You treat them as equals. And now this young man is returning the compliment. Who is it, anyone I know?'

Dear Oliver, I'm sorry I'm such a coward as to hide behind you. But I didn't shop you to Luke and I certainly won't to your mother. 'I don't think so,' she said.

Dinah was filling her glass for the third time. Chloe covered hers.

'Don't worry, he's probably just following fashion.'

'Probably. You don't think we're drinking too much of this wine?'

'No. It fortifies me against *femmes fatales*,' Dinah giggled. 'Listen – "An erect and reckless rector wreaked feckless sex on a wreck inspector." Good, yeah?'

'Ah – yes. As far as it goes.'

'There isn't much further *to* go. It's perfect as it stands.' She grimaced and rubbed her temples tenderly. 'You could be right about the wine. I think I'll take an aspirin.'

At the far end of the garden, hibernating in a woody ball of tangled vines, was a small octagonal summerhouse. In the snug gloom of its interior Helen was smoking a last cigarette and enjoying the familiar comfort of leaning against her ex-husband's shoulder.

'So there it is, my darling. I shall be gone for simply aeons. Is Wednesday still your free afternoon?'

'Yes.'

'Then shall we say this Wednesday? At my house.'

'I'm afraid I can't.'

'Oh Luke, it's been ages. I can barely remember what you look like without your clothes.'

'Then you will just have to use your imagination.'

'Well, if not Wednesday, when can you manage it?'

'I can't.'

'Don't tell me you've suddenly become impotent?'

'No, but I think we ought to give it a rest for a while.'

'It's had a rest for six months. How long does it need, for Christ's sake?'

'Helen – this is just not the time.'

'Ah, I *see*.' She looked at him triumphantly. 'Who is she, Luke?'

He sighed. With Helen, denial was useless. 'I'm not going to tell you.'

'Then I shall have to guess.'

'I wish, very much, that you would mind your own business.'

'Darling Luke, you *are* my business. I still love you madly, you know that.'

'Among a cast of thousands, thank God.'

'Yes, but I have so much to give and I am a very generous woman.'

He laughed. 'You should have been a Renaissance courtesan.'

'I am. The New Renaissance. The one where women are equal with men and some women are more equal than others.' She bit his ear. 'Who is she?'

He shook his head.

'Then *I'll* tell *you*. It's Chloe Olivier.'

'Oh? Why do you think so?'

'You hardly spoke to her during lunch. You avoided her before and after it. And I saw you look at her, just once. That was when I knew.'

Trust Helen. He *had* only looked at her once. 'She's Dinah's friend, for God's sake. You'd hardly expect me to be all over her.'

'But you have been. All over her. Above, behind, betwixt, between – all over.' She smiled sweetly.

So did Luke. 'You may go on as long as you please. I've nothing to say.'

'Then I won't tell you my own little secret. A pity. It would amuse you.'

'No, it wouldn't,' he said, getting to his feet. 'I don't want to know.' He did not want to play this game with Helen. What he felt for Chloe was too important for that. He did not want Helen to touch it. He and she would always be friends, though he was not sure they would ever be lovers again. Now that there was Chloe nothing else mattered.

He dropped a light kiss on the top of Helen's head to signify the end of the interlude. 'Come on, they'll all be waiting for us.'

Helen rose and slipped into his arms with salamandrine agility. 'I'm sure they won't mind being patient until you have kissed me *properly*. Not when we may not meet again for such a long time.'

He kissed her. She was thorough enough for both of them.

'Mmm. That was gorgeous. Do you still love me?'

'In a retrospective sort of way. Come on, let's go.'

In the kitchen, Dinah had routed incipient inebriation and also Oliver who had offered to help with the coffee but seemed more inclined to sit and talk to Chloe. 'Go and be charming in the living-room,' she told him. 'See if they're ready to begin.'

'Anything I can do to help?' Helen's voice came, dove-soft, from the doorway. Her face was radiant.

Dinah made an effort. 'You're all pink and shining. Smoking must agree with you.'

'It does. I took another little stroll, with Luke. Now – what can I do?'

Just bloody well leave him alone, screamed Dinah internally. 'Nothing, honestly. It's all organised.' She swept cups on to a tray and hurried past before Helen could see how near she was to tears.

Helen turned her attention to Chloe, subjecting her to

— 163 —

unabashed scrutiny. 'That dress is perfect on you,' she said admiringly. 'I adore crushed velvet. And that lovely, mysterious green. Where did you get it?'

'Miranda made it.'

'How clever. I'm sure Luke must have told you how delicious you look in it?'

'I don't think so. But Alain has.'

'*Il est bien charmant, ton mari*. You know, you have exactly the kind of beauty that appeals to Luke.'

'Really?' What *was* this? Surely Helen could not know?

'Yes, really. But I'm sure you're well aware of that.'

Chloe felt herself turning into mysterious green jelly. 'Why should I be?' she asked stoutly.

Helen patted her hand. A waft of 'Poison' teased her. 'Don't worry, my darling. I am the Grand Mistress of discretion. I've had to be. Let's face it, all the world's an auditorium when it comes to sex.' She smiled impishly and wandered out of the room, waving as though to lavish applause.

The green jelly sank glutinously on to a kitchen chair. 'I must not panic,' it said.

When her bones seemed sufficiently reconstituted, Chloe went into the sitting-room and sat at the end of the row of chairs facing the makeshift stage. Luke looked at her and smiled like a polite host. She responded primly. The play-reading was well under way. Belle, in the absence of the director – the Junior English master, whom she had not invited – was despotically in charge. They had reached the point where Jack Worthing, read by Adam whose recollection of the play was mercifully vague, proposes marriage to Gwendolen Fairfax, played by Belle herself, who knew every word.

'"You really love me, Gwendolen?"' Adam asked flatly.

'For goodness' sake try to sound as if you *want* me to. Again, please.'

'Don't fuss so. It's only a reading.'

'No reason not to do it well.'

'Oh all right! – "You really love me, Gwendolen?"'

'"Passionately!" – well, go on, react.'

'Shit.' Adam clasped his heart and fell on his knees. 'Will this do?'

'Get up, you fool. You're supposed to kiss me.'

'That isn't in the text.'

'It is in this production. And they did in the film.'

'Very well,' Adam said quietly. He took her by the shoulders and kissed her firmly on the mouth. She did not speak for several seconds.

Then she said in a subdued voice, 'It ought really to be more, well, sensual.'

Luke intervened. 'Can't we move a bit faster? We're here for Helen's benefit, so let's get on to her lines.'

'Yes, of course,' said Belle. 'Sorry, Aunt Helen. Go on, Adam.'

'Right. – "Darling! You don't know how happy you've made me."'

'My own Adam,' cried Belle extravagantly. 'Oh, bugger, I mean "Ernest"!' Everyone laughed and Chloe's heart went out to Belle.

'Gosh, you must be improving, if I can make a mistake like that,' the child said airily, tossing logic to the dogs.

Adam made a face at her. 'But you don't really mean to say that you couldn't love me if my name wasn't Adam – oh no, I don't *believe* this. "Ernest", damn it, I mean "Ernest".' Exasperated he threw his book in the air. Belle fielded it neatly, handed it back and gravely uttered her next line.

'"But your name *is* Ernest."'

They all clapped hysterically.

After that the reading went remarkably well. Helen had the kindness to defer laying the first brick of a new *tour de force*, and Belle, who aimed to keep the magnitude of her own talent a secret until the First Night, concentrated on drawing very creditable efforts from everyone concerned, especially from Tilda who surprised herself by enjoying every minute after the first five.

Miranda, naturally, was given the part of Miss Prism. There was a certain amount of risk in this, given the climactic scene in which Adam must embrace her twice, but the *directrice* considered the danger to be much diminished by the fact that he also had to call her 'Mother'. Adam himself, with his arms around Miranda's delightful body, thought otherwise.

Chloe did not witness this scene because she had been smitten with the sudden uncontrollable need to cry; not just a few drops to be brushed away with her sleeve but great wrenching gulps accompanied, if at all acoustically possible, by howls of anguish.

She waited for the next laugh and fled upstairs to lock herself in a bathroom. Having done so, she was instantly provoked by memories that made her cry all the harder. Grabbing some tissues to do it in, she blundered out of the room and into the next one she came to. It was a bedroom, single, blue and covered with animal posters. Oliver's room. She lay down on the bed and let herself go.

She wept for three minutes and forty-two seconds. The relief was as though a vice had been removed from the upper part of her skull. It left her numb, peculiarly weightless, and bemused by her own behaviour. What on earth had it all been about?

She had not been feeling any sadder, any more confused or guilty or despairing than she had yesterday, or this morning. Why now?

Now, when what she *had* been feeling, while she watched them all working together with such goodwill and humour, had come very near to happiness.

That was it.

It was because they had seemed happy, all of them, during the last hour, linked by the play and their desire for its success. It was because the afternoon had become so exactly as it ought to be. Two families doing something pleasant together, getting to know each other, becoming friends. It was all so right. And she could not bear it because none of it was really true, and that was her fault, hers and Luke's.

She wanted not to love him any more. That was what she wanted but it was not a matter of choice – you can't control what you feel. Only what you do.

'Chloe?'

She jumped. 'Oh, Oliver. I'm sorry. This is your room, isn't it? I felt a bit odd and needed to lie down. I've had a headache all day.'

The boy glowed at her. 'I'm glad. I mean that you chose my room. Lie still. Is there anything I can get you?'

'No, thanks. I'm a lot better now.' She began to get up.

'No, stay a bit. It's nice to have you to myself.'

'Don't they need you downstairs?'

'Not just yet.'

'I thought you and Tilda were really good together. She's usually shy in public. You gave her just the right amount of encouragement.'

'She's a nice girl. But then, she's your daughter.'

'Olly—'

'It's no good telling me again. I love you and I can't help it or stop it. You must know how that feels?'

She nodded, unable to speak. He stared at her, trying to read her expression.

'You can't be still as much in love with your husband as when you married. People just aren't.'

'Relationships change,' she said tiredly. 'The emotions aren't as intense. But other things make up for that.'

'Wouldn't you rather they *were* intense?' He seized her hand. 'Chloe – *please*,' he begged.

She pulled away. 'No,' she said. She stood up. 'Olly, I'm not going to let you go on this way. I'll be your friend and a good one if you want – but I can't be what you want me to be.'

'Why not? You like me. I know you do.'

'Not like that. And even if I did, just think; think what it would do to our families if you and I became lovers.' Double double, and very necessary.

'Why should they find out?'

'I see. So it was just a hole and corner affair you were thinking of?' Brutality as well as hypocrisy. She *was* doing well.

Oliver smiled. 'Sorry. That one just doesn't work.' No. It hadn't worked with herself and Luke either. 'I love you. You can't expect me to be able to see the end of it before it has even begun.'

'It isn't going to begin. You must believe me.' She came close and kissed him gently before he knew it had happened. 'There. That was the beginning and the end of it.'

She left him quickly, running down the stairs.

The phone rang as she passed through the hall. She picked it up.

'Hello.'

'Oh. Is that Mrs Cavendish?' A girl's voice, pitched high with nerves.

'No, but I can get her for you.'

'Oh no, don't do that. It's all right, I—' The line went dead.

Luke materialised in front of her. 'I missed it, but I got you.'

His grin terrified her. She moved backwards. 'No, don't. Not here.'

His brow flew up. 'All right. Who was it?'

'I'm not sure, but I think it might have been Marie de France.'

'Damn. I thought I'd settled that.'

'You've talked to her?'

'Briefly. Unfortunately Philip interrupted the conversation.'

'But you will again? She sounded so – alone.'

'Of course I will. Tomorrow.'

She nodded and made a dash for the safety of the living-room. He caught her wrist as she passed and twirled her into him like a master of the tango. Entrapped, she felt that tug and twist upon her uterus that was like a menstrual pain and which no one else had ever provoked in her. He kissed her, a cruelty under the circumstances.

'I'll see you in three days.' He was punishing them both with this closeness, their bodies an inch apart.

'Yes,' she snapped. Strung up with unfulfilled lust she stalked back to the lesser drama of the play-reading.

'"This suspense is terrible,"' Gwendolen lilted pleasurably. '"I hope it will last."'

Chapter Eleven

❦❦❦❦❦❦❦❦

O N MONDAY MORNING DINAH PHONED Chloe. 'I can't make it tomorrow.' She sounded anxious. They had planned to spend the afternoon doing nothing much and dissecting Sunday.

'That's a pity. Why not?'

'I have to visit the hospital. One of the sixth-form girls has taken an overdose.' Chloe gasped. Her body went rigid, became a pillar of protest and denial. 'Oh please, no,' she whispered.

'Huh? No! God, I'm being so clumsy. It's OK. She's fine now – well, as fine as she can be, she's had her stomach pumped, poor kid.'

'Dinah, who is it?'

'Lisa Latham.'

'Lisa? I can't believe it.' Lisa, with her dreaming eyes and her love of history, who liked to talk to Alain about medieval France, who had told Chloe shyly that she liked her, that her hair belonged to a Celtic princess.

'Chloe? Are you all right?'

'Yes. It's just . . .' She struggled for thoughts, words. 'John and Claudie – they must be in pieces.'

'Yes. Claudie keeps saying she thought she knew Lisa, and how terrible it is to find that she doesn't.'

'Dinah, does anyone know why she did it?' She courted unlikely hope. It need not be because of Luke. Lisa may not be the one. She could have done it because of poor marks, the threat of exams, an imagined disease.

'No. Luke's terribly upset. He seems to think it was over some boy. But Claudie said she didn't have a boyfriend at the moment. Anyway, she can have visitors tomorrow. I've known her for a long time and she has come to me before as School Counsellor. She might talk to me. I hope so.'

'Oh yes. She must be feeling so cut off from everyone. You will let me know how she is? As soon as you can?' She replaced the phone and called the hospital. Lisa was deeply asleep.

Dinah rang next evening to say that she was awake and out of danger. But not out of love, Chloe thought. What a terrible awakening that must have been.

'She didn't want to talk to me about it,' Dinah said.

Wednesday laboured slowly beneath a sky like a dead sea, its stillness streaked with premature rags of red. Friday Street appeared Lenten and judgemental in Chloe's eyes.

Luke was watching from the upstairs window when she arrived at the house. It was cold and the dogs crowded into the hallway at her heels. She had not the heart to keep them out. 'Stay,' she ordered Holmes, as the sensible one. 'Stay in the hall.' She imagined trying to explain their presence to the caretaker. Luke met her at the door of their room.

'Have you heard any more about Lisa?' she asked. 'It is her, isn't it?'

'Marie de France? I'm afraid it is. She'll be discharged in a couple of days. She won't talk to anyone about why she did this. I'd like to see her myself, but it's quite possible it would do more harm than good.' He sighed, closing his eyes. 'I feel so responsible, Chloe, for her frame of mind. If I had spoken to her earlier? Or given her more time.

— 171 —

Obviously I must have said all the wrong things to her on Monday or it wouldn't have happened.'

'What did you say?'

'I told her, very gently, that I couldn't respond to her feelings for me, that apart from anything else, my position prevented it. I also said I liked her immensely and thought her extremely attractive. She seemed to try to work towards a sensible attitude. She said she knew there was no hope for what she called her "inconvenient passion", but that it never seemed to get any less. She asked if she could see me sometimes, alone, so that she had something to hope for.' He frowned.

Chloe waited.

'I said I didn't think that was a good idea. That such meetings would only prolong the emotional connection, and the pain. She looked a bit sick, but she said she understood.'

'Couldn't you have done it more gradually, as she wanted?'

'You think I was wrong?'

'You become an even more romantic figure if you make yourself completely unobtainable. I believe that sort of passion is more easily destroyed by kindness. You offer a low-key friendship, emphasising the mentor relationship, rather than anything more dangerous.'

'*Bore* her out of it, you mean?'

'You're too exuberant. I think you probably give more than you intend.'

'Surely I must be myself with them? I didn't create the image that Lisa has of me. I didn't encourage her to make me into a Rochester or a Heathcliff or whoever it is she fancies.'

'You look right. You're sexy as hell, and you spend half your time with them analysing emotions. You're a walking time bomb for girls like Lisa.'

'God's teeth! Do you think of me like that?'

'I'm not sure. I think I'm too close to you to see you as anyone but you.'

He hugged her. 'Me too. Let's keep it that way. Is it my fault, Chloe? Is it?'

They walked towards the window where they liked to stand and look out over the trees. Today their branches were sullen and motionless, without birds. Chloe turned her back on them, and with them upon her damnable, unreasonable, priest-ridden instinct that told her it *was* his fault, and hers too, or, if not precisely their fault, then their rightful punishment.

'No, it isn't. Suicide attempts are either in one's nature or not. She didn't take anywhere near enough to succeed, so we can't know if she really meant it to. Either way, she needs proper counselling. Everyone experiences unrequited love when they're very young. Not many go to such lengths.'

'So Dinah says. It doesn't make it any less distressing. I can't even put my arms round that poor child to comfort her, as I can with Belle.'

'No, in case of hope.'

'But I can with you – to comfort myself. Chloe, Chloe, I love you. Come to bed and let's shut out the sad, mad world for a little while.'

Their lovemaking was in a sombre mode and they found this strange because it was obviously imposed by exterior forces. They looked more often than usual into each other's eyes, each searching there intensely for the assurance that what they did represented all that was good and necessary, the flowering of the best that was in them, and not merely a worn-weary example of human selfishness that contained the seeds of possible tragedy for the other people they loved.

Their climax brought them to the outskirts of joy, Luke finishing with long, gasping shudders that shook them both, Chloe coming hardly at all. She felt too quiet inside, somehow, for all that. It didn't matter.

'What we need is something to make us laugh, relieve the tension,' Luke said hopefully.

'Let me think. Knock knock.'

'Really? Who's there?'

'Helen.'

'Helen who?'

'Hell 'n' high water.' She told him of Sunday's kitchen mischief.

He laughed at 'the world's an auditorium'. 'Don't worry. Helen loves to tease. But she would never say anything damaging to a third party. That was how our marriage broke up.'

'Tell me.'

'She was having an affair, not the first, but this time she told one of her woman friends about it. She was incandescent with pleasure, the woman said. Unfortunately she said it to her husband, who happened to be a close friend of mine. He, bloody upright citizen as he conceived himself to be, felt compelled to pass the unsavoury parcel on to me. He should have had the sense to see what would happen. He knew how jealous I was about Helen.'

'Perhaps he did. Perhaps it was mischief.'

Luke was scandalised. 'God no. Men aren't like that, *are* they? Anyhow, I lay beside her in bed that night and thought of killing her. In the middle of the night I got up, stripped the bedclothes off her and threw her out of the house.'

'In her nightdress?'

'That and a velvet robe thing that looked as if it were made out of Scarlett O'Hara's curtains. I don't know what I intended, I wasn't rational. But Helen never came back, not as my wife. Her lover got a divorce and she went to live with him. She took Adam with her.'

'How long did that last?'

'She came back after a few months, saying she'd met someone else and that we must always be friends because of Adam and would I like him for a while. He must have been about two. I was still sore, and furious, but I agreed with her. We've shared Adam ever since. It seems to have worked as well as it could. And we did become friends. We always will be.'

Chloe considered asking him if he had slept with Helen during those friendly years, but quickly realised that if he had, and said so, then she would know and Dinah would not, which did not feel right. Anyway, what did it matter? Helen was not an issue between herself and Luke.

'How did Adam like being shared?'

'It hasn't been easy for him. He's had two step-father-figures, each discarded after a couple of years. And many others. Helen can't help it. She must have a double dose of hormones. The trouble is, Adam seems hell-bent on breaking her record.'

'That isn't the impression I get.'

'Well, maybe he's beginning to settle down. Chloe?' He stopped talking, alert. 'Did you hear something?'

'What sort of something?'

'A car. I hard a car, out at the front.'

Heart hammering, she shot up and grabbed at her clothes. 'Oh God, I knew this would happen.'

'All right, take it steadily.' He reached for his shirt. 'No need to panic.'

'There is, there is! What are you laughing at?'

'You. You look like a naughty schoolgirl.'

'You should know.' She struggled with a zip. 'Luke – the bed!'

They threw the cover over it, pulled it straight and raced for the door. They walked silently down the passage and Chloe hovered at the head of the stairs while Luke went to look out of one of the front windows.

'We're lucky,' he reported. 'It's one man in a Land

Rover. He's going off into the gardens on the west side. Even if he comes round to the front, we should be able to get far enough away from the house to look as if we are just careless walkers, rather than willing trespassers. Come on.'

'Trespassers W,' burbled Chloe, thudding downstairs as if they were on fire.

'What's that? Christening your caretaker?'

'Yes. He was somebody's grandfather. I forget whose.'

'Piglet. Winnie-the-Pooh, the soft underbelly of the middle class.'

'Keep your dirty mouth off my hero.'

They reached the hall and received a well-trained muted welcome from the dogs. Only Baskerville longed to bark, but changed his mind when he caught Chloe's eye. Like four comic-strip phantoms they slunk out of the building and along the courtyard wall while Luke secured the door behind them. The way clear, they flitted with supernatural speed across the grass and through the archway, now hung about with skeleton garlands frosted with Old Man's Beard. Then it was a race up the hillside to the woodland path. Baskerville won.

Chloe collapsed on a fallen trunk. 'Thank God.'

'It's damp there.'

'I don't care. My legs have stopped working.'

He sat beside her and held her tightly. The dogs circled them, scenting her distress. Baskerville pressed his nose into her hand.

'Oh Luke, what can we do now? We can't come back here, now that we know he's real.'

'Don't say that.' He turned her and kissed her as though his very urgency could change what had happened – a young man's kiss, sure of winning against all odds. 'Trespassers W arrived at the same time today as he did last time we were here. Since that was a different day, it's probably his regular round. We should be safe enough, as long as we leave in time.'

'*Probably* isn't enough. You can't make love in a state of hideous expectation.'

'*You* can't.' He smiled at her affectionately. 'But why don't we test the theory before we decide on anything we might regret?'

'It's no use.' She shook her head violently. She felt desolate, the sense of loss already upon her. She tried to explain, to herself as much as to Luke. 'It isn't Trespassers W. It isn't the reality of it at all that bothers me. It's that everything seems to point towards an ending for us. Fate, if you like. Those three horrible old women the Greeks invented – they've woven us into their tapestry and we have no choice of action. You and Dinah, me and Dinah, Alain, our children, and now that other poor child in the hospital – everything is lined up against us. We could tell ourselves it wasn't while we could still come here. It was our safe place, what was it, in one of Elizabeth's sonnets – 'A place to stand and love in for a day'. Well, we've had that day. It was very short. It wasn't meant to be longer.'

Luke put her out of his embrace and stood up, confronting her. His eyes glittered. 'That is the most negative, self-destructive piece of nonsense I have ever heard. I'm ashamed of you for giving up so easily. The damn Greeks invented those three meddling old ladies because they were too bloody lazy to work out their own salvation. There's always a way out if you have the energy and imagination to find it. Do you call that loving, Chloe? Giving up? If so, then those dogs know more about love than you do.'

'Don't bully me. I do love you.'

'Don't start crying. It won't solve anything.'

'Then tell me where we are to go from here.'

'I don't think we have any need to go anywhere. But let's look at the possibilities. We can't meet any closer to home, there's too much risk of being seen. We could start registering in hidden hotels as Mr and Mrs Browning, but you would find that sordid.'

'Wouldn't you?'

'It wouldn't matter. Or I could take a flat or a room somewhere. But that is just as risky because if we were to have enough time together it would still have to be too near Sheringham. And nowhere is as securely hidden as this house.'

'So, all you are thinking about is somewhere to go and fuck?' It was a word she did not normally use.

It was ignored. 'Or we could leave our families and live together. And later, when we had organised our lives, we could marry.'

'What?' The shock was like a blow to the chest.

'I love you. You say you love me. You want us to be together for more than a fuck?'

'You know I do.'

'Then living together seems to be the obvious choice.'

'It isn't a choice at all. It simply isn't possible.'

'Why not?'

'I don't have to tell you again. The reasons are people, all of them.'

'And we have to put them first?'

'Yes.'

'Do you know the current statistics for divorce and remarriage?'

'We don't have to take part in them just because they're there. And anyway, do *you* know the percentage of second marriages that fail? Well – you'd be one of them, wouldn't you? I was forgetting.'

'Don't fight me, Chloe. Don't put us on opposite sides.'

'I'm not. But you can't believe we could ever do that. You're just playing with the idea.'

'No, I'm not. I'm just *beginning* to consider it. I hadn't planned to. It's not something I ever expected to think about again. But now I am.'

'Well, don't. I can't bear it.' She stood up. 'Look – let's just go home now and not talk any more.'

'And what then?'

'I don't know.'

'Well, do we part forever, here and now? Can you do that? I can't. And I wouldn't let you do it either. So – do we come back here next week and take a chance? Or shall we skulk in the woods and freeze as we're doing now?'

'I don't *know*. Please. I can't do this now. I feel exhausted. Let me go. I'll call you and we'll work something out.'

'Don't be a coward. I want you to think about this. Seriously.'

'I'm not. I *need* to think. I can only do it properly on my own. I am going now. Don't come with me. I don't want you trying to change anything. Not until I know what I *do* think.'

'If that's what you want. Meanwhile, do you suppose a kiss would burn your flesh?'

'God, I hope so!'

Joel's studio was the gutted and glassed-over attic of a Chelsea mansion flat. Once the home of a minor Pre-Raphaelite, it had been acquired by a popular American painter who preferred, as he was homosexual and enjoyed the sun, to live mainly in San Francisco. Joel, by virtue of the American's friendship with his own mentor and occasional mistress Elizabeth, was his caretaker. He paid a nominal rent for the kind of custom-made space he would never own unless he became very successful or won the National Lottery (he proposed to do the former).

This afternoon Miranda was pacing restlessly up and down the long, skylighted room, looking at things and wondering how to say what she wanted to say to Joel. Usually it was better not to say things at all, but today she felt speech to be necessary.

They had just made love. At least, she had; Joel had probably 'had sex'. There was an afterglow of candles she had placed to cheer the lugubrious cloud-light that slumped against the bare north windows like an old army blanket. Aromatic with lemon grass, the candles gently contested the strength of the incumbent studio scents: the balsamic vinegar-in-the-face exuded by the oils, the bite of varnish, the high kick of turpentine straight to the synapses via the dolorous nose, and underlaying them all the grave emanation of clay. Miranda was fortified by the optimism of candles.

Surrounded by Joel's work, it was possible to imagine how she might feel if she had survived an air crash or stood helpless in the aftermath of battle. Huge gory canvases covered every available surface and sucked her into their terrifying world. She let herself fall into a hideous triptych in which small demonic figures in military uniforms did unspeakable things to each other while the earth around them boiled and fissured. For a moment she gave way to vertigo. Recovering, she was left with awe.

'Who was it said,' she asked, 'that making a picture is like perpetrating a crime?'

'Degas.'

'Oh. Then he was probably thinking more in terms of gentlemen cracksmen than Jack the Ripper or Genghis Khan?'

'Not necessarily. He was deeply engaged by the intricacies of human tissue.'

Miranda shuddered and looked again. 'You know, you are one of the few people who can actually paint the sounds, as well as the sights, of pain and lamentation. Goya did it best. If you only had half an ounce of his compassion, to make sense of all this blazing anger, you might become staggeringly good one day.'

Joel, sprawling naked and pleasantly spent among the wreckage of the bed, cocked a sardonic eye. 'Yeah? Well, be sure to let the critics know, the givers of prizes, the arbiters of fate, the star-gazers into their own Arseholey Pie. And who says I have no compassion?'

'Have you?'

He grinned. 'I'm working on it.'

'Great, because you may need it sooner than you imagine.'

'Really,' he drawled. 'Surely you aren't thinking of giving me a puppy for Christmas?'

'No. I thought a week's tour of the Great Slaughter-houses of England. But perhaps for your birthday. When is it, again?'

'Nineteenth of May.'

'OK, you can have my other present around then. Only it isn't a puppy; it's a baby. I think.' She stopped breathing.

He looked at her. She could not tell how. Her bravado deserted her. She crossed the room and flung herself on him.

'Hold me really tight, Joel. I'm so frightened. I don't know what to feel.'

He lay quite still. Miranda cried. He could feel her tears against his skin. When eventually he moved his arms it was not to wrap them round her but to put her gently away from him. 'This isn't a joke?'

'No.' She sat up and set her back against the wall. 'It isn't.'

He said neutrally, 'I thought you went on the Pill.'

'I did. I am. It mustn't have worked.'

'Or you must have missed one.' His voice was still quiet and expressionless.

'It's possible. But I don't think so. Perhaps it happened that first time.'

Joel got up and began to pull on his clothes. She could not decide whether or not he was terribly angry. She watched him dressing and thought miserably how beautiful he was. His baby would be beautiful too. She wondered if it was a boy.

'You are absolutely certain?' he asked. The rasp of his zip spoke harshly of carelessness. 'You've seen a doctor?'

'No, but I've done a test. It was positive. I'll see a doctor too. Soon.'

'Good.' He held out his arms.

Relief rushed through her and she hugged him gratefully. 'Oh, I do love you,' she said.

He kissed her, which was his customary reply to those words. They sat down on the bed again, leaning against each other and the brilliant row of cushions along the wall.

'So, how far on is it?'

'Just over two months, I think.'

'Uhuh? Then you'd better see the doctor as soon as possible. You don't want to leave it too long. He might not be able to arrange things right away.'

Miranda froze. 'What things?'

'You know, the termination or whatever they call it.'

She had no sense of shock. She supposed that meant she had known subconsciously what to expect.

'I don't know what *they* call it,' she said passionately. 'I call it murder.'

Joel groaned. 'Oh Gawd. I might have known.'

'Yes, I think you might. This is our *baby*, Joel. I'm not going to turn it into one of your paintings.'

'Don't be so dramatic. And don't, for the love of Ada, *cry* any more. You've just got to think about this sensibly.'

'I know. I've been trying to. I haven't had much time to get used to it yet.' There was no point in telling him again how frightened she was. He would only think the less of her.

'You don't have to get used to it,' he said with exquisite patience. 'You have to get rid of it.'

'I've told you, I don't want to. And I don't know how you could, either. It's your baby too.'

'Yeah, well I'm not ready to be anybody's father. I probably never will be.'

'And I'm not ready to have an abortion. I couldn't live with myself if I did.'

'Well, I can't live with you if you don't.'

'But it's wrong, Joel. Doesn't your instinct tell you that?

If it doesn't, you'll never be the artist you want to be.'

'That has nothing to do with it.'

'It has. It's *exactly* what I meant about needing compassion.'

Joel got up and stood in front of her. He looked into her eyes. 'Either you lose this baby or you lose me,' he said quietly. 'Now, I want you to go away and think about that. I'll see you tomorrow in the cafeteria. Usual time.'

'There's nothing to think about,' Miranda said wretchedly, not wanting to leave like this.

'That's up to you.'

He went to the door and held it open for her.

She went home to the flat and allowed herself to cry some more. She needed it badly. She tried to think of the baby in the way that Joel wanted her to, but she ended up simply thinking about the baby. How big was he by now? What ought she to do to make sure he grew properly? What changes should she make in her diet? She was careless about eating, pigging out on special occasions and forgetting about food the rest of the time. What would it feel like to be several months pregnant? Would she be sick much? Would she get horribly fat, apart from the bump? Would she care if she did? Joel would. But there wouldn't be any Joel. Or would there? Surely he wouldn't be able to go on like this when he actually saw the baby?

For a few minutes she became more hopeful. Then the negative thoughts returned. How would she manage to be both a student and a single mother? She did not know anyone in that situation but she had read enough about it to know that it was a very unpopular position to be in. Everyone disapproved of you, from the Prime Minister down to the girl behind the counter at the DSS.

And more to the point, what would her parents say?

They were bound to be disappointed in her, even if they were kind about it, which she supposed they would be, although Mum had been a bit odd recently. Whatever she did, she absolutely must not rely on them to make it all work. If she was going to have this baby, she must learn to look after it, and feed and clothe it, all by herself.

It was then she realised she had no idea exactly what this might involve. There was so much she didn't know, from the mechanics of embryonic growth, which she had learned about at school and then forgotten, to how much it would cost, in time and energy as well as money, to maintain the baby when it had emerged.

Whatever it came to, it seemed unlikely that she could conjure it up while she was still at college. Perhaps they would not even let her stay? It appeared, then, that if she was to keep her baby, she must be prepared to lose not only Joel but also her best chance of developing her talents in order to become competent enough to earn her living.

This was no use. She was running round like a hamster in a wheel. She needed to talk to someone. A friend. Preferably a woman, one who understood the problems. There were three women in her group at college. Cally had had an abortion just after leaving school. But she had spoken of it lightly, as if it had been a nuisance but nothing very terrible. She would do it again, she said. Miranda, who believed that it was in fact a very terrible thing, did not think she wanted to talk to Cally. There was Linda, who had been sleeping with Jack for a term or so and lived in permanent fear of getting pregnant. She would not want to hear about it. And Fiona was a virgin. There was no one else. Tilda was good to talk to, but she was too young.

So it was that she found herself with the phone in her hand, dialling the Cavendishes' number.

'It's Miranda Olivier. Is Adam there, please? Thank you.' She waited, wondering what on earth she was going to say.

'Hi, Miranda. How nice.'

'Um. Yes.' She swallowed. 'How are you, Adam?'

'Is there something wrong?'

'Yes, there is, rather. How did you know?'

'I'd have to be deaf and stupid not to. Are you going to tell me?'

'Well, yes. Only it suddenly seems harder than I expected.'

'Don't worry. Would it be easier if I were there?'

'I think it would. Lots.'

'Fine. I'll be with you in about an hour. It's a good time for traffic. I'll bring some wine and we can weep into it together.'

She decided on a long soak in the bath, which Chloe always said was good for the nerves. Afterwards she examined her body for signs of her condition. Her breasts had begun to feel tender and she thought they looked fuller. Her waist still seemed to be the same, however, and so did the rest of her. She weighed herself. Eight stone, as usual.

Feeling mysteriously reprieved, she dressed in jeans and a sweater, put some plates in the oven to warm and walked briskly down to the Look How Fok to pick up a mouth-watering Mandarin Banquet for Two, to go with Adam's wine. By the time she had returned and set the low table in front of the sofa with glasses, chopsticks and forks for when they gave up trying to be Mandarins, Adam was downstairs, pressing the bell on the intercom.

He hugged her like a very friendly bear. 'Mmm. You smell interestingly different.'

'Ginger Nut bath foam. No, truly.'

'Delicious. If I'd come earlier I'd have applied to lick it off.'

'The nearest I can offer you is Tiger Prawns in ginger sauce.'

'Sounds like a good second. Now, about what's making you unhappy – do you want to talk about it now or would you rather eat first?'

'After. In case I get too emotional to eat at all.'

The corner of his mouth twitched. He touched her cheek. 'Very sensible.'

'Well, I'm hungry. Problems always make me hungry.'

In the end she told him halfway through the meal. He listened without interrupting until she had got it all out. She spoke fiercely, in short bursts, repeating exactly what Joel had said and how wretched it made her feel. For the first time she realised how angry she was. When she had finished Adam gave her another tremendous hug and kissed her in what he hoped was a brotherly fashion.

'He really is a piece of shit,' he said. 'And that means you don't even have to consider him for a nanosecond.'

'I can't help considering him. I love him.'

'Even after this?'

'It doesn't seem to make much difference. Except that it hurts more. I hope *he'll* feel differently when he's had time to think. After all, it must have been as much of a shock to him as it was to me at first.'

'And as much his responsibility.'

'He thinks I forgot the Pill.'

'That isn't the point. You made the baby together.'

'I know. Oh Adam, I can't kill it. How can I?' Her eyes brimmed and she pinched her arm until it hurt. 'What do you think?' she asked.

'Mainly that you've got to be sure, one hundred per cent sure. I'm not interested in trying to persuade you one way or the other, but I do think, for the sake of all concerned, you ought to take a look at all possible futures, not just one.'

'There *is* only one. I know what I think about abortion.'

'What you think, or what you feel?'

'It comes to the same thing. I believe it's morally wrong to take a life once it's conceived; and quite apart from that, I want the baby, very much. The trouble is, I want Joel too.'

Adam, grappling with the sudden insanity of jealousy, wished that Joel might meet Elm Street's Nightmare in a playful mood. 'It probably won't help,' he said, 'but will you let me tell you my own experience? There are some similarities.'

'Of course.' She noticed that even unhappiness gave way to curiosity.

'Last year my girlfriend, Michelle, got pregnant. Just before that we hadn't been getting on so well. She's an anxious, dependent sort of girl, very emotionally needy. I was beginning to feel too pressured by the whole thing. So I was pretty sick when she told me. She said she was going to have the baby, no matter what. She also said she would always love me and that she wanted us to get married. I tell you, right then my instinct was to race for the airport. When I'd calmed down and thought about it, I had to tell her that I couldn't marry her. I didn't love her like that and I knew I never would.'

'Oh, Adam.' Miranda looked woebegone.

'But I understand that she wanted the baby, and I promised to see her through all that, and to help support the child as well as I could. Michelle tried every way she knew to make me change my mind and we went through a really horrible time. And then, when she saw it was no use, she went off by herself one day and had a termination. She thought it would please me, that everything would be all right between us after that. I felt terrible. I knew there was no going back. The relationship simply wasn't strong enough to survive all this. I was right. Her grief for the baby drove her to depression and despair and she blamed me for it. Things went from bad to worse. We were driving each other crazy. In the end I had to finish it. I hated myself for quite a while, but it was the right thing to do.'

'And what about Michelle?' whispered Miranda.

'It's taking her a long time to accept it. She still hopes we'll get together again. I see her sometimes, for coffee or a drink. She rings up two or three times a week. I feel so bad for her – but I know I can't go back to her. It's a bummer.' He stopped and looked at her worriedly. 'Miranda, I'm not sure exactly what I'm trying to tell you with all this—'

'It sounds as though you are saying that Joel and I are finished, no matter what I do,' she said bleakly.

'Not necessarily. I was only talking for myself.'

'I suppose the lesson is that I have to be whole-hearted about what I choose to do. I can expect nothing of Joel unless I have an abortion. And if I did have one, there would have to be no recriminations. In other words, become St Miranda of the Bleeding Heart. God, Adam, what a hopeless mess it is.'

Adam put his arm around her. 'Don't panic. You still have to give yourself more time to think it through. But when you have,' he said shyly, 'I'd like to help as much as I can, if you'll let me.'

'Sounds as if you have enough on your plate.' She kissed his cheek. 'I don't know why you're so nice to me.'

Yes you do, Adam thought, but you don't want to think about it.

'There is one thing,' she said. 'What's your doctor like? I don't want to go to the family one. I'd be embarrassed.'

'She's nice. Very sympathetic, with a sense of humour. I talked to her about Michelle. I'll give you her number.'

'Thank you. That's one thing settled, anyway. Let's not talk about it any more tonight. Let's finish this bottle and have another before I have to give it up.' She raised her glass. 'Sod Joel,' she said bravely.

'With great pleasure. As long as I don't have to do it personally.' He was rewarded by a faint giggle as she cuddled into his shoulder.

Next morning, Miranda was surprised to find Adam deeply

asleep on her sofa. She noted that she had covered him with her spare duvet, and that he looked untidy and romantic. His presence provoked a warm wave of gladness in her.

She decided to leave him to sleep, and let herself quietly out of the flat. She wanted to finish the fashion project she was working on before her meeting with Joel made work an impossibility.

At lunchtime she took her tray to one of the smaller tables in the cafeteria. Joel was late. When he arrived he carried no tray, just a cup of black coffee.

'Sorry. I had an argument with de Witt.' This was his Fine Art tutor. 'So, how are you?' he said lightly.

'I don't remember your ever asking me that before.'

'No? Well, you know – sick or anything?'

'Is this a change of heart? Or just an embarrassed effort at making conversation with a pregnant woman?'

'Give me a break. Of course I care how you feel.'

'Oh. Well, good. I'm OK really. I'm seeing a doctor on Friday.'

'Fine. So we'll talk some more after that.'

'I thought that was why we were here.'

'So did I. I'm sorry, but now I don't have the time. I have to meet someone.'

'Joel!'

'It's important. About this exhibition I might have. It only came up this morning. But why don't I come out to your parents' place on Saturday? That way, we've both had a couple of days to think, and then we can go on from there. Yes?'

'I suppose so. It's probably a good idea,' she said flatly.

'Right. I won't see you before that. I'm going to be a bit tied up. Take care. I've got to go now.' He went. Miranda entertained a small pain of resentment and indigestion.

Chapter Twelve

'COME ON, OLD SON, YOU must've finished by now.'
There was the sound of dry retching followed by a despairing mantra of 'Omigod, Omigod, Omigawd'. A freshening wind rattled a few sympathetic branches among the dark trees.

'It's got to be over soon,' Rufus said helplessly. 'And it's getting better. I mean, you can *talk* to me now, not like when you were right out of it.'

Dwayne was turning his head gingerly with his hands, as if it had somehow got stuck and he was trying to remove it. His torchlit shadow, cast large on the side of the tent behind them, shifted with a mechanical sluggishness, unfamiliar and inhuman.

'Man, I feel weird.'

'What kind of weird?'

'It's like my skull was made of glass – and the sky had got inside it. And it's *trying to make it a different shape*.' His voice cracked on a note of rising hysteria.

'Oh shit. Look, hold on to me. That's right. Then you'll know it's not real and I am.'

Dwayne retched again. 'Why can't I be sick?'

'You've *been* being sick for hours. You've got none left.'

'I wish I could be dead or asleep. I never knew it could be this bad.'

'Me neither. It's the dehydration. Drink some more water.'

'Why don't you feel like this, Rufe?'

'I didn't take any. I told you I wasn't.'

'Wanker. This was *your* great idea.'

'No it wasn't, dickhead. It was you said we should try the stuff ourselves so we could tell the punters exactly what they were getting.'

'Did I? *Did* I? Oh Holy Moly, now I'm losing my marbles. Fucking 'ell, how long is this going on?'

'Not long now, I should think. In fact, you're beginning to look a whole lot better. At least you've stopped shaking. How's the temperature?' He felt Dwayne's forehead. 'Yeah, it's come down a lot. You'll be OK.'

'You reckon? Well, maybe I do feel a bit less terminal.'

'Right. I think we ought to go in now. You don't want to get cold now you've stopped being hot.'

'What time is it?'

Rufus shone the torch on his watch. 'Half ten.'

'OK. If we go now we'll get in before Mum and Dad or the bruvvers. You will stay the night, won't you? I don't fancy it on my tod.'

'Of course, fuck-face. We already fixed all that, remember?'

'No. Oh shit, d'you reckon my memory's gone for good?'

'Don't piss me off. I know when you're just cracking on. But I'm glad you're OK, you stupid shit.'

'No thanks to you, you murdering lunatic.'

On Saturday morning Alain made breakfast for the family before flying to Paris. Everyone ordered whatever they wanted.

Chloe, still in her dressing-gown, had curled up in one

of the wooden armchairs and was attempting to demolish a croissant before it could self-destruct. Tilda was eating a boiled egg with soldiers and Miranda was staring blankly at her plate. At the end of the table, the weekend papers lay in an indigestible and accusing heap, while beneath it Arnie and Grace awaited opportunity.

'Miranda, don't you want that bacon sandwich?' Alain demanded.

'I thought I did, but I don't.'

He frowned concernedly. 'You look tired. You are not working too hard, are you? Or perhaps playing?'

'Not me.' She smiled healthily. 'Anyone else want this? Sorry, Dad.'

'I'll have it,' Tilda said. 'Thanks. Rufus is late,' she worried. 'He'll miss Dad if he's not back soon.' She slid her hand under the table.

'I shall be here for another hour, at least,' Alain reassured her.

'I wish you weren't going. We never seem to have real family weekends like we used to.' She fed a piece of bacon into soft soliciting jaws.

'What about the play-reading last weekend? You enjoyed that.'

'Yes, but I don't count it because of poor Lisa trying to kill herself.'

Chloe, herself still crushed by the event, tried to lift the weight from Tilda. 'We can't *know* she did. Her parents have said she took the overdose by mistake. She had been using a strong prescription for migraine and had kept on repeating it through the night because she couldn't sleep.'

'That's just the official cover-up. Everyone at school knows she did it because of a hopeless love-affair.'

Alain said firmly, 'I think that is Lisa's business, don't you?'

'Yes, of course. I didn't mean – it's just I'm so sad for her.'

'I know.' He cast about for something to alleviate her distress and remembered some of the things Chloe had said to him. 'You are right about family weekends,' he said. 'I miss out on them as much as anyone, you know. Even the small things – for example, tonight you are going to a party, yes? I shall miss seeing how you will look. Why not show me now?'

Chloe rallied and lent encouragement. 'Yes, why don't you put on your new dress?'

'I suppose I could,' Tilda said reluctantly, taken aback by this swing from near tragedy to pure frivolity. But she did feel a certain pleasure; Dad had never shown any interest in *her* clothes before. She gave Grace the rest of her bacon sandwich and trotted upstairs.

Chloe smiled at Alain. 'I found that book your mother wanted,' she said. 'Remind me to give it to you before you leave.'

'And give them both tons of love from me,' Miranda added.

The doctor had confirmed that Grandmère and Gramps could soon be great-grandparents. How would they feel about that? Although both were doctors and liberal in their views, they might not be too pleased to welcome a little bastard into the family. She was not sure anyone would.

Tilda came downstairs slowly, half confident, half in doubt of Alain's reception. She hesitated in the kitchen doorway, lifting her chin and squaring her shoulders as Audrey Hepburn had done – in the video of *Roman Holiday* that Chloe had given her – when she had had to give up Gregory Peck and go back to being a princess.

'Dad?' she said apprehensively.

Alain turned from the coffee machine. His eyes widened. He was genuinely transfixed. A lanky teenager in scruffy, deplorable jeans had left the room, her back proclaiming 'No tories, No tears'. Now, here was this tall, cool young woman in a simple, perfect dress, her hair drawn up and twisted into mysterious coils, exhibiting the excellent bone-structure which he recognised, with humility, to have something to do with him. Her skin, creamy-olive, soft, made him want to touch it. Her shape in the dark silk sheath made him catch his breath and remind himself that she was his daughter.

She stepped forward carefully. 'Do you like it?'

'*Chérie, tu es superbe.*' He briefly kissed the curve of her cheek. 'I confess I had not noticed 'ow much you 'ave changed.'

'Great.' The child reclaimed the woman's body with a wriggle of pleasure.

'I can just see you on the concert platform,' Miranda said, 'not to mention the CD covers and the indispensable interview with *Hello* magazine.'

'I trust not,' Tilda sniffed. 'I think I'll turn back into a frog now.' She made her escape. One could have too much of a good thing. As she departed, her head still held like a crown because that was what wearing her hair up demanded, Rufus made a shame-faced entry by the other door.

'Who was that?' he asked, frowning, by way of a diversionary tactic. It was not a success.

'Why are you so late? I said ten-thirty,' Chloe said.

'Gosh, was it? I thought it was *eleven*-thirty. That would make me a bit early,' he added hopefully.

'I'll write it down for you next time,' she said scathingly. 'You don't seem to have slept very well. And I doubt if you have combed your hair since you left home.'

'I may not have. We were up a bit late, that's all. Talking.'

Miranda examined him doubtfully. 'Are you sure that's all you were doing? You look to me as if you've been *on* something.'

'Get real!' Rufus snorted contemptuously. 'After all that fuss in London?'

'You wouldn't ever try anything again?' Chloe asked anxiously. 'Not even as an experiment?'

'I am quite certain that he would not.' Alain's words contained a threat.

'I'm not completely stupid,' Rufus complained. 'Is it too late for bacon and eggs, Dad?'

Alain examined him dispassionately. 'Your appearance is so revolting that it is no wonder people believe that you are also depraved. Go and make the appropriate transformation and I will consider your request.'

'Terrific. It's not all my fault. They've only got one bathroom at the Cubitts' and Elvis was hogging it.'

Upstairs he washed and brushed up with practised economy and went to see what Tilda was up to.

She was standing at the mirror in her jeans, playing with her hair. Her dress hung on the outside of the wardrobe.

'Hi. Cripes, it *was* you. Nice frock. I like that purple colour.'

'It's aubergine. Don't touch it. Where have you been?' She turned. 'You look a bit moth-eaten, don't you? Your eyes are funny. All piggy.'

'You're as bad as the others,' he said disgustedly. 'Miranda even accused me of doing drugs, would you believe?'

She looked at him narrowly. 'I don't know. I'm not sure I know much about you at all, these days.'

'Whose fault is that?'

'Don't sulk.'

'I'm not.'

'Something is wrong, Rufus. I can tell.'

'I'm perfectly fine. Just leave me alone, will you.'

'You're all wound up about something,' she said more kindly. 'Tell me. You know you can trust me not to say anything.'

Rufus sighed heavily. He could not conceal the state of his mind from Tilda; it was part of being twins, just as he

— 195 —

knew she was a lot happier lately. He would have to throw her off the scent.

'It's nothing really,' he said dolefully, with what he considered to be Machiavellian guile. 'It's just that Dwayne and I are having a bit of an argument.'

'I see. I'm sorry.' Tilda tried not to look pleased. She was wise enough to say nothing further. Argument or not, it would be unrewarding to make any detrimental remark about Dwayne.

Rufus, too, was in favour of changing the subject. 'What's this party you're going to?' he asked.

'It isn't really. Just six of us who are working on the play. We're making a meal. Belle is doing Lasagne and I'm doing chocolate mousse. I'm only the understudy but Kate can't make it. She often doesn't.'

'You're really keen on this play business, aren't you? More than you thought.'

'Lots more.' She smiled at him. 'I'd better go and practise now. Unless you need the other room?'

'I've got homework, but it's OK. The music sometimes helps. Tilda?'

'Yes?'

'Will you make some extra choc mousse for me?'

'Yes, I will.'

She was making it for Paul, really. He had said he liked it. He also seemed to like her, though she was not capable of judging how much. Quite a lot, Belle said. Tilda was guardedly pleased. Paul played the piano as well as she did, and was the first boy she had met who could really talk about music.

Drowsy and disinclined to move, Chloe had remained curled in her kitchen chair, her mind idling between the Saturday supplement and her own concerns. Peace had descended upon the household like a sudden calm at sea. If she listened she could hear the crew at work. The Captain, aloft, was packing his kit and whistling a shanty by Johnny Halliday, whom Allah continued to preserve in unnatural youth. The Petty Officer was washing something into or out of her hair. One ordinary seaman was halfway through the *Twenty-four Preludes*, and the other, one could hope, had reached a similar stage in his history project. The ship's cats, having commandeered the raw remains of the bacon, were napping in the dog's basket. The dog, who had materialised from his native mists to assist them, now lay full-length at the First Mate's feet, snoring delicately. There was a general sense of an engine turning smoothly to internal music, of slow satisfying progress made, that lulled her into a sweet self-deceiving daydream in which all things were well.

She felt, rather than thought – this, just this, is exactly what I want. Then – if I have Luke, I shall not have this.

'Mum, are you asleep?' Tilda's voice apologised.

'Not really.' She uncurled herself. 'Why?'

'I'm going to Belle's now, if that's all right? I'm taking my dress and the cooking stuff with me.'

'Have a lovely time, sweetheart. Not too late home, though.'

'Promise. Bye!'

Next it was Miranda. 'I'm dashing into Guildford. I'll be back in time for Joel. D'you want anything? Only there's something I need.' There was no point in saying this was a book about childbirth. Not yet.

'No, thank you.' Chloe was quite awake now. It seemed that she was to be deserted completely. Unusually, she disliked the idea.

When, a little later, Alain appeared, looking pleasantly dangerous in the black leather blouson he liked to travel in, she saw that he was already inhabiting the small, portable field of energy that surrounded him on these expeditions. The Captain, too, was about to jump ship.

When he gave her his parting kiss, with its customary intimations of affection, regret and promise of amends, a gulf of insecurity cracked open before her with horrible suddenness as though the house itself were breaking apart. About to fall and fall, she held on to him like a woman in a high wind.

Alain noticed nothing amiss. 'Tilda is right,' he said. 'Next week, let's try to make the kind of family weekend she wants.'

'Next week. Yes.' She released him, recovering from her moral vertigo. 'Not long till then.' She smiled and went with him to the front door to wave at his departing car.

As he stepped on to the path, Alain checked and turned back to her. 'I forgot,' he said. 'I meant to phone Luke Cavendish. I'm sorry, *chérie* – but will you call him and tell him I can't do that lecture, not until after Christmas?'

Her lips felt numb. She nodded vigorously.

Rufus waylaid Joel at the usual place and time. He watched in worship as the beautiful bike slid to its skater's halt, but he did not touch it as he would normally have done.

'Hi there, my man. How's it going?'

'Well – it could be better, actually, Joel.'

'Yeah? Why's that?'

'I've had some trouble with those new tabs you gave me.'

'Really? I've had no other complaints. What are the symptoms?'

'It was my friend, Dwayne. He only used one of them and he had a really bad time. Temperature, dehydration, the shakes. The lot.'

'That's serious news. Shit, what can I say, Rufe? I'll check out the source myself and find out what's with this stuff. You're sure he didn't take anything else with it? Alcohol, or any medicinal drug?'

'I think he would have told me if he had. He was pretty

scared. He thought his head was being busted.'

'Poor guy. Look, tell him I want to put it right with him. I've got some excellent dope here. It's baby-safe. Sweet dreams all the way. Give him this from me.'

'I don't know, Joel.'

'What's this, you don't know?'

'I may as well tell you. I don't think I want to go on with this any more – Joel?'

'Yes.'

'I said I don't—'

'I heard.'

'I'm sorry. It isn't just what happened to Dwayne. I think it might get to be too much hassle at home. I looked a bit ropey this morning and everyone noticed. If my parents found out—'

'They won't. Not if you are more careful. At least,' he continued thoughtfully, 'not unless someone tells them.'

'What do you mean?'

'Or someone might even think your headmaster ought to hear about it.'

'I don't believe this! God, Joel, that's really mean.'

'I don't think so. We have an agreement. I am not the one who wants to break it.'

'But that's blackmail.'

'Is it? Well, it won't be necessary unless you behave stupidly.'

'Yeah, well suppose I did the same thing? Told the police about you?'

'You would still be in deep shit, wouldn't you? Expulsion, family disgrace and general odium. No fun for a very long time. You want to go to university, don't you?'

'Yes, but—'

'Then, why compromise your chances? It wouldn't make Miranda too happy, either.'

'Oh shit, shit, SHIT!'

'Lighten up, Rufus. It doesn't have to be this way

between us. I thought we were getting to be friends? Nothing has changed. Young Dwayne had one bad scene, that's all. It happens. He's OK now, isn't he?'

'Yes.'

'Well, then. You're on to a good thing here. It'd be a shame to give it up. You netted a hundred plus, this last time.'

'Did I?'

'Here it is. Just give me back the rest of that sheet, and you can have it. You'll have a substantial down payment on that bike, long before you're allowed to take it on the road.'

'Yes, but do I really want to do it this way?'

'Don't be doleful, kid. This all good news I'm telling you. Jesus, you should have my troubles.'

'Should I?'

'No, not in fact. But you *should* learn to roll with the good times while they're here. Don't you think so, friend?'

'I don't know. Maybe.'

'Maybe is good. For sure is better.'

'OK. I'll go on. Just for a while, though. I mean it.'

'Good man. I knew I could trust you.'

About to make Alain's call, Chloe held the phone self-consciously, aware of a new dimension in the necessity of doubleness.

'Luke? I'm so glad it's you.'

'Me too. Though it ought not to be. The place is full of kids – one of them yours – all too idle to pick up the phone.'

'Dinah?'

'She's gone to a lecture on herbal medicine. And – there's another one tomorrow afternoon.'

'There is?' she whispered.

'And Alain is away.'

'Yes. That's why I called.' She gave him Alain's message and he thanked her.

'Will you come to Friday Street again? Trespassers W is bound to have Sundays off.'

'Are you sure?'

'Meet you there at two.'

The receiver clicked. He was allowing her no room to wriggle. Despite her earlier attack of moral vertigo, she did not want to. Not now that she had heard his voice again. She had forgotten – no, she had been freshly surprised by – its extraordinary power over her, the way she was weakened by his soft musical phrasing with its quick sharp edge of desire that made her want him inside her and let the world go hang.

The emotions released by the call gave Chloe the spurt of energy she needed to send her into the studio. She would work well now. She had begun a new picture in which she combined the village, its church and every aspect of its natural life in a dream landscape where her fantasy of the life of Catherine Chandler was taking shape. She had told Catherine she was going to do it, the last time she had spoken to her, through time and stone and her own disbelief, against the cold north wall of St Mark's. For no reason for which she could possibly account, she had come away enormously encouraged.

Making the best of what light there was, she painted throughout the afternoon. She had no idea of time passing.

At a critical point, Miranda put her head round the door. 'Would you like something to eat? Joel and I are having a snack.'

'No thanks, not just now.'

'We're going to the pub afterwards. Mum?'

'Yes.' Chloe bit her lip, concentrating hard.

'Nothing. It can wait. May I look? Oh Mum, it's like a flying dream; people and animals all mixed up like Chagall, but with such fine detail. 'I can see every stitch in this lace.

Hey, this girl is me! And here I am again.'

'In fact, one of them is a doll called Annalise.'

'I see. No, I don't. What does it all mean?'

'I think it's going to be about freedom and commitment.'

'Tricky subject,' Miranda said soberly.

In the Dark Horse, where the low-beamed rooms were thrumming with Saturday-night cheer, Miranda and Joel occupied a quiet corner near one of the open log-fires. Their conversation, like their surroundings, had its areas of heat and chill.

'I don't understand why it scares you so much. It's not as if I want you to marry me, or live with me. I don't; I just want things to go on exactly as they are.'

'What scares me is that *you* don't understand how impossible that would be. A baby would change your whole life. If you can't admit that, you are being either dishonest or extremely stupid.'

'Don't be so bloody silly! Of course I know it would change my life. What I'm saying is that there is no reason why it should change yours. All I would want from you is a little support. And I don't mean money, I mean ordinary emotional support. As a friend.'

Joel curled his lip. '*Emotional*.'

'All right, so you don't like the word. One of your no-go areas, aren't they, emotions? But you do have them, you know, like everyone else.'

'Really?' He briefly bared his teeth. 'I'm not going to say this many more times. I do *not* want a baby in my life. I do *not* want you with a baby in your life.'

'Well, that's too bad because it's already there.' She clapped her hand to her stomach.

'Don't do that. It makes me feel sick.'

'God, you really are unnatural.'

He lifted his brow. 'Hardly a suitable characteristic for a father-figure?'

Miranda suddenly felt tired. 'I don't want jokes. And I don't want to fight any more. This is too important to me.' Hesitantly, afraid of his defensive anger, she suggested, 'Later – well, you may think differently. People do change.'

'I disagree. Most people simply become more themselves. My self is the one who makes the paintings and the sculptures.'

'Is that all? What about the one who sleeps with me? Eats with me. Even talks to me occasionally.'

'That too,' he admitted. His expression lost some of its detachment. 'And I would like that to go on for quite some time yet.' She saw his eyes take on the lazy slant she recognised. 'In fact, I'm beginning to fancy the first part of it, very much, right now. Arguing makes me feel sexy. Do they have any bedrooms here?'

'Don't be crazy, Joel. It's a pub. We came here to talk.'

'I've finished talking. You know the bottom line. Jesus! If you want a kid so much, why don't you pay it the compliment of planning its arrival like an intelligent woman, when the time and the money are right? Instead of taking on a load you won't be able to carry, and hoping against every signal that I put out that you'll be able to lay some of it on me?'

Miranda shouted, 'Don't you ever listen? That is *not* what I want!'

People turned and stared at her. She tossed her head and glared back. Joel's eye automatically followed the movement of her hair as it caught the light. 'My, but you're beautiful when you're angry,' he grinned. Their neighbours grinned too.

'Especially when I've taken off my – glasses,' Miranda fluted derisively, in the ring-dove coo of Marilyn Monroe. Beneath the table she landed a satisfying kick on his tibia. 'Cocksure bastard,' she hissed.

'Cockadoodledoo,' he carolled amiably. 'I thought you didn't want to fight.'

'I don't,' she said furiously.

'Come on, let's go back to our nice warm dungheap.'

Their quarrel, despite its seriousness, ended, as they so often did, in bed, where Joel discovered an ability to crow like Chanticleer upon reaching his climax. As he had hoped, this proved as disastrous to post-coital tristesse as it did to the nurture of grudges.

Having, as he saw it, restored her mislaid sense of humour, he next set out in earnest to seduce her back to him; for, whatever his behaviour may have caused her to think, he did not want to lose her. He began, in physical terms, to court her, employing every instinct and every aspect of his knowledge of her body and the things he had taught it to enjoy.

There were games they liked, not dangerous ones, but they took them to the edge, sometimes, of cruelty or pain. There was no victim, no perpetrator; they had become equals in the testing of the limitations of pleasure, each wishing to be the one to lead the other further toward the extremes of sensation. Miranda had quickly understood that this was the connection that would provide her with Joel's best means of communication. It was only when they made love that an unspoken code was able to develop between them, its language expanding continually with the increasing number of physical symbols in which it was expressed. This sexual closeness linked them like two spies who worked together in a country where, every day and with perfect ease, they conversed with others in a different tongue, so that they alone knew that they were strangers.

That was what the love between their bodies had accomplished. Between their minds there was another kind of conjunction which was based upon Miranda's desire to comprehend completely, and therefore in a sense to possess, Joel's work. This, she hoped, would give her the whole man. That he completely comprehended hers, they both took for granted. Now, intent and watchful, he took her through the lexicon of their understanding. Following, she wept and cried out, climaxed and wept again, then seized the lead and forced out his own harsh cries as he nearly grasped the element at which he clawed but lost each time to the lesser generosity of orgasm. But though lesser, this was a generosity he prized and upon which he needed to rely. It was his nearest approach – and with Miranda as with no one else – to the elusive mysteries which were the spur and purpose of his work. Truth, certainty, illumination, godhead; he gave it no such name, but felt it only as a perpetual striving.

'It frightens me sometimes, when it's like that. I feel as if I'm being tipped into another dimension and I might not get back.'

'I'll always bring you back,' Joel said. He was kind at such moments.

'Will you? Doesn't it ever frighten you?'

'No. Don't worry about it. We're good together, that's all.'

She kissed his shoulder. 'Too good. Joel, I don't know what to do.'

'Leave it now. Until morning.'

'I can't. I have to make you change your mind. Why are you doing this to us both?'

'Because I can't be any other way. If you are going to carry on like this, I'm going back to my own room.'

'No, don't. Stay with me. I won't talk any more.

In the morning Chloe brought Miranda a cup of tea. She was surprised to find that Joel was beside her. Her manner became grimly polite.

'I see I ought to have brought two cups.'

Joel smiled and stretched. His body gleamed. 'That would be nice,' he said.

'I'll fetch another,' Chloe said curtly.

The sound of smothered giggling followed her out of the room.

'Joel! You are a disgrace – showing yourself off to my mother like that.'

'What did I do wrong?'

'You might have put something on – a penitent expression at the very least.'

'What's with the pursed lips *à la* suburban housewife?' Miranda enquired, helping Chloe with their breakfast while Joel shaved. 'You must have guessed that we sleep together.'

'That doesn't mean I like seeing you in bed together, especially here. It is simply ill-mannered. Would you have done it if Alain had been at home?'

Miranda was puzzled. 'What difference would it make? We do it in other places, why not here? What would be the point of pretending? You're not telling me it shocks you?'

'No. It disappoints me.'

'Only because you dislike Joel. Why do you?'

'I don't, not exactly. He disturbs me. Are you happy with him?'

'People who disturb us are the important ones in our lives. I love him, Mum.'

'I know, darling, I know.'

'I wish . . .'

'What?'

'Oh, nothing. Wishes aren't horses, unfortunately.' She made a wry clown's mouth. 'I'll just have to travel by bus.'

Chapter Thirteen

⟋⟍⟋⟍⟋⟍⟋⟍

IN PARIS, ALAIN RECLINED UPON one of Louis XVIII's better beds. Unlike that unhappy monarch he was in full possession of his head, if not of his pyjamas. Helen was in the tiny kitchen, making coffee and warming pastries on top of the toaster, a revolutionary trick she had invented to complement her laziness.

'Stay there,' she had commanded him throatily. 'I haven't finished with you.'

'Nor I with you,' he agreed. 'So why add crumbs?'

'I need fresh energy. And I want to be wide awake next time.'

Soon she reappeared, offering him a tiny cup which he drained with automatic speed. Helen snuggled beside him with her leisurely *grande tasse*.

'Last time was out of this world, my darling. It's marvellous waking up to find you are being *foutue* from behind, and with such an entertaining blend of *farouche* and finesse. It satisfies one's dear dirty fantasies of being ravished by men whose faces one never sees.'

Alain laughed. 'Would you prefer me to wear a mask?'

'No. I like to see your face. It has an intelligently hungry look that is very sexy.'

Alain wrinkled his nose. 'Does that make sense?' he pondered.

'It does to me. It means you never quite stop thinking, even at the most critical of moments. Luke was like that sometimes.'

'Do you still sleep with Luke?'

'Yes.'

'I thought so.'

'Is it as obvious as that?'

'For myself, I was guessing. But I also thought that Dinah was not happy to see you with him. It seems a pity to be the cause of such unnecessary distress, don't you think?'

'I'm afraid I didn't realise. She is always so sweet to me. And Luke and I are so used to putting up our jokey smokescreen. I thought it worked.'

'It may, in general. It is Chloe who thinks that Dinah minds. They are friends.'

'I see. Then I shall revise my script. I suppose I do tend to be a tiny bit bitch-in-the-manger about Luke. It's a sentimental habit, probably because he is the only one I ever married. And he gave me Adam.'

He looked at her with sympathy. 'Do you regret leaving him?'

Sympathy was a gift she did not permit. 'Darling, I *never* have regrets.'

He kissed her gently. 'Yes, I believe you have mastered the difficult art of living in the moment.'

'How true. Come closer. Mmm. Delicious! And now it is my turn to ask questions. You love your Chloe, don't you, and you are happy together?'

'Yes, I do. We are very happy. At least I am, and I have always thought that she was. I hope so.'

'Then she is likely to remain – what is that quaint old-fashioned word – faithful?'

'Yes. Yes, I'm sure she is.'

'But you are not.'

He smiled, unperturbed. 'Despite appearances, I wouldn't agree.'

'Ah. Experience tells me I am about to hear some outrageous masculine apologia.'

Alain shrugged. 'If that is 'ow you like to see it. But the truth is that I don't make love with other women very often. In fact, I rarely take what I am offered. And I make sure I am never involved in an affair of any length. How can I put it?' He was silent, working it out. 'It is that my infidelities can never go as deep as my marriage. You understand? They cannot touch it – and therefore they cannot harm it.'

'I think I know what you mean.' But she looked doubtful. 'However, I hope you do not expect of Chloe what you will not demand of yourself. How would you feel, would you care at all if she were to be with someone as you and I are now?'

He shook his head at her. 'Helen, you are a mischievous woman. I think you know that, for me, it is a question I would rather not ask myself.'

'Don't worry, darling. Most good marriages are based upon questions that are never asked.' She ran her finger down the thin bridge of his nose, then planted a light kiss on the tip of it. It was a caress with which she used to comfort Adam after applying iodine to his childish wounds. 'You must pay her a lot of attention when you go back to her.'

'I always do,' Alain said mildly. 'But now I am with you. Do you think we could stop talking for a while?'

On Sunday there were gales. A disgruntled Jove hurled hailstones into windscreens and sliced with icy winds at legs.

Chloe, gritting her teeth as she got out of the jeep, was unable to coax Baskerville, shivering dramatically on the back seat, to abandon his nice warm blanket for the mud of Friday Street. 'Stay there, then, you unfaithful hound,' she said grudgingly. He had the grace to look ashamed.

The woodland path had degenerated into a slough. Pinned to the fence near its entrance was a note in Luke's handwriting: 'Try the left bank'. She took it in her hand and he was already with her. Through the trivial agency of a scrap of paper she received as clear a sense of his essential self as if she held his face between her hands.

She began to run headlong, rejoicing, upon the narrow grass bank on the left. She was giddy and out of breath when she saw him waiting beneath the denuded archway, the collar of his greatcoat turned up around black licks of wet hair. Without speaking she came up and pressed the length of her body against his, putting her palm to his face and letting it remember him all over again. At first he did not touch her at all, and then only with his mouth. His lips shaped words upon hers, teasing her to guess their meaning, though she did not even try because what did it matter, there was only one thing they could mean.

Inside the house they found that Trespassers W had become unseasonably parsimonious with the central heating. The temperature in the bedroom was polar.

'I can't feel my toes,' Chloe complained.

At the end of summer he had kissed her feet, scenting the last of the sun on her skin, licking it, salted, from between her toes. Now, in November, he took off her sodden socks and rubbed her frozen bones between his fingers – her winter warmer, her *chauffeur*. Luke was never cold.

They kept on their clothes and wrapped the ancient damask cover round them both so that he could transmit his warmth to her.

'We can't do anything like this,' Chloe protested, laughing.

'Yes we can,' he insisted. 'If we pull your skirt up, and I

unzip – you don't mind if I make a hole in these tights?'

'Apparently not.' She shuddered in reaction.

'There you are. We haven't lost any heat and we're about to make a lot more. But you'll have to keep still or I can't get in.'

'I can't,' she moaned. 'Your hands are driving me mad.'

Need had replaced every cell in her body. She arched her back and took him in. A few fevered seconds and she gave a small grateful cry. Luke, slower, more in control, lifted his head to watch her pleasure.

'I felt that so strongly,' he said. 'Like a hyperactive sea anemone opening and closing around me.'

Something like a smile lightened inside her. 'Animal flowers,' she said softly. 'That's what they used to call them, long ago.'

'Then perhaps they made the same comparison. It would be nice to think so.'

Chloe was enchanted. Once again he had called back the dream that had seemed to foretell his arrival in her life. Like her, he had found his image of love in the depths of the sea.

She floated contentedly on his tide, the petals of her flesh adjusting their pulse to his lazy thalassic rhythms.

'One day we'll be punished for being so happy,' she muttered drowsily, withdrawing her fingers from the cocoon of cloth to wind them in his hair.

'Are we playing a quotation game?'

'No. Wait – yes! It's *Anna Karenina*, isn't it? The film, not the book.'

'That's right.'

'Then I wish I hadn't said it. It makes me feel super-stitious.'

'Don't let it. Why should we be punished? We haven't hurt anyone.'

'How can we be sure? I know that being with you is

changing me. Sooner or later, that is bound to have an effect on the other people in my life.'

'Then, if you are thinking like that,' he said slowly, 'have you considered what I said? About living together.' He took her hand. He would kiss each finger separately, to give her time.

She snatched it back, her stomach plummeting. 'My God, what an astonishing volte-face! First we have hurt no one. Then we destroy them all with a single blow.' She struggled out of the covers. 'That's too fast for me.'

'Don't exaggerate. It wouldn't be like that.'

'How can you possibly know?'

'I can hope. And plan. *Have* you thought about it, Chloe? I need to know.'

'No, I haven't,' she said reluctantly. 'I have tried to – but it's as if my mind simply refuses to recognise the subject. I can't focus, can't seem to get any purchase on the future. The past is easy – a nice straight Roman road marching forward through a well-ordered estate. *Now*, I feel as if I'm standing at the entrance to a maze. The only thing that makes any sense of it, is that I'm there with you. Loving you, making love with you.' She frowned. 'But how can that replace a whole life?'

Recognising the nascent strain exposed by his question, he made her comfortable against him and said nothing, knowing there was more to come.

'Making love,' she continued with a little shake of her head, a hint of fever breaking her voice. 'It's such an odd, unkempt act; extraordinary when you think of it coldly; ludicrous if it were to be viewed by a third party. Yet it is the one occupation we all apparently value above every other. We must, if we are prepared to put our entire existence in jeopardy for it.'

Tears stood sharp in her eyes, of anger, he thought, not distress. He sought to dispel them. 'Oh we do,' he agreed expansively. 'Why not, since it is our greatest pleasure, greater than making money or taking drugs or getting gloriously drunk? Making love is the bee's knees, the cat's pyjamas, the gilt on the liver-spotted lily of life – but it's only a beginning, my best-beloved, a kindly kick-start from Mother Nature. It's up to us where we go after that.'

'I know, I know. But I can't see clearly enough how our life together would be. I can't get past everything Alain and I have built up. He and I have been making love all these years – really making it, creating and recreating it, putting it at the heart of our life as a family.' She put her fist to her mouth, dropping it instantly. 'I still love him, you know.'

'Like this?'

'No, not like this. Like itself.'

'And so?'

'It's no use,' she said miserably. 'I shall only keep going round in circles.'

'I think,' he said gently, 'you must ask yourself what you most want to do – just *want*, not *ought*.'

'But that's just what I can't do,' she cried.

'It might help if you took it one step at a time.'

'You amaze me, Luke,' she said sharply. 'Are you really as certain as you seem? I simply can't believe that you can't feel the same confusion and pain that I feel.'

'I feel exactly the same, I imagine, when I consider Dinah's feelings, or ask myself what effect it would all have on our children.'

'Then why do you talk as if I am the one who has to make the choice?'

'Because I have chosen. There was never any real question for me. I want you more than I want to avoid causing pain.'

'And if I can't say that? You will think I don't want you enough.'

'No. We are different, that's all.'

'We must be! Because if you have really tried, with all the power of imagination you possess, to understand how much you would hurt Dinah if you left her – especially if you left her for me—'

' – Stop this, Chloe. It doesn't solve anything.'

'But it does. Can you actually begin to feel the anguish we would cause and still say that what we want – all right, what we *need*, what we *crave* – can count for more than that? Because I can't. I just *can't*, Luke. I'm sorry.'

'Calm down,' he said, reaching for her. 'Don't do this to yourself. It's all right. Nothing *has* to happen. We can stay as we are. For as long as you like. Until all the children are out of school – whatever you want, as long as we are together somehow.'

'Another three or four years of Trespassers W,' she said shakily, trying to smile. 'I don't think I could.'

'Pessimist.' He stroked her shoulder. 'Don't you see, you need only settle for what you can cope with? We don't have to make any decisions. I've gone too fast for you, I see that now.'

'I'm sorry,' she said dully. 'I panicked.' She wiped her eyes with the back of her hand and pushed at her tangle of hair. She felt incredibly tired.

'There's no need,' he said penitently. 'We'll do anything you please. Just as long as I don't ever have to be without you.'

'I suppose I'm a coward,' she said sadly. 'I feel safer with what I know. So shall we just go on meeting in this very desirable Grade Two Listed Limbo, putting my animal flowers through their paces? Until one day Trespassers W comes down like a wolf on the fold and gobbles them up.'

Luke gave a shout of laughter. 'We'd better not explore *that* idea too closely. And really, he won't. But if it will make you less anxious I'll fix up an early warning system. And just think,' he finished, his voice furry with persuasion and renewed desire, 'how lovely it will be here in the summer.'

The weather changed, an indolent sun making a late

appearance in a sluttish ensemble of wispy clouds tacked across a pale denim sky.

Thus invited, Joel and Miranda took the bike out and swooped about the countryside in search of an undiscovered wilderness in which to walk. Half an hour's airy mapless meandering deposited them outside the Thomas à Becket, which Miranda remembered someone had recommended to her. They parked the Harley and went inside, where they shared a hot toddy with a steaming group of hikers. Taking their advice, they were afterwards faced with a dozen suitably woody and muddy walks. On the hopeful grounds that no one else would, they picked the muddiest of all.

Quite soon, they were standing on the path overlooking Arden Court, admiring the Italian extravaganza of its rooftops.

'It is the same house,' Miranda said. 'I recognise the cupola.'

'So do you want to go down and look around, or what?'

'I don't know. It seems like Mum's private thing, somehow.'

Joel shrugged. 'I thought you were curious. And it's nice to have an objective.'

'Other than sorting out the future?'

'Anything other than that.' But he smiled.

Not only had they had really good sex twice already that day, which had left him in a benevolent mood, but there were signs that Miranda might come round to his point of view about the baby. She had promised, after their second and highest ecstasy, that she would seriously consider the possibility of having a termination. She would study the procedure and its physical and psychological effects, and would think about the freedom it would restore to her. She would also think about what Joel wanted. After all, she claimed to love him, didn't she?

'Come on, then. Let's go,' she decided now.

Chloe would not know, and why should she mind if she did?

'It's no good. They're locked.' She gazed in disappointment through the wrought-iron gates.

'We'll find another way.'

It was not long before they discovered the thorny path that Holmes and Watson had opened.

'It's like "The Sleeping Beauty".'

Joel grinned like a satyr. 'Poor girl. Fancy hanging on to your virginity for a hundred years.'

'It wasn't her idea,' Miranda said testily. 'It was the Enchanter. He was some kind of jealous father-figure.'

'More likely to have been an over-protective mother, judging by the look on Chloe's face yesterday morning.'

'Shut up, Joel, or I will knock out one of your best teeth.'

'Oh yeah?' He picked her up and held her, kicking, above his shoulders, until she gave in and consented to laugh with him.

'Hey, we should be quiet now,' he warned. 'We don't know who might be here. I mean, technically, we're trespassers.'

'Trespassers W.'

'What?'

'Winnie-the-Pooh. Didn't you have him when you were little?'

'Sure. The drawings were fun, but I thought the stories were crap.'

'Who read them to you?'

'No one. I read them myself. Some teacher gave me the book because she thought I was deprived.'

'You were.'

'Stuff it, will you?' he said furiously. His locked and private prejudice had been invaded by the vision of

Miranda as a triumphant Madonna, relating the adventures of the imbecile bear to a small figure with unruly red curls, a child who was loved enough not to regard that smug, sweet, safe world of friendly animal psychiatrists with an envy that cut new wounds across the scars of his stepfather's strap.

Miranda, whose thoughts ran on similar lines, chose to evade them with a sudden burst of speed. It brought her to the front of the house, which she found both lordly and forlorn, and then into a courtyard where there were several doors, one of which, she soon established, had been left carelessly and invitingly ajar.

They entered the house and moved silently about it on their rubber soles, barely whispering, so that they might immediately detect any further presence.

When they reached the upper floor it was Joel who glanced through the half-open door of the bedroom. Instantly assimilating what he saw, he threw up an arm to hold Miranda back. Turning to her, he laid a finger on his lips.

Puzzled, she saw that, although the injunction to silence was deadly serious, his eyes were alive with delighted irony. He gave her a little push, then held her still.

She gave one half-smothered cry she could not help. Then he pulled her away and made her take her time and keep the silence while they gained the stairs. In less than a minute they were crashing through the shrubbery.

'If you tell anyone – *anyone* – about this, I'll kill you, do you hear?'

'I hear you. Look where you're going. Hang on, you're caught on something. OK, you're free. Now, stand still for a second and take a couple of deep breaths. Oh, now – for God's sake, what is there to cry about? It's not the end of the world if Chloe wants to have some fun, is it? She's as much entitled to it as the rest of us.'

'No, she isn't!'

'Why not? Because she's married? Because she's your mother? Why?'

'Oh, go to hell. You don't understand anything.'

'And you do? So tell me.'

Miranda's response was to sob harshly. 'What's *wrong* with everyone?'

'Come on now, it's not so bad. Who was her friend? Good-looking guy.'

'Luke Cavendish,' she spat.

'Why is that so outrageous? Who is he?'

She shook her head.

'Listen, you mustn't get so upset about this. It's your mother's business, not yours.'

'Oh, leave me alone, Joel! How could she do it?' she demanded of the world at large. 'I can't believe it. How could she?' She continued to shake her head from side to side, unable to escape the scene she had been forced to witness, the lovers, wrapped in each other's arms, the lax grace of their bodies as remarkable as the appalling innocence of their sleeping faces. It had been a picture of great beauty, as tender and luminous as a Correggio. That made it worse, somehow.

She would not talk at any point on the journey home. Joel accepted this, awed by the compacted energy of her anger. Why, he wondered, did Chloe excite such a passion of condemnation, far greater, it seemed, than anything she had unleashed upon himself? She had been angry with him, certainly, was still. Her anger and hurt ran beneath the surface of their time together, ready to break out and confront him at any opportunity. But it had never been this tight, white, absolute obloquy that she had turned upon her mother. Did she expect Chloe to conform to some blue-print of maternal perfection she had drawn up? Or had Chloe herself passed on such a blueprint and had now abandoned it in favour of a new and more alluring construct, one of human imperfection and pleasure set in an Eden of wintering trees? Whatever the case, he was sorry for them both. He would try to go easy on Miranda for a while.

When they arrived back at her house she stopped him as he was following her to the door.

'No. Don't come in until you've heard what I'm going to say.'

'Can't you say it inside?'

'No. I have to draw a line somewhere and I'm drawing it out here. I may not want you in this house again.'

'Don't be so damned childish, Miranda.'

'Just listen, will you? And remember as you do, that I am not going to change my mind about this.'

'I see.' Sympathy began to seem less appropriate. 'Well?'

'I am going to have this baby, Joel, and there is nothing you can do about it. I don't want you ever to come near me again unless you intend to accept my decision and give me the minimal amount of support I've asked you for. Do you understand?'

'But you said this morning—'

'This is now.'

'I think you are making a big mistake.'

'No. *You* are. Are you going or staying?'

'If you mean have I changed my attitude in the last half hour – no, I haven't. And I won't.'

'That's it, then. Have you left anything in the house?'

'Some stuff in the bedroom. Miranda, do you really—'

'I'll get it. Stay here.'

'For fuck's sake!'

She reappeared and thrust his bag into his arms. Then she went into the house and closed the door without looking back. As she ran upstairs she heard the Harley's engine roar away.

After a time she washed her face and combed her hair and packed her own bag, not the one Joel had given her, with the things she would need to take on the train.

Then she went downstairs and made herself some coffee and sat down to wait for Chloe.

'I know, boy, I know. It was horrible of me to forget you. I'll make it up to you, honestly. You can have minced turkey for dinner, and I'll let you sleep on the bed.'

Baskerville was not mollified. He was horribly thirsty and his feelings were hurt. On top of that, he had almost been forced to the indignity of relieving himself in the jeep. Forgiveness would not come cheap. He stalked into the kitchen before Chloe and clouted the insolent Arnie out of his basket with a magisterial swipe of his paw. Miranda was sitting at the table, her posture abnormally neat.

'Hello, lovely. On your own? Where's Joel?'

'Gone.'

'I thought you were leaving together?'

'Mind your own business.'

'Miranda, what on earth—?'

'Joel is nothing to do with you. As a matter of fact he is nothing to do with me either, not now.'

'I see. Oh, my love, I'm so sorry. You must be—'

'No, you don't see. You don't know anything about it.'

Chloe was winded. Her instinct was to take Miranda in her arms but that was obviously not what was wanted. Searching her white, closed and impervious face, it was hard to tell what was.

'I can see that you have been upset,' she said neutrally, 'but do you really have to be so unpleasant?'

'Oh, I think so. It is how I feel. At least it's honest.'

'If that's the case, perhaps you could direct your honesty towards the proper target.'

'I am doing.' Her gaze was hard and concentrated. There was no doubting her hostility.

'What am *I* supposed to have done?' Chloe asked, annoyed. 'If this is because I didn't like finding you and Joel in bed—'

Miranda made a short savage sound. 'No. It's because *I* didn't like finding *you* in bed with Luke Cavendish.'

In the slow-motion second after she had spoken, Chloe was able to hope she had misheard. Her daughter's eyes, bright with bitterness, told her she had not.

They looked at each other across the silence.

Chloe sat down. Arnie jumped into her lap. She did not notice, though she stroked him automatically.

'Will you explain?' she asked quietly.

'That house. We found it. I saw you together. Now *you* explain.'

'If you saw us,' Chloe said, wondering what words, if any, she could find to defend herself, 'then I don't need to explain.'

'Don't you? You seemed to think *I* ought to, yesterday. So now I want to know. Why have you been fucking Luke Cavendish?'

'Because I love him.'

'I don't believe it.' The censorious green glare wavered to disillusion. 'You can't! What about Dad?'

'I haven't stopped loving Alain. It isn't as simple as that.'

'You bitch. You're a filthy bitch, do you hear?'

'No, I'm not. I'm an ordinary woman in quite an ordinary situation, who happens to be your mother.'

'God, I wish you weren't!'

'Don't. I'm sorry that you should have found out like this – even sorrier that you feel this way about it. But please, give yourself a little time to think about it. You have had a shock. So have I. Please, don't let's say things to each other that we shall regret.'

'I shan't regret anything. I do think you're a bitch and I do wish you weren't my mother.' She paused. 'And I wish

— 221 —

to hell you weren't going to be my baby's grandmother.'

Chloe closed her eyes. When she opened them Miranda's look of triumph shocked her more than the truth it confirmed.

'You're pregnant?' she said weakly, as if it might even yet be denied.

'Obviously.'

'How long?'

'Nearly three months.'

'It's Joel's, of course?'

'It's mine.'

'He is the father?'

'He was. But he isn't going to be. This baby doesn't need a father. It will get everything it needs from its mother.'

'You're completely sure you want to have it?'

'I'm *going* to have it.'

'Oh, my dearest child, I'm so sorry.'

'Why? Because I'm pregnant or because you're an adulterous bitch? I'm *glad* I'm pregnant, so you needn't worry about that. But I think you should start to worry, pretty desperately, about your own predicament.'

'Miranda, how can we talk if you're going to be like this?'

'How can we talk at all? I don't know you any more.'

'I haven't changed. I just love someone, that's all. It doesn't make me a criminal, or even a bitch. I didn't want it to happen.'

'Then why did you let it?'

'I couldn't help it.' Chloe's patience snapped. 'Why did you get pregnant?'

'I don't know. Maybe I forgot a pill, maybe not. I'll never know and it doesn't matter. What you did does matter. Not just to me, to all of us.'

'I don't think it is your business to say these things,' Chloe said firmly. 'As for having the baby, if you can't be sensible with me, I suggest that you stay overnight and discuss it with your father. He will be home at eight this evening.'

'Are you going to discuss Luke Cavendish with him?'

'That must be my decision. The two things are not connected.'

'Aren't they?'

'No. You need to talk to us about the future, to Alain alone if that's what you want. You know that we will both give you all the love and support you will accept. But Luke and I have nothing to do with that. You could do a lot of damage to this family if you are mischievous enough to talk to anyone else about it. I need time to think things over, just as you do.'

'Are you going on with it?' Miranda demanded.

'I don't know.'

'You can't, not now.'

'It is not your concern. I repeat, you may cause more harm than you intend if you try to interfere.' She had no idea where her strength was coming from, was grateful that it came at all. 'You must give me your word about this. For Alain's sake if not for mine.'

Miranda looked at her with contempt. 'That makes it easy for you, doesn't it? You know I'd do anything rather than hurt him. It's a pity you don't feel the same. That's one of the things love is about, if you didn't know. All right, I'll give you my promise, but I'll never give you my respect, or my love, ever again.' She dropped her head as if this had been too sorrowful to speak, then looked up, meeting Chloe's eyes with a coldness that hurt her more than she could bear. 'How could you, Mum? With Luke Cavendish. Dinah was getting to be your best friend.'

Chapter Fourteen

W HEN ALAIN CAME HOME HE did not immediately
sense any grave change in the expected tenor of
the household. It was, indeed, blessedly quiet,
but he ascribed this to the absence of both twins rather
than to the fact, which he failed to notice, that Miranda did
not speak to Chloe unless first addressed by her.

When Chloe departed unobtrusively for her studio, and
Miranda asked if he were not too tired to talk to her for a
while, he inured himself good-humouredly to the prospect
of another conference on the 2CV.

'*Mon dieu, mon dieu, mon dieu*!' he exclaimed, as she had
known he would, when she had finished speaking. 'Have
you truly thought about this, Miranda, with common
sense, with logic?'

She grinned. 'I don't think logic comes into it; but yes,
I have. You'll soon get used to it,' she added cheerfully. 'I
have, almost.'

Alain was pulling the short hair on top of his head into
little peaks, a thing he did when he was perplexed. 'But this
is a bombshell,' he pronounced.

'You sound like Inspector Clouseau.'

'I *feel* like him. I don't know what to say to you.'

'Just say *bonne chance*, or whatever.'

'Hmm. Whatever, eh?' He took both her hands and squeezed them hard.

'*Quoi que ce soit?*'

'I don't think one can translate. Now – tell me everything you have thought about this – again, from the beginning, how you feel and what you want. And then we will make a plan.'

She got up to kiss his smooth cheek. 'You are never so happy, are you, as when you're making a plan?' She sniffed appreciatively. 'Mmm. You've changed your aftershave.'

'Have I?'

'Yes. I like it. It's more feminine than the last one.'

'Then I may change it again.' He would. It was Helen's perfume, transferred during a passionate leave-taking in the taxi to Charles de Gaulle. At the airport itself she had, of course, behaved with perfect circumspection. He was not sure what he was going to do about Helen.

Chloe confronted her painting and could make it mean nothing to her. She knew this was because she was presently inhabiting some cut-off region between grief and despair, but she had come here instinctively, if not for comfort, for confirmation of who she was.

When Alain came in later, he found her standing at the easel, staring without seeing. There were changes in her face, a premonition of ageing. When he held her, at first she stiffened, resisting.

'It isn't as bad as you think,' he said. 'In a year we will all be besotted with this baby. We won't know how we existed without it.'

'I hope so. But what if Miranda doesn't want that? If it takes her away from us?'

'That won't happen, why should it?' He was certain. 'You know, when she first told me I almost suggested an abortion. That would have been a mistake, wouldn't it? She has always been so much against it.'

'Yes,' she said.

'You look tired, *chérie*. Will you come to bed soon?'

'Yes. I just want to . . .' She made a meaningless gesture at the picture.

'Don't worry. We are going to make this something to celebrate. Miranda and I have already started on a plan.'

A plan. Her painting was also intended to encompass a plan; of Catherine Chandler's life, of her own. It was to have explained them, each to the other, to have made sense of the past and reconciled their hopes and fears for the future. It was ambiguous and difficult and she had barely begun to understand what she was doing. She looked into it and could find nothing of what she sought. Her gaze returned again and again to the little white, disembodied head, its sweet face shining like a star in a corner of the midnight sky.

She had to talk to Luke. He must be told what had happened. But first there was the night to get through. Alain would want to make love. She did not want it. She felt sick, fragmented, incapable of taking part. But she would; and she would make quite sure that Alain could have no idea of her reluctance.

In the morning she waited till eleven to call Luke. After his initial surprise, which he expressed by a brief silence followed by a thoroughly masculine curse, his only concern was for her and for Miranda.

'It must have been a hellish shock for the poor girl. No wonder she turned into the Avenging Angel in full feather. How does she feel now?'

'Outraged. She won't speak to me, Luke. I think she hates me.'

'Give her time. She's probably reacting to her own

situation as much as yours. She can't hate you forever, she's going to need you too much.'

'I don't know. What worries me most of all is that her feeling about me may have influenced her decision to keep the baby. She says my relationship with you isn't just a betrayal of Alain, but of her too – of the whole family. An unforgivable selfishness on my part. I think she sees abortion, and even adoption, in the same light. As if she's determined not to betray her child as I have betrayed mine. Something like that.'

'She may find that a useful stick to beat you with just now, but I think she will have the baby because she wants it, not for any other reason.'

'Luke, I don't know how to deal with this.'

'You can only take it as it comes and try to stay calm, if you can. Is Miranda still with you?'

'No, she went back to the flat.'

'Good, that gives you both some space.' He hesitated. 'You know, Chloe, from our own point of view, all this may turn out to be not such a bad thing. We were heading towards stasis. It may provoke some action.'

'For God's sake! I've told you – I don't want action. Stasis is fine.'

'Maybe, but it has never been known to last.'

She thought tiredly that he sounded almost exhilarated.

At lunchtime, Rufus made a lucrative trip to a specific oak tree in the wooded area behind the school playing-field. He emerged to find Tilda waiting for him.

'Fancy another little walk? I want to talk to you.'

'What about?'

'This and that.'

Rufus looked knowingly. 'Won't Paul Hughes take you for a walk, then?'

'Do you have to be such a prat?'

'You like him a lot, don't you?'

'Mind your own business. It's you I want to talk about.'

'You're blushing. You *must* have had a good time last night.' He added solicitously, 'I thought Paul Hughes was going out with Fiona Thompson in five A?'

'That finished ages ago.'

'So it's all on, then? He really fancies you?'

Tilda, with whom last night had rated somewhere between Rachmaninov's Second and Prokofiev's *Romeo and Juliet*, smiled mysteriously. 'He told me something about you.'

'Yeah? What?'

'That you're selling drugs.'

Rufus leaped. 'For Christ's sake, be quiet! You don't know who might be around.'

'So it's true, then?'

'No, it isn't!'

'There's no point in lying. One of Paul's less intelligent friends is one of your customers. Look, I don't want to get you into any trouble. Just tell me about it. Where do you get the stuff from?'

'Bloody hell, Tilda. This is nothing to do with you.'

'Of course it is, stupid. Look, too many people know about it. It has to stop. Are you using Depraved Dave in the Sixth? Because if you are, I'm going to tell him just what I think about it, right now.'

'No, I'm not, so you can take that Joan of Arc look off your face. Just forget it, will you? Because if you start interfering, you'll only get me into deep shit.'

'You're in it now. I suppose Dwayne's part of it too?' she asked thoughtfully. 'If Dad gets to hear of this, you realise you won't be allowed to go around with him any more?'

'You wouldn't tell Dad?'

'Not if you tell me.'

'You're just as bad as – you really are disgusting.' But he wanted to tell her, really. It was all getting too heavy for him. 'OK. I get my supply from Joel. Now are you satisfied?'

Tilda groaned. 'You are an idiot. I should have guessed. All those bike rides. And he's exactly that sort of person.'

'He was all right at first. He was trying to do me a favour. So I could save up for my own bike.'

Tilda rolled her eyes. 'So, what now?'

'Well, it's all gone a bit wrong. I'd kind of *like* to stop now, honestly. But Joel says he'll make sure Mr Dacre knows about it all if I do.'

'Poison. He always was, pure poison. I'll never understand Miranda.'

'Yes, but what am I supposed to do? I don't have any choice. I've got to keep on selling.'

'Pushing,' Tilda said clearly. 'That's what it is. You're a pusher, just about the lowest form of pollution on the planet.'

'I don't have to push,' Rufus muttered. 'The punters practically *pull*.'

'Well, you're at the end of your rope,' she informed him grimly.

'Are you crazy? Joel will do what he said.'

'We'll find a way to stop him.' Was this Tilda talking, the girl who had been singed by the faintest spark from Joel's coal-burning eyes? Where had this confidence come from? 'What I'd love to do,' she continued, 'is to tell Miranda what he's been up to. But there's no guarantee she could stop him, and every chance she would tell Mum and Dad. But what I did think of was – Adam Cavendish is keen on Miranda too, isn't he?'

'Yes, I suppose he is.'

'Then why don't we get Belle to tell Adam about Joel? He'll be so mad. He'd try really hard to get the better of Joel.'

'Why is he more use than Miranda?'

'He's an outsider, and he's a journalist. Joel won't know what he might do. Maybe he can turn the blackmail on to Joel. What do you think?'

'Why not just put up a public notice?' Rufus demanded tragically. 'You may as well. Did you ever wish you'd never been born?'

'Not recently. Cheer up, Rufe. I'll make it all right, I promise.'

Belle, privately, was unenthusiastic about any activity which might have the undesirable side-effect of casting Miranda Olivier into Adam's arms. On the other hand, Tilda was her closest friend, Rufus was Tilda's beloved brother, and Joel Ranger was very bad news, except, you had to admit, to look at. If Adam, despite his denials, was really in thrall to Miranda and her Medusa curls, it could even be a good idea if he were given the opportunity to get her out of his system. He obviously considered Belle herself far too young for him, quite apart from any conservative doubts about sibling relations, but she would soon be old enough, and faster than he might think.

She would be magnanimous. She could afford to be. Time was on her side.

'What will you do?' she asked. 'Don't forget you mustn't drop Rufus any deeper in it. So, if you tell Miranda, you must swear her to secrecy.'

'I'll be careful.' Adam smiled and pulled her hair. Which was degrading but better than nothing. 'I'm glad you told me, Belle.'

'And grateful?'

'Naturally.'

'How grateful?'

He sighed. 'You tell me.'

'You take me out to dinner and that new play at the Royal Court Upstairs. Just the two of us.'

'As grateful as that? Will next Tuesday suit you? If I can get tickets.'

'Great. And wear that lavender-grey shirt. You look dishy in that.'

'Your lightest wish is my command.'

It will be, one day, she thought, presenting her cheek to be kissed. When Adam obliged she turned her head very quickly but somehow managed to miss his lips. *Damn!*

Miranda, in her dressing-gown, with her wet hair wrapped in a towel, sat hugging her knees on her living-room floor. She looked defeated and rather ill, her large eyes haunted by what she had just heard.

'If you want to shoot the messenger,' Adam said, 'I'll understand.'

'You had to tell me, I can see that.' Her mouth trembled. 'I knew he could be cruel, but this is something so different. So demeaning to him. Why would he do it? He doesn't need money, not *that* badly. He's already selling his work – and he's bound to do really well after this exhibition he's having. What makes him need to do something like this? He hardly even touches drugs himself, except hash. And to use Rufus—' Her voice rose and broke. 'Why hurt Rufus? Is it because of the baby? Is he as angry as that?' She shuddered and began to weep. 'I loved him so much. Why did it make him so angry?'

Adam knew better than to take heart from the past tense. He knelt beside her on the floor and wiped her wet cheek with his hand. 'I don't know, love,' he said. 'Maybe I'll understand better when I've talked to him.'

'I'm not sure you ought to,' she said nervously. 'Or that you could make him stop. I don't know what to do for the best.'

'We could go to the police,' Adam said doubtfully. 'They'd probably let Rufus off lightly, concentrate on Joel.'

'No. Nothing public. Not yet. Please.'

'Of course not, if you don't want it.'

'I don't know what I want.' Her face crumpled and she burrowed her head into her knees. He wanted to scoop her into the crook of his arm and fly up with her above the rooftops like Beauty and the Beast at the end of the Cocteau film they had seen together. More practically, he took the towel, which was slipping off her head, and began to blot dry the ends of her hair. She stopped crying and looked at him gratefully.

'You do that very well,' she said.

'I've had lots of practice. With Helen.'

He was controlling anger because anger was not what she needed while she was so weak, but he was eager to go where he could express it freely.

'Why don't we get this over?' he said. 'Give me Joel's number. I'll check if he's home and go over to his place, now.'

'You can't,' she said anxiously. 'There's something else.' She twisted bits of towel between her fingers. 'I didn't want to tell you this, but I can't let you see him unless you know. He could use it somehow, like he's doing with Rufus. Maybe you have some idea already?'

'What is it, Miranda?' he said patiently.

'Your father and my mother are having an affair.'

Adam stared at her. He laughed. 'Is this a dream you had?'

'You didn't know. I'm sorry.' Her voice was small and sad.

'No, I didn't,' he said flatly. 'You had better tell me about it.'

She told him all she knew.

'I could have killed my mother when I saw them.'

'Why would you want to do that?' he asked mildly. To her astonishment he smiled. 'Luke and Chloe, eh? I think I can get my head round that. They certainly make a remarkable couple. If neither were married you'd say they were made for each other. Chloe is gorgeous, as well as one of the nicest people I have ever known. I can see her fatal attraction for Dad.'

'Adam!' It was a protest.

'Can't you? The other way?'

'Your father? I suppose he is kind of charismatic. And terrific looking. Probably sexy as hell. But they're our *parents*, Adam.'

'That doesn't make them saints. People can't help falling in love. That's why it's called falling, because it's something you don't choose, it just happens. You know that. So do I.' He smiled mischievously. 'Do you suppose it will be easy to remain faithful to one person for – oh, maybe fifty years of married life? And if you think so now, do you believe you'll still think so in twenty years? At their age?'

'I don't know,' she muttered, subdued. 'I hadn't thought about it like that. I just couldn't take seeing them that way, all wrapped up in each other on the bed.'

'OK, it was a shock. But give them a break. They're human too.'

'You are a constant surprise, Adam.'

'Good.'

'I would expect you to feel differently, what with your parents' divorce, and living with Helen and everything. And what happened to the romantic idealist who declared himself ready to die for love?'

'He's still there, really,' he said wistfully. 'Of course I want to live with someone I love, and stay in love till the end of the world, but I'd be dishonest not to admit that even my brief experience of that world offers less than an even chance.'

'Mine too,' Miranda said bleakly.

He gave her a hug. 'Don't give up. Love is a risk. But we have to take it, or we're dead. D'you see?'

'Yes I do.' She nodded. 'That's how I feel about my baby.' She got up and stood looking out of the window.

'You can ring Joel now, if you like,' she said resolutely. 'I'll go into the bedroom and finish off my hair. I don't want to hear.'

'What the fuck business is it of yours?' Joel responded pleasantly to Adam's compassionate request.

'I like Rufus. He's a nice kid. He can't be very big in your scheme of things. Why not let him off the hook?'

'How would you like to go to hell?'

'Put it this way – not much can happen to Rufus as a result of your attentions. He's too young. But a lot could happen to you.'

'Could this be a threat?' the contemptuous voice wondered.

'A suggestion.'

'Not interested.'

'Then maybe the police will be. Look, I don't care what you do with your life; just leave Rufus out of it, unless you want to hear more.'

'I haven't time for this.' Joel's voice tightened. 'I'm trying to work. But get hold of this, asshole – any more hassle from you or anyone else and I won't just tell that effete aristocrat who runs the school that your little ginger friend is dealing; I'll also tell him his top man can't keep drugs out of the playground or his prick in his own pants. Right? Oh, and I have friends, too. One of them works for the *Sun*.'

As he heard the phone slam down, Adam wondered if this were true. He could always find out. Helen did have a friend on the *Sun*, more than one, probably.

When Miranda reappeared, looking wan and apprehensive, he told her regretfully, 'You were right. It looks as if we're going to have to put Luke in the picture before we go any further.'

When Adam had left, she decided to try talking to Joel herself after all.

'I've said all I'm going to say,' he pronounced succinctly. 'So that was your friend Adam? Seemed a bit sartorially stressed to me.'

'What?'

'Underpants over his tights, my dear Lois. Aching to do good deeds in a naughty world. And to you, in bed, natch.'

'Don't be such a stupid shit, Joel.'

'Don't be such a silly bitch, Miranda. When are you coming to see me?' he enquired amiably.

'Are you crazy?' Why couldn't she just drop the bloody phone?

'No, just hot. Suppose I come over there, instead. Will you be warm, wet and welcoming, or is all that just for Adam now?'

This time she did drop it.

'You wouldn't mind, would you?'

Luke became aware that Dinah had spoken to him. He looked up from the book he was pretending to read and regretfully dismissed the unseen presence, shimmering between the eye and the page, of Chloe.

'Would I mind what?'

'If the discussion group meets here, in the afternoon. You would probably never meet them.'

'You aren't, by any change, providing cover for a coven?'

'Idiot. Quite the opposite. It's an exercise in demystification. A few of us keep running into each other at various lectures and workshops, and we want to try and work out which of all these theories and practices we feel like taking seriously and which are way off the wall.'

'You mean it isn't always immediately obvious?' Luke said, grinning.

'No. Why should it be?'

'I don't know.' He shrugged. Something more seemed to be expected so he asked, 'What's next on the agenda?'

'The concept of psychic energies. Auras, body meridians, blockages.'

'Sounds nasty. Does one take pills for it?'

'Don't make fun of what you don't understand. Even the acceptable faces of the New Age – the acupuncturists and herbalists and homeopaths – believe in the existence of psychic energy in one form or another. For example, there's a really nice theory that says plants have energy fields that can interact with our own.'

'*The Return of the Triffids*?'

'Oh, you. Don't be so mean. I think it's an interesting idea. After all,' she hazarded wildly, 'if everything is made up of atoms, maybe one form of energy can turn into another?'

'Dinah, you know better than this. Why don't you go and talk to Olly? He's a whizz at physics.'

'I'd rather talk to you. You're hard to catch, lately. And *is* it physics,' she demanded enthusiastically, 'or something else? Something outside everything we know, that we'd be mad to pass up?'

'I don't know. I want to read,' Luke said, turning back to his book. This was untrue. He had been quite unable to read. All he could do, or wanted to do, was to think about Chloe. He was rarely so lacking in self-discipline and it made him angry with himself.

'Never mind, I expect there's a cure for it,' Dinah replied tartly. Obscurely hurt, though she could not have pinned down the reason for this, she went away and left him to it.

'What's wrong with Dinah?' Adam enquired, wandering into Luke's room with a carelessness that was more studied than achieved.

Adam sighed. 'Nothing, as far as I know. Why?' He put the book aside again.

'She nearly bit my head off just now. I only asked if she

could make me a good herbal love potion.' He ran his fingers over a row of green volumes in the bookcase and opened one at random, rifling through its pages without looking at them. 'Does she really take all that stuff seriously?'

'It's my fault. I was teasing her. I shouldn't. I think what she feels is three-parts healthy curiosity to one-part irrational optimism. But you haven't come here to tell me your step-mother doesn't understand you. What's this about a love potion?'

'Nothing.' Adam felt his throat drying up. 'Just give me a minute, Dad. This is going to be embarrassing.'

It was, although Luke helped him by hearing him out calmly, without interruption. The calm was entirely superficial. Beneath it swelled Wagnerian surges of angst.

'I'm sorry I had to invade your privacy like this,' Adam concluded, with relief.

Luke, between waves of ungainly emotions, tried to grasp at the implications of what he had heard. 'Not privacy,' he said automatically. 'Secrecy.'

'Oh Lord, I feel as if I were outing a bishop.'

Luke's brow lifted. 'A bad shepherd, who will probably lose his crook?'

'God, I hope we can prevent it coming to that.'

'Thank you. You are being very good to me. Adam, I am more sorry than I can say that my affairs should have caused you so much trouble. I particularly regret Miranda's distress.' He paused, pushing back the waves. 'But I am not going to apologise for my relationship with Chloe, because that isn't how I feel about it.'

Adam shook his head. 'I'm not making any judgements, Dad. I understand, at least I think I do.'

'I am in love with her.'

'Yes. I thought you must be.'

There was a longish silence which neither knew how to fill.

Eventually Adam said, 'Am I allowed to ask questions?'

'If you like. I probably won't know the answers.'

Adam wavered, then went bullishly for the china. 'Does this mean there's going to be another breakup?'

It was the adjective which jolted Luke's precarious balance. It was sixteen years since he and Helen had divorced, yet their son spoke as if it had been last week. As if it were a permanent possibility. *Another* breakup. *Another* divorce. *Another* attempt at parenthood abandoned. Everyday life.

'I can't tell you that,' he said very gently. 'It depends on so many things. I don't even know, yet, what all of them are. This business with Joel Ranger has been rather a shock; I need to find out how far it will affect the situation.'

'One hell of a lot, unless we get our skates on,' said Adam warmly. 'Why don't you and I go over there and call his bluff? Persuade him that we have more clout with the tabloids than he does. With our fists, would be nice.'

'I'm sure it would, from what I've heard of him. But don't be in too much of a hurry, Adam. I have the school to think about, as well as the family. And I'll have to find out what Chloe wants to do about it all. I don't need to tell you how serious it will be if the whole thing explodes.' He pressed his hands to his temples for a second, the first sign he had given of his grim recognition of the direction in which they might be going. 'I shall see Chloe tomorrow,' he said. 'I'll talk to you again after that.'

Adam thought of their meeting in that deserted house, as Miranda had described it to him, and looked shyly away. 'I suppose Dinah has no idea,' he asked hesitantly, 'about Chloe?'

'No. No one does. Did, rather.'

'Dad – it is the real thing, isn't it, the one you want to go on forever?'

'Yes,' Luke said quietly, 'I'm afraid it is.' He smiled sadly at his son. 'You've been kinder than I probably deserve. Thanks.'

'That's OK,' Adam said awkwardly. 'I can't help feeling sympathetic. I think the same thing is happening to me.'

'Thus the love potion.'

Adam grinned foolishly. 'Yes.'

'For Miranda Olivier?'

'Well, yes. Funny, isn't it – mother and daughter? I'd kind of like the idea, if things were a bit different. I mean, we'd still be a family.'

At nine o'clock Miranda called Adam. She was weepy and excitable and would barely allow him to speak. 'He isn't going to listen to you. He doesn't care about you or your father or anyone else. But he does – did – care about me. I know that. If I can't talk him out of this, no one can. I don't want to go there on my own, Adam. I'm terrified it won't work. Come with me?'

'Sure, but I'm the last person he wants to see.'

'You don't have to come in, just be there. Please.'

'I'll come and get you. Wrap up well. It's cold.' He had noticed that, despite her pregnancy, she seemed to be getting thinner.

'You're sure you'll be OK? We ought to have a signal, in case you need me.'

'Don't *worry*, Adam. I'll be fine. Just wish me luck.'

She got out of the car and looked up at the dark bulk of the house, her heart beginning to thump uncomfortably. She let herself in with the keys she still possessed and began the ascent to the studio. Instinctively, she used the stairs rather than the lift, a Pre-Raphaelite paean in wrought iron whose centenarian song could be heard all over the building. She had no precise idea of what she was going to say to Joel. She was not even certain for whom she wished to plead. She wanted to protect her family, to rescue Rufus and keep Alain from the knowledge of Chloe's betrayal, but she had no desire whatever to help her mother. She had tried to go along with Adam's kinder and more liberal attitude, but her efforts fell into a boiling of hurt, revulsion and soured love every time Chloe came near. She ought to be punished, and almost certainly would be, by a method as yet unforeseen, but it must not be the awful Roman kind of punishment whereby the whole family was forced to suffer with the evildoer, as in *Ben Hur*. No, not *Ben Hur*; he was innocent. Unless she gave the Charlton Heston role to Alain, who had a tendency to drive his chariot at full thunder. Oh my God, what was she thinking about?

This was no time to lose all her marbles and send them scattering down the stairs. She stopped. She took several of what Dinah Cavendish – poor Dinah, also betrayed – called triangular breaths; in for a count of seven, hold for seven, out slowly for seven. They *were* ever so slightly steadying. They took her, numb if not calm, to the top floor where she found Joel's door unlocked, which must mean that he was in.

She pushed it open and went into the kitchen. He had fried a steak and made a wine-and-mushroom sauce, some of which remained in the pan. The good smells fortified her with their ordinariness and she moved on into the studio. At first, she thought there was no one there. The long room was in shadow, a single lamp glowing in a corner of the work area.

She was about to call out, in case he was in the bathroom, when there was a low sound, perhaps an intake of breath, which made her look toward the bed.

'Joel?' She took half a step, then froze.

Déjà vu. It had to be. The only other explanation was that Joel was physically present on that bed, naked except for the grin he flaunted like a banner of insult, one arm resting upon the Botticelli abundance of Cally Baker's hair.

Cally, who used abortions as means of contraception, slept with the world and his dog, and had always wanted to get her legs round Joel.

Now Miranda had a magnificent experience for an artist. She saw red. Ferrari red. Saw it in all its pristine, garish, gory glory, hazing before her in a scarlet gauze, pin-pricked with twinkling points of light. It was staggering, stupendous, it summoned up her blood, a calefaction devoutly to be wished. It gave her *carte rouge*. She leaped for the bed. Bending, she thrust both hands into the polished abuse of that golden chevalure, got a good grip, and hauled for all she was worth.

Cally screamed and screamed. The noise was dreadful, like a vixen fucking, Miranda thought aptly. She was astonished by the apparent level of pain. Mercifully, the red rage made her strong enough to drag her victim from the bed in less than two seconds. Cally lay quivering on the floor, clutching her head.

'Well, well, Miranda,' Joel said satirically, 'was there something you were trying to say?'

Miranda burst into tears.

'Oh sweet Jesus!' Joel was disgusted. 'Not both of you.'

He rooted about the bed and tossed a handful of garments over the side. 'Cally, I think you'd better go,' he said firmly.

'Why should I?' She glared hatefully at Miranda. 'Are you going to let her do this?'

'She seems to have done it without my permission. Hurry up, there's a good girl. I believe Miranda wants to talk to me.'

'Fuck you, then!' Cally sat on the bed and furiously pulled on her clothes. 'You really are thirty kinds of shit, Joel,' she hissed.

'Now where have I heard that before?' He sounded bored.

Cally readdressed herself to Miranda. 'You won't get

away with this, you bitch. I'll see you later.'

Miranda had recovered from her bout of reactionary tears. 'Don't bother,' she said. 'I might do it again. I enjoyed it.'

It was true. It had been exhilarating. The unfortunate thing was that she could see quite clearly that she ought to have made her onslaught on Joel himself. Oh well. Jealousy, for she recognised its green and unpleasant hand in this, could misdirect one's traffic.

Cally, dismissed and humiliated, could think of no sufficiently wounding words of farewell, and performed instead a telling mime of tossed locks and lost illusions as she attempted, somewhat shakily, to stalk to the door. After she had slammed it, Joel, grinning, patted the pillow next to him. 'Why don't you get in?' he invited cosily. 'She's made it nice and warm. Ah, no. Please don't attack again. I'm a lot stronger than Cally. And I should not make any allowances.' He reached for the tobacco tin under the bed and began to roll one of his fat cigarettes.

Miranda realised that, unless she got as good a grip on herself as she had on Cally's hair, she could have no hope of anything resembling a serious hearing. She fetched herself a chair and placed it opposite the bed.

'Very businesslike,' Joel approved, licking his cigarette paper lovingly into place.

She watched him lick. She had often thought Joel's tongue ought to be arrested for soliciting. She shivered. She must not let him get to her. He finished licking and offered her the neat result.

'You look as though you could do with it. Or a good fuck,' he added generously. 'Both, if you like.'

'Neither, for the moment, thank you,' she replied. 'You know why I'm here.'

'Do I?'

'I want you to stop this game you are playing with my family, before it turns into something nasty that you didn't intend. I don't believe you really want to hurt me.'

'Uh-uh.'

'And it's difficult to see why you should want to harm my family or their friends.'

'So what am I up to, then?'

She shrugged. 'I think you're just punishing me a bit, because of the baby. Teasing really – but a pretty vicious form of teasing. You obviously don't mean to let yourself be publicised as a sleazy little voyeur who gets off by telling tales on illicit lovers. It wouldn't do much good for your relationship with Mr Yamamoto.'

'Indeed?' Joel remarked courteously.

'What I can't take,' she said with a spurt of anger, 'is the way you treated Rufus. That was genuine blackmail. You shouldn't have done it. It was despicable.'

'I think you'll find Rufus got a little bit confused,' said Joel quietly. 'I simply showed him where his best interests were. There was no question of any heavy persuasion until Adam Cavendish shoved his nose in. You shouldn't have let him, Miranda. It was between you and me.'

'No. You made it wider than that. Luke Cavendish is Adam's father, for goodness' sake. He's a public figure and you had threatened him. You wouldn't talk to us. I couldn't decide what to do.'

'Yeah? Well, you have poor instincts. You should have known your friend's interference would make me angry. I was already angry with you.'

'So why not attack me? Why my family?'

'Oh, perhaps I just wanted to shake them up a bit, bring a taste of insecurity into their smug little world. Give them a touch of excitement? Force them to make some unexpected choices?'

'What right have you to do that?'

This was ignored. 'You see, Miranda, what an interesting problem I have set for your mother and her lover?' He watched her face closely. 'It's called a double bind. If

— 243 —

they do their moral duty as a parent and a teacher, and inform the school about the drug traffic, they take the chance of their love affair becoming Sunday breakfast for their family and friends, the school, the village, in fact the universe as they know it. If they don't tell, they could probably go on keeping their secret – unless, of course, *you* felt like shopping them. Neat, isn't it?'

She managed not to hit him. 'No, just malevolent,' she snapped. 'And doesn't it give you exactly the same choice? If you force them to go public, they will certainly take you with them. Do you really want to go to jail?'

'No chance.'

'Why not?'

'Without hard evidence there is no case against me. There isn't a single shred of evidence anywhere in my life, unless you count the comparatively innocuous contents of this tobacco tin. Nor is there any possibility of tracing either my supplier or the people I supply.'

'Oh, come on – you can't believe you would get off scot-free. The accusation alone would be damning. And the drug squad are not fools.'

'I could be willing to take the risk. Are they?'

'I don't believe you will. Not out of simple spite.'

'Spite?' He gave her a hard look. 'If we're talking spite, you might like to think about your own behaviour. You treated me like shit, Miranda. First you make me think you were taking what we had going together seriously enough to have the abortion; a couple of hours later you turn around and say you're having the kid instead and will I get the hell off of your doorstep!'

'All right, it was a bit extreme. But you know why – what we'd just seen. And you know I never wanted an abortion. I was just trying to want it. For you. That made me angry too. OK, I shouldn't have acted as I did, I was upset.'

'So was I.'

Her stomach turned over. 'What do you mean?'

'Don't bother,' he said grimly. 'The truth is that you are as much to blame for the situation as I am. Your selfishness is every bit as strong as mine. You shut me out in more ways than one when you closed that door. As for blackmail, what were you trying to do to me?'

Was that true? And was it hurt, rather than spite which had sent him on his potentially disastrous course? She was shaken and disoriented.

'If you really believe that,' she said seriously, 'then I'm sorry. But I want to put it right, now. Won't you help me? Give it all up. Hurting other people isn't going to make anything better for us.'

Joel grimaced. 'If I did, could you guarantee I'd get no flack?'

'I don't know,' she said honestly. 'I expect they would want the drugs to stop. I can't say what they would do about it.'

'That's not good enough.'

'I'd do all I could to get them to leave you alone.'

He stretched, sat up and reached for her hand. Surprised, she let him take it. He pulled her on to the bed and kissed her with a tenderness she had forgotten he possessed. Her whole body rejoiced in this reunion, she could not prevent its hallelujahs of response.

He held her face between his hands and whispered warm against her ear, 'You know all you have to do to make everything OK – don't you?'

She went cold in his arms. 'I can't,' she said. She thought, I am a fool. I should have expected this.

'And that's your last word?'

'Yes.'

Their arms fell from each other. Joel got up and put on his jeans. 'Come here,' he said. 'I have something to show you.'

She thought of leaving, but even now the pull he exerted was too strong for her. Now especially. It was probable that she would never be so close to him again.

He flicked the switches and the lights went on at the other end of the studio, revealing a large rectangular shape covered with a sheet. Joel padded down and whirled away the cloth.

'I wanted you to know what an inspiration you have been,' he said sweetly. Miranda approached through a minefield of doubt.

She was looking at a glass tank standing on a table. About a yard in length, two feet wide and eighteen inches tall, it was filled, to a depth expressive of the golden mean, with faintly bluish water. Suspended and seeming to float halfway below the surface was a large object made of rubber or some other plastic material. Coloured pink, grey and shades of indigo, it was a scale enlargement of a resting penis. To one side, apparently the focus of the singular and understandably mournful eyeball set in the end of the glans, the tiny figure of a woman was swimming busily away from it, using its testes for water wings. She was naked, her body was quite delightful and she had a mass of dark red hair streaming on a cleverly installed current.

Miranda walked around the tank. She thought she might be going to laugh. Or possibly cry. Or both. She did neither. 'What does it mean?' she asked.

Joel chuckled. 'Whatever you like. How about: "The Increasing Isolation of Man from Woman as a Result of Man's Emasculation by Feminism"?'

Miranda gave him a severe look. 'You mean: "Get a Load of This said Adam proudly. Bollocks, said Eve and went to have a Good Conversation with the Serpent".'

Joel laughed. He pressed a button on the side of the tank and the tiny woman made swimming motions like a plastic bath-time frog. She looked foolish, lovable and very determined.

'Good likeness, isn't it?' he said.

'Very. But whose side are you on? It's difficult to tell.'

'There are no sides. Neither is a winner because they have not learned how to get it together. They probably never will.'

'Generally? Or personally?'

'Either.'

'If that's how you feel,' she said sadly, 'then I'm afraid they won't.' He did not reply. To fill the silence she walked once more around the tank. 'I like it,' she said. 'I think it will cause quite a stir if you put it in the exhibition. Have they given you a date yet, by the way?'

'Not yet. It'll be sometime next summer.'

'Good. Well.' Words were becoming painful. 'I'm sure it will be a success.' He did not give her any help, so she said with a rush, 'I have to go now. You haven't told me, yet, what you're going to do.'

He looked at her steadily. Then he showed his teeth. 'Nothing has changed,' he said. 'It's still up to you.'

Contempt struggled with habitual love.

'You can keep your bollocks, Joel,' she told him. 'I can swim without them.'

It was some time since Adam had seen Cally fly out of the house and down the street as if pursued by furies. He left the car and sat on the low garden wall until he heard the front door slam a second time.

'You were so long, I was beginning to – Miranda? What is it, sweetheart? What did he do to you?'

Finality had overwhelmed her on the stairs. The wave had passed, but it had left her spirit silted up with little stones of hopelessness.

'Don't look like that,' Adam pleaded.

'He doesn't love me,' she said. 'He doesn't know how to love anyone.'

'Sit down, here. That's right. Here's my scarf, mop up your mascara. Now tell me what he said.' He pulled her against him and listened to the fractured tale.

'It's all right, you're allowed to laugh,' she said at the end of it.

'I don't think I want to,' Adam said. 'Have you still got the keys?'

'Yes. I meant to give them back.'

'Give them to me.'

'There's no point.'

Adam held out his hand.

'I'd rather leave it.'

'We can't. It isn't just us.'

She sighed. 'I suppose you're right.' She handed him the keys.

'Wait in the car and keep warm. I won't be long.'

Seventeen minutes later it was Miranda's turn to offer him the scarf. 'Are you hurt?' she asked.

'It's not as bad as it looks.' Adam's eye was inflamed and he breathed in sharply as he bent to get into the car.

'Him?'

'About the same.'

'Shall I drive?'

'No, I'll be fine.'

'He used to do karate.'

'I noticed.' Joel had kicked him very prettily in the ribs. He was not sure if any were broken. In return, he had managed to give Joel's right shoulder a wrench that would prove extremely painful. Lucky for Joel; what Adam had wanted to do was to break his painting arm.

In the matter of name-calling they were also more or less even. Yet neither had mentioned Miranda's name.

'It was a bum move,' Adam admitted as they drew away from the kerb. 'He called the guy on the *Sun*. He's seeing him tomorrow.'

Miranda groaned and covered her face. After a while she asked, 'What can we do?'

'Not much, on our own. I'll talk to my father again. He's

— 248 —

had some time to think. Maybe he has some ideas.'

'It certainly was a bum move,' Luke agreed when Adam followed him into the bathroom at half past eleven that night. 'I sympathise, no one more so, but I think you had better keep away from Joel in future.'

'Depends on what happens,' said Adam darkly. 'There may have to be a Last Battle, one day.'

'Sufficient unto the day,' Luke replied dryly. 'Leave it with me. I'll see what can be done.'

Chapter Fifteen

⊙⊙⊙⊙⊙⊙⊙⊙

WHEN CHLOE WAS A CHILD her greatest treasure had been a 'snowstorm', a globe of Victorian glass which contained a miniature English village with a church, a school, a shop and half a dozen houses. She had called it Melton Parva. It was inhabited by tiny people made of lead; the priest standing at the open church door, the schoolmistress at the gate of the school, a family walking home past the blue pond with its pair of infinitesimal ducks – she had christened them all. The old priest at St Jude's was Father Anselm, a medieval scholar with a rigorous mind and a kind heart. The schoolmistress, Miss Charlotte Manderley, was a rose-and-gold beauty whose lover had mysteriously disappeared. Every day she watched for him, taking solace from the children she taught, longing for children of her own. One day he would come back to her, his saddlebags stuffed with silver and experience. The family were the Pargeters. They lived in the largest house, the one with the lovely garden. George Pargeter, who had lived there all his life, was a famous artist. His wife, Eleanor, was a musician and a mouth-watering cook. William, the son, was at medical school, intending to set up practice in the village. His young sister, Tess, was a mass of imagination and emotion who did not yet know what she might turn out to be. Chloe identified strongly with Tess and had kept a diary of events in the village as recorded by her.

For several seasons, Melton Parva was her second home. Only very rarely did she exercise the godlike power by which, with two shakes of the glass that separated her from the microcosmic lives within, she could bestow on them an instant Christmas of sparkling white flakes. She did not like to do this often because she considered it too great a disturbance to the equilibrium of the tiny world. She was able to ignore the snow that must lay year-long upon the ground. She had learned to tap it towards the circumference of the parish, so that there remained green grass, brown earth, blue water.

By some paradoxical quirk of memory, it was that small, controlled world which entered her mind now, as she stood in appalled abstraction at the upper window of Arden Court, trying to take in what had happened. Below her lay a very different winter scene; pale light on a skeleton guard of trees, shrubberies thick with twisted sticks, the bared stone of the empty archway – a landscape stripped to the bone.

'I need a few minutes,' she said. 'It's – there's so much to think about.' It seemed to her, as she heard Luke trying to find words which did not cut and stab, words with which to communicate and not confound, that Joel Ranger had, with hideous irony, become godlike as she had once been, had maliciously shaken up the snowstorm in which she and her family had made their modest dispositions, and had released a blizzard which threatened to engulf them all in an avalanche of lost content.

Was that how it was? Or was it, now as in childhood, she herself who had first created order and then brought down the storm? Probably the answer lay in some ramshackle compromise between guilt and chance.

'Are you all right?' Luke had come to stand beside her.

His arm encircled her, warm and solid, but, for the moment, incapable of comfort.

'Can he be stopped?' she asked. Her voice seemed to come to her from a distance, like the soundtrack of a movie.

'I don't know. Will you let me tell Philip Dacre everything? He has uncles and cousins in all the right places. He'll be able to help.'

'Will he want to help,' she asked doubtfully, 'when he's heard it all?'

'I think so. He's a good friend.'

'Then tell him,' she agreed. 'Luke?' Her stomach churned.

'Yes?'

'Joel will have to be charged, won't he? No matter what happens to us as a result of it?'

'I'm afraid so, yes. Can you face that?'

'I shall have to. It may be far harder for you. I'm sorry if this sounds selfish, but – Rufus will have to give evidence. What will happen to him?'

'It isn't selfish. I can't be sure, but my guess is that he'll be put on probation.'

'Will he be expelled?'

'Philip is against drug expulsions. He doesn't think they address the problem. So far, we have only had to deal with a few isolated cases, and we've managed to be discreet about them. I imagine, this time, a lot will depend on how much damage Joel is able to do.'

'I see. Thank you.'

'Chloe, I wish I could do something – anything, to stop you being hurt like this.'

She smiled. 'If only it were just me.'

She wanted to touch him now, to offer the comfort she could not receive. She kissed him, not with passion but with a deliberate seriousness that parcelled up everything they shared together and sealed it against all prying hands and eyes.

'I can hardly bear to ask you this,' she said, 'but I must know. Is there a chance that you might lose the headship, or even what you have?'

'It's possible,' he said levelly. 'If the whole story is presented to the governors – officially that is, including the part played by our relationship. Or if it all becomes public knowledge. But that may not happen – or the governors may not give a damn.'

She was not convinced. 'This is a nightmare.' She shuddered, overcome by the humiliating inevitability of their situation. 'I have never felt so powerless. And to think that evil little monster has fathered Miranda's child.'

'Don't, love.' He wrapped his arms around her and held her until the panic left her. 'I know it all looks bleak at the moment – but at least what has happened brings us right up against our choices for the future.'

'Choices? What choices? Luke, we no longer *have* any choices.'

'Of course we have, I've told you, I can get a job three hundred miles away tomorrow. A thousand miles, if you like. Look, I've got a friend who runs a language school in Verona. He's looking for someone to take it over for him so he can retire. It would be perfect. We could take whichever of the children wanted to come along, and lead an idyllic life together. Sun, music, celestial architecture, a truly civilised society and *l'amor che muove il sole e l'altre stelle*. Why not?' His smile invited her, triumphant. He threw open his arms. 'Why not?'

For a glorious moment she thought she would run into that operatic embrace and burst into a rapturous aria of acceptance. He read the thought and laughed exultantly before he saw her eyes change and watched the vision fade.

'You know why,' she said dully. 'Because we can't just run away. Because we are ultimately responsible for all that has happened. Because we have to tell Alain and Dinah everything. Now. Too many people know about us; we

— 253 —

can't take the chance that they might hear it from someone else.'

'All right, I can see that. But doesn't that make it more urgent for us to decide what we might do – so that we can tell them we are going to be together? I know it will be hard, but . . .'

Chloe sighed. 'In three or four years' time, that might have become possible. But now – you must see how it is. We have run out of time. We have brought sudden and horrible trouble into everyone's lives. We can't just turn our backs on them. It isn't *about* us any more.'

He seemed dazed. 'You really mean that, don't you?'

'Yes, I do.'

'God, I can't stand this.' He took hold of her and shook her. 'Don't, Chloe. Don't rush so single-mindedly towards destruction. Can't you at least wait and see what happens, like any other reasonable being?'

It sounded like a reprieve. Was that what she wanted?

'I don't know. I don't think I can keep up –' she reached for the words '– the perfect selfishness that this sort of loving requires. It's like a clenched fist. What I have I hold. Nothing else, no one, matters. But we can't go on like that, not now. We have to turn away from each other and do what we can to limit the damage.'

'Turn away?' he said incredulously. 'This isn't some bloody bus we can catch or not, as we please. This is the rest of our lives. Of course love is selfish, it's a biological necessity. How else can it move the sun and stars? Does it suddenly count for nothing because a vile-minded little drug-trafficker thinks he can get away with blackmail?'

She said quietly, 'When I see myself reflected in Miranda's eyes, I feel shame.'

'You have an over-active conscience.'

'I can't help that. Any more than I can help loving you.' She faced him and looked into his eyes, begging him to understand. 'I can't even imagine not loving you. And the idea of being without you is the most painful thing I have ever had to face. But I know the most important thing is to deal honestly with the life I've already made. The future will have to be dictated by the past. There's no way out of that.'

Luke was exasperated. 'You're talking nonsense. Haven't you ever heard of change? It's what creates progress. Have a little courage, can't you?'

'Love, please. Don't go on with this.'

'How can I help it,' he said desperately, 'when I can feel you slipping through my fingers?'

'It's the same for me,' she cried.

He groaned. 'I know. I'm sorry. I'm angry because I'm afraid of losing you.' He sat down heavily on the bed.

Chloe remained at the window, drawing her finger nervously up and down the pane. Outside, a pair of white doves flew on to a parched branch and settled into a connubial huddle.

'Alain comes home on Friday evening,' she said unsteadily. 'Will you tell Dinah then?'

He suddenly saw that there was nothing he could fight. 'I suppose I must,' he said. He caught at a last gleam of hope. 'Let me speak to Philip first, though. He might think of something.'

She sighed. 'I wouldn't hope for any miracles. Oh Luke, I am so sorry. I want to put us first, you must know how much. But I can't.'

'Sorry?' He almost laughed. 'Have you any idea how ridiculous that sounds?'

She went over to the bed and sat beside him. She took his hand. 'Don't begin to hate me. However convenient it might be, morally speaking, I don't think I could bear it.'

His face relaxed and he opened his arms again. 'Come here. I'll show you how much I hate you.'

They held each other as though they had already been visited by some great natural disaster and were now at the centre of a spurious calm. Moving their hands lovingly over ungiving cloth, they kissed with a will towards passion which they found themselves unable to fulfil. Tenderness had become more necessary than desire. It was difficult not to regard this as a form of defeat.

Chloe said, 'This is going to be wretched. We can't sit here thinking that this may be the last time. And we can't make love because that *is* what we are thinking.' Luke could not speak. He stroked her hair and her face. 'So – I think I'd like to leave now, if you wouldn't mind. If we stay, it can only get worse.'

'Is that what you really want?'

'For now. Yes.'

'Then, when shall I see you?'

This was the bad moment. 'I don't know.' She tried to smile, quoting him. 'So much is going to happen. Let's wait and see?'

'But I *will* see you?'

'Yes. I love you.' She kissed him quickly and broke away.

Chloe fled down the lane accompanied by demons of anguish and regret, her thoughts knocked out of her in hard gasps as she ran. She ought to have said, 'No, you will not see me. We shall not come here again. This really is the last time. Believe it. It is true.' That was what she ought to have said.

When she reached the road she stopped and stood still. Even now, she could turn round and run back to Luke, tell him she would never leave him again.

She crossed the road and sat on the bench beside the lake. She would remain there until she was sufficiently in control of herself to drive. Looking across the water, she saw a couple emerge, arm in arm, from the woods behind it. Their heads were close together, their whole demeanour expressed pleasure in each other. She had never seen the man before, but she felt the fateful glass turn over again as the woman's rich laugh rang out, suddenly, happily, startling several browsing ducks. It was Mrs Cubitt.

They skirted the water, coming towards her. She presented a polite face as they drew level with her, maintaining a pleasant blankness as she caught the flicker of warning in the lively brown eyes.

'Not a bad day, despite the cold,' she said.

'Ever so nice, really,' was the agreeable reply, which seemed, by some sympathetic magic, to contain a wink.

Just before Chloe reached the carpark, she came upon Luke's old navy blue Citroën, of the type dear to lovers of *romans policiers*. He had left it off the road, but perfectly visible, in a small scrubby clearing. Mrs Cubitt would certainly have recognised it and, meeting Chloe, have drawn her conclusions. Thus the wink.

Chloe smiled. However hellish her present prospects might be, there was still amusement to be found in such an unexpected and unspoken exchange of guilty secrets.

Back in Sheringham, she was alerted by the domestic alarm that lives in women's heads and is proof against any shock the world can throw at it. It reminded her to call at the post office to collect the dry-cleaning. The counter was busy so she idly began to inspect the food alleys. She turned the corner and there at the other end of the row, wrapped in a purple cloak, dreamily contemplating the dogfood as if it were the French Lieutenant's frigate, stood Dinah.

Scalded by surprise and an abject, pitying love, Chloe wrenched her eyes away and tore out of the shop.

Five minutes later she arrived at her own back door with a hunted sensation and a need for imminent collapse.

As she entered the kitchen, both twins flew at her, leaping and babbling, with Baskerville in enthusiastic support.

'Kittens!' they yelled. 'Three kittens!'

'Oh God.'

'Mum!'

'Oh God, how wonderful. Where are they?'

'In Baskerville's basket. He's being awfully sweet about it,' Tilda said. 'I think he thinks he's their father.'

'That's what you get for giving up Biology,' Rufus snorted. 'Look, Mum. Aren't they absolutely ace?'

Of course they were. They always are. There lay Grace, looking older and somehow stately, proudly suckling a row of furry sausages – one black, one red and two torty.

'Four!' they cried in admiring unison.

'Which one can we keep?' asked Rufus artlessly. 'We both like the spotty ones and we've got the other colours already.'

'No one said anything about keeping any of them,' Chloe said. It was then that she remembered, looking at his bright, expectant face, what it was that he had done and what that, in turn, had caused to happen.

'Well, no,' said Tilda nicely, 'but people always do.'

With astonishing self-control Chloe said, 'I'll think about it.'

When the phone rang after supper on Thursday, Rufus got to it first.

'Hello, you useless old fart,' he said confidently. 'Oh cripes! Yes. I'm really sorry, Sir. I thought it was – yes, Sir, right away.' Green-gilled, he handed Chloe the instrument of torture. 'It's for you. It's Mr Cavendish.' His eyes were enormous.

'Serves you right,' said Tilda gleefully.

Chloe carried the phone into the sitting-room. 'Luke?'

'Oh cripes, eh? He must have been reading Richmal Crompton.'

'How kind of you to ignore the more obvious influences, such as *Viz*, or Ben Elton.' She heard his rich chuckle.

'I'm sorry to catch you just now, but I thought you'd

want to hear what Philip Dacre had to say. He's talked to his press baron uncle.'

Coldness hit her stomach. 'Yes. What *did* he say?'

'He was surprisingly angry. More on Dinah's behalf than out of any moral disapproval. But Uncle Ned will do his best to keep your name and mine out of the papers, at least as far as our private relations are concerned. He's making calls, pulling strings. He thinks the drugs story may have to come out, but the *Sun* isn't going to print anything until they've found out all they can about Joel Ranger. So, he might end up wishing he'd never started any of this. If that's any consolation.'

'Not much.'

'Have you talked to Rufus about it yet?'

'I'm waiting till I've told Alain everything.'

'Tomorrow night?'

'Yes.'

'I don't know what to say to you.'

'No.' She drew a sharp breath and hurried on. 'Mrs Cubitt is coming tomorrow morning. Can I give her some warning? Dwayne is bound to be involved.'

'I'd rather you said nothing until we know exactly how everyone stands.'

Chloe sighed. 'If you say so. But I shall feel pretty shitty, watching her clear up our mess and thinking of the one we've got her into.'

'Don't overcompensate. Dwayne made his own mess, like the rest of us. Chloe, I need you.' His voice descended to familiar warm depths. 'When can we meet?'

Her body responded eagerly like the well-trained animal it was. 'I don't know. Soon.'

'*How* soon? We really need some time to—'

She pressed the cut-off button and returned the golden tones to the ether where they could do no harm, unless a passing angel were to be inadvertently seduced and fall like a pound of feathers, at precisely the same speed as a pound of flesh. One hundred and twelve pounds of flesh, while we were being precise.

'Was that something about me?' Rufus demanded innocently.

'No. Should it have been?'

When, as was her impeccable habit, Mrs Cubitt arrived on the stroke of ten, Chloe found herself inanely demanding an account of the weather, which she could see perfectly well for herself out of any one of a dozen windows.

By way of reply, Mrs Cubitt sniffed and shook out a slightly spotted red umbrella. Then she drew herself up and spoke quietly. 'I shan't mention it again. But I did want to say something, just the once, about the way we met the other day.'

'Oh. Yes,' said Chloe nervously.

'It ain't often life turns round an' makes you a free offer of a bit of real happiness. Not in my experience. You'd be a fool not to accept.'

'Yes.' And they *had* looked happy, coming arm in arm out of the woods, all lit up with their pleasure in each other. 'Yes, you would.'

'It's not always been easy at home, not these last few years.'

'No. Then I'm glad that's the way it is now. The only thing is,' she added shyly, because she could not help it, 'what if it doesn't stay like that? What if it begins to affect other people. Your family?'

Mrs Cubitt's smile was sad and kind. 'In that case, my dear, I'm afraid it'd 'ave to stop.'

Their eyes met without winking. Chloe nodded, her eyes filling with tears. 'Yes, I'm sure you are right.'

She grabbed the damp umbrella and up-ended it in the Chinese vase where it would be company for Tilda's riding crop, Rufus's divining twig and the walking stick with the duck's head handle she had given Alain when he sprained his ankle. She felt a rush of love and guilt towards all of these objects, seizing hold of the duck's head and stroking it frantically.

'What shall I do today, then, Mrs Olivier? Bedrooms and bathrooms?' The sympathetic voice reverted to professionalism.

'Yes, please.' Chloe blinked and wiped her hand over her cheeks. 'And maybe you could tidy Alain's study a little. Not so that he would notice, of course.'

''Course not. I know better than that by now. Back soon, is 'ee?'

'Yes, this evening.'

'Then I'll give the desk a bit of a polish. And by the way...'

'Yes?'

'My name's Adèle. I'd like you to call me that.'

'It's a lovely name,' Chloe said gratefully. 'Old-fashioned and dignified. It reminds me of lace dresses and flowery straw hats.'

'You're not far wrong. My mother called me after Adèle Astaire, the dancer. 'Course, *he* always 'as to call me Del Girl. Thinks it's funny.' Her tone suggested this was a complete explanation of the freely-gifted woodland walks.

'What a waste,' Chloe deplored.

'Not very romantic,' sighed Adèle.

'No, it isn't.' Chloe gave her a fierce little smile. There you are Dr Freud, Siggy. The answer to your question. It hasn't changed. Not yet. What do women want? They'll take romance. I will. Adèle will. Miranda would if she could. Tilda wants it. Belle demands it. Dinah misses it without even knowing it's gone. Helen Cavendish manufactures it and sells it. We must all be barking mad, mustn't we, to invest so much of ourselves, to risk so much of our lives for anything so fragile and insubstantial, something that will never be anything more than just an idea we all keep inside our heads. It may be a different idea for each one of us, but we share the knowledge of its existence, and the value it has for us, and that makes us sisters. 'I should like to call you Adèle,' she said, 'and I think you ought to call me Chloe in return.'

'Well, I don't know about that,' Adèle said, but she sounded pleased. Sisterhood had been acknowledged and strength was mysteriously derived from this.

When Alain came home Chloe was sitting at the kitchen table, forcing herself to make some sketches for her painting and slugging her way through a bottle of wine on the grounds that it might settle the nervous swooping of her stomach. Each sketch, of a dark and leathery-winged figure reminiscent of Milton's Satan, blackly increased its power to threaten and command.

She heard the car and waited, heart thumping, for him to come in. He seemed to take a very long time.

'*Chérie*!' He dropped his bag and held out his arms.

Her legs would not work. 'There you are,' she said, remaining seated. She did not know how she was going to get through this.

Alain stood behind her chair and wrapped his arms around her, briefly holding her breasts. 'Here I am. *Tiens*! Who is that?' He tapped a drawing.

'God. The Father.'

'Really? He does not look as if 'e 'as a very Christian attitude.'

'He's pre-Christian. He's the thing you worship out of fear, not love. He may even be a devil instead, I'm not sure yet.'

'Is he why she locked herself up, your friend Catherine?'

'Perhaps, the second time. I'm just trying things out.'

They were taking a wrong direction. She did not want to begin a normal conversation.

'Are you hungry?' she asked.

'Not really, but I'll have a glass of your wine. Where are the children?'

'Both gone out. Do you mean you don't want to eat, or just not yet?' It was ridiculous, how instinctively she wished to get the business of eating over before she told him.

He shrugged. 'I'll make myself some toast later if I want anything. Let's just drink. Is there another bottle of this?'

'Yes.' She began to rise from her chair.

'No, stay there. I'll get it. I want a quick wash anyway.'

While he was out of the room she began to grasp at words of explanation, but they came to her in unrelated fragments like the pieces of a jigsaw where no whole picture was provided. She could not make them fit. She felt sick and afraid.

When he came back she waited until he had refilled the glasses, then until his was half empty, before throwing the pieces into the air.

'I have some things to tell you. None of them are good. I don't know what to put first.'

He looked at her thoughtfully. 'I sensed there was something. You are very tense. I thought it was your work.'

He reached over to rub her arm sympathetically. She flinched. Surprised, he nevertheless said calmly, 'Perhaps the worst should be first?'

'Very well. The words aren't right, but—' *Mon enfant, mon frère*, what have I done to you? '—but I'm, I've been making love with Luke Cavendish.'

He hit her across the mouth, his knuckle slamming hard against her lips. She tasted blood. The shock reverberated through them both and Alain shook his head as though it were he who was stunned.

'Is this true?' His face had changed. He looked like a stranger. His eyes were very wide and bright, feral.

'Yes.'

He hit her again, punching his fist into the side of her neck. This time the pain propelled her into some kind of self-preserving protest.

'Don't do this, Alain. It can't change anything.'

In a way, she was glad of the pain. It was the least she could do, to suffer a little physical pain. Alain stared at her and drove his fingers distractedly through his hair. His face became his own again and he groaned in horror.

'I'm sorry, Chloe. I didn't want – I shouldn't have done that. But it is such . . .' He waved his hands in despair. 'It's so much. I can't take it in. It's as though you are talking about someone else. Not you. It's not you, Chloe.'

So she was a stranger too. Twenty years of marriage, transformed in twenty seconds.

'No, I know. But it has happened. It wasn't planned or sought for. It just happened. There's no point in saying I'm sorry.'

His anger leaped from hiding. 'Why? Because you are not?'

She had to finish as quickly as possible, tell him all of it. She must be calm and forget nothing.

'I'm sorry for the outcome,' she said quietly. 'Alain, I'm not sure if you've heard the worst or not.'

He looked dangerous. 'You are going to tell me you are pregnant?'

'Oh, no! No, of course not.' She was foolishly relieved, then shamed by it. 'No, it's about Rufus.'

He frowned, but relaxed attentively. 'Continue.' In French, that was the natural word to use. In English, it sounded cold and formal. But Alain knew that.

Piece by piece, as logically as she could, she managed to lay the whole sorrowful picture before him. When she had finished and saw how it had grown together in his eyes, she realised that she had never even begun to envisage how ugly it would look.

She wept, collapsing completely. 'I *am* sorry,' she cried.

'I am. I can't bear that I've made these hideous things happen. I wish that Luke and I had never had to meet.'

'But not that you had never slept with him. That, I suppose, was irresistible.'

She said nothing. She could not speak with dignity. She had no dignity. He ignored her, his head bent between his fists.

'Alain?' His pain was hers too, she could not prevent that.

'Wait.' His hands held her off. 'I need to think about all this. Would you mind just leaving me alone for a while?'

'If that's what you want.'

'I want it.'

She needed to say that she still loved him, loved him very much at this bitter moment she had created for him; but she had the good sense not to use the word.

She went to wait it out in the studio. The canvas was a dominant presence now, crowded and complex, babbling with busy lives and ghosts. Her unfatherly God-figure would only cow them all into an institutional submission, fill them with the fear of death and sin, the withholding of joy. Perhaps she would not use him, or would diminish him, limiting his power. Would that be dishonest? Didn't he belong there, as well as the anchoress and her guardian angel? Or had she invented him because he represented something in her own life, which by now was inextricably mixed up with Catherine's? If so, could love ever deserve such a judgement as his, such a harsh promise of punishment?

It *was* love. Whatever her doubts, that was not one of them. She loved Luke in a whole and inevitable way, so whole that she could not divide it to analyse it, any more than she could understand its origin or necessity. It just was. It existed. Complete and perfect. And in a place of its own. That was it. Its boundaries were inside them both, and it had nothing to do with the world in which they had lived until they met. But if she chose, it could have everything to do with the future. She had only to lift the phone, said the soft voice of the serpent. Catherine Chandler, she begged the clear-faced young woman, straight as a candle in the north-east quadrant of her picture, give me your strength. If that was praying, then she was praying.

Alain came in quietly and took her hands.

'Forgive me,' he said. 'I regret striking you more than anything I've ever done.'

'It doesn't matter.'

'It does. It will never happen again.'

'I don't care about that. You were shocked, that's all.'

He sighed. 'Yes, it was a shock.' He made her sit down beside him on the old horsehair *chaise* opposite the canvas. 'But perhaps I might have expected it.'

'Why?' Her voice lifted in surprise.

'Because I leave you alone too much. Because my work is too important to me. I get tunnel vision about it.'

'But that's nothing new. So do I. It's how we are. It's partly why we've done so well together, that we each have our own obsession.'

'And now you have a new one.'

'Alain, I don't think I can—'

'No – and I don't really want to hear any details. But I do need to know what you want to do.'

She hesitated for a second. 'Nothing.'

'Nothing?'

Nothing comes of nothing. A void, in which Luke was not. Courage, now.

'I want things to stay as they are, or rather, to go back to what they used to be. I mean, I don't want to leave you or anything. Unless you wanted me to?'

'Of course I don't,' he said vehemently.

'Are you sure? You might feel differently tomorrow, or next week.'

'I won't. You're my wife. I love you, whatever has happened. How can it make any sense to break up a good marriage for a single affair?'

Gratitude and his discounting of his own pain caused an excess of honesty. 'It's been, well, it's more than just an affair. I don't think I even know how to have an affair.'

Again that lift of his hand, staving off what he would not hear. 'Just tell me – is it finished, Chloe?'

She nodded.

'Completely? No loose ends?'

'Not that kind.'

So that was it. Only now that she had spoken the words could she begin to believe them, and to know that what she had decided was the right thing for all of them and that she might be able to stick to it.

Alain looked at her fiercely. 'Do you still want to sleep with me?'

She wanted to weep for the hurt and pride that made him ask.

'I haven't changed towards you. It isn't like that. I couldn't bear not sleeping with you. I would feel so lonely.'

'So would I.' He pulled her to her feet and kissed her roughly. 'Now. I want to have you now. I want you naked and I want to take off his fingerprints.'

You can't do that, she thought sadly, they are indelible.

He made love to her with a solemnity that came from sorrow and the attempt to avoid desperation. Chloe responded with a tenderness that she hoped did not seem maternal. Each found that they were, after all, a little lonely during this over-careful coupling. It would be better next time, they said.

They sat up and held each other kindly, limbs finding the comfort of custom.

After a while Alain said, 'I can't blame you, Chloe. I don't have the right. But did you need him because of something that is wrong with us?'

'No, there was nothing wrong. That's what makes it hard even for me to understand. I've been as happy as any reasonable person could expect.'

'So have I.' He moved restlessly. 'Why is it, I wonder, that our lives are not enough. We seem to have a compulsion towards something else, something forbidden, apart from the pattern we have made. A genetic need, perhaps? A gene for excitement?'

She wanted to say no, really, that was not why it had happened, but she would only hurt him again.

'Is that it?' she mused. 'I don't know.'

'I think that is what it is for me, at least,' he said deliberately.

'You?' she said, stung by surprise.

Alain did not wish to hurt her, only to show her they were equal in this, and if possible to allay a portion of her guilt. Partly, he wished to persuade himself. Equality, if only imaginary, must surely feel less painful.

'You too?' she said shakily. 'Then, perhaps I should also have expected it. I mean –' she smiled tightly, self-mocking '– you are away so much, and my work is probably too important to me.'

Her jealousy warmed him. 'They were just – interludes. Sex. No beginning, no end.'

'Oh. Really.' Anger flared. 'Anyone I know?'

He lied whitely. 'No. They were strangers in strange beds. Abroad. In Hong Kong. Malaysia.'

'How many?'

'Not many.'

She did not press him. The knowledge made her oddly shy with him. Depression closed on her like the leathery wings she had drawn. She understood what he was doing, that he was offering her his own guilt in order to free her from her own. But this was not what she wanted, this neat, bloodless exchange that nullified all transgression, a kind of horribly sophisticated sexual plea bargaining, modern morality packaged like a convenience food. She accepted no comparison. The idea offended in the place where she was most herself. If she allowed him to mend matters in this way she would be guilty of dishonesty, as well as adultery, as well as love. But if she told Alain how she felt, it would damage his pride even further. Obviously, this was her time for sacrifice. She may as well lay her honesty on top of the funeral pyre she was earnestly building for her inconvenient love.

'I don't like it,' she said. 'I hate the idea of your penetrating other women, giving them your time, your charm, touching them.'

Alain made what Tilda would call 'one of his French faces'. 'Well, I am not exactly enraptured by the picture of you lying beneath Luke Cavendish. I could kill him, you know that?'

'Yes, I know.' She looked at him helplessly. 'That is what is going to make everything so difficult. The future. How on earth are we going to deal with what has happened? Living together, all of us, in the same close community? The children being such good friends. Rufus, and the school and the whole damned mess. I just don't know how we can.'

Alain smiled. 'We shall be "civilised", isn't that it? I shall not kill Luke Cavendish – and you will not sleep with him. As for the children, they will simply go on as before. Perhaps not Miranda, she must do as she pleases. She didn't need this, Chloe, she has enough to trouble her.'

'Please. You must know how badly I feel about her. I'm not sure if she will ever forgive me. That's one of the really bad parts.'

'So I imagine,' he said coldly. 'Are there any good parts?'

'I hope so, eventually,' she said humbly.

'I'm sorry. I will try not to be bitter. The good part is that we *can* get over all this, if we are really determined and work together.'

'Do you really believe that?'

'I'm sure of it,' he said confidently. 'But right now, what you and I have to do is to put our personal feelings aside and concentrate on the children. Rufus has been a great fool and will probably receive a healthy fright and some sobering judgements. Miranda has been badly hurt. They need us, both of them, to be strong and united.'

'We will be,' she whispered.

'*Bien.*' He rolled over and sat facing away from her on the edge of the bed. Without turning he said, 'Promise me it's really over, Chloe.'

'It's over.' She hesitated. 'Except that we may have to cope with the publicity, if it happens.'

'Should I go and talk to Philip Dacre?'

'No. Leave it to Luke.' Her voice was steady on his name. This pleased her. 'Alain, how much ought we to tell Rufus?'

'You mean, do we give him the whole convoluted story, or just stick to the bits that affect him?'

'Yes. Providing that nothing does get into the papers.'

'Then I think we should tell him that Adam felt he had to see that Joel was put out of business – I'm sure Adam will agree to that – and that Rufus will have to pay for his foolishness in whatever manner the law and the school may decide.'

'Poor little boy.'

'He is not a little boy,' Alain growled. 'He is a young Machiavelli and he needs exactly this, right now. For all we know he's been smoking and dealing ever since he was in the kindergarten.'

'Oh, I don't think so, honestly.'

'Well, I am certainly going to find out. The other thing we must consider is Miranda's baby. She will have to tell the twins about it, sooner rather than later.'

'Oh God, I hadn't thought of that.'

'Don't worry, I'll talk to her.'

'Thank you. It might help to improve the atmosphere when she's here. She still won't speak to me. I don't know how to behave with her.'

He took her hand and pressed it encouragingly. 'It will all work out, you'll see. Just follow your indubitable intuition.'

She laughed, lightened by gratitude. Impulsively, she pulled him nearer so that she could hug him. She was thankful for his wisdom in failing to probe the state of her emotions, or to test his own any further at this point. She appreciated the tough, adult quality of his affection for her and the children.

'Would you like to see something nice?' she asked.

'What kind of something?'

'Come and see.'

Chloe put on her kimono and Alain, already dressed, followed her along the landing to the airing cupboard. He was mystified.

'It's more peaceful than the kitchen.'

She opened the door and there were Grace and her kittens on top of a pile of towels. They hung over them, stroking and tickling, congratulating the smugly purring mother.

'Innocence,' sighed Chloe, conscious of envy.

Alain chuckled, a happier sound than she would have expected to hear. 'Which one shall we keep?' he asked.

It was in the dead hour of the night that Chloe awoke and began to panic. She had dreamed the undersea dream again, and thought that she still held Luke in her arms. Then he had begun to slip away from her, to melt into the water and the weeds as though he had never existed. She felt an anguish such as she had not imagined to be possible. Come back, she cried silently into the dark. I don't want you to go. I can't live without you.

Chapter Sixteen

DINAH WAS KNEELING ON THE rug in front of the fire with her arms round Oliver. 'It will get less painful, I promise you,' she said. 'Not yet, but one day. You'll meet a girl you like, or it will simply fade. It does, you know, or how would any of us live?'

'It hasn't yet. It's getting worse. I feel sick every time I see her. And she's so fucking nice to me, it *makes* it worse. I'm sure I'd have a chance if only she would let it happen instead of running away.'

'Oh, Olly. This won't do, you know it won't.'

'Oh, hell. What's the point of anything?'

'Listen, I'm not saying that what you feel for Chloe isn't special and different – but something like this happens to most of us while we're growing up. God, I fell in love with one of my cousins. It was really embarrassing, he was about fifteen years older than me. I was convinced he was crazy about me. I made a complete idiot of myself, played the vamp, wrote him letters. Eventually I got drunk on cider and waited for him one night in his room in my nightdress. He was horrified. And then he laughed at me. I'll never feel as bad as that again. I wanted to die.'

'Yeah? so that's where I get it from. Doomed to love an Older Woman. Why d'you marry Dad?'

'He was the sexiest thing I ever saw.'

'OK, so you know how I feel.'

'Yes, I do. And I also know you'll feel that way again. But I'm glad you told me what it was that was turning you into a crabby monster.'

Oliver grinned sheepishly. 'Sorry, Mum. Listen – you won't tell Dad about this, will you?'

'I wouldn't dream of it.'

'Only I'd feel such a total asshole. Promise?'

'I've said so, haven't I?'

'Come for a walk?' Luke asked her later. 'There's something I need to talk to you about.'

'It's freezing out there,' Dinah protested, regretfully putting down the autobiography of Shirley Maclaine. 'We can talk just as well if we're warm.'

'It was just – where are the kids?'

'Belle's rehearsing. It's only a couple of weeks or so till the first night. Adam has gone to see Miranda, and Olly's upstairs organising his Animal Rights campaign. He's trying to persuade the local Hunt Sabs it's in their interests *not* to behave like thugs if they want to get involved.'

'I wish him luck.' Luke continued to stand restlessly in front of the fire.

'So, what was on your mind?' Dinah turned a page, unwilling to abandon the psychic star on her South American mountain top. He looked at her warm, relaxed body, the contentment in her face. In a moment he was going to wish he could put back the clock.

'Something pretty unpleasant is probably going to happen. It's my fault and I have to try to explain it to you.'

'Wow. You sound serious.' She put down the book.

'It is serious. I'm sorry. I wish there was any way I didn't have to tell you.'

'What is it, Luke? Is one of the kids in trouble?'

'No. I am. We are. No – don't say anything yet.' She saw

him gather himself as if for a parachute jump. 'I've been – seeing Chloe Olivier. We've been, well, lovers.'

Dinah shook her head. 'What?' She was laughing, that shaky, this-can't-be-true laughter that plays for time and begs for denial.

'I'm so sorry.'

'Luke this *is* some kind of joke?' She put out her hands and felt for the cushions on either side of her.

'No, it's – I've been meeting her since early in August.'

'I simply don't believe it.' But she did. She had only to look at his face and she did.

'I'm sorry,' he said again.

'Are you in love with her?'

'Yes, but—'

She flew at him, arms flailing, nails raking at his face. He put up a hand to fend her off and she drove her fist in between his ribs with an impact that left him swimming with nausea.

'Dinah!'

'Shut up. Shut up. Shut up! You filthy, whoring bastard!' She began to strike out wild and fast, landing blows wherever she could, kicking his legs and shins and clawing at his face. 'I hate you!' she screamed. 'I wish you were dead.'

'Please – I know how you must feel –'

She howled.

'– but we have to talk about it, love.'

'Love! Love?' She screamed in earnest then. 'How could you do this? How could *she* do it? Christ, Chloe! I'd like to kick the hypocritical shit out of the foul little bitch. Pretending to be my friend – not just a friend, a real friend – when all the time you were fucking each other rigid.'

'Dinah, it's finished,' he shouted. 'I won't be seeing her again. I would never have told you if it hadn't become imperative. Now will you sit down and let me tell you why. We have to get through this.'

'Don't tell me what to do, you lying bastard. God, the

pure gall of it. I'll just *bet* you wouldn't have told me.' Nearly hysterical, she began hitting him again – dogged, stubborn blows whose force dwindled and dissolved in misery. He got hold of both her hands and held them still. She panted, glaring at him, tears falling and soaking her shirt. 'You're still in love with her, aren't you?'

'That isn't what I want to say to you.'

It was the best he could do. A simple 'yes' would probably have been better. She screamed again, allowing the sound to tear open a path for the pain to rage into her. She keened aloud, giving an almost musical shape to grief and betrayal. Luke, shaken by the strength of it, could do nothing to help her.

Upstairs, Oliver heard his mother scream. He knew at once that she was not in physical pain. He left his room and went to the top of the stairs. He heard his father's voice rumble beneath the storm. Slowly he crept downstairs to the living-room door. He did not consider that he was eavesdropping. It was a simple compulsion.

'Of all the women in the world,' he heard her cry. Her voice was strident, brave and pitiful. 'And would you believe that I actually thought you might still be sleeping with Helen?' She broke on a laugh. 'Maybe you are. I'm sure your cock and your ego are big enough to satisfy her as well as that bloody bitch. Chloe! I should have recognised that cream-fed, glossy-eyed look of hers. The dirty, thieving slut.'

'Dinah,' Luke implored. 'You've just got to calm down. You'll make yourself ill if you go on like this.'

'Calm down?' She swooped up and down the scale. 'I need to go out and commit a particularly obscene form of murder, and you tell me to calm down?' She lifted her foot and aimed a vicious kick at his groin.

'No, you don't.' He swerved and backed off. 'All right, maybe I deserve it but—'

Oliver erupted into the room. 'Too right, you deserve it, you fucking scumbag.' He confronted his father, chest heaving, barely able to stave off the humiliation of tears. Chloe. Chloe and Luke. Something important was breaking down inside him.

'Oliver.' Luke was suddenly in control. 'This is nothing to do with you. Get out.'

'Isn't it?' The boy trembled. 'What would you know?'

'Oh my God,' said Dinah, suddenly quiet. 'Leave him, Luke. Olly, I'm desperately sorry you had to hear any of this. Leave us alone now, please. I'll talk to you later.'

'What, and leave you with *him*?'

'It's all right.'

'Really? And is it all right for him to fuck Chloe Olivier?'

'You are offensive and hysterical,' Luke said flatly. 'I suggest you go away and ask yourself just what you have achieved by bursting in here like this.'

'I heard my mother scream. What would you have done, left her to scream?'

'For God's sake, can't you see you're only making things worse?'

'He could hardly do that,' Dinah said. She went to Oliver and put her arm round him. 'Go on, Olly, just for me.'

'Well, OK,' he agreed reluctantly, 'but don't think I'm not going to beat the hell out of him.'

'Not necessary,' Luke told him with an unsuitable whiff of levity. 'Your mother has just done that.' He could not help feeling that the scene had been on a descending curve from low drama to high soap since the moment it began.

Oliver threw him a look of killing contempt and left. Luke took a deep, deep breath. Now they had the rest of it to get through. He looked sidelong at Dinah. He had forgotten she could be like that. Her language was a shock.

She saw him looking and smiled, though not kindly. 'All right, tell me,' she said.

'May you live in interesting times' goes the subtle Chinese curse.

That weekend, Chloe felt she was learning the precise measure of that subtlety. It began with Rufus, who appeared in his parents' bedroom at nine o' clock on Saturday morning, wearing his halo and carrying two mugs of coffee. It was uncomfortable to accept this largesse in the knowledge that the halo would shortly be confiscated for an unspecified period.

At breakfast, conveniently, the conversation revolved around Tilda, who was spending all her free time in rehearsal but was now worried that she might be developing stage fright.

'Belle says it's natural and it means that I'm a really sensitive player. We're going to work on my entrances today; she thinks that will help. If that's OK?'

'*Chez* Cavendish?' Alain enquired.

'Yes.'

He nodded. Chloe felt unpleasantly self-conscious.

'As long as you are back this evening to see Miranda.'

When she had gone he grimaced at Chloe and invited Rufus, who was deep in his computer manual, to accompany him to his study.

'Is something wrong?' Rufus intuited, wondering if they had, after all, heard him come in at half past one last night.

'I think so, don't you,' Alain said calmly.

There followed several very bad moments for Rufus.

'Oh shit,' he said, when his father had laid out the facts for his shame-faced confirmation. 'Joel will murder me.'

Alain raised his brows. 'I might. But not Joel. He will quite possibly be in jail.'

'Oh *shit*!' repeated Rufus even more emphatically.

His father looked at him as if he was something interesting at the end of a microscope. 'What distresses you most?' he asked. 'The fact that you have been engaged in something that is stupid, dangerous and against the law – or the destruction of your relationship with Joel?'

Rufus struggled to approach the truth. 'He was my friend, Dad. He just doesn't think the same way as you do.'

'And what about you? Do you think as he does?'

'I'm not sure. I think so, except I don't like being blackmailed.'

'That seems to me a pretty big exception. Would a true friend really descend to blackmail?'

'I suppose not. But I still don't want to dob him in.'

'I'm sure you don't. But this young man is doing too much damage to be allowed to continue. It may be necessary for you to give evidence in order to stop him. It is also possible that charges may be brought against you. I'm sure you understand how that would affect your future?'

'Yes, Dad.'

'I should also like to remind you that we have gone through all this with you on a previous occasion. You caused us considerable distress then, and it is all the more considerable now because it is evident that you have learned nothing from your earlier experience. It seems to me that we have been altogether too lenient with you. And therefore I am going to leave your fate in the hands of those whose profession it is to deal with such misdeeds.'

'D'you mean the police?'

'Probably. And your headmaster, naturally.' He sighed and looked at his son with distaste. 'You are very young to be a criminal, Rufus. I am very disappointed in you. You may go. Please stay in the house.'

'I am sorry, Dad. Honestly.'

Receiving no reply, he left, downcast.

Oh shit and piss and fuck! How had he got himself into

such a mess? A more immediate bind was that he and Dwayne had been going to spend the day hanging out with the bikers at Newlands corner. Fat chance now. Perhaps, if he waited a bit, he might be able to sneak out later. For one thing, they'd better shift all the stuff they had in hand; he didn't want any evidence hanging about.

Watching his face, its changes no longer quite those of a naughty schoolboy, Alain had wondered if he had grasped all the implications. He would, in time. He was intelligent enough to work them out. In fact, the first really important thing that Rufus worked out for himself was that he was now unlikely to get the longed-for Harley before he was sixteen. Unless he could think of some other means. Later, of course, when all this had blown over.

Miranda arrived in the late afternoon, deposited by Adam Cavendish who followed her into the house and greeted Alain and Chloe with every evidence of pleasure and none of any constraint. He left almost at once, breaking Chloe's heart with his derivative smile, promising to run Miranda back to London on Sunday evening.

'Is that 'eap of yours off the road again already?' Alain demanded.

'No. Adam just likes looking after me, so I let him. I rather like it too.' She smiled and kissed Alain's cheek.

Chloe, who had so far managed to produce only a reasonably casual 'Hello, darling', which had been ignored as if unspoken, now wanted to say something nice about Adam. 'He must be a great help to you, just now,' she tried apprehensively.

Miranda said to Alain, 'You said there was a special reason for this visit?'

'Yes,' he said shortly, 'and part of it is to tell you that I will not have you being rude and unpleasant to your mother. You should be ashamed.'

'*I* should be ashamed!' Miranda was outraged. She

turned on Chloe. 'Have you told him yet? Because if you haven't—'

'I have. I told you I would, in my own time.'

'You don't have to explain yourself to her, *chérie*,' said Alain softly. 'As for you, Miranda, don't be such a self-righteous little bigot.'

Miranda burst into disbelieving tears and Chloe rushed out of the door. Alain spent a diplomatic hour mopping them up in separate rooms.

It got a little better after that.

Chloe declined to be present while the twins were told about the baby, but to her surprise Miranda asked her, rather primly, to remain.

'After all, it affects everybody,' she said. True, it was the only remark she volunteered to Chloe for the rest of the evening, but she did reply, if somewhat over-politely, when Chloe spoke to her. It was progress, of a sort.

The twins' reactions to the news were characteristic in both cases.

'Gosh, I'll be an uncle!' Rufus said proudly. 'I'll be able to teach him things. When he's bigger, of course.' He was not so keen on the nappies and burping aspect. He supposed he did not mind Miranda not being married. People didn't seem to bother much about that these days. Dwayne's brother, Clint, had a baby with his girlfriend, and they didn't even live together.

Tilda kept very quiet while Rufus enthused. 'Congratulations,' she offered colourlessly when it was her turn. 'Do you mind saying – I mean, who is the baby's father?' Please God, let it be Adam.

'You know very well. There's only one person it *could* be. It's Joel's baby, technically speaking.'

Tilda flushed crimson. 'That's disgusting! You can't have his baby. You can't!'

'What do you suggest I do? Spit it out?' Miranda snapped.

'Well, couldn't you – is it too late to—?'

'Get rid of it? Yes. It was too late the second it was conceived. I'm ashamed of you, Tilda. I thought better of you than that.'

Tilda had shocked herself. 'Oh no,' she cried, horrified. 'Oh Miranda, I'm sorry. I didn't really mean that.' She began to cry. 'I just want everything to be all right for you.'

Miranda softened. 'I know that. And it is, really it is.'

Tilda shook her head and ran out, brushing at her wet face. She reached the downstairs bathroom just in time to be sick. She cleaned herself up and scrubbed at her teeth with her fingers, then sat on the chair until she felt a bit less shaky. Lifting her chin, she stood up and composed herself for her entrance and went back into the kitchen. There, she apologised to everyone, especially Miranda, and asked if anybody would mind if she were to go up to her room and try over her lines for the rest of the evening.

Lying on her bed, she put aside the new security of repeating her lines to consider what had happened to Miranda. She did not want it to happen to her. The problem was that Paul had asked her to go out with him 'seriously'. She interpreted this as meaning that he wanted her to go all the way with him. The very thought of what this entailed made her feel sick again. It was Joel's face, not Paul's, that she imagined, hanging over hers, grinning as he thrust himself into her, intruding, invading, taking her over, stealing a part of herself. Joel, with his smile, his darkness and his anarchic messages about the world and its pleasures. She moved rhythmically, pressing her hand between her thighs, feeling his hands on her hair, on her breasts, tearing off her clothes. She felt herself grow warm and wet and made little gasping sounds of fear and lust.

In bed, Chloe worried on a large scale.

'Relax a little,' Alain comforted. 'At least everything is out in the open now.'

'Not everything.'

'Well, all that needs to be.'

'You don't think Miranda would tell the children the rest of it, do you?'

He said grimly, 'I have made sure she will not.'

She woke late, feeling limp and exhausted. She ran a bath and lay in the scented water longer than usual, mulling over the events of the weekend and trying to find some encouragement in them. There was only confusion. She had just got out and begun to towel herself dry when she heard the front door knocker. She ignored it, hoping whoever it was would simply go away. The knocking became more insistent, however, so she wrapped herself in her kimono and went down to answer it.

She opened the door and gasped. 'Dinah!'

'Bitch!'

Dinah thrust past her and into the kitchen. Anger accompanied her like a dangerous pet, bulky and unpredictable. Chloe followed her, her head spinning. She was met by a wall of contempt.

'I see you are dressed for the part. Does he like you permanently ready for him, no bra, no knickers? Or perhaps he prefers you like this?' Dinah seized the ties of the kimono and yanked it right off, sending Chloe staggering naked across the room.

'Not bad,' she said, making an intimate appraisal of breasts and loins, 'if you care for mellow fruitfulness. I'm sure you make a very professional whore.' She bared her teeth like an animal. 'How many times have you done it with him?'

Chloe tried to rally a little. 'I wasn't counting,' she said. 'You could ask Luke, but I don't suppose he was either. This is just stupid, you know that.'

'Stupid?' Dinah's face crumpled and she made claws of

her hands. 'Do you have any idea what you have done to me?'

Chloe waited.

'Can you imagine how it feels – how demeaning, how pathetic, how unbelievably belittling it is to have the man whose life is your sole centre suddenly turn round and tell you he is in love with someone else? And not just anyone. Oh no. Only the friend you thought would be the closest, the one you trusted, the one you were beginning to love.'

'Dinah—' Unconsciously Chloe stretched out her arms.

'And not content with that – you had to have my son too. You were so far gone on heat for Luke that there was plenty left over for Oliver. You've led him on until the poor kid doesn't know what the hell to do with himself. Do you know what you are? A first-class example of the mythological female monster. A hydra, a Medusa, a Melusine, an all-devouring, come-all, fuck-all legendary monster. I loathe you. I'd like to kill you. If I can think of a way of doing it without being found out, I *will* kill you.'

The greater emotions, Chloe thought, cannot stand much ordinary daylight. 'If it would make you feel any better, I wish I could say I recognise your picture of me. But I don't.' She was very tired. She picked up the kimono and put it round her shoulders. She went to the table and sat down. Dinah watched, but made no move to prevent her.

'Don't you? Well, I would hardly expect you to recognise the truth when you see it. You must have told so many lies since meeting Luke.'

'Oddly enough, I haven't had to. Look, Dinah, if he has told you everything then you know that all he wants, or Alain and I want, is to try to leave it behind us and make things work again as they used to. Our children are friends, why should we destroy that for them? We have both been strong families, even happy ones, before this. I can't undo what Luke and I have done – but I can tell you that I have hurt myself, perhaps as much as even you could wish, in hurting you and Alain. I'll never cease to regret doing that.'

'What good is that to me?' cried Dinah. 'I've lost my husband. I've lost my son.'

Chloe frowned. 'That isn't true. And why Oliver?'

'Because he can't bear to be in the same house as his father. I told Luke to get out, but he won't so Oliver has. He's going to live in the rooms over the vet's surgery.'

'I'm so sorry. I did try to tell him—'

'Go to hell. I still don't think you can really *see* what you've done to us. And what about your own family? Didn't you ever think of them while you were stuffing my husband's prick up your greedy little cunt? Did you think at all, either of you? There isn't a single one of us who won't suffer for your selfishness. You've turned your two "happy families" inside out just to satisfy your dirty little itch.'

'It wasn't like that.' She couldn't help saying it.

'Oh, of course not. It was the real thing, the grand passion, the splendour in the grass. The great love that was worth a lifetime of regret. Well, was it?'

'I'll talk about anything else you like, Dinah, but I won't answer that.'

Suddenly Dinah seemed to run out of power. 'No?' she said wearily. 'I don't think I want to hear it, anyway.' Bereft of her anger, she looked younger, defenceless. 'I wanted to hurt you, even physically, if I could. But I guess you've hurt yourself almost enough. I hope so.'

Chloe looked at her in anguish. She could find nothing to say.

Dinah shook her head sadly and left her to her silence.

That evening Philip Dacre received a phone call which surprised him.

'It's Dinah. I'm miserable and I need cheering up. Can I come over to see you?'

'My dear, of course. Come right away. I've talked to Luke. I know you must be very unhappy. We must see what we can do about it.'

What they did was to drink a great deal of Philip's delicious Condrieu, eat smoked salmon and soda bread and listen to Brahms.

The fatalistic surges of the Fourth Symphony expressed Dinah's emotions far better than she could have done herself, and she found that she did not want to talk about Luke at all, but simply to sink into the relief of getting drunk on wine and music and the knowledge that she was with a man who both desired her and cared about her.

Philip was not drunk when he told her that he had been in love with her for longer, probably, than he even knew himself, and nor was Dinah, not quite yet, when she said that he was the only man she wanted to be with at that moment. When he kissed her she responded more passionately than he had imagined in his most optimistic fantasies, so that any scruples he may have had about taking advantage of her seemed unnecessary and ungrateful. When he took her into his large and comfortable bed, every one of those fantasies was realised to the crest of its potential, and after that they made up new ones as they went along.

In the early hours of the morning, Dinah was nudged into consciousness by throbbing temples and a parched throat. Still half-asleep, she edged carefully to the side of the bed to avoid disturbing Luke. As she sat up gingerly and swung her legs to the floor, she became aware that something did not feel quite right. She blinked and rubbed her eyes. Her head did not like this. She must have drunk an awful lot last night. Then she remembered. The Condrieu.

'Oh, no. Philip.'

She could hardly bear to turn and look at him; she just

might have imagined it. He was breathing deeply, unaffected by any panic-stricken vibrations of hers. His face had that smooth, boyish surface that men seemed to recover so easily in sleep. Luke had it too. But Luke was in the spare room at home. She got out of bed and dressed. She wondered if she should wake Philip but decided against it. She hardly knew what she wanted to say to him. She crept downstairs and found a biro and some paper next to the phone in the living-room.

Dear Philip,' she wrote, 'I have to go home. I have not stayed out all night since I was a rebellious teenager. Thank you for last night. I'll call you. Dinah.'

It wasn't much but it would do for now. The real reckoning would come later, when she had worked out what the devil she felt about what she had done.

Belle and Adam sat at a candle-lit table in the floor-length window of La Grenouille, eating cassoulet and racing each other through a cheerful Côte du Rhône. Belle had taken a lot of trouble with her appearance and thought justly that she should be placed where as many people as possible, inside and out, could appreciate her efforts. She wore a startlingly adult scarlet dress from the theatrical costumier whose cast-off box she rifled regularly, a mouth to match, and a heavy black lace shawl. Adam, in black trousers and the lavender grey silk shirt as commanded, told her she looked like Carmen. Taking the single red rose from the vase on the table, he laughed and put it between her teeth. She removed it, brushing it tantalisingly past her lips, snapped its stalk and tucked it into his top pocket.

'There. Now we're a pair.'

'So who am I supposed to be?' he asked, grinning. 'Escamillo or Don José?'

'It depends.'

'On what?'

She rolled her eyes. 'On whether you could kill me for love.'

'For love? No. For the sheer pleasure of it – possibly.'

'Be careful. You have to be nice to me tonight. Can we have some more of this wine?'

'Yes, if you give a sober performance when we get home.'

'I always do. So you are sleeping at home tonight?'

He looked surprised. 'I do live there.'

'You didn't on Sunday. Or Monday.'

He frowned. 'Stop fishing, Belle.'

'What if I am? I'd probably only catch an old boot.' She smiled sweetly.

Adam lifted one brow severely, a habit that always made her feel faint with lust. 'If you're thinking of Miranda, what does that make you, a raddled young hag?'

She protested. 'What do you mean?'

He touched her lips. 'Raddle or reddle, a coarse red pigment. You don't need it, you know. You are quite colourful enough without it.'

'Is that a compliment?'

'Only if you stop being nasty about Miranda. She needs friends just now. I thought Tilda might have told you, she's going to have a baby.'

Belle froze in horror. 'Oh, no! Adam, how could you be such a dickhead?'

'I haven't been, you idiot! It isn't mine, it's Joel Ranger's.'

'Oh, thank goodness.' She flopped with relief. 'Don't *ever* give me such a fright again. Is she going to marry him?' She looked hopeful.

'No, she isn't,' he said testily.

'I see.' She paused. 'So *were* you with her, then, these last two nights?'

'That is none of your business.'

'Yes it is. You care what happens to me, don't you?'

'Yes, but—'

'Then why shouldn't I care about you? I want you to be happy, that's all. You must admit you haven't been too clever at picking girls, so far?'

'I've had my moments.'

'They haven't lasted long.' Not that she objected to this. 'I don't expect Miranda will, either.'

'I don't know. It's different,' he said seriously. 'More of a grown-up undertaking. Heavier.'

Belle's heart sank. 'Because of the baby?'

'Partly. But more because she makes me think about things. I like talking to her. It's comfortable being with her. There's no strain.'

'Sounds like Darby and Joan. I suppose you *are* sleeping with her?'

'God, you are insatiable.'

'Don't you mind scraping up Joel's leavings?'

'OK, that's it. End of conversation. Why don't we talk about you, instead?'

'It's only my second-favourite topic. I haven't finished with *you* yet.'

He sighed impatiently. 'I don't know why it is you think you own my soul.'

'I have a pact with Satan. One day, when you're capable of looking after it, I'll give it back to you, with interest.'

He shook his head. 'You are a strange creature. I wish I understood you.'

'It's just as well that you don't.'

'You are always so – extreme.'

'I know.' She nodded sagely. 'It's because I don't want my life to be *little* and inconsequential, even for half an hour. I want it to blaze. Can you understand that?'

'Yes, I can. That's the way I sometimes feel about writing.'

'You have to feel it all the time. D'you think I'll make it, Adam? Do you think I can be like Helen?'

He took her hand and squeezed it. 'Yes, I think you can.'

His look of affection made her ache. She raised his hand and laid it against her cheek. 'I love you, Adam,' she said.

'I love you too,' he smiled and released her hand.

She would treasure this moment. The trouble was that she might have to treasure it for an unconscionable time, through a whole string of Mirandas and lesser lights, until he eventually realised that his soul was simply the other half of hers. It would give her plenty of time in which to build up her blaze. But it seemed such a waste. If only she could have him now.

At home, when they got out of the car, she said, 'Kiss me goodnight. Properly. Just once. I want to know what it's like.'

'You mean you've never . . .?'

She shook her head, her eyes enormous in the moonlight. She crossed her fingers behind her back.

Adam kissed her with care and tenderness. It was only when her soft mouth opened under his and he felt the unmistakable pressures of her body, that he realised what she had meant by properly. It was a bit of a shock, but for some reason which he could not fathom, either then or later, he made no attempt to draw away from her.

Chapter Seventeen

L UKE CALLED CHLOE. HE WOULD not allow her to speak. There were things they must talk about, but not on the phone. He would meet her at Arden Court at two o' clock on Wednesday.

They met in the courtyard, embracing fiercely, like collaborators.

'I was afraid you wouldn't come.'

'So was I.'

'Shall we go inside?'

'I think I'd rather hear your news first.'

'It's cold.'

'Never mind.'

'Very well. It's good, on the whole. First, Philip says the police have persuaded the paper not to print Joel's little hate-tale. They think he is worth watching for a month or two, to see if he will lead them to a bigger fish. If they published the story now, it would only warn off his suppliers.'

'That's marvellous. Oh, God, the relief. I can't believe it.'

'The next thing is that any eventual court case will come up in Joel's bailiwick, not out here, and Rufus may not have to be involved. Our local Chief Inspector will want to talk to him, however. He and Philip are going to hold a very thorough and very discreet investigation into the prevalence of drugs in the school. Rufus and Dwayne and their customers will be given a series of hefty penalties which will make their lives seem rather grey for a year or so. I don't know if this is justice, exactly, but whatever it is, I hope it will work.'

'We'll make sure it does. I'm glad Joel will be punished, except for Miranda's sake. As for you and me, perhaps we are more fortunate than we deserve.'

'What, because we are not to be victimised? As we once said, love is not a crime. Can we go in now, Chloe? You must be freezing.'

She hung back, hesitating. 'I don't think we ought to make love again.'

'For God's sake, why not? Don't you want to?'

'You know I do. But we made promises. We ought to honour them.'

'We will, we will, but as the excellent saint suggests, not yet.' He reached for her. 'Come here, will you!' He grabbed her and held her by the scruff of the neck. He pulled open her coat, tugging and unbuttoning until he had got his hands on her again. 'Do you know how angry I am about what you're doing to us?'

'Yes.'

'Then do as I say, or I will undo everything you are trying to mend; your marriage, mine, everything. Right now, I don't give a damn about any of it.'

'Have you turned blackmailer now?'

'I'll take you any way I can get you.' There was the pirate's smile.

'You can't.'

'I can for this afternoon. One last hour or two before the howling desert of time and regret and unbearable temptation that you've chosen for us to look forward to. Surely you aren't so scrupulously conscientious as to refuse us that?'

'You make it sound small-minded. I don't see it like that.'

'I don't care how the blazes you see it. Come on. And shut up.'

He dragged her after him into the house and up the stairs. Soon she began to laugh, she couldn't help it, his set face was so absurd. At the door of the bedroom she checked with a murmur of surprise. 'Look at this. The revenge of Trespassers W.'

The bed had been stripped. The rose brocade had gone, only the grey mattress and an uncovered bolster remained.

'Don't waste time looking for symbols. Get your clothes off.'

'Luke, why are you behaving like this?'

'Like what?'

'Like a gangster in a B-movie, cool and brutal and overdoing it.'

'I'm protecting myself. God, woman, hurry up, you're killing me.'

She obeyed. There seemed to be no point in pretending, now that they had got as far as this.

She lay down beside him and he kissed her with a slow eroticism which was as near as he could come towards making her suffer. If she thought this was going to be the last time, a thing he still did not want to accept, then this must be the time that would keep her awake at night and eventually, surely, bring her back to him?

'Are you too cold?'

'No.'

'Good. I want to look at you.'

He spread her upon the mattress and travelled her with his fingers, stroking every centimetre of skin, gently forcing every orifice.

'No, be still,' he said when she tried to respond. 'This is

my private odyssey. I want to be sure my hands will remember you. For once, I don't want anything to depend on words. I deal in them all the time, I don't want them to be between us now.'

Silently she thanked him for that.

When he covered and came into her he was not cold, neither was he brutal unless in the excess of passion. He searched her face, as he had always done, to see how she liked it, and found the same bright affirmation that was there the first time they had done this, and all the times between. He saw her smile and close her eyes and knew she was diving down into the blue-green depths she had dreamed for them, where seaweeds swayed on the current of their blood and animal flowers opened and closed. He followed her and the astonishing, common miracle occurred; the present fell away and they were timeless again, as easy as sleep.

He did his best to hold her to him, to make it absolutely unthinkable that this should end, but she knew what he was doing and made herself strong in spite of his determination.

He leaned on his elbow and gazed into her eyes with the shameless seduction of a matinée idol. 'We *could* go on like this,' he said in tones of deep reasonableness. 'If we are much more careful than we have been. However rare our meetings might be, they must be better than nothing.'

Chloe sighed. 'That would be cheating.'

'How can you be so relentless? It amazes me.'

'I have to be, because you won't help me.'

'You used to be such a romantic. What has changed you?'

'Romance,' she said shortly.

'Why?'

'Because it can only survive in a vacuum. It perishes in the common air we breathe. And not Byron or Shakespeare or the blessed John Donne himself can do a thing to alter that.'

'That's a desperate thing to say. Nothing has changed between us. We *feel* the same, don't we?'

'Yes, but we no longer have a separate place in our lives in which to be lovers. Our vacuum has been filled up with the consequences of our actions.'

'So you intend to consign us to the past, now, today, as if we had never happened?'

'No.' She caught his face between her hands, begging him to understand. 'You will illumine the rest of my life. I don't believe you will ever fade for me. I can't make myself stop loving you – but I'm not going to deceive myself or anyone else, or tempt myself beyond bearing, by letting this go on any longer.'

'Don't worry,' he said, with the familiar curl of amusement in his voice, 'you can safely leave the temptation to me. My conscience is Neanderthal in comparison with yours.'

'You won't listen to me, will you?' She was near anger now. 'All right, you could probably undermine me one day. Perhaps you will. But I will hate myself for it if you do.'

'Only for two minutes. Take today, for example.'

'I mean it, Luke, and this *is* desperate. If you won't let go, Alain and I will leave Sheringham and you will never see me again.'

This alarmed him. 'Chloe, you wouldn't?'

'Alain has already asked me if I want to leave. I don't. I want to be near you. I want our children to keep their friendship. I want to see you sometimes, and talk to you. It may be a special kind of torture – there will always be the wound within the body – but it would, as you say, be better than nothing.'

'It would be next to nothing.' He groaned. 'You terrify me. You are a monster, an entirely female, masochistic monster.'

She gave a vinegar grin. 'Dinah said something like that.'

'Dinah?'

'Didn't she tell you?'

'No.'

'Then neither shall I. You will try to make it work, won't you?'

'Trying is instant death to situations such as ours. Either it will work or it won't. I believe it will because that, despite some melodramatic appearances to the contrary, is what Dinah really wants.'

'I'm glad.'

'Are you? And since I am apparently not to have what I really want, I am content, or perhaps inured is a better word, to keep what I have.'

'Oh Luke. Is it worse for you than it is for me? I can't tell.'

'Nor can I. All I know is that we are wasting time which has become precious beyond the jewels of avarice. Can we stop now?'

'Yes. Kiss me, Luke. Come into me again. We won't talk any more. Talking is for beginnings.'

She sensed that she had spoken their elegy.

It was with Dinah in mind that Chloe decided she would visit Oliver in his bolt-hole above the vet's surgery. It might prove to be an embarrassing mistake; on the other hand she might be able to do some good. She chose a time in the early evening when Olly was likely to be at home, left a spaghetti sauce to simmer, and drove round to the flat.

The surgery was a newish brick building with the traditional black-slatted upper storey reached by an exterior stairway. She climbed this slowly, nerving herself for an emotional reception. As she knocked on the door, a lamp came on above her head, revealing a light, parsimonious rain.

'Chloe!'

'Hello, Oliver. May I come in?'

'What the hell do you want?'

'I want to talk to you, if you'll let me.'

'It's my mother you should talk to. You should talk to her on your knees.'

'It's partly because of her that I'm here.'

He hesitated, then stood back to let her pass.

'In here.' He stalked ahead of her into a warm room furnished as a bed-sitter, and motioned her into an armchair. Several expressions chased each other across his thin face. 'Well?' he demanded.

'Are you going to give me any real chance at all, or are you just going to stand there and hate me?'

'You don't deserve any chances.'

'Why not?'

He gaped. 'Because you've done what you did with my father and just about ruined my mother's entire life.'

'What I did with your father, you think that was an evil thing to do?'

'What else?'

'And yet, wasn't it the same thing that you wanted me to do with you? I'm putting it a little crudely, I'm sorry.'

He glared. 'It isn't the same.'

'It is. I fell in love with your father, Olly. If I had fallen in love with you, you would not have called it evil, would you?'

'You're twisting everything,' he cried, his face working. 'It's not fair!'

She smiled gently. 'Nothing is very fair, just at the moment. Perhaps we shouldn't expect it to be. Do you really hate me, Olly? Because I wish you wouldn't. I'd like your friendship now; it would help a lot.'

'Friendship? You've got to be joking. But I'll tell you what I *would* like from you – a really good fuck, like you've been giving my father.' There were tears in his eyes.

'Oliver, don't. I know how badly this has hurt you, but you must believe that I am deeply sorry for that. Can't you try to forgive me?'

'Maybe, if you'll sleep with me. Will you? I'm sure Luke and I do a lot of the same things in bed. Close your eyes and you won't know the difference'

It was time to toughen up. 'That's enough. You're acting like a spoiled brat.'

'Spoiled?' His voice shook. 'My father sleeps with the first woman I have ever loved and you call that spoiled!' He was on the verge of breaking down.

'I agree that it has been a terrible experience for you.' Her voice was kind again. 'But I won't allow you to speak to me like that. You only degrade yourself, not me.'

'You've already done that. So has he.'

She ignored this. 'I understand that Luke has dealt a blow to your masculinity and hurt your pride. But what about your mother? You've got to get over this if you want this business ever to become part of the past, if you want to help your parents put things right between them.'

He gave her a bruised look. 'What do you mean?'

'You have to stop looking at it from your own point of view. If you are outraged by your father's behaviour, consider how humiliating it must be for him to know he is the object of your contempt. And your mother – by leaving the house you have added to her problems. You know, if you are honest with yourself, that she really wants to make peace with Luke, but you make it more difficult by dividing her loyalties.'

'I can't believe you are blaming me.'

'I'm not, I'm saying you are not helping. Dinah needs you at home. You're the only one she can count on just now. Adam isn't close enough and Belle is too young, and anyway, she knows nothing about all this.'

'I don't want to go back. I don't want to be anywhere near him.'

'I know, but won't you please think it over, for Dinah's sake?'

Oliver's stance became less combative. He looked at her grudgingly. 'You really think it would help?'

'I think it would make her happier if she didn't have to worry about you as well as the rest of it.'

Now he abandoned his offensive entirely and dropped to his knees beside her. 'Oh Chloe, why couldn't you have loved me instead? There would have been none of this trouble.'

She smiled. 'There would have been plenty of trouble, believe me. And while we're throwing hypothetical questions about, why couldn't you have been ten or fifteen years older? Who knows what might have happened. Of course, we might have had a few complaints from your beautiful wife and children.'

'That's not funny.'

'No, but at least you've stopped hating me.'

'I don't hate you. I'm jealous and it hurts like hell.'

Impulsively, she hugged him. 'I wish I could take it all away. I can't, but I do love you, very much, in the way you don't care about just now.'

'Don't say that. It's like you want to be my aunt or something. You'll just have to put up with the way I feel.' He sighed deeply. 'Look, I will go home, if you like, if it'll make Mum feel better.'

'Will you?' She was delighted. 'That's terrific.'

'Well, I do kind of miss everyone – almost – and I can't stay here much longer without paying Alastair some rent.' He knelt up and touched her cheek, his green eyes insisting on this minor indulgence. 'I shall miss you too,' he said. 'Until I knew about you and Dad, I could always tell myself I had the ghost of a chance.'

The 2CV announced itself with its usual mechanical fanfare. Chloe prepared to be contemned or ignored, depending on how Miranda felt that evening. She was getting a little tired of walking on eggshells.

'Here, boy.' She addressed the dog basket. 'Come and give me some moral support.' Baskerville, nothing if not a moral giant, shook himself and ambled over to nuzzle his head into her lap.

'Hi, Mum.' The greeting was subdued but polite. A new multicoloured haversack was tossed into a corner. 'Sorry this is such short notice. Only Adam asked me to a party tonight, but he didn't know about it himself until this morning. Hello, Baskerville, my old darling. Who's a great big softie, then?'

Miranda bent to scratch the dog behind his eager ears. Her hair, scented with lemon balm and wrapped with beads of many colours, settled cloudily over Chloe's knees, a closer contact than she had allowed since their rift. Chloe began to feel a humming inside her chest.

'Would you like some coffee or something?' she asked.

'I ought to sort out my stuff, first. There's a dress needs hanging if I'm going to wear it tonight.'

Nervous, wanting to get it over, Chloe said, 'Miranda, there's some news. We've been told that Joel may soon be prosecuted. Rufus won't be involved.'

There was a hiatus, as if the words had taken longer than usual to travel. Miranda's face was as clear of content as that of bodiless Annalise. 'Oh, right. Thanks.'

Chloe continued awkwardly. 'I don't know how you feel about Joel now, but it can't be good to think of him going to jail.'

There was another lapse. Then Miranda said brightly, 'Where are the kittens? How's Baskerville coping with them?'

'Look under the table. They have a new basket. Draught-proof. Baskerville is the perfect godfather. He even lets them sleep with him while Grace takes a break.'

Miranda did not look under the table. The china face

cracked and she burst into heartbroken tears. 'Oh, Mum.'

Chloe suppressed the rising hosannas inside her and took her daughter in her arms. Miranda resisted and the carolling stopped, then her sobs redoubled and she cast herself on Chloe's breast as she had not done since she was six years old.

'It's Joel. Baskerville cares more about those kittens than Joel does about his own child. I just don't know how I feel any more,' she wailed. 'I never knew anyone could hurt me so much. It's as though by getting pregnant I'd attacked everything that's most important to him, offended something really deep in him. I think the whole blackmail thing is about that. I wouldn't give him any power about the baby, so he punished me by showing he could exert power over you and Rufus instead.'

She stopped to wipe her eyes, ringed with kohl like a Greek tragedian's. They made Chloe understand Dinah's urge to kill the perpetrator of pain.

'I think I hate him now,' Miranda finished, more in hope than certainty. 'But he is the baby's father. I can't change that. I just pray heredity is only a few per cent of our characters, the way some scientists think.'

Chloe smiled, gently letting her go. 'Don't worry, lovely. Your baby will be loved to pieces by so many people. That will easily balance a few negative genes. And Joel does have more than a touch of genius. His child could inherit that.'

Miranda shuddered. 'His genius is almost all on his dark side. I wouldn't wish that on a helpless infant.'

'Look, the baby will be himself. Or herself. Which do you want, by the way?'

'I can't decide. It's kind of a sexual thing, isn't it? Not just gender. I'll be living with another male or female psyche. Do I want a little live-in lover or a really close girlfriend and rival?'

Chloe laughed. 'It's exactly like that for the first few

years. The fights are similar too. But you'll be horrified by how quickly he or she decides to become an independent person and challenge everything you say.'

'I think I'd better just take it as it comes. No sexual preference, no preconceived ideas about How to Bring Up Baby.'

'Sounds right to me.'

'Good.' Shyly she sought Chloe's eyes. 'Mum?'

'Yes?'

'I'm glad we've, well, cleared the air a bit. I'm afraid I freaked about a few things. I must have been hard to take recently.'

Chloe waved the subject into the ether. 'Me too,' she said.

Miranda glowed with relief. 'OK. Will you come upstairs with me and tell me if you think I can still wear that dress? I think I'm starting to show around the waist. I seem to have stopped being sick, though,' she added with a woman-to-woman pride.

Chloe felt she might rise into the air on a cloud of euphoria like some ecstatic mystic. This is my well-beloved daughter who has come home. When, later, Alain came in, shrouded in tweed and complaining of the British weather as if he had not lived in it for twenty years, he found the two of them bent earnestly over the table, giggling and stitching. They were applying floating panels of butterfly silk to Miranda's expectant black dress.

'*Mon dieu, mon dieu, mon dieu,*' he said, transported to France by delight.

The evening relaxed and stretched to become one which Chloe would remember with grateful wonder. It seemed to her, during the few hours that followed Miranda's home-coming, that a process of self-healing had begun, that they might still become again the family they had been before she had risked their destruction.

When Adam blew in to wait for Miranda, he took the chair he usually sat in and was soon engaged in a satisfying discussion with Alain on the idiosyncrasies of the French press. Chloe, meanwhile, employed the loaves and fishes method with her roast chicken, adding a package of frozen seafood and a sachet of saffron, so that the delicate *poulet au riz*, *sauce mousseline*, became a refulgent, resplendent paella.

At the exact second of its perfection, the door flew open on a draught of night air and noise, admitting Tilda and Belle, who had, of course, been rehearsing, and with them a politically subdued Rufus, whom they had pressed into slavery as their prompter.

'Everyone will be eating, I hope,' Chloe called above the ensuing racket.

'Adam? Are you doing anything afterwards?' asked the loudest voice, Belle's.

'Miranda and I are going to a party.'

'Oh. Only I thought you might run us back to school. We've absolutely got to get the second act right by tomorrow. We need every minute we can find.'

'I'm sorry,' Adam blandly refused to be managed.

Alain was watching in amusement. 'Don't worry, Mademoiselle,' he said. 'I will take you.'

'*Merci bien, Monsieur Olivier,*' Belle said sweetly. '*Vous êtes trop gentil.*'

'*Mais je vous en prie!*' Alain had the distinct impression that she wanted him to kiss her hand again. She would cause trouble in the world, that one. Helen must have been much the same at her age.

'Hi, Rufus the Red-handed.' Miranda spoke from the doorway where she had paused for maximum effect. 'How's the Fine Young Criminal? I hear you've escaped the hangman's noose.'

'Hi, fatty,' Rufus returned joyfully. 'Looks as if you could do with one round your waist.'

'Shut up, you're making Tilda blush. And you can't even see my waist under all this froth.'

'Everything makes her blush. It must be some weird disease. Yes, I can. It's under your armpits.'

Miranda came and cuffed him cheerfully. 'I expected,' she said to Alain pointedly, 'to find him languishing in his room with some old bread and a glass of water, preferably in chains.'

'Good idea,' approved Tilda, recovering. 'I'll keep the keys.'

'That is, indeed, still possible,' Alain growled. 'But this is a pleasant occasion, so we will be nice to each other, yes?'

Tilda shrugged. 'OK, but we'll only let him out to do the prompting.'

Sending her an affectionate glance, Chloe thought that, tonight, nothing could possibly be nicer than to listen to them behaving the way they had always done. It was premature to hope, but it was beginning to appear probable that a whole layer of their life together, perhaps even the foundation layer, had remained magically intact.

Dinah's initial instinct had been to tell Luke that she had slept with Philip. This would have the advantage of serving the dual purpose of confession and revenge, both of which she felt to be necessary if they were to go on being married.

She planned the confrontation for Saturday morning, when the two of them would be alone in the house. Just as she was about to begin confronting, however, Luke announced that he had arranged to go and talk to Philip about their forthcoming liaison with the county constabulary.

The pre-emptive mention of Philip's name had a far stronger effect on Dinah than she would ever have bargained for. It was bizarre. She found her pulse leaping, her breath constricted; her breasts and, good Lord, her vaginal tissue were swelling with the languid heat. She said nothing to Luke except to bid him an abstracted goodbye. Then, still in her alarming but by no means unwelcome state of arousal, she lay down upon her bed to reconsider her options.

She cast her mind back – her body was evidently there well in advance – to the night they had spent together. There was no doubt that Philip had been a good lover – more than a good one, a considerate and enthusiastic one. His bedroom practices had been astonishingly liberal for a man who daily presented himself as the epitome of British restraint. He had, in fact, been a little perverse, which she found extremely exciting. It was quite a long time since she and Luke had done anything unusual in bed, and even longer out of it.

Philip, now that she had awarded herself the freedom to think about him, began to exude for her the musky and compelling sexuality of a Bluebeard. There he sat, in his great dark house with its memories of his dead wife and its heavy treasury of art, and he thought of her, of Dinah, of things he might do to her body, and perhaps eventually, she thought with a *frisson* of apprehension and appetite, to her mind.

She wanted him. There was no doubt; the moisture between her labia proved it bountifully.

Well, then, why not take him? And let him take her. It would be her first adult adventure. Perhaps she was guilty of romanticising, but what of it? It was indubitably her turn for such an indulgence.

It was just after she had arrived at this satisfactory and life-enhancing decision that Oliver returned to the fold, with his woolly heart on his sleeve and his laundry in a pillowcase. She was so pleased with him and with her afternoon's progress towards the self-improvement she had lately been seeking in various less entertaining ways, that she was overcome with a wave of generosity towards the whole of silly, sexy, misbehaving mankind.

It was in this spirit that she telephoned Chloe.

Was it? Surely it couldn't be? Chloe could hardly believe her ears. The voice sounded exactly like Dinah.

'Chloe? Are you still there?'

'Yes. Yes, I'm here.' Her jaw was frozen as though by novocaine.

'I thought you would want to know.' The tone was removed and oddly heady. 'Oliver has come home. He tells me I have you to thank for it.'

'Oh. Has he? I'm so glad. I didn't do much, really. He was a bit confused, that's all.'

She waited. Dinah did not reply. Chloe didn't blame her. 'Well – how are you?' she asked, conscious of further inanity. 'I've been wanting to—' To what?

'No, Chloe,' Dinah said firmly. The connection was gone.

Chloe did not know whether to be depressed or elated.

Later, Dinah also phoned Philip, who was amazed and delighted in equal parts when he heard what she had to propose.

'You seem cheerful tonight,' Luke said, testing the water, which had lately been hot and turbulent.

'Do I?' Dinah smiled, catlike, twisting tendrils of her hair round her finger, a habit she had when enjoying herself. 'Oh well, one can't be miserable *all* the time.'

It was such a Dinah-like remark that Luke began to feel that life might begin to shake down into its old pattern sooner than he had thought. It was not what he wanted. He wanted Chloe.

But he was not going to get her. At least, not yet.

*

'I'm going to play Cecily,' Tilda said. She had tried to sound casual but the sentence curled up at the end in pleasure.

Chloe smiled. 'What happened?'

'Well, last week, Kate got this zonking attack of stage fright. Belle was furious with her, and even Mr Day was a bit fed up. We all thought she would be better next time, but she wasn't, she got worse. Mr Day gave her until tonight to pull herself together – it's the first full rehearsal, the whole play. But this morning Kate's mother sent a note saying Kate had been worrying about it all so much that there was no question of allowing her to continue. And, well – I'm the only other person who knows the part,' she finished modestly.

'Tilda, my goodness. And do you feel confident about it?'

'Not too bad. I mean, I really do know the lines because Belle has been so obsessive about rehearsing. She's thrilled, of course. You'd think, to listen to her, that she had arranged it all herself. In fact, it was probably her fault that poor Kate started freezing completely on stage, when at first she was only nervous. She's such a perfectionist.'

'Is she now?' murmured Chloe politely.

'Anyway, I think I might not make too bad a job of it. I'm certainly going to do my best.'

Was this her hesitant child?

'I can't wait till the first night. We're going to get a terrific kick out of seeing you all out there, watching us; all the Oliviers and the Cavendishes lined up to support Helen and Belle and me. I'm looking forward to it like an extra birthday, aren't you?'

Chloe had indeed given some thought to the occasion. It terrified her. 'We all are,' she said.

'Mr Cavendish is coming to rehearsal tonight, so I'd better be good. I don't want to disappoint him.'

'You won't, you'll be a nice surprise.'

She must somehow train her body to refrain from reacting in any one of a dozen treacherous ways when Luke's name was spoken. This time there had been a deep throb under her breastbone, as though someone were trying to coax a note out of a main artery.

'I'll need every spare minute,' Tilda frowned purposefully. 'Would you believe there are only ten days left?'

The throbbing came again. Perhaps this was what was meant by a panic attack. Chloe had never quite believed in those. She would be more sympathetic in future.

Ten days. Ten days to put her shaken world back the way it had been before Luke had come smiling down that hillside and failed to tell her, until too late, much too late for either of them, that he was the guardian of her children, thus handing her a ready-made relationship which would have involved safe pleasantries, parents' meetings, little chats about academic progress, possibly even friendship, but not love; never the demon love that feeds on fire and cares for nothing but its own perpetuation.

Or was she deceiving herself? Yes, certainly she was. No social structure yet devised was proof against pheromones and an English romantic education.

Nevertheless, in ten days it would have to be. They would all be together, as Tilda had described, she and her husband and her lover and her lover's wife and several of their children, in celebration of the talents and friendships which were important to all of them. It had to work. It would work, surely, if everyone wanted it to.

And then the fire struck again. And yet, she thought. *And yet* rendered her instantly helpless.

And yet, it is all wrong, is it not? We ought to be together, oh my best beloved. How shall I bear it, how will you, if we are never to be together? She felt a heaviness in her breasts and touched them because Luke could not. She had no control over her body's responses. Such a humiliation left her without dignity, but then that had long been gone.

Empty and raging, she called his name.

She cried. She could not stop herself. She cried as a child does, weeping freely and angrily, giving herself over to pain.

It seemed to her in the unexpected reversal of this breaking down that the whole reality of her life was contained in the hours she had shared with Luke. Now each jewel-bright second was split and splintered, refracted through tears, the broken shards of absolute perfection. They entered her heart like knives of glass. They had been a necklace of rare beads, snapped and spilled in anger by the malign magician, Love, whose high powers had come to nothing, who watched her perfect hours go rolling across the sunlit floor of Arden Court.

When she had regained what would pass for command of herself, Chloe took refuge in her studio. Here, the painting was a silent, supportive presence, a witness to her acknowledgment of grief, the only one she could tolerate.

At ten, Alain looked in, wondering that she should be working so late. When he saw her face he went quietly away.

It has happened only now, she thought, while she scattered brilliant beads of colour across the skies, the graves and the millefiori gardens of her visionary village. I did not know it. I thought it was already accomplished, but I was wrong. It was only a blind, a lure for Luke to follow where I needed him to go. But I did not go there myself. All my morality was for him, to prick and persuade. It is only now that I know I must truly give him up.

Love is a wound within the body. Even that is too much. Die, love, die. Love is dead. Long live love. It's dead but it won't lie down. I may be going a little mad, but not so mad that anyone will notice. I may even, if I am lucky, find a certain amount of freedom in it.

*

In the morning, while Chloe was at her maddest and lowest, Luke phoned. She could only weep.

Destroyed by her sorrow he asked if he could come to her. She would not allow it.

'What will we do?' he asked. His voice was stripped and raw so that she mourned for its lost cadences of piracy and persuasion.

'We will do what we said we would do. I'll see you at the First Night. Goodbye, Luke.'

'Chloe, don't go.'

Chapter Eighteen

❦❦❦❦❦❦❦

THE MOVEMENTS OF THE CAVENDISH household were difficult to choreograph. The rules were unwritten and breakable on pain of some discomfort. They were as follows; Luke and Dinah might occupy a room at the same time, provided that it was not their bedroom or that it did not also contain Oliver. While both of them could behave quite normally with Belle, Dinah was no longer comfortable with Adam, whose involvement in adult affairs was embarrassing to her, while Luke naturally felt the same about Oliver, who, helpfully, had devised a policy of see-and-flee in relation to his father. Dinah and Olly went into partisan huddles in the kitchen, Adam treated everyone exactly as he had always done, and they all colluded to bamboozle Belle, who would barely have responded had she been told that every room in the house had been mined, so consummate was her preoccupation with her own drama.

Indeed, when Helen Cavendish arrived, with her usual drums and trumpets, to stay with them throughout the week of the play, Belle was the only one to greet her with a pleasure undiluted with relief and gratitude such as can be expected on the arrival of a bomb-disposal unit.

Helen, who had found a new hairstyle, lost another five

years and had countless adventures to impart, had so far defused the situation by the end of her first evening that everyone was talking to everybody and nobody was rude to anyone. This was a matter of some satisfaction to Watson and more so to Holmes, who was of a neurasthenic disposition and hated scenes. They knew whom to thank and followed Helen about, sinking their large heads on her knees at every opportunity and helping her with her dinner.

The next day being a Sunday, Belle announced that she was going over to the Oliviers' and suggested that Helen might like to accompany her and deliver a timely boost to Tilda's confidence.

'Love to, darling,' Helen said readily. 'It will be nice to meet Alain and Chloe again. And that lovely girl, Miranda wasn't it?'

'Yes. She probably won't be there.' Or so one hoped.

'I might come with you,' Adam offered.

'Great.' (Belle hoped more fervently.)

'Anyone else?' Helen asked.

'You might take the dogs. They need a walk,' Dinah replied.

Not for the first time, she smiled sunnily at Helen, whose mind whizzed busily, visiting possibilities that might explain this sudden popularity. She could settle on none, so she summoned the adoring dogs and returned the smile, accepting her luck where it was found.

Her first impression was that the Oliviers were considerably more relaxed than the Cavendishes. But even here there was something, a scent in the air of almost too much kindness. She noticed that Adam was also a part of it. Like all good actors, Helen had a deep and merciless curiosity about other people's business. When she found that Chloe, like Dinah, was disposed to be more friendly towards her, she began to make out what must have happened. It was serious then? A trapdoor opened and unceremoniously dumped an established part of her emotional security. She felt a little sick, but it was only jealousy. She knew how to deal with that.

'How is Dinah?' Chloe was asking her, too casually, as they drank their second cup of coffee.

'She's fine. Looking forward to seeing the play.'

'Good.' Chloe could think of nothing to add.

'Aunt Helen,' said Belle importantly, 'would you mind if we did just one scene together, right now? I think it would help Tilda if she got a bit of practice with you before she has to do it on stage.'

It was by no means pure kindness that animated her, though she did indeed want to banish every trace of nerves in Tilda; the scene she had chosen was the one in which Adam would have to kiss her again. Miranda, who had not had the grace to be absent, could reprise Miss Prism.

Helen was happy to oblige, while Tilda, who had worked on her role with such dedication that she no longer suffered from any nerves to speak of, would not have dreamed of saying so.

Adam, who remembered the scene and also the last time Belle had kissed him, suggested that, this time, Alain should read the part of Jack Worthing. Contemptuous of his cowardice, Belle determined to make him pay for it. She kissed Alain with a swooning ardour that shocked, surprised and delighted him in roughly equal parts. He noted the sideways slide of her remarkable eyes towards Adam and felt a wistful sympathy for that honest and decent young man. This wicked and skilful child would probably prove capable of keeping up her obsession until both she and her half-brother were old and grey, in Adam's case prematurely.

To punish her he kissed her back. She appeared to enjoy it. Chloe was not watching, though Helen was.

When the scene was over and Belle had stopped flirting

with him, he invited Helen to smoke with him again, in the garden.

They tramped amicably along frosted paths. There were berries to admire, and evergreens. Alain held her arm very lightly.

'You have no summerhouse here,' she regretted.

'None.'

'Perhaps it is just as well.'

He smiled. 'Possibly.'

She blew a smoke-ring at him. 'Paris was delightful,' she said.

'It was.'

'I shall be there again in April. Like the song.'

'I will remember that.'

It was not a promise, as it had been before. Neither was it a rebuff. She laid her hand on his arm. 'I like to keep my friends, Alain. As friends, whatever else they may or may not be.'

He covered the hand with his own. 'You always will. You have a gift for friendship.'

'I have a gift for turning lovers into friends. And while this means my life is never quite as interesting as my reputation, I would recommend the habit.'

Alain sighed. 'It's an admirably positive attitude, but I'm not sure it would always work as well as it does for you.'

She looked at him attentively. 'Why not?'

He grimaced. 'Perhaps I had better tell you what has happened here.'

'I think I can guess.'

'Not all of it.'

He was brief and comprehensive. Helen became visibly more shocked. 'My God, Alain, I had no idea you'd all been going through such horrors. I'm so sorry. Poor Miranda. She is enormously brave to have this baby. I just hope that little psychopath pays for everything he's done.'

Alain shrugged. 'That's in the lap of the gods. But

Miranda will do very well. Like all of us, she is learning that she is much tougher than she had realised. I expect your family is finding the same.'

'My family?' Helen looked surprised. 'Yes, I suppose they are the nearest thing I have to one, now that my parents are dead. Odd, but I hadn't thought of it. And yes, they seem to be coping. They were a bit shell-shocked when I first arrived, but they are recovering. The play helps.'

Alain smiled. 'It's true. The play holds us all together, whether we like it or not. But I still don't believe I could watch Chloe turn your ex-husband into a friend. Too much trouble has come out of all this for me to forgive him easily.'

'I understand that – but I hope you're not making the mistake of confusing the two elements in the story. The blackmail and Miranda's relationship with Joel are quite apart. As for Luke and Chloe, well, you should be the first to admit that this is life; it happens. And what would you prefer? A nice, tidy boredom? Don't worry too much. The pain will fade in time. It always does. Thank God, everything changes.'

'I know. I have changed myself. I have become afraid of losing Chloe.'

'What a very salutary thing.'

'I might have known you would say that.'

'I have said it before, if you remember, in Paris.'

'So you did. Do you have any more of this sterling advice?'

'Oh yes.' Helen grinned unashamedly. 'Never let yourself be found out.'

'How romantic you are, Hélène.'

'My darling, it is the only way to *stay* romantic.' She looked at him wisely. 'Think about it.'

One of the many good things about Sheringham school

was its purpose-built theatre and concert-hall, a modern building set back among trees at a distance from the main house, and containing a level of mechanical, electrical and acoustic excellence which many public arenas might covet. The seats were comfortable too.

Tonight, the auditorium buzzed on a high note of expectancy. As a compliment to Helen, the audience presented themselves at their brightest and most decorative. There was a sense of occasion. There were hats, there was scent, there were fur, fake and feathers. The noise was deafening.

On the stage, at the crack in the blue velvet curtains, Rufus, who had no costume to get into, stood watching people arrive. He was surprised to find how many faces he recognised. It made him feel he belonged here.

'Are they here yet?'

He was joined by Tilda who was already dressed, though she would not come on until Act Two.

'Do I look OK?' she murmured.

'No need to whisper. Listen to that lot out there, like cows that need milking.' Critically, he looked her up and down. 'Yeah, you look good. Pretty,' he added magnanimously.

'Really?' She gave him a grateful smile. 'I'm glad you're here.'

'*You* don't need me. You know it all backwards.'

'No. I just meant – I'm glad you're here.'

'Oh, right. Thanks. So am I. It's fun to be doing something together again, even if you're a top dog and I'm only a dogsbody.'

'I'm not a top dog. Only Helen can be that. Hey, look, there's Dwayne, with his mother.'

'Cripes, she's even got Elvis to come, and his girlfriend. She looks like she escaped from a zoo in that spotty frock. Poor old Dwayne, he's in the doghouse too. And right now, he's the underdog and no mistake.'

'He must be, he's wearing a suit! Oh look, the parents have arrived. There, talking to the Cavendishes. Mum looks great. A bit serious, though.'

Rufus became guilty. 'I expect she's still pissed off about me. And Dad's got that sort of prowly look he gets when something's bugging him. God, I hope they soon forget Joel and all that. I'm in agony till they do.' Most of his agony was accountable to the donation Alain had induced him to make to a charity for drug-damaged children. It was goodbye to the Harley, for some years to come.

'Honestly, I bet they're thinking about something else entirely,' Tilda comforted. 'There you are, they're smiling now. They've said hello to Mrs Cubitt and they're finding their seats. Oh, no! The seats on either side are already taken. And Adam and Miranda are miles back, on their own. What a shame. I thought they would all sit together, us and the Cavendishes, like a real theatre claque.'

'I expect the Cavendishes have to sit with Mr Dacre.'

'I never thought of that. OK, I'd better get back to the dressing-room. It's nearly time for curtain-up. Wish me luck.'

'Of course I do, you silly old fart. Break a leg. Break both of them.'

'I wish they'd hurry up,' Miranda fretted. 'I can't relax until they've met.'

'Just don't expect too much,' Adam advised her. 'They're only going to exchange two polite words, not go into a grand reconciliation scene.'

Miranda bit her lip. 'But isn't that what tonight is meant to be about? Reconciliation? Public proof that we can all get on together.'

'Maybe, but it's better not to put too much weight on it, not just yet.'

'Don't, you're making me nervous. And it's so hot in here.' She fanned her face with her programme.

'Are you feeling wobbly?'

'No. Well, only for them. I just wish they didn't have to do this stupid handshaking.'

Her eyes, like Adam's, were riveted on the right-hand entrance to the stalls, where families, friends and local inhabitants were receiving a warm and personal welcome from Luke and Dinah.

'Why can't Philip Dacre do it? He's the Head,' Miranda said querulously.

'I think he feels it expedient to his eminence to maintain a certain *gravitas* on these occasions,' Adam mocked Philip's rotund style. 'Besides, this is Dad's departmental showcase, not his.'

Miranda laughed, then stiffened and clutched his hand. 'Here they are.'

They watched avidly as Alain and Chloe came in together, Chloe a little ahead. She hesitated infinitesimally, and moved forward to touch the hand Luke held out to her, their fingers barely connecting. Then she turned to Dinah, who was regarding her with a fierce smile, while Alain nodded to Luke who did not, this time, extend his hand. Dinah evidently said something amusing, for they all smiled before Alain and Chloe passed on to look for their seats.

'That wasn't so bad, was it?' Adam asked.

'I guess not. I bet it felt awful, though. Poor Dad.'

'Poor everyone.'

'I suppose so. Oh well, it's over. At least, until the interval.'

'Don't think about that now. Oh look, there's Olly.'

Oliver had arrived late on purpose. He feared embarrassment and would not have come at all did it not mean that he would see Chloe again. He exchanged a few words with his parents and looked round for her. She was just about to sit down in the third row back. Good, he would be able to sit behind her and watch her instead of the play.

He stood at the end of her row until he caught her eye, then nodded and blushed in her direction. She waved and smiled just like anyone else's mother. She looked wonderful, in something long and soft in midnight blue, and her hair was plaited into a kind of coronet. The sight of her made him want to fall on his knees.

Chloe saw very well how he felt. She hoped she had not looked like that when she had been forced to touch Luke's hand. The electric exchange had brought to mind Michelangelo's hand of God.

Beside her, Alain studied the programme. 'Gwendolen – Matilda Olivier,' he read proudly. 'I just can't believe how completely she has changed. A year ago she would barely go out of the house.'

'A year ago, she didn't know Belle,' Chloe said firmly.

'You are right. It is a good friendship.' Alain was eager to be generous where he could. 'I 'ope,' he added, recalling Belle's less scrupulous side, 'that the influence flows both ways.'

'The affection does, and that is the important part. Alain, I think the curtain is about to go up.'

The first act was a revelation. Helen's Lady Bracknell was new and rather startling. One could see in her not only the beloved gorgon of happy anticipation, but a woman of wit and intelligence confined by an aristocratic marriage within the strictures of a society as narrow and suffocating as a cruelly-laced corset. Her revenge for this, and her chief pleasure, was to employ the power awarded her station in manipulating that society according to her whim.

What Helen did was to allow half-caught glimpses of the younger, less acerbic woman, one who, like her daughter, could be conscious of her attractions and certain of her worth, a woman with something to look forward to. In Gwendolen one could see precisely what she once might have been, for Belle played her as every inch her mother's daughter. She knew it, the audience recognised it, Oscar had even laid it out in so many words; only poor besotted Jack Worthing remained unstruck by the lightning realisation that to marry Gwendolen would be one day to wake up and find himself married to her mother.

'Isn't she wonderful?' Dinah said, wiping her eyes in the interval.

'Astounding,' Luke marvelled. 'I had no idea. Every time I looked in on a rehearsal she seemed to be telling someone else what to do. I saw nothing like this. Little witch.'

'I guess she was aiming at hitting us over the head with it. And I, for one, am sufficiently stunned to take her seriously from now on.'

'That sounds like Belinda. But how on earth did she and Helen manage to work it all out in the short time available to them? Beats me. Anyway, come on. Let's circulate and collect sheaves and garlands of congratulations upon having such a gifted daughter.'

'Yes, let's.' Forgetting everything outside the gratifying moment, Dinah linked her arm in his.

'I never thought she would be as good as this,' Chloe said, glowing. 'So elegant, and far more presence than I expected.'

'I thought she might surprise us,' Alain smiled.

'And as for Belle – my goodness, what a prodigy! It looks as if we're present at the birth of a new theatrical dynasty.'

'You're forgetting; she and Helen are not related.'

'Oh, no. They aren't, are they? Funny how alike they are.'

'Are they? *Alors, chérie*, shall we make an attempt on the bar?'

'If you like. No, just a minute. Here's Rufus.' She welcomed the reprieve, being none too enthusiastic about repeating the earlier unnerving experience with Luke and

Dinah. 'Hello, darling, are you enjoying it? Aren't they all marvellous?'

'It's terrific. Loads better than the dress rehearsal. Here, I've got an invitation for you, from Helen Cavendish. She's having a celebration party in the bar after the show. There'll be food and everything.'

'Oh. Thank you.' Chloe became nervous again. 'What do you think, Alain?'

'I think we could not possibly refuse,' he said pleasantly. 'Thank you Rufus. We'll see you later, then.'

'Fine. Do you know where the Cavendishes are? I've got to deliver their invitation too.'

'They'll be at the bar,' Chloe told him. 'Adam and Miranda too, I expect. I'm not sure about Olly – oh, there he is, behind us.' She smiled at Oliver again and he waved happily back.

'That boy seems to like you,' Alain remarked.

'He's a nice boy. He likes everybody. Do we have to go to the bar?'

'Not if you don't want to.'

'I don't. The party will be more than enough. Do you think Helen did it on purpose?'

'Did what?'

'Kept the invitations back until the interval, so that it would look really ungracious to refuse?'

'Oh yes. I am absolutely sure of it. I think there is an additional role which she is eager to play tonight. That of the Good Fairy Catalyst.'

'Really? What makes you think that?'

'Just that I have an idea that Helen is a far nicer person than many people would give her credit for.'

'I don't see how you can deduce that from smoking a couple of Gauloises with her and listening to her banging on about the French theatre.'

'No? *Eh bien*, per'aps I am mistaken. It may be that she simply likes parties.'

Helen had extended her invitation to the families of everyone who had worked on the play. This meant that although the crowd would be large enough to cover any awkwardness between the Oliviers and the Cavendishes, it would still be small enough to prevent their avoiding each other. With Adam's discreet help, she had provided them with some delicious food, sent over by John and Claudie's chef, and an absurdly generous amount of wine. She was also ready to perform any social engineering that might be necessary. Meanwhile they could all get on with it for half an hour while she signed autographs and gave interviews to a couple of TV channels.

'Here. I hope there's enough. I know how hungry you get when you're nervous.' Adam presented Miranda with a very large plateful of hot, crisp and creamy delicacies, and removed a bottle of wine and glasses from his pockets.

'God, it looks wonderful.' Miranda seized a glistening vol-au-vent and demolished it in two bites. 'Oh, yum.'

They had spread themselves and their feast halfway up the curving staircase that led from the bar to the upper offices of the theatre. Its rails were minimal and they were well-placed to observe the festive chaos below, including any further performances by their relatives.

'Hello, here's Philip Dacre. He's decided to socialise, after all.'

'He's helping himself to a whole bottle, just like you,' Miranda noticed with amusement. 'And *two* glasses.'

They watched the imposing figure mow his way slowly through the crowd, shedding pleasantries on either side, until he reached the recipient of the second glass.

'It's Dinah,' Miranda said. 'He's made her laugh, that's good. They're touching glasses. Looks a bit conspiratorial to me.'

'Perhaps he's managed to persuade her to take on some

more work. She said he had asked her. Apparently he wants a sort of full-time psychiatric housemother.'

'Does she want to do it?'

'I think she does. She seems to have become bored or disillusioned or something, with her trips into the alternative life. And it would give her less time to brood. If she is doing.'

'Can't you tell?'

'Oddly enough, I can't. She seems OK, a bit hectic, but she always was.'

'Have another glass,' invited Philip.

'Two is enough for the first ten minutes,' Dinah said. 'At this rate, I shall be completely blotto in half an hour. Most unsuitable, but not altogether unlikely. You know, there's something about you that makes me want to go to extremes.'

'You are not the only one,' Philip murmured.

'Good. Hadn't you better go and talk to people? This is getting dangerous.'

'I don't want to talk to anyone but you,' he said even more softly. 'And I don't want to *talk* to you.' He smiled at her politely.

'In that case, you may as well go home.'

He filled her glass whether she wanted it or not. 'There is just one thing we do have to talk about.'

'What?'

'The time and place of our next meeting. Something that will fit in with your domestic arrangements.'

Dinah found herself swaying slightly towards him. She had a sudden vivid picture of his unclothed body, large, powerful and priapic. She straightened, took a deep breath and thought quickly. 'Tuesday evening. Seven forty-five. Your place.'

'That will be very satisfactory, Mrs Cavendish,' he asseverated in his headmaster's voice, regretfully letting himself be importuned by a parent.

I know it will, Dinah exulted, gracefully giving way. And the wonderful thing about it is that I shall not feel even the tiniest twinge of conscience. Funny, I suppose I have Luke to thank for that.

It was not, she had decided, because she loved Luke any the less that she was able to allow herself to sleep with Philip; it was because his infidelity had hurt her so deeply that, in the end, it had set her free from her utter dependency upon that love and its reciprocation.

She would never leave Luke. She hoped he would not leave her. But if he should, it would not be the end of the world, although she did not deceive herself that it would seem anything less than that in the event.

The crowd parted before Tilda like a benign Red Sea, depositing her, lapped in congratulations, before her parents. The boy who had played Algernon to her Cecily followed in her stately wake.

'Mum, Dad,' she said, holding fast to the new-found confidence derived from her role, 'I'd like you to meet Paul.'

Alain and Chloe, she was relieved to find, behaved as though she introduced young men to them every week, and her father quickly discovered that Paul shared his own fascination with the more recalcitrant examples of the internal combustion engine.

'So it's all right if I ask him round on Sunday?' she asked Chloe quietly.

'I was just about to,' Chloe smiled. 'Come here, you beautiful creature. I've been waiting all evening to give you a hug. We're so proud of you.'

'Dad too?'

'He'll tell you himself, as soon as he gets the chance. He seems nice, your friend, easy to get on with.'

'Yes, he is. Thanks, Mum.' Tilda returned the hug.

'What for?'

Oh, I don't know.' She smiled shyly. 'Thanks, anyway.'

The thing about Paul, she had discovered to her intense relief and pleasure, was that, although he had admitted to finding her unbearably desirable, he had no intention of hurrying her. What was interesting was that she thought she might soon quite like him to hurry her. She found him immensely attractive and her physical response to him was strong but in no way frightening. He was an accomplished musician and was even beginning to compose. There seemed to be nothing missing in the recipe for a good relationship – except, perhaps, a certain element of danger. It was not Paul who figured in some of the dreams that came to her when she was not quite asleep.

Chloe circulated for a while to give Alain his opportunity to set the stars in Tilda's crown by telling her what he had thought of her performance. She was about to join the group containing Mike and Maggie when a woman moved away in front of her and she suddenly saw Luke. He stood, glass in hand, laughing at someone's joke while his eyes roved about the room in a restless, hungry search. She looked too long and they found their rest. The commotion in the room receded, leaving her with him at the centre of a charged stillness.

'My God,' said Adam. 'Will you look at that. Talk about "Across a Crowded Room".'

'Oh no, please no,' Miranda moaned. 'They can't. They mustn't look at each other like that. Anyone can see how they feel.'

'Wait,' Adam said.

Chloe smiled faintly. She felt as if she was coming apart. She raised her hand in a vague salute and turned away.

'Excellent,' approved Dinah, who was standing behind

her. 'Quite admirable.' She waved her glass in emphasis, splashing her dress. 'But can you keep it up?'

Chloe assimilated shock. 'I think so,' she said gravely.

'Good. Because I don't suppose *he* can.' She thumbed over her shoulder towards the space where Luke had been. 'Men are not as accustomed as we are to denying themselves what they want.'

She knew that, in her present circumstances, this was not quite playing the game, but she had given up that particular game. On the other hand, Chloe's distress was a palpable thing. To her surprise, she derived no satisfaction from this.

'I thought Tilda was just perfect,' she said warmly. 'I wouldn't be surprised if she ends up at RADA or somewhere, with Belle.'

Chloe was grateful, though bewildered by the warmth. It was difficult to keep up with Dinah. It was probably best simply to follow her lead. 'As far as I know, she still favours the Royal College of Music.'

'I know, but Belle is developing this grand life-plan for the two of them. She wants them both to go to RADA and also to share some space, as she puts it, in some desiccated dive in one of the more depraved parts of the city.'

'I see.' Chloe smiled. 'Couldn't they share the space but go to different colleges? Supposing any of them will take either of them.'

'Yeah, I guess – but you know what it's like. Best friends and all that? Never apart, thick and thin, shoulder to shoulder, what's mine is yours—' Dinah spurted into laughter. 'Oh Lord, what am I saying? I didn't mean – well, sorry. Anyway, that's Belle's plan. It'll be interesting to see what happens when the time comes.'

'Yes, it will,' Chloe agreed, shaken once more. 'I suppose they will still be friends.'

'I'm sure they will. For one thing, no man will ever come between them.'

'Oh. Why?' She met Dinah's eyes which were slightly blurred and definitely mischievous.

'Because Belle has the good sense, quite remarkable at her age, to be so single-minded about acting that boys just don't get a look in. The minute they get serious, she chucks them. Very wise. Friends are different.' The blurred eyes narrowed. 'She really values her friends. She hasn't had one as close as Tilda since she was ten. That was Beth. She moved away. They still write.' She sighed sharply. 'I suppose what I am really talking about is you and me.'

Chloe entered a spiral of apprehension. 'How do you mean?'

Dinah emptied her glass. 'I mean that you and I were on the way to a really good friendship. Damn it, we were almost there. And then you and Luke had to go and mess it all up. It's such a waste, Chloe, a shame and a waste.'

'Yes, it is.' So let's try to do something about it. 'Do you think – might it be possible to rescue a bit of it? I mean, we are all going to meet, almost daily, some of us, for as long as the children make it happen.'

'I don't know. It couldn't be the same, how could it?' Dinah backtracked for the sake of her pride. 'But I suppose we ought to try to salvage something. Otherwise it's going to be permanent hell having to pretend in front of the children every time they devise one of their devilish compulsory family treats. Then there's your grandchild, whom Adam seems intent upon godfathering. He's actually started buying baby clothes.'

'He really is the paradigm of the New Man. Miranda is very lucky.'

'Yeah. One of those cute little Babygro things, striped like a bee.'

Chloe felt the nudge of unreality. How Luke would laugh if he could hear. 'The thing is,' she said, with false calm, 'do you really mean any of this? Or are you just a bit drunk?'

'I mean it, I think.'

'But can you trust me enough?' This was what Dinah really needed to ask herself.

'Oh, I think so,' she drawled. 'After all, you have already produced the equivalent of the brewer's dray for this incarnation. I'm probably safe with you now. Come on, for God's sake, let's have another drink.'

'You drink too much,' Chloe said.

'I know. I enjoy it.'

'The last time I saw you drinking like this,' Chloe returned with painful honesty, 'you were doing it so that you could tolerate Helen. I just hate to think that now you are doing it in order to tolerate me.'

'I am not,' Dinah insisted cheerfully. 'I'm simply having a good time. That is what I've decided to do, from now on.'

'This is incredible,' Miranda said, with tears in her eyes. 'I can't believe they're talking to each other. Dinah must be a saint.'

For herself, she could not imagine ever speaking to the unspeakable Cally Baker again, unless to tell her exactly what breed of bitch she was.

'That's why the party was such a good idea. People show their real feelings more when they've had a drink. Especially Dinah.'

'Maybe. I'm never sure about that. Hey, look, there's more.' She pointed.

'Now that, I didn't expect.'

Alain had taken note of everyone's position in the room, including that of the recording angels on the stairs, and judged this to be his best opportunity to combine what he saw as his duty to one situation and his penance for another. He made his move accordingly.

'Luke – *si vous avez un moment*?' He was unaware of

using his native tongue, having done so instinctively out of nervousness.

Luke turned quickly at the accents of the *Troisième Arrondissment* and concluded that Damocles had chosen an unsportingly public place in which to make his suspended strike.

'As many as you like,' he said courteously.

'I will not keep you long.'

Alain wondered if it was possible to abhor the thing a man has done without feeling the same abhorrence for the man. He would have liked, very much, to knock Luke down, here and now, but he also entertained the quixotic notion of helping him up afterwards. Chloe must have brainwashed him with her gentle but determined blackmail on behalf of the children. He sighed and did what he had to do.

'I have been thinking,' he said, with careful attention to his aspirates, 'about that talk you asked me to give to your students. You will remember?'

Luke was amazed. The sword, it seemed, was no longer pending. 'Of course I remember.'

'*Bien*. I regret that I have been unable to do it before now. I have simply not had the time. But if you would like, we can discuss a date for it, early next term?'

Luke produced a dazed smile. 'That is really very kind of you.'

'I suppose it is,' Alain agreed.

This caused Luke to reflect upon the smallness of the satisfaction derived from doing the right thing. Especially, since he was not at all convinced that it was the right thing.

Surely it would be more honest, and therefore more moral, to obey his instinct to sweep Chloe up and carry her off in his navy blue Citroën to some attractive and economically viable end of the earth, preferably Mediterranean, than to deny that instinct and allow her to deny it too, and tamely submit to the fiendishly painless traps of

Dinah's and Alain's good nature?

Evidently some of his reasoning was obvious to Alain, who drew deeply on his Gauloise and looked amused. 'I would prefer it to be mid-week, if possible,' he said.

'I'm sure we can work something out. I really am very grateful.'

Alain shrugged. 'It's a good idea. I shall be glad to do it.'

'Right. Well. I'll call you, then?'

'Yes, do.' Alain hesitated. 'Have you – did you enjoy tonight?'

'Very much.'

'So did I.'

They both nodded, not quite smiling. As they were about to part, honour if not honesty satisfied, the scent of the casbah was suddenly with them.

'Darlings!' Helen kissed each one soundly on the cheek. 'My two favourite men in the world. I want to hear you tell me again how wonderful I was. The BBC man said a sexy Lady Bracknell was a wicked conjuring trick that only I could perform. Alain, *chéri*, will you give me one of your horrible cigarettes? I've run out and I'll smoke anything.'

He tapped one up and offered it to her. Before taking it she opened her tiny bag and produced a gold lighter which he recognised as his own.

'Nice, isn't it?' She smiled innocently. 'A friend left it at my Paris flat. I forgot to return it last time we met, but I expect he will come and collect it one day. It's far too good to lose.' She dropped it back into the bag and snapped the clasp.

'Indeed it is,' Alain agreed, with the finest edge to his voice.

It had been a present from Chloe when he had given up giving up smoking. He had not known where he had left it. He would certainly have to recover it, one way or another.

Luke, watching Helen's smug expression, had the oddest presentiment that she was in some way making fools of them both; but the only way that occurred to him was patently absurd. Surely? God knew, he was accustomed to her teasing by now, but tonight he could not bring himself to join in her mischief.

He patted her on the arm and excused himself.

He had to look for Chloe. They had still not spoken except at the door, when her fingers had vibrated against his and rendered him savage with resentment at what she was doing to them both. He could only assume she was avoiding him.

He found her at last, talking to Claudie. She looked pale and tired. She caught sight of him and her face softened in that lovely way she had, and he forgave her everything. Claudie was waving her arms in exasperation. 'He is a charming boy. I simply do not understand Lisa. It's not as if we're asking her to form any relationship she doesn't want. But it's time she began to go out again. It isn't right for a young girl to stay in and mope for months on end. He has only asked her to a party. All her friends will be there. They have been so supportive, all of them, coming to see her, bringing her schoolwork, records, gossip – but she can't expect that to go on forever. I wish you would talk to her, Chloe. She is so fond of you. Luke – hello!' She seized his arm and kissed him on both cheeks. 'Come and tell me what to do with Lisa. I simply have to get her out of the house and back to school after Christmas.'

Luke accepted the kisses without returning them and smiled gently at Chloe. 'I think you should let her take whatever time she needs. But I agree that Chloe should speak to her. She seems to have a way with young people and their problems.'

Claudie nodded. 'I'm so sorry that she wouldn't let Dinah counsel her.'

He shrugged. 'Probably too much like an official shrink.'

'I'll talk to her, if you like,' Chloe said. 'Though I can't promise it will be any help.'

They debated the problem until, providentially, John appeared and whisked Claudie away to introduce her to someone.

'Thank God,' Luke breathed. 'How are you, my love?'

'Don't look at me like that.'

'I can't help it.'

'Please try.'

'If you're worried about people reading our minds, why don't we move closer to the wall? We can pretend to admire the pictures.'

She followed him and they stood facing each other, half-turned towards a watercolour landscape with towering trees and a stone pavilion.

'Actually, it's rather fine,' he said. 'It reminds me of one of those first sketches of yours, the one you were working on the day we met. It has the same blue-green sadness about it.'

'Thank you. It's by John Piper,' she said, feeling unsteady. 'This is not fair of you, Luke.'

He sighed. 'I'm sorry. I don't think I shall ever be able to talk to you like a parent, or a stranger.'

'You don't have to. Why not treat me as a friend, for God's sake, like Claudie, or Maggie. But without the flirting.'

'They do the flirting, not me. I suppose I could try. But the trouble is – oh, Chloe, I don't know if I can really manage any of it. I've been so bloody, purgatorially miserable without you.'

'Don't. You must know how that makes me feel.'

'We've got to meet,' he said urgently. 'I can't bear to stand so close to you and not be able to touch you. It makes me want to tear off all our clothes and fuck you to pieces, right here in front of everyone.'

'Luke.'

'If you want to prevent something like that, you had better agree to meet me. Will you come to Friday Street next week? It will be the only chance before the Christmas break.'

She sighed helplessly, wanting to laugh, needing to weep. 'Would you promise me that it would be the last time, *really* the last time?'

'I'd promise you anything you wanted.' His eyes shone.

'And then break your word.'

'Only if I were *in extremis*, as I am now.'

'I believe all it will do is to stretch out the pain, further and further each time we meet. It makes it twice as unbearable. No, I won't come.'

He moved closer to her. 'Don't you want to?'

She could smell him, now, not just the residual tang of soap or aftershave, but the true scent of him that she loved and missed and wanted all over her.

'You know I do.'

'Then, please. I beg you.'

'Hush. Someone is bound to notice us, soon.'

'I don't give a damn if they do.'

She saw the pirate behind his smile and felt herself weakening. She glared at him. 'Well, I do. We have to be able to do this properly. You can't ruin everything now.'

'It's you who ruins everything,' he said bitterly, 'by denying what there is between us. No – I'm sorry. I know that's not true. Oh God, this is horrible.'

'Yes, it is. If you can see that, why do you let it happen? I don't want to remember us like this, our words and our way of being with each other reduced to such pathetic poverty. Let go, Luke, before we shame ourselves and what we really are, what we really feel. I want to remember you when every word you spoke made me drunk with pleasure, and I had never seen you angry. I want to think only of the loving, not of the pain.'

'Isn't that cheating? Isn't the whole truth the only truth?'

'What do you mean?'

'I mean,' he said, disturbing her with his intensity, 'you are tearing something up by the roots, and yet you still insist it is a healthy plant. I call that hypocritical.'

'Is that what you think? I'm sorry.'

He saw how much he had hurt her and said quickly, 'Look, we obviously need to talk, perhaps to be more honest with each other. We can't leave it there. Say you will meet me.'

Chloe hesitated. She had been sure of her way when she came here, but Luke had always possessed the ability to turn her certainties into doubts. Perhaps he was right. If he felt like this, then they did need to talk.

'All right.' She met his eyes. 'I will come to Friday Street. And now, I'm going to talk to Mike and Maggie. I can't stay with you any longer.'

He caught her arm as she turned away and bent his head above hers. 'I love you,' he whispered.

She was shaking so much as she left him that she was afraid someone would think she was ill. She stood still for a moment near the foot of the staircase, dazedly trying to collect herself. As she lifted her head to take in more air, something colourful caught her eyes. It was Miranda, sitting on the stair with Adam. They waved to each other. Miranda blew her a kiss.

She went downstairs to the foyer and sat on a chair in the deserted coffee bar. She had never been so tired. This schizophrenic existence was wearing her out; keeping up a pretence of some little strength for Luke, showing a different kind to Alain, another – a counterfeit of daily serenity – for the children, neighbours, friends; while all the time she was drained and wretched with weakness, with sorrow, and a love that no longer had a lap in which to lay its head.

It was almost as if she were in mourning, except that, whatever Luke pretended to think, nothing had died.

Chapter Nineteen

ON WEDNESDAY, LUKE WAITED AT the end of the
woodland path until he was quite sure that she was
not coming. Then he walked over to the Thomas
à Becket to use the phone.

At home, Chloe sat waiting for it to ring.

'Why aren't you here?'

'It was the only way. I had to show you. Telling you
doesn't work.'

'I'll give you one last chance to do what you really want
to do.'

'I am doing it, only you won't believe me.'

'No, I won't. Meet me here in twenty minutes. I've
decided what we must do. I'm going to take that job in
Verona, and you're coming with me.'

'No.' The phone in her hand was slippery with tears.

'The love that moves the earth and stars? Oh, Chloe.'

'No.'

'Just get here, that's all. Or, I'll come and fetch you.' He
rang off. She went to the studio, dried her eyes and sat
looking at nothing. Later, she drove round to Maggie's
house.

Perhaps, when he came, with his energy and his beauty

and his voice that was going to torment her every time she heard it, to try to take possession of her life, a second absence would convince him that this was something she would not allow him to do.

On a morning early in February, Chloe and Baskerville walked through the village in frosty sunlight among the early intimations of a spring their noses knew to be false. Yesterday the cold had rung like crystal, tomorrow it would do so again.

They came to Holly Cottage and Chloe glanced superstitiously over its wall. The garden was neat and bare and there was no sign of the child, Rosie, or of any part of Annalise.

When they entered St Mark's churchyard, she shivered as they passed between the leaning rows of gravestones in their verdigris great-coats. For the last few days a death had preyed upon her mind.

Unable, this particular morning, to face muscular kindness, she hoped she would not encounter the Reverend Nicholas Bannister. Beneath the vault of the porch she ran her fingers down the latest roster of lay duties and pressed them against Dinah's name in a pointless bid for reassurance.

'Stay here, boy,' she commanded Baskerville. 'I won't be long.' The great dog subsided obediently on a piece of matting designed to receive parishioners' boots, and nuzzled happily among the intriguing smells.

Chloe pushed open the west door, which barely complained in the cold weather, and found the church to be mercifully empty. She hoped it would remain so. She went slowly down the aisle without her usual affectionate acknowledgement of the praying hands of the arches as they closed above her head, or the rows of woodland eyes watching her from the kneelers.

In the chancel, in the space before the altar, the dead

knight slept on in the faint, stained light from the east window. Careful out of custom, she did not step on his worn brass silhouette. She took a chair and placed it beside the quatrefoil stone hearing-aid that assisted her in spirit across the centuries to the ear of Catherine Chandler.

'I am here because there is no one else I can talk to. You will not like what I came to tell you, but you will have heard such things before. The anchoress was the first resort of desperate women.

'However, let us not begin with desperation. Catherine, at last I have finished our painting. It is very beautiful; I think you would like it. It is beautiful not only because it is sumptuous to the eyes – though it is, oh, prodigally – but because it has a kind of spiritual balance to it which you would understand. Above all, it is a celebration, like a mass, composed in paint instead of music. The composer I had in mind was called Marenzio, but he lived later on than you did. It begins by celebrating the life of the senses, as a hedonist does, the young life of a girl who has not yet learned how to be unselfish, or indeed, why she should be; the girl you once were, and I was, and Miranda. We are all there, on the canvas. All our lives are there.

'But the picture also honours the life of the spirit, the life of sacrifice made in the name of love, the kind of sacrifice you made when you let them seal up all your abundant young life inside these breathless stones. You were far too young to know what you were doing. How do I know? I don't. I mix intuition with statistics and wishful thinking. Your father was still alive when you went into the wall, so you were unlikely, given the averages of your time, to be much over twenty. An age to be passionate about a man, not about God

'Yes, I know. I have *said* I cannot know. I can only approach you with my imagination, though it has always felt like something deeper, if there *is* anything deeper than the human imagination.

'It doesn't matter. You became an anchoress and I became a married woman, a step which, far from requiring any sacrifice on my part, seemed to me a glorious indulgence.

'But I am right, am I not? You were not yet ready to make the sacrifice. You survived three years of continence and chastity and the light of small candles and then you burst out into the eye of the sun. You can see it all in the painting, you look like a bride.

'And I, twenty years older, look out with the same singing gaze from another part of the canvas because I have broken out of my marriage, which was neither chaste nor cold, and frequently luminous with shared pleasures. And so there we are, you in your part of the village and I in mine, setting up shock waves of happiness that rocked our little world. I don't know what happened to you in those months of liberation, but what I discovered in loving Luke, apart from the sheer exhilaration of it, was a sense of perfect unity with another being. It has been the truest and purest of passions.

'I know, the general opinion, drawn from the inexorable evidence of human history, is that passion does not endure. Oh, I hope it does not. What you found in your freedom, it seems, was the way back to God. You learned that you had not been mistaken in your vocation, only premature. You also, perhaps, experienced perfect unity. You returned to your stone home, here, just behind my hands, and you praised the Lord and were happy because you had been able to make the sacrifice willingly, out of love.

'And that, in my godless, modern fashion, is what I am trying to do now. It is not a parallel but there are certain correspondences between us. I want more than anything else to remake my marriage, although it is sometimes difficult to maintain that desire against the sustained battery of temptation launched against me over the phone. You see, Luke has not given me up yet, except in public and

— 337 —

the eyes of his family. He calls me once or twice a week, to let me know that Rufus has done some creditable piece of work or that the temperature yesterday was 17°C. He has stopped asking me to meet him because I always put the phone down when he does that. I ought to put it down anyway, but I can't. He knows that.

'But I am trying. I will not give in.

'And now something has happened which makes everything different and terrible and far more difficult for me. It is the worst thing of all. I am carrying Luke's child.

'There is no question that it is his. I have worked out precisely when I must have forgotten to take my pill. Ironically, it was the very last time we made love. I missed the first period just over a week later. It should have happened during the week of the play, but what with all the family excitement and my own grieving over Luke, I didn't even notice. When I missed the second one I knew right away, before I'd even taken the test. I had it confirmed by a doctor. I went to the one who is treating Miranda. I didn't want to go to my own, here in Sheringham. Catherine, I cannot give birth to this child.

'I know. You would tell me it is the very worst of sins, and, believe me, I am not far from agreeing with you. You will say I shall be damned forever. My reply is that I already feel something of the torment which you envisage for those who are damned.

'Yet it is the only way. I can see no other choice.

'If I were to let Luke know that we have made a child, he would get up on his white horse and ride roughshod through the fragile supports of my household until he had reduced it again to the rubble from which we are slowly seeking to rebuild it. Yes, yes. He is the child's father. I could go with him to Verona and – and what? Be happy? Knowing what agony I had left for every other person whom I love. An agony which I would share, and Luke too, though at first he would not admit it. Indeed, our share would be the greater, and it would not end.

'And if I were to tell Alain? I honestly don't know what would happen. He might consider it too much to forgive, in which case we would part. If we were to do that, the family would be destroyed as surely as if I were to go away with Luke.

'Alain might, himself, suggest a termination. I suppose I think this the most likely outcome, knowing his generosity of spirit. In which case all I would have accomplished would have been to cause him great and unnecessary pain by revealing the pregnancy.

'If his generosity were that of a saint, he might accept the child as his own. I am the one who could not accept that. I would love not only the child but his father in him. Alain would know that and he would suffer permanently from my infidelity. And more; it would be a betrayal of Luke to leave him in ignorance of his living child, as it would be a crime against the child to deny him the knowledge of his father. So you will see how I am trapped? There *is* only the one way.

'Please try to understand, as I am trying.

'I have thought, although it is not in my nature, that I would like to kill myself, as well as the tiny creature who is folded inside me in what is now such perfect security. Perfect unity. Ah, God.

'But I shall not do that. I would be ashamed.

'There is a horrible logic about it, Catherine, in the end. It isn't much to cling to, but it is all I have. What I am going to do will undoubtedly bring about the greatest happiness for the greatest number of those who share my life. I am compelled by a utilitarianism of the heart.

'You ask, does that give me the right to take a life already begun? I have debated the issue so many times in my life. I have always maintained that, in the early weeks, a woman must have the right to choose what she will do. If it gives you any satisfaction, this choice is the hardest one I have ever made. I am going about my daily life in the knowledge that I carry within me a life and a death.

'I would like to ask for your blessing, Catherine. You may not wish to give it, but I have great need of it.'

She knelt close to the wall and thrust her hands through the leaves of the quatrefoil. It seemed that some cold comfort came to her through the stone.

Outside, in the equivocal sunlight, Baskerville was becoming impatient. He had abandoned the porch and was rooting about in the churchyard, turning over clods of earth and grass. As Chloe came out of the church he gave a deep bay of recognition and raced off in the opposite direction. She was mystified until she saw Miranda coming through the lych-gate, clad in a velvet rainbow and carrying a plumber's bag. The dog was leaping up to lick her face and herding her joyfully back towards the porch.

Chloe willed a transformation upon herself.

'Hello, my lovely,' she called shakily. 'What are you doing here?'

'My timetable has altered. I get Wednesdays off now to work on exam pieces, so I thought I'd come and take some expert advice.'

They kissed, holding each other a while.

'That's wonderful. How did you know where to look for me?'

'I met Mrs C in the post office. She said she saw you come up here.' She frowned. 'You haven't been crying, have you?'

'No, I've just got a bit of a cold.'

Miranda put her arms around her again. 'Oh, Mum. Doesn't it get any better?'

'I'm not sure I know how to answer that.' She smiled weakly.

'I saw him, last weekend. I wasn't going to tell you. He gave me a wicked grin and called out, in the middle of the village street – "Be sure to remember me to your charming mother". No wonder it's hard for you.'

'Never mind, sweetheart. I'll survive.'

'You'd better. I'm going to need you. And so is Moriarty.'

'Who?'

Miranda patted her thickening waist. 'It was Adam's idea. He said it would add some excitement to the lives of Holmes and Watson.'

'How thoughtful of him. What if it's a girl?'

'It's only a nickname. It would be even better for a girl. She could be the heroine of a cult movie. Hey, wait till I show you what's in here.' She knelt and searched vigorously inside her bag, assisted by Baskerville, and pulled out a diminutive blue jumpsuit scattered with yellow stars. There was also a yellow hat and a tiny pair of trainers with a criminally expensive label.

'Adam bought them. He's always buying things. Moriarty will be the best-dressed baby in Britain.'

Chloe smiled. 'Leave something for us to do, won't you?'

'Don't worry. That is partly why I came home today. There is something I want to ask you. It's pretty enormous, so you'll need some time to think about it. And we'll both understand if you say no.'

'You and the baby, or you and Adam?'

'All of us.' Miranda looked both smug and shy. 'We're going to be a family. Not marriage or anything, of course. But the girl who rents the loft next to mine is moving out, so Adam is going to take it. We're going to share everything, including Moriarty. It'll be just the same as having two parents.' Her eyes shone.

'I'm so glad, darling. Adam will make a perfect father-figure.'

'Yes, it does feel as if it might work. But we are going to need some help.'

'Tell me.'

'Well, I'm really keen to finish these two years at college, now I know I've got my grant. Adam will finish his course this year and he'll try to get a job right away. The thing is, until I do leave, I'm not going to be able to be a very good mother. However hard I try, there won't be enough time. It will be the same for Adam. We both want to do really well and get the best possible start afterwards. So, although I know I'm not going to want it this way, the best thing would be if there was someone else to look after Moriarty. You do see?'

For a split second her daughter's smile reminded Chloe of Joel, whom neither of them wished to mention. 'I'm beginning to,' she replied. Her heartbeat developed a disturbing stutter. 'You think I might do it?'

'Well, yes.' Anxiously Miranda tried to gauge her reaction. 'As I said, I know you will need to think about it.'

Chloe sat down on the bench the church fathers had thoughtfully provided for such apocalyptic moments.

'So you did,' she agreed. She needed to take this slowly. 'What exactly did you have in mind?'

'I thought, if you and Dad could work it out, that Moriarty might live with you during the week. And I could come out here on Wednesday afternoons and make up my college work in the evenings.'

'Wednesday afternoons?' Chloe repeated. Momentarily, the conversation slipped from her grasp.

'Yes. I know it would mean a lot of disruption for you, with your own work and everything. But it's got to be so much better for any child to be with its grandparents than with overstretched parents, much less some complete stranger you don't even know you can trust. Don't you think?' she added hopefully.

Chloe could not reply.

'Mum?'

She held her off with a small gesture. 'It's a lot to take

in, all at once. A kind of shock, I suppose.' The nature of which would never be fully known to Miranda.

'I'm sorry. I should have thought.'

'Don't worry. Just give me time to get used to the idea.'

'Of course. Look, I know it must seem as if I'm just being pig-selfish. Wanting to keep the baby and then loading the responsibility on to you. But that really isn't how I feel. I have to try to make sensible plans or I won't be able to cope. And this seems like the very best thing I could do for Moriarty.' She finished on a burst of passion.

'I know, my love, I know,' Chloe murmured.

Miranda looked at her, worried. She seemed vague, no longer quite present. She must be brought back.

'There is another dimension to it,' she said enticingly. 'I thought perhaps you might actually enjoy having another baby around after all this time.'

Chloe smiled, a stiff minor triumph over despair.

'I mean, you've always told us how nice it was when the three of us were little. But don't think – it's not that I don't know it's a huge thing to ask.'

'You don't, in fact,' Chloe sighed. 'Not yet. It's all right, Miranda. You don't need to say any more. It's a very sensible idea, you are right. But it does need a certain amount of consideration.'

'I know,' said Miranda humbly.

'Right. Look, why don't you take Baskerville for a walk along the stream and leave me to mull it over for a while?'

'OK. Fine. He'll be glad of the exercise.' She was eager to please. 'Come on, boy. Water!'

Chloe leaned against the wall behind the bench and closed her eyes. Contrary to her promise she tried to think of nothing. She would have liked to become a husk without content, flesh or thought, something which would blow away on the next lift of air, break down and disperse into unfeeling particles of universal dust.

But the very fancy cheated her desire and respite was not given. There was no escape. Like Miranda, she must make positive plans for a future or she would not survive. She had always known, her own mother had made it a first principle, that the simplest and most satisfactory method of survival was to involve oneself in the plans of others. Well, then?

She thought first of Wednesday afternoons. To be dedicated, in that planned future, to a different kind of loving.

Herself, her daughter and her daughter's child.

Behind her closed eyes there rose a rich vision from the Renaissance. She saw the child, dressed in starry blue garments, reaching out, laughing, from his seat in his grandmother's lap, to grab a handful of his mother's cinnabar hair. A modern version of Christ, the Virgin and St Anne. Without God, but containing all that could be required of love.

She thought of that other child, curled inside her, unnamed now and forever. She thought of his father and of the path not taken.

She had been right when she had said to Luke that there could be no great love that did not end in tragedy. What she could not have predicted was that the tragedy, though it would be of their making, would not, in the end, be their own. There was, she saw, a sad poetic justice in what must happen now. And afterwards?

There was to be no indulgent abandonment to grief. For here was Miranda, who would give no time or truck to tragedy, waiting to cram her arms full of her shared gifts of life and hope.

She began to tremble. She did not deserve such gifts. Surely this was not the impartial mask of justice come to trial?

It was not. With a lift of the heart, she recognised a different, a gentle face. It was what Catherine might have wished for her.

It was mercy.

Soon, she got up and went to look for Miranda. She found her crouching on the narrow footbridge over the stream that bounded one side of the churchyard. Baskerville was in the water, playing out fantasies with the sticks and stones she threw for him.

Chloe stood watching them. She envied their whole-hearted commitment to the moment, an instinct that now, sadly, seemed lost to her.

Baskerville saw her first. Belling his greeting, he splashed his way towards her through the heavenly playground of water. She smiled at him. He was a dog who could make you smile.

Behind him, through the tossing spray of his passage, she saw Miranda straighten and tense, her face still; waiting to be told.

Still smiling, Chloe lifted up both arms in a motion of affirmation and acceptance. 'It's all right,' she called. 'It's yes!'

Yes to all of it, the tragedies, the everyday and the astounding, unexpected glory such as I have known and must now account for. What other choice is there?

Other best selling Warner titles available by mail: